SLOW BUT DEADLY

SLOW BUT DEADLY

The Second Novel in the Alan Ericsson Series

HENRY FAULKNER

ISBN: 1540790703
ISBN 13: 9781540790705
Library of Congress Control Number: 2016920285
CreateSpace Independent Publishing Platform
North Charleston, South Carolina

Contents

Conventions

Distance and Time

Distances are in nautical miles. Times and dates listed in the text are local to the action, except as noted. The first part of the narrative takes place east of the International Date Line, although the task forces did go west of the line briefly to conduct the Marshal and Gilbert raids. In chapter 8, on March 6, 1942, the setting moves west of the International Date Line until near the end of the story. Thus during this period, the dates are one day later than in Hawaii and the rest of the United States.

Real and Fictional Names of Historical Persons

I have used the real names of persons that are part of the history in two cases: (1) prominent persons about whom I have enough biographical information to have some understanding of their character; (2) peripheral persons whose part in the story is small enough so that it is not necessary to understand their character. Otherwise, I have used fictitious names for historical persons, which may have some resemblance to the real names of the persons. In parts of the story, the leading character takes on the role of a known historical person. I hope I have not offended anyone by making that substitution.

Aircraft Nomenclature

Army and navy aircraft types were known chiefly by alphanumeric designators, which are explained in appendix A. Most of the time, in conversation these designators or various nicknames were used. A few months before the United States joined the war, the navy officially recognized the names used by the manufacturers, such as Wildcat or Dauntless. To make it easier for the reader not familiar with World War II aircraft, I have decided to use these names for the airplanes, even though US military personnel did not usually use them in conversation.

Introduction

This novel, the second in the series, is set in the first six months of US participation in World War II. It is nearly entirely set in the Pacific theater. It begins a little over a week after the Japanese attack on Pearl Harbor (a few days after the first novel ends) and finishes about a week before the Battle of Midway.

This first part of the war in the Pacific was arguably the least predictable and, hence, is fertile ground for an adventure story. The rapidity of the Japanese advance to the south came as a shock to the Allies, and its stunning success surprised even the Japanese themselves. As they continued into operations beyond what they had carefully planned, they began to make mistakes.

For the US military, without recent experience, it was a time of climbing a steep learning curve. It was also a time of making do with existing equipment. Rearmament had been started some years previously and was accelerating rapidly, but only a trickle of new equipment arrived in the Pacific theater during this time. Transferring assets from the Atlantic theater to meet the Japanese threat was in direct conflict with the overall strategy of giving higher priority to defeating Germany, which had been agreed upon before the United States entered the war, and was therefore limited.

Airpower had been emerging as an indispensable part of military operations, both in Europe and in Asia. Land based aircraft did not have enough range to conduct two way combat operations over more than limited areas of the vast Pacific. Thus the aircraft carrier became the most important strategic weapon during this period. By this author's reckoning, the United States and Japan each started hostilities with six fleet carriers, the larger, faster ships that determined the strategic balance, and no new ones became operational during this period.

The crippling of the US battleship fleet by the Japanese attack on Pearl Harbor turned out to be much less of a setback than it first appeared, because the US aircraft carriers were absent and hence undamaged. Of the six US fleet carriers, however, one was urgently needed in the Atlantic and kept there during this period. Another was brand new with a green crew and needed much more exercise before being ready for combat operations at the start of this period. That left four, three of which were in the Pacific and one of which came from the Atlantic early in the period.

When the United States joined the war, most of the top officers of the US Navy felt that the six to four Japanese advantage in carriers in the Pacific was acceptable because our equipment and training were superior. This evaluation gradually eroded during the period, as the Japanese equipment and training proved to be roughly equal. In addition, one of our carriers was laid up for repairs during most of this period after being torpedoed by a submarine in January 1942. Thus, with a six to three disadvantage in strategic assets, the US Navy faced an uphill battle in just trying to restrain further Japanese advances, let alone taking the offensive and satisfying the public thirst for revenge for the surprise attack on Pearl Harbor.

INTRODUCTION

This is the story of a fictional carrier pilot during this period, as seen from his point of view. Nearly everything in the story that involves more than this pilot and his acquaintances, however, actually happened at the places and times given.

CHAPTER ONE

Departure for the Pacific

Tuesday, December 16, 1941

Lieutenant j.g. (junior grade) Alan Ericsson was on the hangar deck aboard the aircraft carrier USS *Yorktown*, navy ship designation CV-5. She was scheduled to depart late that day from the Norfolk Naval Operating Base in Virginia for San Diego, California, via the Panama Canal. She had been transferred from the Pacific to the Atlantic the previous May, in response to increasing tensions with Germany. Now, with the outbreak of war with Japan, she was urgently needed back in the Pacific. Cranes on the pier were loading supplies onto the flight deck, which were then lowered to the hangar deck immediately below by the forward elevator. Alan was helping to supervise the stowage of supplies in his squadron's storage area.

USS *Yorktown* (CV-5) at dock, 1940
(US Navy/PD-USGOV-MILITARY-NAVY)

Around 0700 Alan heard the sound of a truck pulling up on the pier outside and shouting. Next he recognized the whine of the machinery that operated the large crane just aft of the island, the superstructure on the starboard side of the flight deck. Then the klaxon warning horn sounded, and the ship's bullhorn network announced, "Now hear this. Stand by to hoist aboard and strike below the cargo fighter planes." About ten minutes later, the midships elevator came down with the first of the Wildcat fighter airplanes, which were to be taken to San Diego as cargo, its fuselage on one dolly and its wings and propeller on another. Alan occasionally glanced aft to watch the airplane stowage activity.

The ship's executive officer, Commander Joshua Clapp, was pacing up and down the starboard side of the hangar deck, occasionally giving orders to the petty officers, who were really running the show. Teams of mechanics from each of the four squadrons aboard were assigned to the various operations. The dollies were pushed forward, and the fuselages were hoisted to the overhead, between the girders that supported the flight deck, where they were made fast. The wings and propellers were stowed in the storage areas on the side of the deck. Then the dollies were pushed aft to go back up on the elevator. After a few airplanes had been stowed, Alan thought it was going fairly smoothly, but Clapp was not satisfied. He had a stopwatch in his hand and was urging the scowling petty officers to speed up the process. As the hoisted aircraft filled the spaces between the girders, the stowage activity worked its way aft.

Hangar deck of USS *Lexington* (CV-2), 1941
(US Navy/PD-USGOV-MILITARY-NAVY)

After ten Wildcats had been stowed under the overhead, Alan could see that the men were starting to tire, working hard for two hours without a moment's break in the action. At one point Clapp came out to where the hoisting was going on and shouted directly up to the men above to pick up the pace. Alan saw that each of the top enlisted men in the squadrons had an animated conversation with Clapp and came away looking disgusted. While a crew was securing the twelfth Wildcat to the overhead, Alan started aft with a question for his boss, the squadron's engineering officer, Lieutenant Angus "Scottie" MacAllester.

Alan was about halfway back to where the hoisting activity was happening when there was a twanging sound from directly above. Fear gripped him as he sensed that something large was falling toward him. He saw a dark blur and felt a glancing blow on his chest and hands, which threw him backward, and almost simultaneously there was a crash that echoed around the hangar. He landed on his back on the deck and banged the back of his head. He saw stars but jerked up on his elbows to see that his feet were only inches from the nose of a Wildcat, which had come to rest at a steep angle on the deck, while the tail remained fastened to the overhead. His head, chest, and hands hurt, but nothing seemed to be broken. The stowage activity on the hangar deck had immediately stopped, and men converged on the Wildcat as he sat up.

As the shock of hitting the deck wore off, Alan began to relax and understand how lucky he was—he could have been killed or consigned to a wheelchair for the rest of his life. His mind reeled at the thought. He knew well that carrier aviation was a very dangerous business, in the air and on the flight deck. Now it seemed like the hangar deck was not very safe either.

Scottie ran up with a worried look on his face. "Alan, are you OK?" he asked breathlessly.

"A few sore spots, but otherwise I think I'm OK."

"Damn, that was close!" exclaimed Scottie.

Two pharmacist's mates appeared with a stretcher. After they checked Alan over, they asked him to stand up. Alan stood up slowly while they watched. Except for the sore spots, he felt he was fine. They told him to walk over to the port side and sit on a crate, and watched him as he walked, with Scottie following. They seemed satisfied and departed. Alan felt OK, but his mind was still spinning from his brush with death.

"Stay here and take it easy for half an hour, and then see me, OK?" said Scottie.

"OK." Then Alan said, "The men are exhausted from the rushed nonstop work. They must not have gotten that Wildcat secured."

"That's right. Clapp rushed them so much they cut corners, which is bound to lead to accidents. One hell of a fucking ship's executive officer," Scottie said with a belligerent look.

Scottie was easygoing, and Alan had hardly ever seen him angry. There was no mistaking it now, especially since he was not given to foul language. Alan nodded. *Not a good start to the voyage to the Pacific*, he thought.

Scottie went back to work, and Alan started watching preparations to raise the nose of the Wildcat so the fuselage could be lowered onto a dolly. Clapp was there, watching with an angry expression. *I wonder if he realizes that he has actually slowed everything down by rushing the men too much*, Alan thought.

Alan's mind wandered back to what had happened since the ship had arrived back in Norfolk two weeks earlier. So much had happened that it seemed like months ago.

Yorktown had arrived at Norfolk on December 2, after a busy fall serving in the undeclared war against Germany. She shadowed important convoys and patrolled the western part of the North Atlantic. A complete overhaul of the ship had been postponed twice and was then scheduled to occur at Norfolk in December. When she arrived, all hands had looked forward to a period of rest in port and spending time ashore. Many of them, including Alan, had been thinking about going home for Christmas.

All that had gone out the window on December 7. The surprise Japanese air raid on the navy base at Pearl Harbor in Hawaii had changed everything. Alan's first reaction had been anguish about whether his wife, Jennifer, had been injured or killed in the attack, and feeling intense regret that he had agreed with her when she decided she wanted to make the move to Pearl Harbor.

She had been working as a civilian for the Office of Naval Intelligence (ONI) in Washington in the spring and summer, and then she had transferred to the Combat Intelligence Unit at Pearl Harbor. The last letter Alan had received from her was sent just before the attack. After the attack, all forms of communication between Hawaii and the mainland had immediately become choked. The mail had been suspended, and access to telephone and telegraph had been limited to the highest-priority users. Alan had felt intensely helpless and frustrated at not being able to do anything but wait to learn what had happened to Jennifer in the attack.

The attack had changed the mood in the country completely. Alan had been amazed at the suddenness of the change. After a long period of gradually increasing tensions with Japan and Germany, with no end in sight, the country was suddenly and totally at war. After a few days of confusion, the military and most of the public had settled into a grim determination to seek complete victory, no matter what it took. Before the attack, the country had been deeply divided on whether to join the war. Now the country was united, and the previously strong isolationist movement, which advocated staying out of all overseas wars, was reduced to insignificance.

On December 10, the men of *Yorktown* had received the news that the ship would depart for the Pacific in six days. There was no attempt at secrecy, and all the ship's men set about making arrangements to be away for an extended period.

When Jennifer had been considering the move to Pearl Harbor in July, she and Alan had talked about the probability of war with Japan and of *Yorktown* being sent back to the Pacific as a result. Now both had happened, sooner than they expected. He missed Jennifer very much, and he was delighted to be headed her way, although he still did not know if she was all right. He would be in the same ocean at least, and the ship was likely to go to the fleet naval base at Pearl Harbor sooner or later, so he would be able to see her, at least briefly. These thoughts eclipsed any thoughts about going home for Christmas.

That evening, Alan had called his parents to tell them he was leaving for the Pacific and to arrange for his father to collect his car and take it to their home in Brookline, near Boston, for storage.

The urgency of getting *Yorktown* back to the Pacific had been too great to allow time for an overhaul, but in two days she was to go into dry dock in the Norfolk Navy Yard, to receive hull maintenance and much needed upgrades in her antiaircraft armament and radar. The *Yorktown* men had plunged into hard work to get ready for the long voyage before she left the pier for dry dock.

On December 11, Germany and Italy had joined Japan in declaring war on the United States, and the United States reciprocated. Alan was puzzled about why Germany wanted war with the United States, just when its invasion of the Soviet Union seemed to be bogging down.

In the evening of December 11, Alan had received a telegram from Jennifer, the six words exquisitely chosen to convey that she was unharmed and hinting that she was undaunted. It was such a huge relief that it took a little while to sink in. The glow in his heart grew until he was bursting with joy, and he had some trouble calming down enough to pass the news on to their parents. Afterward he realized that she had probably used her position in intelligence to get special access for that one short telegram, and he was deeply grateful that she did. He thought it would be many weeks before he heard from her again.

While *Yorktown* was in dry dock, Alan and Scottie had kept busy organizing supplies ashore to be loaded when she came back. She returned to pier 7 early in the morning of December 16. Alan had reported to Scottie on the hangar deck soon after. Scottie had described in a disgruntled tone how the ship would be taking twenty Wildcats and nine Dauntlesses to San Diego as cargo, overcrowding the hangar deck.

Scottie had also said that Clapp would be supervising the stowage of airplanes on the hangar deck, because he had been dissatisfied with the pace of stowage when the air group was last loaded by crane in September. By this time it was well known among the aviators that, although Clapp was the senior naval aviator aboard, who got his wings of gold in 1926, he was grouchy and unable to share his expertise. He also seemed to think that almost every activity in the ship could be done better if he were put in charge.

Alan's mind came back to the present when he noticed a tall gray-haired man, whom he recognized as the ship's captain, Captain Ellington Buckthorn, slip into the hangar over on the starboard side. A much shorter man, Commander Murray Arnham, the assistant air officer, was with Buckthorn. Alan had met Buckthorn, and he knew Arnham fairly well because he had been the skipper of Alan's squadron for the first four months after Alan had joined it. Buckthorn conferred with the top enlisted men in each squadron. Then Alan saw Arnham gesture to Scottie to join the group. Scottie spoke to them for a few minutes, and then Alan saw Scottie looking and pointing in his direction as he spoke. Finally Buckthorn left the group and came across toward Clapp.

Clapp had been busy trying to speed up raising the Wildcat's nose and had his back to the captain. He was clearly startled when Buckthorn appeared at his side. Buckthorn began speaking, while Clapp's face gradually turned redder and redder. Finally, Clapp turned abruptly and strode over to the starboard side and out of the hangar. Buckthorn went back over and spoke to Arnham and then left the hangar. Alan gathered that Buckthorn had put Arnham in charge, relieving Clapp.

Arnham and Scottie came across to Alan, who stood up as they approached.

"Hello, Alan. How are you feeling?" inquired Arnham.

"A few sore spots, sir, but otherwise fine," answered Alan.

"No dizziness?"

"No, sir."

"While they are getting that Wildcat back down and off the ship, we need to double check to make sure all the stored airplanes are properly secured. I want to put you in charge of that, if you feel up to it. After what just happened, I don't think you'll miss anything, and the men won't want you to. Be sure to stop if you start to feel bad."

"Yes, sir. Thank you, sir." Alan felt he was up to it and was glad to personally check the attachments. The teams that had been doing the hoisting reported to Alan, and he conferred with them briefly. They were intensely relieved and grateful that Alan blamed Clapp rather than them for the accident. He went with them up a ladder to the catwalks that ran among the girders supporting the flight deck. The men were meticulous in examining the attachments, but he looked over each one himself. It took about half an hour to check everything, and the men found two more attachments that were done hastily and might have come loose eventually, which they secured.

Meanwhile Arnham quickly took over the aircraft stowage with his commanding presence and booming voice, which more than made up for his short stature. The men moved quickly, and there were no more scowls from the petty officers. The damaged Wildcat fuselage was placed on a dolly, which was joined by the dolly with the wings and propeller, and the two went back up the elevator and off the ship. Additional teams of mechanics were recruited, so each could rest briefly before the next operation. Then the loading of cargo airplanes was restarted, filling the overhead. Four cargo airplanes were stowed on the port side of the hangar and secured on their dollies, so they could be moved if necessary. Mess attendants brought lunch, consisting of sandwiches and coffee, up to the hangar, and the men consumed them in brief breaks while work continued.

Then Alan recognized the low growl of radial aircraft engines coming from the shore, and the carrier's aircraft began arriving, after the long taxi across the naval base from East Field at the Norfolk Naval Air Station. They were also hoisted aboard by the ship's crane and lowered to the hangar deck by the midships elevator. Around 1830 all the air group airplanes were on board. The teams had secured twelve Wildcats on the flight deck and filled up the hangar deck with all the other air group airplanes. All hands on the hangar deck took a supper break to partake of the additional sandwiches and coffee that had been brought up and then went back to work stowing equipment and spare parts.

Yorktown got underway a little after 2100. At 2200, Arnham called it a day, leaving some more to be done while underway the next day.

When Alan went off duty, he went up to the starboard gallery, the narrow deck that ran along the side of the flight deck a few feet below it. Although he was tired and still sore, he wanted to get a last look at the Virginia shore. It had been a cloudy day, but the air underneath the clouds was remarkably clear, with the temperature in the forties. *Yorktown* had passed slowly through Hampton Roads and was now crossing the south end of Chesapeake Bay, headed for the open Atlantic.

Alan saw that the shore was lit up the same as ever, with no sign of a blackout yet. Alan had spent four years in the Submarine Service, and he realized that probably some German submarines had enough range to do at least short patrols along the East Coast of the United States. The large volume of unescorted merchant shipping along the coast would provide easy pickings, which had previously been off limits while the United States remained neutral. It was too soon now for them to have crossed over, but it seemed likely they would arrive before many weeks passed. Would the shore still be lit up, inviting attack and silhouetting any shipping near the shore? He hoped a blackout was getting organized.

He also hoped the navy was rapidly making preparations for escorted convoys, just like the ones that had been organized in the North Atlantic. He knew there was a shortage of escort ships, but protection for the coastwise traffic seemed just as important as for the transatlantic traffic. For the United States, the Atlantic submarine war seemed likely to be the first place where the results of joining the war against Germany would be felt, particularly by civilians.

Alan had feared for some time that the United States would get into a war with both Germany and Japan, known as the "Two Ocean War," before it was ready, and now it had happened. The navy's unreadiness for war against submarines in the western Atlantic and unreadiness for air raids in the Pacific were signs that this fear was justified.

Alan had learned at the naval academy that the United States had a war plan for Germany, known as "War Plan Black," and one for Japan, known as "War Plan Orange." The navy had focused most of its planning for the last twenty years on war with Japan, and Alan was familiar with the Orange plan. That plan anticipated a Japanese offensive, which would capture US possessions in the western Pacific, including the Philippines. Then the US fleet would sortie to the western Pacific and overwhelm the Japanese navy. He thought the Orange plan seemed simplistic, having a strong resemblance to the Russian effort to send a fleet from Europe to crush the Japanese navy in 1905, which ended in disaster for the Russians.

The fall of France in June 1940 made it clear that the United States could no longer rely on the European powers to contain Germany, and the survival of Britain was not assured. This led to discussions that produced a new war plan during 1941, called "Rainbow Five," for war against both countries simultaneously. Germany was perceived to be the greater threat, and Rainbow Five called for remaining on the defensive in the Pacific until Germany was contained. What this meant in terms of actual operations in the Pacific was far from clear to Alan. He suspected there would be a period of confusion before a plan emerged.

In the few days that Alan had been back aboard, he felt the new atmosphere in the ship. Although the Atlantic missions had some possibility of combat with submarines, now the ship was off to war for sure. Most of the crew had a more solemn, determined demeanor.

Alan looked forward to getting to the Pacific. In addition to being closer to Jennifer, *Yorktown* and her air group would be able to make a much bigger contribution to the war effort there than in the North Atlantic. In the North Atlantic, he had been one of the few who had dropped a depth charge on a German submarine, but, as often happened, the results were unknown. In the Pacific, *Yorktown* would probably go into combat against Japanese aircraft, ships, and shore bases, where the results would usually be obvious.

There would also be much greater risk because the Japanese would be shooting back. Alan knew he could be injured or killed, but like most young men, he believed the odds were strongly against it. He was aware of the conflict between wanting to prove himself and fear of injury or death.

How good were the Japanese pilots and airplanes? The prevailing view before December 7 that they were definitely second rate had softened a lot after they showed their stuff at Pearl Harbor and the Philippines, but it still prevailed. Alan, who had been reading aviation magazines for the last ten years, was skeptical about this view. Occasionally there were disturbing articles about the capability of Japanese aircraft and the rigorous training of their pilots, which Alan thought might be closer to the truth. Alan was fairly confident, nevertheless, that the Japanese would not easily overwhelm US naval aviation in the way that they had overwhelmed the Chinese air force and the US Army Air Force so far.

Alan could just make out the shadowy forms and white wakes of the starboard two of the four destroyers steaming in an arc formation ahead of *Yorktown*. The destroyers were there to protect the big carrier from submarine attack. They were modern destroyers of the *Sims* class: *Hughes*, *Walke*, *Russell*, and *Sims*, who would be accompanying the carrier to the Pacific. Alan had a particularly warm feeling for *Sims* because he and his gunner had been picked up out of the frigid North Atlantic and well treated by her men, after he had crashed in October.

USS *Sims* (DD-409), 1940
(US Navy/PD-USGOV-MILITARY-NAVY)

Now Cape Henry was passing abeam to starboard. Alan wondered how long it would be before he got back to the East Coast of the United States again. It could be a long time, possibly years. He had grown up in the Boston area and had spent most of his navy career on the East Coast. He had been assigned to serve in the Pacific, however, for his two year tour on a surface ship, which was a requirement for new graduates of the naval academy. He would miss his family and navy friends on the East Coast. He was nostalgic and looking forward to the future at the same time.

Before climbing into his bunk, Alan retrieved the telegram he had gotten from Jennifer on December 11 from its special place among his personal effects, and read it one more time:

SAFE SOUND TELL ALL YOU RASCAL STOP
JENNIFER

"You rascal" was a term of affection that she used only with him. To him this use of it conveyed her love, along with an upbeat note, which suggested that she was undaunted by what had happened. It captured two of the things he liked most about her: her capacity for love and her determination. He went to sleep with the vision of her as he had last seen her in August.

Wednesday, December 17, 1941

Alan slept like a log and rose at 0430. His head, hands, and chest felt much better, but he found that his stomach muscles in front were now quite sore. Thinking of his narrow escape the day before, he thought probably his stomach muscles had instinctively tensed very hard to pull his shoulders forward as he fell backward, to help protect his head. His head still hurt a little bit, so it was good that it had not hit the deck any harder.

Alan was a pilot in Bombing Five, one of the four squadrons that were normally assigned to *Yorktown*. All of the pilots in the squadron were assigned an additional duty when they were not flying. Alan had been appointed assistant engineering officer shortly after he joined the squadron, helping the engineering officer, Scottie, supervise the maintenance of the squadron's air-planes, and it was a job he enjoyed. He had always been interested in machinery and vehicles, and he had worked as a car mechanic during the summers in junior high school. He considered Scottie to be a friend and mentor, as well as his boss.

Like all the ensigns and j.g.'s, Alan shared a tiny state-room with another pilot in the squadron. His roommate was Lieutenant j.g. James "Jolly" Lowery. Jolly was in the class of 1935 at the naval academy, one year behind Alan, but had been in Bombing Five about twice as long. He was short but handsome, with an appearance of innocence. He was a dedicated pilot who scored well in dive bombing and gunnery practice. He also had a spontaneous and rebellious sense of humor that accounted for his nickname and that Alan greatly enjoyed. As Alan had gotten to know Jolly, he came to understand that his relaxed, humor-ous side complemented his serious, dedicated side, and he could switch very quickly from one to the other.

On shore Jolly lived with his wife, Irene, in a rental house near the Norfolk NAS. Alan had met Irene several times when the squad-ron was based at Norfolk. She was an attractive blonde who seemed like a good fit for Jolly, with a similar irrepressible sense of humor.

When they first went aboard *Yorktown* in September, Alan had won the coin toss and took the lower bunk. Now in a different stateroom, it was Jolly's turn for the lower bunk. Jolly was already up, and Alan mumbled a greeting before going off to the head.

Alan was a fairly junior pilot in the squadron, having joined the previous June, right after graduating from the navy flight school at Pensacola, Florida. Most of the junior pilots were en-signs, reservists who went into aviation when they joined after college, or academy men who had chosen to go directly into aviation after their surface tour. Alan, however, had chosen at that point to join the Submarine Service and had transferred to aviation in 1940. In the navy, naval aviation officers were known as "brown shoes" because they wore brown, rather than black, shoes. The rest of the navy officers were known as "black shoes."

The carrier's squadrons, collectively known as the "air group," comprised all of the offensive and most of the defensive capability of the ship. The air group carried by *Yorktown*, as with most of the US Navy fleet carriers in 1941, consisted of a fighting squadron, a scouting squadron, a bombing squadron, and a torpedo squadron. The fighting squadron was Fighting Forty-Two, or VF-42, with an assigned strength of eighteen Grumman F4F-3 Wildcat single seat fighters. The number 42 indicated that this squadron was one of two fighter squadrons normally assigned to CV-4, USS *Ranger*.

The scouting and bombing squadrons were Scouting Five (VS-5) and Bombing Five (VB-5). The "5" meant that these squadrons were normally assigned to CV-5, USS *Yorktown*. Each had an assigned strength of eighteen Douglas SBD-3 Dauntless two seat scout bombers. Some dive bomber squadrons on other carriers still had some of the earlier SBD-2 version, which did not have self-sealing fuel tanks, a bulletproof windshield, and armor for the crew, but was identical in appearance.

During the 1930s, the distinction indicated by the "Scouting" and "Bombing" labels had gradually faded away, so that by 1941 both squadrons were equally proficient in both the scouting and bombing functions. In addition, during the summer of 1941, both squadrons were reequipped with the same airplane type for the first time.

The torpedo squadron was Torpedo Five, or VT-5, with an assigned strength of twelve Douglas TBD-1 Devastator three seat torpedo bombers. There was one additional Dauntless for the commander of the *Yorktown* air group (CYAG).

Grumman F4F-3 Wildcats in formation, 1941
(US Navy/PD-USGOV-MILITARY-NAVY)

Douglas SBD-2 Dauntless, 1941
(US Navy/PD-USGOV-MILITARY-NAVY)

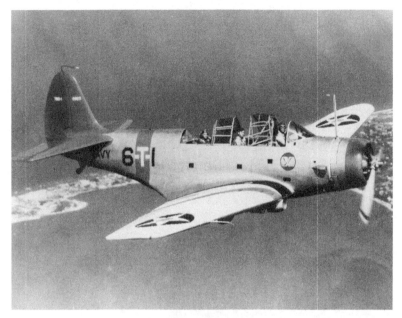

Douglas TBD-1 Devastator, 1938
(US Navy/PD-USGOV-MILITARY-NAVY)

During the fall, Scouting Five had been assigned to dive bomb-ing exercises with the army in the southern United States, while the other three squadrons had been aboard *Yorktown* during her tour of duty in the North Atlantic. Alan was therefore acquainted with many men of the rest of the air group, but he was just starting to get acquainted with the officers and men of Scouting Five.

Alan was glad to be in US naval aviation and not the US Army Air Force or the British Royal Air Force. He thought the navy had done well overall in developing fighters and other spe-cialized combat aircraft, such as dive and torpedo bombers, in the thirties. The navy had little interest in heavy bombers, which, in Alan's opinion, preoccupied the US Army Air Force, leading to lower priority for fighters and other smaller combat aircraft. The

British Royal Air Force seemed to be similarly preoccupied with heavy bombers until the late thirties. This led to a near disaster because they barely had time to catch up in fighter strength before the Battle of Britain in the summer of 1940. Their fighter planes and pilots were excellent, but there were barely enough of them. Unfortunately naval aviation in Britain had been put under the Royal Air Force and much neglected, so they lagged far behind in carrier aircraft.

Alan decided to become a naval aviator partly because he admired carrier aviation. A large group of combat aircraft that could suddenly appear anywhere in the world that was within range of the ocean seemed to him to be a much more versatile and potent weapon than a similar number of aircraft flying from land.

When Alan had graduated from the navy flight school at Pensacola, Florida, he had had a preference for flying fighters, but dive bombers were a close second, so he was not disappointed with his assignment. Before transferring from submarines to aviation, he had had duty at the Newport Torpedo Station for nine months. There he had come to doubt the reliability of American torpedoes, so he was glad that he had not been assigned to a torpedo squadron.

The officers of carrier squadrons all participated as pilots, and a few squadrons also had enlisted men who were pilots. A squadron would normally have a few spare pilots and airplanes beyond the assigned strength but might have less, depending on circumstances. Each squadron also had a body of enlisted men, most of whom were assigned to the squadron's engineering department, maintaining the squadron aircraft. There were 120 enlisted men in Bombing Five. Some of the enlisted men in the scouting, bombing, and torpedo squadrons also flew in the back seats of the dive bombers and torpedo bombers as gunners/radiomen and bombardiers. Each squadron, as well as the entire air group, was a self-contained unit that could, if necessary, function ashore or on any US Navy fleet carrier.

Part of the underway routine was that the squadrons started the day, usually slightly before dawn, with flight quarters, which was announced over the ship's bullhorn. This meant that all aviation related personnel reported to their duty stations, which for pilots were their ready rooms. There the plan for the day and any information needed by the pilots were announced.

Today flight quarters was at 0600, and afterward Alan went to the hangar deck, to continue supervising the process of stowing everything away. The hangar was below the flight deck and extended about four fifths of the length of the ship. Most of this space was equivalent to three decks in height to allow storage of aircraft suspended from the overhead and still have enough height to move aircraft around freely on the deck.

The stowage process proceeded slowly, allowing Alan moments when he could relax a little and let his mind wander. His thoughts turned back to Jennifer. He imagined the intelligence unit where she worked was in turmoil after the Pearl Harbor attack, and she was probably very busy.

Alan and Jennifer had first met in July 1936, and Alan found her extremely attractive. She was then dating a classmate at submarine school, however. Soon she was engaged, but her fiancé broke the engagement. Then she plunged into her graduate studies and mostly declined social life until after she got her master's degree in February 1940. Alan ran across her in April in Newport, Rhode Island, when Alan was working at the Newport Torpedo Station, and Jennifer was working at the Naval War College there. Jennifer was attracted to Alan; they had dated over the summer and had gotten engaged in August. Then in September, Alan had left for flight training at Pensacola, Florida, and Jennifer had gone to work for the Office of Naval Intelligence in Washington, DC, in January 1941. They had been married in May 1941, right after Alan finished flight school. Alan had been assigned to Bombing Five, based in Norfolk, Virginia. They were too far apart to live together, but they had been able to visit each other frequently on weekends over the summer.

By July, Jennifer had become discouraged because ONI's work was being subverted by the bureaucratic fighting in the Navy Department in Washington. She also had heard that the Pearl Harbor intelligence group under Commander Joseph Rochefort was looking for people. Rochefort, whom Alan had met, had an excellent reputation among dedicated intelligence people, including Jennifer. Using her intelligence connections, she had found out that Bombing Five would be aboard *Yorktown* patrolling in the North Atlantic through the fall. Wherever she was, they would not be able to see each other during that time. Both she and Alan had been feeling that war with Japan was likely, and in that case *Yorktown* was likely to go back to the Pacific. Putting all this together, they might be able to see each other more often if she was at Pearl Harbor. With Alan's approval, she applied for transfer to Pearl Harbor. Her transfer had been very quickly approved, and she had departed Washington for Pearl Harbor in late August. They had kept in touch by airmail during the fall.

The evening meal was the first time the squadron had been together off duty since the war had started with the Pearl Harbor raid, or even since the ship had returned to Norfolk from the North Atlantic. Supper was served in shifts from 1700 to 1900. It was remarkably formal unless the ship was in a state of alert. The officers wore dress uniforms. They were seated in the wardroom at long tables with linen tablecloths, and they ate with silver marked with the ship's monogram. The food was good. It was carefully prepared and then served by diligent colored and Filipino mess attendants. Alan sat with his friends, at one of the tables for ensigns or j.g.'s. The higher ranking officers had a separate table.

Yorktown Wardroom
(US Navy/PD-USGOV-MILITARY-NAVY)

As the food was being served, Lieutenant j.g. Einar "Teeth" Jensen smiled and said to Alan, "Stringy, what's this story we're hearing about you being attacked by a Wildcat on the hangar deck yesterday?"

Most of the academy men, called Ringknockers by the reservists, had received a nickname from their classmates, which had a tendency to stick through their navy careers. Alan's nickname, Stringy, came from his shape: he was six feet one inch tall and weighed 155 pounds. Teeth had gotten his nickname because his grin revealed a mouthful of large, crooked teeth. He was a big bear of a guy from Minnesota, class of '35, and had spent two years as an enlisted man before attending the academy. He had been in the squadron for about a year.

"Well, the nose of one that had been poorly secured to the overhead suddenly fell down. It brushed by me in front and knocked me down on my back. I was sure lucky not to get smashed."

"Jesus, were you hurt?" asked Ensign Cedric "Slick" Davis. Slick, class of '37, a thin craggy guy from Arkansas, had been in the squadron about a year and half.

"I had some sore spots, but I was fine."

"Whew! How come the Wildcat wasn't properly secured?" asked Teeth.

"Clapp was running the show on the hangar deck, and he was trying to speed up the operation, continually hounding the men, instead of making sure there were enough of them for the job. I think the men began to get careless."

"No soap! So, besides putting men and airplanes at risk, he actually slowed everything down?" asked Jolly Lowery with a chuckle.

"That's right," said Alan. "The captain came down and put Arnham in charge, relieving Clapp. Arnham had me supervise a thorough check on the attachments to the overhead that had already been made. The men were as anxious as I was to make sure they were secure."

"I bet," said Teeth Jensen.

Slick changed the subject: "Well, Stringy, the Japs attacked the Philippines just like you said they would last summer."

Alan added, "And we should be evacuating as fast as we can."

Ensign Edward "Ned" Morris jumped in: "What? The news said a lot of airplanes were lost on both sides when the Japs attacked. It sounds like we're holding out OK, like the British in the Battle of Britain." Ned was a tall, dark, and handsome aviation cadet (AvCad) from Arizona who had joined the squadron right after Alan did. Alan did not look down on reservists as some academy men did. He and Ned were the newest rookies for a while and became friends.

The AvCad program, with its combination of officer training and flight training, being much shorter than the four-year naval academy, was quite intense. When they finished flight school, AvCads were commissioned as ensigns in the reserve. Many of the AvCads had also picked up nicknames along the way.

Alan replied to Ned, "The British never lost control of the air. Their air bases were never put out of action. There was an article in the *New York Times* a couple of days after the attack that said our air bases in the northern Philippines had been put out of action for the time being. That meant we had lost control of the air, and since we'd lost a lot of planes, we were not likely to get it back before they invaded. Very likely we've lost the Philippines and all our men who cannot get out fast." He still had not gotten used to the idea of such a total debacle.

"Aw, g'wan, Stringy, the B-17s probably have attacked their bases on Formosa. Maybe they've been put out of action too," said Ensign Mike Burke. Mike was a red haired AvCad from Chicago, and he had also been in the squadron for about a year and a half.

Alan responded, "With all the bad news, don't you think we'd hear about it if there was any success on our side? I think either the B-17s were destroyed by their air attack, or they fled to the southern Philippines, or some of each. Any that are in the southern Philippines are out of range of Formosa, so they can't help with regaining control of the air. They could try to hit the Japs when they invade. But if the Japs have control of the air, the B-17s are going to get chewed up, like the Germans did over England and the British did over the continent, when they tried daylight bombing with no fighter escort."

Teeth weighed in: "I suspect Stringy is right. It may take a while, but I think nearly all of the army personnel stationed there will be killed or captured. This is a disaster worse than the attack on Pearl Harbor! And they had nine hours' warning!"

Jolly's taste for irony came through: "The witch hunt over responsibility for the failure at Pearl Harbor has already started, and it's getting plenty of attention in the press. Meanwhile, the greater disaster in the Philippines is going almost unnoticed."

Ned said, "Pearl Harbor was a big surprise. But everyone was expecting that the Japanese would attack the Philippines. Why were we so unprepared?"

Alan replied, "For thirty years, up until last July, we knew we couldn't defend the Philippines against a Japanese attack. We planned to evacuate and take them back after we defeated their navy. Last July the army bomber people convinced Army Secretary Stimson and President Roosevelt that B-17s could hold off the Japanese. Roosevelt had been anxious to call their bluff if they went into Indochina. When they did, the army plan gave him what he thought he needed to freeze their assets, which evolved into the oil embargo."

Jolly added, "The heavy bomber people still believe in Billy Mitchell's theories, that heavy bombers can attack and defend anything. And they still think they can do it without fighter escort. That's why they've been emphasizing heavy bombers over fighters for years."

Alan continued, "So we started sending B-17s out there, but I suspect there weren't a great many on Luzon all ready for combat on December 8. But I still don't understand why they couldn't use them to attack the air bases on Formosa before the Japanese attacked them, when they had nine hours' warning. It's hard to believe, but I suspect that MacArthur is still fighting World War I and doesn't understand the importance of controlling the air. I think he believes he can fight the Japanese on the ground with no air support."

Ned replied, "I didn't realize that only six months ago, we wouldn't have even tried to defend the Philippines. Now I see why you are saying we should evacuate."

Teeth added, "Once the brass thought they could defend the Philippines, I think it made them feel like Pearl Harbor was five thousand miles behind the front lines, and they didn't have to worry about it being attacked at the start of hostilities."

"I hadn't thought of that, but it could explain the big surprise," said Mike.

Slick Davis said, "Going back to the witch hunt, I heard today that the ship was notified that Admiral Kimmel has been relieved as CINCPAC. Admiral Pye is the temporary CINCPAC, until the arrival of Admiral Nimitz, who has been the head of BuNav, to take over as the new CINCPAC. Nimitz will not be CINCUS, as Kimmel was, and they haven't announced who will be."

Alan replied, "Yeah, I heard that too. I haven't heard very much about Nimitz. I've heard mostly good things about Kimmel. There was an intelligence failure. I know Kimmel's intelligence officer, Layton, and I bet he was watching everything he could get his hands on. I suspect the failure was in Washington, and so they couldn't warn Kimmel or Layton, but Kimmel makes a convenient scapegoat, turning attention away from Washington."

Alan suspected Admiral Turner, the director of the Office of War Plans, and his fight with rival ONI had a lot to do with the intelligence failure, based on things he had heard from Jennifer the previous spring and summer, but he could not talk about that.

"That sounds pretty sour, but it seems likely," said Teeth Jensen with a grimace.

There was pause while they all ate in silence.

Ned cleared his throat and said, "That was something when the Japs sank *Repulse* and *Prince of Wales*. That pretty well shoots down the argument that aircraft can't sink battleships in the open ocean." Alan was in complete agreement, and he smiled and nodded. The British battle cruiser and battleship had been operating off the coast of Malaya without air cover, in a desperate attempt to repel the Japanese invasion of that colony, when they were sunk on December 10.

Mike chimed in, "That's right. They were land-based airplanes, but I don't see why carrier aircraft couldn't do the same thing. That means the aircraft carrier is the new capital ship. The Gun Club must be in a funk." They all laughed. The Gun Club was the informal name for those who revered the battleship, which had ruled the waves up from the 1880s until the 1930s, when the aircraft carrier began to challenge its supremacy.

CHAPTER TWO

Through the Canal

Sunday, December 21, 1941

The air was warm and humid before dawn. Alan remembered it was the winter solstice, the shortest day of the year in the Northern Hemisphere, and a primeval cause for celebration in a great variety of cultures. Now *Yorktown* was approaching the Panama Canal, close enough to the equator to have warm weather year round and little variation in daylight. He recalled the previous winter solstice, when he had been at Pensacola and had enjoyed a one time long distance telephone call with Jennifer.

As a geography enthusiast, Alan appreciated what the existence of the Panama Canal meant. It and the Suez Canal were the two great canals that cut through continents and shortened trips enormously. Alan had passed through the Panama Canal aboard the battleship *Pennsylvania* when he was serving aboard her during his surface tour. She was the flagship of the US fleet, based then at San Pedro, California. As the flagship, she always participated in the big annual navy exercises called the Fleet Problems, held in the spring in tropical waters. Fleet Problem 17 had been held in the Caribbean in April 1936, so ships based in the Pacific traveled through the Panama Canal both ways to attend. Unfortunately, Alan's duties on both transits had required him to remain below deck most of the time, so he had seen little of the canal. He hoped to get a better view this time.

After Alan first went aboard *Yorktown* in September, he heard about her passage through the canal on her way to the Atlantic the previous May, which had been entirely at night. All markings peculiar to the ship had been covered up, and only a minimum of duty personnel had been allowed on deck. This attempt to conceal the operation turned out to be a surprising success, but few aboard saw anything of the canal. Many of the air group and the ship's company, who had not made the ship's earlier transit back in April 1939, were interested in seeing the canal.

Just before dawn, right after flight quarters, Alan liked to go up to the bow of the ship, one deck up from the hangar deck, to take a look around and enjoy the fresh air. The bow was open all around. There was a tub for a 20 millimeter antiaircraft battery that sat elevated about five feet off the deck on pillars, a few feet back from the bow itself, but there was room to walk all around it.

Today Fighting Forty-Two would be sending thirteen fighters to land at France Field, Canal Zone, to be able to act as combat air patrol (CAP), fighter cover in case of an enemy attack, during the ship's transit of the canal. During the transit, the ship would not be able to steam at high speed into the wind and therefore would be able to launch airplanes only by catapult, which was too slow to respond to an attack. At 0630, as he was leaving for the hangar deck, he heard the growl of the engine of the first Wildcat going to full power. He paused to watch. Shortly afterward the airplane roared over his head. The other fighters followed at twenty second intervals. Alan was a bit jealous that those fighter pilots would get an aerial tour of the canal.

That day Alan was on duty on the hangar deck. Although it was hot and humid, he thought it was a very pleasant change from the cold North Atlantic. The steel curtains on the sides of the hangar deck were all open to allow fresh air to come in. These curtains could be closed in foul or cold weather and could also be used at night to black out the ship while allowing activities to proceed on the hangar deck. The mixed odors of gasoline, lubricating oil, solvents, paint, and other liquids used in maintenance could become strong when the hangar deck was closed, but now the open sides ventilated the space completely.

Alan was able to look up from his work occasionally and watch what was happening around the ship. Now the sun was well up, and Alan could just make out the low shore of Panama. Soon they passed through the opening in the breakwater into Colon Harbor, going in a southerly direction. Alan recalled the surprising fact that, going toward the Pacific, the canal ran in a generally *southeasterly* direction, because the canal was in a reverse curve in the Isthmus of Panama.

There were a number of ships scattered around the harbor that appeared to be idling, waiting for their turn to enter the canal. The Canal Zone and the canal were US possessions, and Alan knew that US Navy combatant ships had priority. Soon the destroyers approached the channel to the Gatun Locks. These locks had three stages running in a southerly direction and raised the water level eighty-five feet up to that of Gatun Lake. There were two sets of locks side by side, allowing traffic to proceed in both directions simultaneously. *Yorktown* entered the first lock a little before 0830. Alan noticed that the ship was a fairly close fit in the lock. He could understand why the crew had spent the previous day removing and stowing anything that protruded over the side of the ship. He thought about the new Essex class carriers being built, which were larger than the Yorktown class. They were still supposed to fit in these locks, but they would be an extremely tight fit. *Yorktown* continued through the three lock chambers and entered Gatun Lake around 1015.

Off to the right less than half a mile, Alan could just see the top of the giant Gatun Dam, which held up the Chagres River to create Gatun Lake. He noticed the thick tropical forest covering the shore, and the smell of rotting vegetation. He watched occasionally as the ship followed the buoyed channel southeast through the lake and turned east into the valley of the upper part of the Chagres River. The ship passed up the river valley and then swung right to go southeast into the Culebra Cut. The cut was a man made channel cutting through the Continental Divide, which rose to 280 feet above the water. Alan could see that digging the deep, steep sided channel through the ridge, amid tropical heat and diseases and using the equipment of 1910, had been an enormous undertaking.

At the end of the cut were the Pedro Miguel Locks, with only one stage on each side, lowering *Yorktown* thirty-four feet to the level of Miraflores Lake. This lake was very small and not much wider than the cut itself. After the lake came the Miraflores Locks, with two stages on each side, lowering the ship back down to the level of the Pacific Ocean. The actual amount of the descent in these locks varied considerably because there were twenty foot tides on the Pacific side, unlike the tiny tides on the Atlantic side. Alan had heard that during the night transit of the canal the previous May, bumping into the sides of the Miraflores Locks had damaged some of the underwater protuberances of the ship. This transit seemed to go smoothly.

Yorktown exited the Miraflores Locks around 1630, and Alan went off duty. He followed what had become his usual routine, getting some exercise by jogging around the flight deck, before showering and changing for supper. He had a good view as the ship continued southeast in the channel to the city of Balboa, where she tied up to pier 18 at about 1730. No liberty was granted. Only a group of men who had been helping load the ship at Norfolk and who had been unable to get off in time were allowed to disembark for the trip back. Then the ship began fueling and taking on aviation gasoline. Alan went to his stateroom to change out of his sweaty clothes and shower for supper.

While in Balboa, word circulated that Japanese submarines had attacked two US tankers off the coast of California, and one was sunk. Their submarines had also sunk several freighters near Hawaii and shelled the islands.

Alan had been wondering for the past year or so if the United States or the Japanese would engage in unrestricted submarine warfare, in which submarines were free to attack unarmed merchant ships and do nothing for the survivors in the event of a sinking. The Germans had been doing this against Britain for over two years, and previously in World War I, and now would do the same against the United States. The United States had long condemned the practice and cited it as the principal reason for joining World War I.

The vulnerability of the island nation of Japan, however, with its dependence on supplies arriving by sea, provided a strong incentive for the United States to reverse its policy in the event of war with Japan. Alan had heard from submariner friends before the Pearl Harbor attack that the US Navy was considering it. Then, before leaving Norfolk, Alan ran into a submariner friend who told him that it was generally understood in the Asiatic Fleet as early as October that there would be unrestricted submarine warfare in the event of war with Japan. His friend also said that, only hours after the attack at Pearl Harbor, the order had gone out to all of the Pacific naval commands to execute unrestricted submarine warfare against Japan.

Although the attack on Pearl Harbor provided a convenient excuse, the decision to make this major policy change had evidently been made weeks, if not months, earlier. The attacks off California and Hawaii showed that the Japanese had no qualms about it either. Alan had come around to the view that it was not immoral, as long as the merchant seamen were treated more like the military, including being properly paid for the additional risk. He knew this would be a major shift, so it would not happen quickly.

Monday, December 22, 1941

Alan was again on duty in the hangar the next morning. He continued to occasionally take a moment to look out through the open sides of the hangar deck and see what was going on. The ship edged away from the pier around 0800. Ahead of the carrier, he saw the two light cruisers *Richmond* and *Trenton*, which had now joined the task force for the voyage to San Diego. Alan thought their presence was welcome, although they were obsolescent ships from World War I. They had four stacks and looked distinctly different from newer light cruisers.

After steaming through the channel to the Pacific, the harbor pilot was dropped off soon after 0900. The task group continued going only slightly west of due south, starting to cross the Gulf of Panama before rounding Mala Point during the evening and heading west to parallel the coast of Panama. Early the following morning, after passing Coiba Island, the task group would be able to turn to the northwest, toward San Diego.

It would take eight days to get to San Diego. Alan realized San Diego was farther from Panama than Boston, because Panama was due south of South Carolina, so the ship would be traveling west a distance equivalent to crossing the United States, in addition to going north.

Enemy combatant ships had always been fair game for submarines. As the task force passed through the canal, the threat of German submarines had been exchanged for the threat of Japanese submarines, bringing home the concept of the two ocean war. The threat of German submarines had still not materialized on the western side of the Atlantic. The Japanese submarines, however, had been preparing for war with the United States and had been active near the coast of North America already. *Yorktown*'s escorts moved into a cruising formation with the cruisers ahead of the carrier on either side and the destroyers in an arc farther ahead. This formation was used because the ships would be moving fast enough that it would be difficult for a submarine to approach from the rear.

A half hour later, the *Walke* depth charged a suspected submarine contact with unknown results. Captain Buckthorn, who was also the commander of the task group for this voyage, did not want to delay its progress by turning the carrier into the easterly trade wind to launch aircraft, so the cruisers catapulted floatplanes to watch for submarines. The floatplanes were Curtis SOC Seagulls, one of the few biplane types still operational with the fleet.

Alan was off duty in the afternoon, and he went to the wardroom to see if the ship had received any recent newspapers and magazines from the United States while it was docked in Balboa. He understood that, as a naval aviator, the navy had no need to keep him informed of world news or the strategic situation. But he was very curious and looked for anything available to learn what was going on. He particularly wanted to learn about the extent of the losses at Pearl Harbor. The news he had seen so far had been vague, with unofficial estimates of 1,500 killed. The scuttlebutt was that a number of battleships were very badly damaged, and a lot of aircraft had been destroyed, but none of the three carriers in the Pacific had happened to be there. The word was that *Saratoga* (CV-3) was finishing an overhaul at the naval shipyard in Bremerton, Washington, and *Lexington* (CV-2) and *Enterprise* (CV-6) were on reinforcement missions to outlying islands.

Alan saw there were new magazines, and he grabbed the latest issue of *Time* magazine, dated that day. He settled in a chair and turned to an article labeled, "World Battlefronts: BATTLE OF THE PACIFIC: Havoc at Honolulu." The article reported that the navy had released casualty figures, showing 2,700 navy men killed and injured. Also the secretary of the navy, Frank Knox, had made public some details after he had returned from a one day fact finding trip to Pearl Harbor. He admitted that the battleship *Arizona* had been sunk and some other ships badly damaged. However, there had been little damage to the harbor, and the oil storage tanks were unscathed. Toward the end of his remarks, he said, "The essential fact is that the Japanese purpose was to knock out the United States before the war began…In this purpose the Japanese failed…The entire balance of the Pacific Fleet with its aircraft carriers, its heavy cruisers, its light cruisers, its destroyers and submarines are uninjured and are all at sea seeking contact with the enemy."

Alan was sure that wartime news control had carefully tailored this report. The number of casualties suggested that the damage to ships and aircraft was greater than admitted, which agreed with the scuttlebutt. He was particularly interested in whether there had been damage to aircraft carriers. He knew that if there had been any carriers in or near the harbor, the Japanese would have given them at least as much target priority as battleships, which seemed to have taken the brunt of the damage afloat.

He also knew the layout of Pearl Harbor and its surroundings from his visit there in 1935 during his surface ship tour. Because the harbor was surrounded by hills, it would be nearly impossible to conceal damage to aircraft carriers from civilian observers on shore. Thus he was fairly sure that the navy would feel compelled to admit it if there had been damage to aircraft carriers. *This means that the scuttlebutt is basically correct about the carriers being absent,* he thought, *a very lucky break. Given the general shortage of oil tankers, the lack of damage to the oil storage facilities is also a very lucky break.* Alan was relieved to feel that the United States was not in such a bad situation as some of the news suggested.

The magazine also confirmed that shortly after the attack, the army had taken over the Hawaiian territorial government and declared martial law. Soon they also took over the larger businesses. All dependents of military personnel were ordered to evacuate. That left Alan as one of a very few active duty personnel in the Pacific who might get to see his wife occasionally, provided *Yorktown* visited Pearl Harbor. As he left the wardroom, Teeth and Jolly came in and went straight for the magazines, as he had.

At 1500, Alan was walking along the port gallery. He noticed that the ship was turning into the east-northeast trade wind. He looked around and saw the thirteen fighters that had provided CAP in the Canal Zone returning to the ship. They landed aboard in the space of a few minutes. The ship then turned back out of the wind toward the south-southwest.

Before supper, Alan took a walk up to the bow of the ship. Just before he left, he enjoyed the beautiful rapid tropical sunset.

Alan thought it was a handsome scene, with the starboard sides of the cruisers and destroyers lit up in the pink light.

At supper Alan was with his friends again, and he thought the news from the fresh magazines would be an important topic.

Teeth Jensen spoke up: "We got some new magazines at Balboa. There was more detail about the damage at Pearl Harbor but nothing about damage to aircraft carriers. It sounds like they were not there, which was damn lucky."

Mike Burke added, "If that's true, and the aircraft carrier is the new capital ship, maybe the Japanese didn't hurt us so much at Pearl Harbor. It's terrible that we lost so many men, but we could probably get along without the battleships, which can't keep up with the aircraft carriers anyway."

"I was thinking the same thing," replied Alan. "Knox's statement after he came back from Hawaii had an optimistic note at the end. Perhaps it had some justification."

Jolly added, "You know Mahan always advocated concentrating all your heavy ships in an overwhelming force and using them offensively. It looks like the Japs took that advice to heart, because that is exactly what they did—only they used carriers instead of battleships. If we had had some warning, probably we would not have lost so many men, but the damage would have been similar, because they had so many carriers that we were outnumbered. If our three carriers had been there, they probably would've been sunk, even if we had a warning, and then we'd be in worse shape." Alfred Thayer Mahan was the famous turn of the century American naval strategist, who was revered in many navies.

Alan said, "I agree. However, we did have a warning, in November 1940, when the British raided the Italian fleet at Taranto. If we had paid close attention to that, which I suspect the Japanese did, we would've understood how vulnerable a fleet of battleships in harbor is."

Alan smiled as Teeth Jensen chuckled, thumped the table with his fist, and said, "Dammit, you're right. I had forgotten all about that."

Ned Morris chimed in: "The army wasn't much help either. In theory they're supposed to protect our ships when they are in port."

"I suspect a lot of the planes they usually have in Hawaii had been sent to the Philippines," replied Slick Davis.

"Very likely," said Alan.

CHAPTER THREE

Northwest to San Diego

Tuesday, December 23, 1941

The normal shipping lanes from Panama to California ran parallel to, and not very far from, the west coast of Mexico. All hands had been told that, for this voyage, the ship would steam well offshore, away from the normal shipping lanes, to reduce the chance of encountering submarines. They had already steamed out of sight of land and other ships, and the smell of the land had faded away. Alan hoped that the absence of submarines would provide an opportunity to hold much needed dive bombing practice during the voyage.

The news circulated through the ship that the Japanese had taken Wake Island, a sad sequel to the heroic repulse of the initial invasion attempt on December 11. Also that day one of Scouting Five's Dauntlesses crashed on takeoff, and *Russell* rescued the pilot and gunner. Accidents during carrier flight operations were fairly common, and often the disabled plane ended up in the water, rather than on the flight deck. Therefore, during flight operations, plane guard destroyers were stationed off each quarter of the carrier, where they were in a good position to rescue the occupants of such planes.

Thursday, December 25, 1941

On Christmas Day there was a muted celebration on the carrier, with a special dinner. On the previous Christmas, Alan had been at Pensacola, where the students were only given two days off, so it hadn't been a very festive occasion either. That day the ship's newspaper also reported on the talks in Washington between President Roosevelt and Prime Minister Churchill of Great Britain, and the gallant defense of Wake. Alan had been thinking that, like the Philippines and Guam, Wake's position far west of other American bases and within range of Japanese land based aircraft actually made it so vulnerable that it was a liability, and it should have been evacuated.

Saturday, December 27, 1940

Now *Yorktown* was about halfway from the Panama Canal to San Diego. She was 300 miles offshore from Acapulco, and there had been no sign of submarines. It was 0600, and the Bombing Five pilots were gathered for flight quarters in their ready room, right under the flight deck. Each squadron had a ready room where the pilots gathered for briefings, educational sessions, drills, and to stand by for flight operations. Relaxing and sleeping sometimes occurred during standby periods.

The ready room was in a typical naval ship compartment, painted white. Under the overhead there was the usual assortment of pipes, ducts, wires, lights, loudspeakers, and so forth. The deck was covered with red linoleum. On the surrounding bulkheads, there were hooks for flight gear, life vests, and clipboards, and shelves for manuals. The room was pretty well filled with large chairs for twenty pilots, five rows of four with a center aisle. The chairs were sturdy metal ones that were fixed to the deck, each with a folding arm that created a writing surface in front of the chair. They were upholstered with leather, comfortable, and could even recline a little. There was space underneath each chair for personal gear. On the bulkhead in front, there were large blackboards, with several sections ruled off to show mission rosters and flight information. Also in front there was a small lectern and a teletype machine. The ready rooms were the only spaces in the ship that had air conditioning. Alan thought that added a lot to the comfort, but he wished it would remove more of the cigarette smoke, he being one of the few nonsmokers.

Recent photo of the World War II aircraft carrier ready room
exhibit at the National Museum of Naval Aviation
(Author Photo)

Dive bombing practice was scheduled for Scouting Five and Bombing Five. Scouting Five was going first, at 0730, and Bombing Five would begin taking off at 0900.

Alan had practiced dive bombing on a moving towed target sled a number of times during the summer and fall. He had found it much more difficult than dropping on fixed targets on land, such as the ones he had trained on at Pensacola, where he made excellent scores. The tow ship would go into a hard turn, simulating the radical maneuvering of a ship under attack. The dive bomber pilot had not only to maneuver to stay on target; he also had to allow for the drift caused by the wind, whose direction relative to the target path was constantly changing as the ship turned.

So far Alan had been very disappointed with his bombing scores, which were near the lowest in the squadron. He suspected his standing in the squadron suffered as a result. He had had several sessions in the fall with his roommate, Jolly, and Scottie MacAllester, both of whom were among the top scorers, to learn their technique. Since then he thought he knew what he had to do to improve his score, but he hadn't been able to try it yet.

"Atten-shun!"

The pilots rapidly stood while Bombing Five's commanding officer, Lieutenant Richard Armiston, came in at the rear and strode up the center aisle.

"As you were," said Armiston.

The pilots settled back down. Armiston went over the plan for the practice. They would dive from 15,000 feet. They would be using the usual small practice bombs, which would be aimed at a target sled towed by *Hughes*. The standard target was a 50 foot diameter circle, smaller than the *Yorktown*'s hangar deck width but larger than the beam of the ship at the waterline. The squadron would take off and make their dives in a specified order. Observers on *Hughes* would note down the location of hits and misses by number in the dive sequence.

Alan scanned the ruled blackboard in the front of the ready room to see where his place was in the order. Eighteen aircraft were listed with pilots, but his name was not there. Anger welled up as he realized this was probably a deliberate move by the squadron flight officer, Lieutenant Kelly "Bull" Durham.

Alan thought Durham was very competent and diligent, but he did not seem to have much respect for anyone but himself. He rarely smiled and had little apparent sense of humor. Durham hated his nickname, but it had become popular as his abrasive manner took its toll of goodwill. Bull Durham was a popular tobacco, and as a result, "Durham" had become a slang word for "bullshit." No one dared call him Bull to his face, however. He was a big man who routinely used his size for intimidation. Durham openly brown nosed his superiors and tended to bully anyone he outranked, although he made some effort to get along with most of the pilots in the squadron. Alan had been included in that group until about two months earlier. Then he, as acting engineering officer, had grounded Durham's airplane, which Durham took as a personal affront. The airplane turned out to have a dangerous defect. Durham's gunner had pointed out the symptoms during their last flight, but Durham had ignored the tip. The word had circulated around the squadron that Alan had been correct to ground the airplane, adding to Durham's irritation.

Since that event, Durham had been seething with anger toward Alan. As flight officer, scheduling planes and pilots was Durham's responsibility. On this voyage until now, the only flying for Bombing Five had been antisubmarine patrol, considered a bore by most of the pilots, and Durham had not kept Alan out of this duty. Now all the pilots were looking forward to dive bombing practice, and Durham had pulled Alan out. Durham had tried to pull Alan out of a mission once before, back in November, but the skipper had overruled him. *I guess he thinks he can get away with it this time. We'll see.*

Since then, Alan had seen that Durham was currying favor with Armiston, and, with less success, the squadron executive officer, Lieutenant Gordon "Gordie" Bellingham. As exec, Bellingham outranked Durham in the squadron, even though Bellingham had more recently been promoted to lieutenant and thus was junior to Durham in the navy. Alan liked Bellingham and thought he was a good exec. A good exec should be aware of the personal relationships in the squadron. Alan thought Bellingham was well aware that Durham was wearing out his welcome with a number of the pilots.

All the pilots in the squadron were expected to attend and absorb any briefing, whether or not they were on the roster for that flight, so that last minute substitutions could be made. At the end of the briefing, the pilots were dismissed until 0845, to be ready for the 0900 launch. Alan wanted to find out for sure why he was not included. He would probably get no satisfaction from Durham, but he would have to follow procedure and talk to him first, before going up the hierarchy. Durham ducked out of the ready room as soon as the briefing was finished. Alan tracked him down in the squadron offices.

A smirk appeared on Durham's face as soon as he saw Alan.

Alan came right to the point. "Why wasn't I included in today's practice, sir?"

Durham's smirk remained. "Close the door, Ericsson."

After Alan closed the door, Durham continued, a smile spreading on his face, "You're not really cut out for combat flying, are you, Ericsson? You just don't have the aggressive spirit. We're thinking of taking you off flight status permanently. Pushing paper seems like a job you would be more suited for."

"I see, sir," said Alan evenly, controlling his temper with some difficulty.

"Now get out, Ericsson. I've got work to do."

"Yes, sir," said Alan and left Durham's office. He had thought his place in the squadron was fairly secure, in spite of his low bombing scores, and that Durham's threat was an idle one. Now he was not so sure. As he headed into the passageway, Bellingham was coming toward him.

"May I have a word with you, sir, in private?"

"Sure, Alan. Come into my office." They went into Bellingham's office, and Bellingham closed the door.

"Durham has taken me out of today's practice, sir. He said, quote, 'We're thinking of taking you off flight status permanently,' unquote. He says I don't have aggressive spirit."

"Must be the royal 'we' because I've never heard of this bullshit. I was on my way to ask him why you were not on the roster. He's never gotten over that time you grounded his plane, has he? Take Robbins's place in the practice today, and I'll tell Durham and Robbins. If Durham throws you any more screwballs, let me know."

Ensign Lewis Robbins was the most junior pilot in the squadron, having been in the squadron less than a month. Robbins's place in the order for the practice was last, flying wing on Lieutenant j.g. Jeremiah "Jerry" West, one of the more senior pilots in the squadron.

"Thank you, sir. Do you have any complaints about my performance in the squadron, sir?"

"No, Alan. You need to improve your bombing scores. Your gunnery is excellent, as is your work on the hangar deck, and you did depth charge that submarine. Considering you're only eight months out of Pensacola, I think you've done pretty well. You're a little older and wiser than many of the others."

"Thank you, sir. I can see that being exec isn't an easy job."

"No, Alan, it's not. But it can be very satisfying. When you get some more experience, you might make a good exec."

"Thank you, sir."

"Good luck in the practice, and get a hit. See you back in the ready room."

"I'll do my best, sir," said Alan as he opened the door. He was grateful that Bellingham was a thoughtful and friendly officer, and Alan felt somewhat relieved as he went back to the ready room. He was still worried because he knew if his bombing scores did not improve, his place in the squadron might not be secure.

The pilots were back in the ready room at 0845; a little later the klaxon sounded, and they were ordered to man their planes. Knowing it would be cold at high altitude, Alan grabbed his sheepskin flying jacket on the way out. As he stepped through the door out of the island onto the flight deck, the wind struck him and set his pant legs flapping. *Yorktown* and her escorts had turned off their base course of west-northwest to steam into the east-northeast trade wind for flight operations. The speed of the ship added to the speed of the wind to produce a wind over the deck of about 35 knots. Alan was inspired by the beautiful day, with bright sun, a few puffy clouds, and temperatures in the sixties. His quick scan of the sky found Scouting Five off to starboard, waiting to land back aboard.

Above him as he came out of the island was the air control station. The air control station was a compartment high on the port side of the island behind the bridge. Its large windows projected out from the island to provide a complete view of the flight deck. This station was where flight operations were controlled in a manner roughly analogous to a control tower on land.

He looked over Bombing Five's aircraft as he walked aft to his plane. They were spotted for takeoff on the aft end of the flight deck, with the deck cleared ahead of them. They were in rows of two, staggered so the tail of one airplane fit between the noses of two in the next row. Neither the Dauntlesses nor the Wildcats had folding wings, but the larger Devastators did, so they could be spotted closer together. He thought the squadron's aircraft made an impressive sight, lined up with the ship's wake spreading out behind them.

Yorktown at sea, February 1942
(US Navy/PD-USGOV-MILITARY-NAVY)

Taking Robbins's place, Alan would be flying wing on Jerry West, along with Ensign Otto Meyer, who, like Robbins, had joined while the ship was in Norfolk. Carrier squadrons, except for fighter squadrons, used three plane sections consisting of a leader and two wingmen, who normally flew on either side of the leader. Two sections constituted a division. There were three divisions in the typical scouting or bombing squadron, normally led by the skipper, the exec, and the flight officer. West was leading the last section, the second section in the last division, led by Durham.

In July 1941, US Navy fighter squadrons had switched over from three plane sections to two plane sections because they were more flexible and maneuverable. In these squadrons, three sections constituted a division. Some pilots were advocating that the other carrier squadrons make the switch to two plane sections. This seemed like a good idea to Alan, but it had not happened yet.

The pilots on the regular flying roster each had an airplane assigned to them, and the name of the pilot was stenciled on the side of the fuselage, below the forward cockpit canopy. Five Baker Twelve (5-B-12) had become Alan's airplane. However, for the sake of flexibility, pilots should always be ready to fly any airplane of the same type and not become too attached to any one airplane. Alan found that his airplane for this mission, the airplane spotted in last position, in the last row on the starboard side, was 5-B-12. *Perhaps Durham hoped it would become Robbins's airplane when I was grounded.*

The brown-shirted plane captain, Aviation Machinists Mate First Class (AMM1c) Karl Klein, was standing on the left wing outside the front cockpit, having finished the engine warm up and shut down the engine. All the enlisted men who worked on the flight deck had colored shirts and cloth helmets in colors that identified their function. The plane captains were in charge of maintenance and preparation of one plane. Alan respected Klein and made sure Klein knew that. Klein reciprocated, and they had a good relationship. Alan walked up to the left side of the fuselage behind the wing and climbed up onto the black nonskid walkway on the wing next to the fuselage.

"Good morning, Klein," shouted Alan over the wind and noise from engines still running. "All set to go?"

"She's ready to go, sir. I heard Ensign Robbins would be taking her today," said Klein.

Alan smiled and said, "That was Bull's plan, but it got changed."

"Good deal, sir," said Klein, grinning.

As Klein climbed down off the wing, another enlisted man climbed onto the wing.

"Good morning, sir," said Aviation Machinists Mate Third Class (AMM3c) Alvin Kidd, "I was told to report as gunner on this airplane."

Alan knew Kidd as a mechanic. Alan also knew Kidd had recently qualified as a gunner, but Alan had not flown with Kidd. He wondered if Kidd would be as chatty in the air as he was on the hangar deck. Aviation Radioman Second Class (ARM2c) Wayne Parker had been Alan's usual gunner, but Durham knew that Alan and Parker got along well together, so he assigned Parker to fly with other pilots.

"Very good, Kidd. I'll be flying this airplane, instead of Ensign Robbins. Welcome aboard."

"Thank you, sir. Glad to fly with you, sir."

Alan climbed into the front cockpit, while Kidd climbed into the rear one. Alan quickly strapped in, checked the adjustment of the seat and rudder pedals, and stowed his charts and notes. He had been flying the Dauntless now for five months and had become thoroughly acquainted with it. He was completely at home in the spartan military interior, with the black instrument panel in front of him, a thicket of levers and knobs on the left side, many smaller levers and controls on a shelf on the right side, and the control stick sprouting up in the middle. The cockpit was as familiar now as his office had been when he had had a desk job.

1. CONTROL STICK
2. CARBURETOR AIR CONTROL
3. COWLING FLAP CONTROL LEVER
4. AUTO-PILOT "ON-OFF" SWITCH
5. PARKING BRAKE HANDLE
6. TRIGGER SWITCH
7. COCKPIT VENTILATOR
8. ENGINE PRIMER
9. OIL COOLER AIR SCOOP CONTROL
10. IGNITION SWITCH
11. STARTER MESHING PULL
12. WINDSHIELD HOT AIR CONTROL

PHOTO NO. 12942 - PILOT'S COCKPIT - FRONT

Dauntless pilot's cockpit, from pilot's manual
(US Navy/PD-USGOV-MILITARY-NAVY)

CHAPTER THREE ~ NORTHWEST TO SAN DIEGO

The company name for the SBD was the Dauntless, but it was also known to the pilots as the "Slow but Deadly," the "Speedy D," and a few other more derogatory names. Alan thought the Dauntless was by far the best dive bomber in the US inventory, and he was very pleased to be flying it. It was a big improvement in handling characteristics and performance over its immediate predecessor, the Northrop BT-1. When Alan had joined Bombing Five, they were still flying the BT-1, and Alan had done his carrier qualification in it.

Alan liked the Dauntless so well that he wondered whether he would have an equal regard for its planned replacement, the Curtis SB2C Helldiver. The Helldiver was a larger, faster airplane with an internal bomb bay and folding wings. The Helldiver had first flown over a year earlier in December 1940. After the prototype was destroyed a few days later, many changes were made. However, the navy was in such a rush to get the latest aircraft to the fleet that they had ordered the Helldiver into production before that. This was an unusual and possibly counterproductive step in Alan's view. After that progress slowed down, and the first production aircraft was still many months off.

The Grumman TBF Avenger, on the other hand, the new torpedo bomber, first flew eight months after the Helldiver. The Avenger's development, however, had proceeded much more smoothly and rapidly than that of the Helldiver. It was now starting production and was due to reach the fleet in a few months. It could carry a torpedo internally in a large bay in the fuselage, and it seemed to be a big advance over the obsolescent Devastator.

The flight deck of an aircraft carrier was in effect an airport, although it was much smaller than anything but the tiniest of land airports. It was also surrounded with good places to watch operations, from much closer positions than available at a land airport. So the pilots had a large audience at close range for some the most difficult parts of their flying.

Alan looked out over the squadron's airplanes ahead, an impressive sight from this angle as well. The right wing of West's airplane was directly in front of his propeller. He started watching the deck signal officer, called Fly One. After a few minutes, Fly One gave all the pilots the signal to start engines. Alan followed the warm start procedure and soon had the engine idling contentedly.

Alan turned on the intercom between the two cockpits. He picked up the microphone, pressed the push-to-talk button on the side of the microphone, and said to Kidd, "Ready for takeoff?"

"Oh yes, sir. Great to get back in the air, ain't it, sir? I have been looking forward to this. Are we going to beat Scouting Five?" Kidd was referring to the squadron rivalry for most hits in the dive bombing exercise.

Alan knew he needed to nip the small talk in the bud. "Kidd, I like your enthusiasm, but I want all the talk on the intercom to be strictly business, unless we're on a long boring mission. Tell me anything you think I might need to know, and ask about anything you need to know to do your job, but hold the chitchat, OK?"

"Yes, sir. I…" The intercom went silent. *He's trying*, thought Alan.

Dauntless being launched from a carrier, 1941
(US Navy/PD-USGOV-MILITARY-NAVY)

The skipper would be the first to takeoff. Fly One was signaling with his flag and then sent Armiston on his way. One by one, Fly One sent the rest of the squadron on their way, with Meyer being the last before Alan. Fly One now stood to the right of Alan's plane. Seeing that Alan was looking toward him, he waved his checkered flag over his head, the signal to hold the brakes and go to full power. Alan pulled the stick full back with his right hand, pushed hard on the top of the rudder pedals, which activated the brakes, and moved the throttle lever smoothly to full power with his left hand. The engine roared, and the airplane shook in the propeller blast at full power. Like most aircraft engines, the engine had no muffler. There were two exhaust stacks appearing from the lower cowling, about eight feet away from the pilot's open cockpit on either side. Although Alan usually enjoyed engine noise, he was glad his leather helmet and earphones protected his ears somewhat from the deafening roar.

Alan looked over the engine gauges. The acceptable range on most of the gauges was marked with a green arc, so they could be rapidly scanned for trouble. Fly One was holding his hand cupped to his ear, the signal that the engine sounded OK to him: Was the pilot ready to go? Alan thought it sounded like all 1,000 horses were present and accounted for, and he nodded that he was ready to go. Then Fly One brought the flag smartly forward and down. Alan released the brakes and eased the stick forward as the airplane accelerated rapidly.

With its light load, the airplane lifted off about halfway down the deck and quickly passed over the bow of the ship. Alan shifted his left hand to the stick, and with his right he moved the landing gear lever aft to the up position. He then pushed the hydraulic power lever, which activated the hydraulic system for enough time to retract the gear. He waited for the plane to accelerate more and then followed the same procedure with the flaps. Switching hands again on the stick, he used his left hand to reduce power to the normal climb setting by pulling the throttle and propeller levers back, while the roar of the engine subsided slightly. He banked to the right to cut inside West's turn and join up in formation. He slid the front cockpit canopy forward to close it, and Kidd closed the rear canopy by sliding it back. The canopies were kept open for takeoff and landing to enable a quick exit in case of trouble. The squadron continued into the long spiral climb to 15,000 feet, engines still loud under climb power, while the ships below became steadily smaller.

Squadron procedures said that oxygen was not required for a climb to 15,000 feet, followed by an immediate practice dive bombing run. If they stayed above 12,000 for more than 30 minutes or climbed higher than 15,000, oxygen was required. Alan enjoyed the view from high altitude on a clear day, and he liked the higher speed and longer range when the airplane was operated there. However, the fact that the oxygen mask became uncomfortable fairly quickly took a lot of the fun out of it.

Below them, *Yorktown* was still headed northeast while she took Scouting Five back aboard. Then she turned left back to the west-northwesterly base course she had been following, with the destroyer screen and two cruisers maneuvering to keep their positions relative to the carrier. The tow ship and target were off to port of the task force. Alan found that it was always a pleasure to watch these evolutions from the air.

Passing through 11,000 feet, following squadron procedure, Alan throttled back, shifted the supercharger control lever smartly to high blower, and brought the throttle back up to the climb setting. The higher supercharger speed caused the compression of the air going into the engine to increase, overcoming the loss of atmospheric pressure at higher altitudes.

After about fifteen minutes, Alan joined the rest of the squadron orbiting at 15,000 feet. He throttled back to low cruise, and the roar of the engine was subdued. It was a very nice sunny day. *Yorktown* was a small gray rectangle far below, with her wake more visible than the ship itself. On a hand signal from the skipper, the formation shifted from sections into a single line astern for each division, to get ready for the dive.

From the thumps and vibrations, he could sense Kidd swiveling his seat around to face aft and opening the rear cockpit canopy. Alan pulled down his goggles and opened the front canopy. His outside air temperature gauge read 9 degrees Fahrenheit, making him glad of his jacket. Dives were always made with both canopies open, in case of trouble, and the wind in the cockpit rose to the point where goggles were needed. To get used to what it would be like in a combat situation, the gunner swiveled his seat and slid both the top and rear canopy sections forward to open the rear cockpit completely. He then removed the rear flexible machine gun from its stowage in the aft fuselage, set it up on the ring mount facing aft, mounted an ammunition box on the gun, and set up the ammunition belt feed.

Alan keyed his mike. "Ready for the dive, Kidd?"

"Ready, sir," Kidd replied.

After Armiston's and Bellingham's divisions had dived, Alan shifted the supercharger to low blower in preparation for the pullout at the end of the dive. Then he moved the propeller control to full low rpm, to prevent engine overspeed during the dive. Next he moved the mixture control to full rich and turned on carburetor heat, which kept carburetor ice from forming at very low power settings. Then he switched the stick to his left hand, and with his right he moved the dive flap lever aft to the open position. This lever controlled both the lower flaps, or landing flaps, and upper flaps, or dive flaps, on the trailing edge of the wing. The landing flap lever controlled only the lower flaps. However, the flaps would not move until the hydraulic power lever was pressed.

Alan saw Durham suddenly roll inverted and pull the nose down into a near vertical dive. One by one, the others followed as they came to the same position. Alan glanced back and forth between the line of aircraft ahead and the target sled, which he could see by looking next to the fuselage and just in front of the wing on the left side. There was a small window in the bottom of the fuselage in front of the control stick, intended to help keep the target in view before the dive. However, it was usually obscured with engine oil, which naturally collected on the bottom of the fuselage behind the engine. The oil came from minor leaks around the engine and various vents in the oil system.

As West went into his dive, Alan pushed the hydraulic power lever to open the landing and dive flaps. These were perforated rectangular panels along the trailing edge of the wing, which opened up like a clamshell to an angle about thirty degrees from parallel to the airstream, providing a lot of aerodynamic drag. These flaps had been developed for the BT-1 and were one of the few items that were carried over to its successor. This extra drag permitted the clean monoplane dive bomber to dive vertically without exceeding 240 knots airspeed. Going any faster meant that the pullout at the bottom of the dive would have such high g-force that it might cause the pilot to black out and the wings to be permanently bent, or the pullout had to be started so high that a hit would be very unlikely.

Meyer went into his dive. Now it was Alan's turn. "Here we go," he cued Kidd on the intercom. Alan then made a very quick series of control motions to enter the dive. He switched hands on the stick and pulled the throttle to idle. Then he rolled the airplane upside down and pulled the nose down into a steep dive. He found his tiny target and maneuvered to fly a straight line toward a point upwind of the target, using the sun for direction and knowing the wind was east-northeast. The tow ship had gone into a hard turn to the left, with it and the target sled each at the head of a wake that looked like a comma, a typical maneuver of a ship under air attack. In making the hard turn, both the tow ship and the target sled were skidding sideways, as usual, in addition to turning. This made it more difficult to visualize where their paths were going and where the target would be when the bomb arrived.

His dive felt like it was straight down, but he knew that it was probably in the 70 to 80 degree range. The sound of the air rushing past the cockpit quickly built up to a roar, drowning out the engine. Alan felt his adrenaline rise rapidly as he hurtled down at 400 feet per second, and the size of the ships below grew quickly. The seat belt, which he had carefully tightened, and his feet on the rudder pedals kept him from sliding off the nearly vertical seat cushion. He kept the upper part of his body from falling toward the instrument panel by using his left arm braced against the glare shield above the instrument panel. He leaned forward and put his right eye up to the bombsight. He watched the ball instrument in the sight and tried to keep it centered, to avoid any sideways skidding of the airplane, which would cause the bomb to diverge from the direction the airplane was pointed. At the same time, he kept the cross hairs of the sight on the aiming point.

Alan watched the altimeter with his left eye. At 4,000 feet, he took his left hand off the glare shield, using his muscles to keep from falling into the instrument panel, and reached down with his left hand for the bomb release lever. He knew that the high-scoring pilots went lower in their dives, around 1,500 feet, before releasing the bomb and pulling out. Alan had released as low as 2,000 feet, but it made him nervous. He had decided to try 1,750, prolonging his dive by about a half a second. Passing through 2,000 feet, he had the sight on the aiming point. He pulled the bomb release lever. He felt nothing because the practice bomb was very light, but he saw that, while pulling the lever, he had allowed the ball to wobble off center.

Immediately, he started pulling the nose up with his right hand on the stick. As the g-forces built up, he felt pulled down into his seat. He pulled the nose up until he began to lose his vision. As the blood drained from his head into his feet, the image in his eyes became gray and smaller with the onset of tunnel vision. He kept the nose coming up at a rate that kept his tunnel vision moderate, maintaining somewhere around four g's, or four times the normal force of gravity.

The horizon came into view at the top of his vision. Now Alan was being pulled into his seat instead of into the instrument panel. He was able to put his left hand on the stick and use his right hand to move the dive flap lever forward to the up position. By then he had leveled off at 500 feet, not a lot of room to spare, but he realized that, in a combat situation, he would have to take more risk and go lower, to increase the chance of a hit. Then he quickly pushed the hydraulic power lever, so the flaps would retract. The roar and the airspeed fell quickly. He quickly switched hands on the stick, pushed the propeller control to climb rpm, opened the throttle to climb power, and turned off the carburetor heat. The tension subsided, and he felt the cold sweat inside his clothes. He climbed back to 1,000 feet and joined up with the rest of the squadron. Now he had time to reflect that he had very likely missed because the ball was off center, and he felt deflated.

The formation then turned and headed back for the ship. The ship was steaming east-northeast into the trade wind again for flight operations. The squadron flew about 1,000 feet off the starboard side of the ship at 800 feet above the water from stern to bow in right echelon formation. Then came the break, the standard military method for spacing out the formation for landing. Even with the bow of the carrier, Armiston, leading the formation, abruptly banked to the left and made a 180 degree turn to the left to enter the downwind leg of the traffic pattern off the port side of the ship. As he did so, he lowered the landing gear. At five second intervals, each pilot followed in succession. With the landing gear down, each plane slowed in the turn from cruising speed, about 150 knots, to pattern speed, about 100 knots. Then the canopies were opened, and the landing checklist followed. Alan was the tail end Charlie, and he had gone around three miles beyond the carrier before it was finally his turn to swing around into the landing pattern.

Alan flew back toward the ship, following Meyer, and went through the carrier landing checklist. He felt the tension rising, as he always did before a carrier landing. He flew past the stern of the ship on the downwind leg and continued for about half a mile. Then he turned 90 degrees left onto base leg and flew until he was nearly lined up with the deck, slowing to 65 knots, about five knots above stall speed for the airplane's typical landing gross weight. Then he made a gradual left turn again onto the final approach leg, headed toward the stern of the ship from straight behind.

Dauntless coming aboard with LSO
(US Navy/PD-USGOV-MILITARY-NAVY)

Now he kept the airspeed constant by moving the nose up or down with his right hand on the stick. At the same time, he controlled the angle of the shallow glide with his left hand on the throttle. He began closely watching the signals from the landing signal officer (LSO), Lieutenant j.g. Norwood "Soupy" Campbell, who was standing on a special platform on the port side above the aft end of the flight deck and giving correction signals with large paddles held in each hand. Soupy was giving Alan small corrections, which he followed. As he approached the aft end of the flight deck, Soupy gave Alan the "cut" signal, which meant the approach was good and he should close the throttle and land. There were nine arresting wires stretched across the aft half of the flight deck. Alan plunked down near the fourth. The arresting hook dangling from the tail of his Dauntless bounced and caught the fifth wire.

The wire hauled the airplane's speed down very quickly, so that it came to a stop in about 100 feet. The rapid deceleration threw Alan forward against the seat belt and his left arm braced against the glare shield. He narrowly missed bruising his forehead on the gunsight. Alan had become used to these scary sensations, and in fact relished them, because they signaled a successful landing. Moving forward, the resistance of each wire was higher than the previous one, because there was less space to stop before the crash barrier. Thus it was easier on the body to catch one of the first few wires. However, Alan's crash the previous October was caused by trying too hard to do this, and afterward he had broken that habit quickly. As the airplane stopped, the tension came off the arresting wire, and the airplane's tail came down on the deck. He began to relax.

A yellow-shirted deck control man signaled Alan to taxi ahead because the green-shirted arresting gear men had disengaged the arresting hook from the wire. He pulled the lever that raised the hook and taxied forward, the arresting wires and barriers having been folded down into slots in the deck by a chief petty officer operating controls in the gallery. Another yellow-shirted deck control man directed him where to park. Blue-shirted plane handlers then placed chocks around the main wheels to prevent the aircraft from moving. He shut down the engine and climbed out into the 35 knot wind. He pulled off his flight jacket and felt his sweaty clothes quickly cool. The deck started to tilt to starboard as the ship heeled in the left turn out of the wind to resume its course toward San Diego.

The Bombing Five pilots were given some time to have lunch and relax, and told to be back in the ready room at 1300 for another dive bombing practice. Alan got back to the ready room at 1255. A large diagram of the target sled had been made and posted at the front of the room. The positions where each practice bomb fell in the morning practice had been marked on the diagram with the sequence number of the airplane. Alan's bomb had missed to starboard by about 50 feet. Only three pilots missed by a greater amount. Among these were Lieutenant j.g. Winfield "Pooh" Featherstone and Ensign Sherwood "Slippery" Simpkin, who fell near the bottom of the squadron in most respects. Armiston, Bellingham, Durham, West, Jolly, and Scottie had gotten hits. Durham's was the best, near the center of the target. Scouting Five had gotten five hits, so Bombing Five was ahead in the rivalry. Alan was disappointed, but he knew what he had done wrong. He had to go lower and keep the ball centered. He resolved to try to go steadier and lower in the next dive.

Armiston went over the plan for the next practice, which was essentially a repeat of the morning exercise, except that Bombing Five would launch first at 1330. Alan noticed that Durham had made a change to the gunner assignments, assigning Parker to be his own gunner. *That looks like trouble*, he thought. When Alan came onto the flight deck, he noticed Bellingham and Parker talking to each other as they walked around to the forward end of the island, away from the other pilots and gunners and out of sight. The cumulus clouds had become larger and closer together.

This time the practice dives were a little different, because the clouds at around 5,000 feet sometimes obscured the target. As Alan popped out of the bottom of the clouds, he found he was close enough to being on target that he could get back on. He managed to keep the ball centered, and he dropped near 1,500 feet. He pulled out harder, causing his vision to almost disappear. He finished at 500 feet, so he still had a little room to spare. He had a good feeling about this dive.

After landing and parking his airplane, Alan started walking aft on the starboard side of the flight deck toward the island. With flight operations complete, the ship started a left turn back to base course, and the flight deck canted to starboard. He was about halfway between the forward elevator and the island when he paused to watch the other ships of the task force maneuver toward their new positions on the base course.

Alan turned to look back at the navigation bridge. He was startled to see an officer dart across the bridge to the starboard wing, a strong indication that something was not going well. Alan watched as the same officer ran to the port wing of the bridge and then back to starboard. He was shouting orders, but Alan could not hear them from his position. The bridge was usually a place of calm, deliberate action, the navy at its finest. He smiled in amusement at this scene, which seemed to be the opposite.

Alan looked to starboard and saw the light cruiser *Richmond* turning left toward the carrier. If she turned to the right, she would easily miss *Yorktown*, but there was a destroyer off her starboard side in a parallel turn. If her turn continued, she would be on a collision course with the carrier. Alan stared in fascination, as the cruiser continued her turn. It would not be so amusing if there really were a collision.

The officer on the bridge was a burly man, not particularly tall, so he was not Captain Buckthorn, who was tall with an average build. Normally the officer of the deck (OOD) had the conn. Alan did not know all the officers in the regular rotation for OOD, but he could not remember one who was burly. He walked toward the island to see if he could recognize the officer who apparently had the conn.

The collision alarm sounded with a loud blare. Men on deck stopped what they were doing to see what was happening. *Yorktown* and *Richmond* continued their left turns, with *Richmond* now off the starboard bow with a course perpendicular to *Yorktown* and only about 300 yards away. Then Alan noticed turbulence in the water on *Richmond*'s port quarter. He figured she was reversing her port screw in an attempt to tighten the turn. Alan looked up at the bridge. The same officer appeared in the middle of the bridge and leaned over the rail to shout to someone on the flight deck. It was the ship's executive officer, Commander Clapp.

The ships continued their turns, with their courses gradually moving from perpendicular toward parallel. It was going to be a very near thing whether they hit or not. As they came closer, Alan grabbed a stanchion and unconsciously held his breath. Finally *Richmond* swept down *Yorktown*'s starboard side, going in the opposite direction, only about 10 yards away. As Alan released his breath, he heard sailors on both ships exchanging insults. Petty officers on both ships barked out reprimands to their men.

Alan looked at the bridge again. He recognized Captain Buckthorn, and then he and Clapp moved aft into the wheelhouse and out of sight. What had happened? Alan was very curious, but he was pretty sure such an embarrassing incident would never be explained.

The excitement seemed to be over, and Alan went to the hangar deck to see if there were any problems, known as "squawks," reported with the airplanes. When he came into the hangar, he ran into Parker, who seemed to be both scared and angry.

"Hello, Parker. How did the flight with Bull go?"

"It was the shits, sir. He hardly said a word to me. He made the worst dive I've ever seen. He was wobbling around the whole way down. Then after the flight, he accused me of keeping my seat facing forward during the dive and getting all over the rudder pedals to mess it up. He told me he was going make sure I was demoted and never flew again."

"I am very sorry, Parker. You're getting caught up in Bull's feud with me. It has nothing to do with your performance. I'll have a talk with the exec."

"Thank you, sir. Lieutenant Bellingham already has an idea of what is going on. He pulled me aside before the flight and asked me about flying with Bull. I told him I expected that Bull would find some reason to take me off flight status. He looked disgusted and said to let him know if that happened. I am going to ask Chief Patterson to do that."

Aviation Chief Machinists Mate (ACMM) Roy Patterson was the senior enlisted man in the squadron and acted as the official liaison between the enlisted men and the officers.

"Good. I don't think Bull will get away with this in the end. But you may have to put up with some more crap in the meantime. Good luck, Parker."

"Thank you, sir. The way things are going, I will need it."

Alan went to check in with Scottie, and Parker went to report to his plane captain.

The Bombing Five pilots were told by the bullhorn to gather again in the ready room at 1600, when the results of the afternoon practice would be posted. This time Alan got a hit! His pleasure was tempered by the fact that it was only a hit by about two feet, and Armiston, Bellingham, West, and Jensen had done better, but still he felt a glow of satisfaction. Bellingham's was the best, about three feet from the center. Scouting Five got seven hits, so they won the contest. Durham had missed by 40 feet, about average for the misses. Durham's miss was explained by Parker's story, but Alan wondered what caused Jolly to miss. Both were among the high scorers in the squadron.

At supper, the day's practice naturally came up in conversation. Jolly started off, "Did you see Bull in the second dive? I was following him. I thought maybe his rudder cables had come loose. He was fishtailing around so much I lost my concentration. I've got to make sure to try to keep my concentration no matter what happens."

That explains Jolly's miss, thought Alan. Durham had caused Bombing Five to lose the contest with Scouting Five. Lying about Parker's actions was a much more serious offense, however.

Alan said, "I was so far back I couldn't see what happened with Bull in the dive. But I have an idea of what was going on. He assigned Parker to be his gunner, and he was planning to find a reason to bilge Parker as a gunner, because he knows Parker and I get along well. So he deliberately messed up his dive. Then after the flight, he accused Parker of having his seat facing forward and messing up the dive with the rudder pedals. He wants Parker demoted and permanently barred from flying. I ran into Parker, and he told me about it. Luckily Bellingham was already expecting trouble between Bull and Parker, and he talked to Parker before the flight, so I doubt Bull will get away with it."

Jolly said, "I remember seeing Bull's gunner in the dive. He was facing aft."

"Bull sure is a pill. I'm startin' to think the squadron might be better off if Armiston bilged him, even though he's a good pilot," said Slick in his Arkansas drawl.

Teeth Jensen replied, "Gordie is a damn fine exec. He picks up on things like that and tries to shield Armiston from all the petty stuff. But I wonder how long he'll be able to do that with Bull, especially with Bull being senior to him."

Alan changed the subject: "Anybody know what caused the near collision with the *Richmond* around fifteen thirty? Clapp seemed to have the conn for some reason."

Jolly replied, "I was wondering about that too. My gunner is a friend of one of the quartermasters. I asked him about it later. He said Buckthorn had the conn at first. Then he gave orders to go back to base course and gave the conn back to the OOD. Then he went below. Very shortly Clapp appeared on the bridge and took over the conn himself. He proceeded to screw up the maneuver to the point where there nearly was a collision with *Richmond*. When the collision alarm went off, Buckthorn rushed back to the bridge. He told Clapp to wait in his sea cabin, took the conn, and got everything straightened out. Sometime later there was a shouting match in the sea cabin."

"That would've been fun to see," said Mike with a smile. The others grinned.

"I hear Clapp disapproves of almost everything the captain does, which is why the captain avoids him as much as possible," said Teeth.

"Some exec," said Slick.

CHAPTER FOUR

San Diego

Tuesday, December 30, 1941

Flight quarters was at 0600, with the pilots of all four squadrons gathered in their ready rooms. Seeing Armiston at the front of the room reminded Alan that Bellingham had been unable to avoid involving Armiston in the question of Parker's flying status. There was a rumor that the matter was concluded with Durham getting dressed down in Armiston's office. *Durham's behavior is getting him into trouble with the skipper*—a gratifying thought. Durham's feud with Alan continued, but now Alan was somewhat relieved that he was no longer the sole object of Durham's anger. Each pilot who had flown with Parker as his gunner—Mike, West, and Ned—had stood up for Parker when Bellingham asked around, so now Durham hated them also. Jolly clinched it when he told the exec that Parker was facing aft in the dive, so now Durham hated Jolly almost as much as Alan.

It had been announced the previous day that the whole air group would be flying into the San Diego Naval Air Station, located on North Island in San Diego Harbor, while the carrier approached the harbor. It was another clear day with the temperature in the mid-fifties at dawn. *Yorktown* was now about 75 miles southwest of San Diego, coming straight in from well offshore to minimize time in the coastwise shipping lanes. Flying the air group in from offshore was an alternative to unloading them by crane and taxiing them to the naval air station.

It had also been announced that the ship would be spending about a week in San Diego, before departing on her next assignment. Now, while he was waiting for the briefing to start, Alan recalled what he knew about San Diego. Although Alan had taken a bus trip to Tijuana when he was stationed on *Pennsylvania* based at San Pedro, he did not see much of San Diego Harbor or the navy facilities as he passed by. He had heard a fair amount about that aspect from navy friends.

Naval aviation on North Island went back to the earliest days before World War I, when Glenn Curtiss owned it. Ever since then, North Island had been the hub of naval aviation on the West Coast. Now the air station had become a very large facility.

Like Norfolk on the East Coast, San Diego was also the traditional naval fleet headquarters for the West Coast. Unlike Norfolk, major shipbuilding and major repair were all done at other ports, mainly Mare Island, on San Francisco Bay, and Bremerton, across Puget Sound from Seattle. This was because the natural harbor was too shallow for large modern ships, and only in the last two years had it been dredged to accommodate them.

Alan's attention returned to the briefing as Armiston began with some background. He reminded the pilots that the civilian airport, Lindbergh Field, was directly across the harbor to the north of North Island, only about two miles away from the naval air station, and it should be avoided. Durham, as flight officer, presented the weather, which was excellent. Jolly, as navigation officer, gave the course and distance for the flight.

Then Armiston discussed the air group procedure for this flight. Since they left Norfolk, the *Yorktown*'s air officer, his assistant, and the air group commander had been considering what types of launch and departure sequences they would use in a combat strike against enemy carriers.

Alan knew that the original doctrine was to use what was called a "normal departure." The squadrons were launched one by one, and they departed for the target as soon as each squadron was complete and in formation. Usually the fighters going on the strike were launched first, because they had the shortest takeoff roll, and thus could be spotted in front. Also there was a preference for having the fighters engage enemy fighters and strafe the target before the bombers arrived. The torpedo bombers were launched last, because they required the longest takeoff roll. Since the fastest airplanes were launched first and the slowest last, the squadrons would definitely not arrive at the target at the same time.

Later a preference developed for all the strike aircraft to arrive at the target together, with the torpedo planes down low ready to begin their runs, the dive bombers up high ready for their dives, and the escorting fighters divided between the two groups. If that were achieved, the torpedo bombers and dive bombers would attack simultaneously, dividing the defending fighters and antiaircraft fire.

The standard doctrine intended to accomplish this result was called a "deferred departure." In this, all the strike aircraft took off and assumed squadron formations near the carrier and then departed for the target as one large group. The idea was that the whole group would remain together and arrive simultaneously at the target. The pilots had been pointing out for some time that there were several flaws with this procedure. First, the planes circling over the carrier, waiting for the last to take off, used up a significant amount of fuel, cutting into their combat radius.

This was particularly true if all four squadrons were involved, because that required more than a full deck load, and there was an extra delay while the second deck load was brought up from the hangar. Second, the three aircraft types that were now in service cruised at different speeds, so they would slowly draw apart or the faster types would have to make S turns to stay with the slower ones, which would reduce their range. For the flight to the target, the torpedo planes cruised at about 100 knots, the dive bombers at 130 knots, and the fighters at 140 knots. Third, with the dive bombers cruising at high altitude, 12,000–20,000 feet, while en route to the target, it would have to be very clear weather to remain in visual contact with the torpedo planes at 1,000 feet. Therefore, being together at the beginning of the flight would probably be of little help in arriving simultaneously.

The air office and group commander had come up with an alternative procedure, a modification of the normal departure, called a "running rendezvous." The slow torpedo bombers would take off first, the dive bombers next, and the fighters last. Each squadron would form up and depart for the target as soon as possible. The idea was that the faster squadrons would tend to catch up as they flew to the target.

Alan liked the idea, but he realized that there was a problem because the torpedo bombers needed most of the deck length to take off when they were carrying torpedoes, so they could not have airplanes spotted behind them. The easiest solution was to launch them separately first and then bring the rest up from the hangar and launch them together. The delay while the others were brought up from the hangar seemed to roughly compensate for the big speed difference between the torpedo planes and the dive bombers.

The air office decided to use the opportunity of the flight to San Diego to try out this procedure. Although it was a relatively short flight compared to a combat situation, where the target would likely be at least 150 miles away, it would be useful to see how it worked out.

With the bombers not burdened with bombs, torpedoes, or gunners, it was also decided to try a full deck launch, in which all of the aircraft were on deck before departure. When Alan came onto the flight deck at 0645, he was greeted with an impressive sight. Rows of airplanes were spotted close together from just aft of the island all the way to the aft end of the flight deck, sixty-one in all. Most had their engines running as the plane captains warmed them up. Torpedo Five was in front, followed by Scouting Five, Bombing Five, and twelve from Fighting Forty-Two farthest aft. Six from Fighting Forty-Two were still on the hangar deck, kept on board for CAP over the carrier as she made her way into the harbor. *Yorktown* was turning around to steam into the west wind for flight operations.

Alan worked his way back to his airplane. He was in the middle of Bombing Five, flying wing on West again, with Morris as the other wingman. Alan waved to Klein, who was sitting in the cockpit of 5-B-12, shutting down the engine. Klein climbed out, and Alan climbed in and settled himself. He saw Fly One give the signal to Torpedo Five to start engines. Soon the CYAG led the launch in his Dauntless, followed by the skipper of Torpedo Five. Even with the short distance available, the Devastators lifted off easily well before the forward end of the deck. As Scouting Five started to launch, Alan got his engine started.

Soon Alan was on his way, and he slid in on West's left as West closed with the rest of the squadron. For the short flight, the Dauntlesses climbed to only 8,000 feet. Alan could make out the Scouting Five formation ahead, but Torpedo Five remained too far ahead to be visible. He looked to his left and could see San Clemente Island about 30 miles away. He then twisted farther to the left and looked farther away at eight o'clock and was just able to make out San Nicolas Island in the hazy distance. The pilots had been briefed that both islands belonged to the navy. San Clemente had a small air station with two runways, and San Nicolas had two unpaved emergency landing strips.

Now Alan could see the coastline ahead. The graceful curve of the harbor entrance became visible, and even some mountains east of the city. After about fifteen minutes, the hand signal was passed for the squadron to begin its descent. Alan could still see Scouting Five ahead in its descent, but not Torpedo Five. The flight had apparently been too short for the running rendezvous to be completed. Armiston came on the squadron frequency, having talked to North Island Tower, and said the wind was 280 degrees magnetic at 10 knots, and they would be using runway 29. The squadron would approach the air station on the south side in a wide left downwind leg, make a 180 degree turn, and then fly west over the runway threshold, before executing the break. As they approached, each three plane section shifted into right echelon, stepped down. Now Alan was on West's right and below, while Ned Morris was on Alan's right and below.

They turned and flew parallel to runway 29 about two miles offshore. They then made a very gradual 180 degree turn to the left to fly down the runway centerline. Armiston initiated the break procedure as he crossed the threshold, and the squadron followed. The last of the Scouting Five airplanes was on the final approach leg to the runway. Alan quickly looked over the air station. It occupied a lot of area and had a confusing array of taxiways between runway 29 on the south side and the ramp areas in the northeast corner. Alan could see the rest of Scouting Five taxiing northward.

Alan made his break, opened the canopy, and ran through the checklist for landing on shore. He made sure the arresting hook remained stowed and the tail wheel swivel was locked. As he turned onto the final approach leg toward the runway, he saw a green light from the control tower, clearing him to land. Alan noticed there were several large transport ships in the harbor to his right, and he recognized a navy tanker, known as an "oiler" in the navy, by all her extra gear topside for refueling ships while underway. Soon he was rolling down the runway, feeling that the landing was trivially easy compared to landing on a carrier. After he turned right off the runway, he was glad he could simply follow the airplane ahead on the long taxi to the ramp. He arrived on the ramp, and a lineman showed him where to park. The squadrons were side by side on the spacious ramp. He shut down the engine and climbed out at 0800. The skipper directed the Bombing Five pilots toward a hangar, where their shore ready room was located.

Yorktown at dock, North Island, San Diego Harbor, 1939
(US Navy/PD-USGOV-MILITARY-NAVY)

As Alan listened to the chatter among the pilots while they walked toward the hangar, he realized the long voyage from Norfolk was complete, and everyone was looking forward to a little time ashore and some relaxation, including himself. They were also wondering what their next assignment would be. He thought of Pearl Harbor and Jennifer.

In the ready room, Armiston made several announcements. Admiral Ernest J. King, formerly commander in chief of the Atlantic Fleet (CINCLANT), had taken over as CINCUS. He had immediately changed the acronym for that office to COMINCH because he did not like the sound of the earlier acronym. It was also announced that there would be practice sessions for all four squadrons that afternoon and the following morning. The practice for Bombing Five and Scouting Five that afternoon would be another dive bombing session. The next morning they would have gunnery practice, firing both fixed and flexible guns at targets towed by airplanes based at the air station. Gunnery and dive bombing practice could be set up more easily at a naval air station than on the carrier at sea. Then came the welcome news that there would be liberty in San Diego for all air group personnel for the afternoon and evening of New Year's Eve until 0200 New Year's Day. *Yorktown* would be departing on January 6, as the nucleus of a task force that would sortie from San Diego on an undisclosed mission. Rear Admiral Frank Jack Fletcher would be in command of the task force, and he would hoist his flag in *Yorktown*. *Yorktown* and her escorts came into the harbor later in the morning, and the carrier tied up to the pier before noon.

In the dive bombing practice that afternoon, Bombing Five got six hits. Alan was disappointed that his bomb was not one of them, but it was a very near miss. He had to content himself with the fact that the trend of his bombing results was positive. Durham again had the best hit, and Jolly also got a good hit.

By suppertime the pilots had gotten their rooms at the Bachelor Officers' Quarters (BOQ) on the air station, and the air group scuttlebutt had tapped into the local rumor mill. The word was that a lot of the shipping in the harbor was slated to form a convoy to reinforce the American outpost on Tutuila Island in the eastern part of the Samoa island group with a contingent of marines. *Yorktown*'s next assignment would be to escort the convoy to Samoa and then go on to Pearl Harbor. It sounded logical. *Well, if that's true, we aren't headed into harm's way for now,* Alan thought. Most of the pilots had had a full day and retired early to their rooms. Alan fell asleep with the delightful thought that, if the ship went to Pearl, he might be able to see Jennifer soon.

Wednesday, December 31, 1941

Alan was happy that, as usual, he was among the top scorers in the fixed gunnery exercise. He, Teeth, Jolly, and Durham were grouped so closely together it was essentially a tie. Armiston, Bellingham, MacAllester, West, and Davis were not far behind. Alan's gunner was again Kidd, and in the flexible gunnery exercise, he tried hard, but his inexperience resulted in a low score. Alan tried to be encouraging and pointed to his own bombing scores as an example. Parker was a high scorer, flying with Bellingham.

Alan was beginning to like Kidd, and it seemed that Kidd would be his regular gunner. Unlike many of the pilots and the navy hierarchy, Alan believed that gunners should get some training in how to fly from the rear seat, so the gunner might be able to bring the airplane back if the pilot was disabled. On the way back to North Island from the gunnery exercise, he decided to give it a try.

"OK, Kidd, I think it would be a good idea for you to have some practice flying the plane, so you would have a chance to bring her home if I could not. What do you think?"

"Ahhhh, yes, sir. I…I would like to give it a try, but when I started striking for gunner a couple of months ago, it was the first time I had ever been up in an airplane. I don't know anything about how to fly."

Alan could tell Kidd was startled and taken aback. "Well, let's just give it a try for a little while when we have a chance, like now. We'll take it one step at a time. The first thing is to locate the stick where it's stowed on the port side and mount it in the socket between your feet."

"OK, sir." After a minute: "Stick is mounted, sir."

"OK, now reach down and adjust the rudder pedals so you can use them." Another minute went by.

"Rudder pedals adjusted, sir."

"I am going to make some gentle maneuvers, and I want you to put your right hand on the stick and your feet on the rudder pedals and gently feel what I am doing without resisting it, OK?"

"OK, sir."

Alan moved the stick first sideways, rolling into banks in either direction. Then he moved it forward and backward, causing the airplane to nose up and down. Then he moved the rudder pedals, causing the airplane to yaw to the right and left. Meanwhile, he told Kidd what he was doing. "Now I want you to repeat what I did and keep telling me what you are doing. You move the controls, and I will keep my hand and feet on them to feel what you are doing, OK?"

"Yes, sir." Kidd did a reasonable job of repeating and gave a running commentary on what he was doing. After he finished he said, "Hey, that was OK. I think I'm starting to get the idea, sir."

"Very good, Kidd. Now we'd better catch up with the squadron, but we'll keep at it whenever there is a chance. If we go on a single plane search, we can get in a lot more practice."

"Yes, sir. Looking forward to it."

They caught up with the squadron as North Island came in sight and landed uneventfully.

After lunch, most of the pilots from the air group showered, changed their clothes, and boarded shuttle buses that would take them southeast over the causeway across Spanish Bight to the city of Coronado and the ferry terminal. There they would catch the ferry across the harbor to San Diego.

Alan went with Jolly Lowery, Teeth Jensen, and Slick Davis, catching the ferry at 1430. He was looking forward to a little fun and entertainment. It was another beautiful sunny day. As they crossed the harbor, Alan noticed that among the larger ships there were no fewer than three Matson luxury liners—*Monterey*, *Matsonia*, and *Lurline*. He remembered that Jennifer had made the voyage from San Francisco to Honolulu the previous September in *Monterey*. He knew that up until the United States entered the war, the Matson line had a monopoly on the shipping of civilian cargo and passengers between the mainland and Hawaii. He suspected that after the army took over Matson, along with other large businesses in Hawaii, their ships were put to military use. The ships here might be slated to carry the marines to Samoa, presumably in a somewhat less luxurious style than Matson had provided. Also in the harbor, besides the cruisers *Richmond* and *Trenton* that had come with *Yorktown* from Panama, Alan recognized a heavy cruiser of the *Northampton* class and a light cruiser of the *St. Louis* class.

Alan also got a closer look at the navy oiler he had seen from the air. She was *Kaskaskia* (AO-27), commissioned in 1940, one of the 18 knot modern oilers of the *Cimarron* class. Alan was interested in logistics in general and underway refueling in particular. Thus he had learned that the navy had realized in the mid thirties that it would need new high speed oilers to keep up with the newer, faster ships of the fleet, particularly the aircraft carriers, and he followed their development. Under the leadership of a former navy admiral, a successful example of industry government partnership got the Cimarron class, or "T3," oilers designed and built. They were bought by oil companies and went into service as civilian ships, but they could be taken over by the navy in case of war. The navy paid for their special features that were not needed for civilian use. At the time these were among the largest tankers in the world. However, what really distinguished these tankers from their commercial cousins was that they were 50 percent faster, able to cruise at 18 knots instead of 12 knots. It took 13,000 horsepower to move these ships at 18 knots, compared to 5,000 horsepower to move them at 12 knots, so the power plant was about two and a half times larger. Alan thought these fast oilers would be crucial in moving the fleet over the great distances of the Pacific Ocean. *Unfortunately, there are only a handful of them operational right now,* he thought.

USS *Cimarron* (AO-22), 1965
(US Navy/PD-USGOV-MILITARY-NAVY)

As the ferry approached the city, the buildings shone brightly in the low winter sun. Alan and his companions spent the rest of the afternoon wandering around the downtown area, doing a little shopping, and writing postcards to friends and relatives. Alan wrote postcards to Jennifer's parents and his parents, and to their friends the Peckhams, who had welcomed Alan to their home in Newport, Rhode Island, on many occasions. He found out that the mail to and from Hawaii had resumed a few days earlier. He was eager to write a real letter to Jennifer, but that would have to wait until he had some quiet time. He wondered how long it would be before she got her Christmas present from him, which he had mailed from Norfolk just before the Pearl Harbor attack.

They chose to have dinner at Top's Nightclub, a block from the waterfront just north of the downtown area. The owners had built a brand new building, with what Alan considered to be amusingly flashy modern architecture, and recently opened the club. The entertainment and dinner were good. Afterward, Slick steered them to a bar with hillbilly music that he had heard about. Alan and Slick enjoyed the music immensely. They stayed for about an hour, but it became clear that hillbilly music was not the favorite of Teeth and Jolly.

At about 2100, Jolly suggested they try another bar down the street. They went in and found a merry atmosphere with a jazz band playing. The place was pretty crowded, and they began looking for a table.

"Uh-oh, looks like this place is contaminated with Bull," said Jolly, looking at a table in a back corner. Alan followed his glance and saw that Durham had a table with Featherstone and Simpkin. The only obvious open table was right next to Durham's.

"They've seen us. We can't just leave like a bunch of scaredy-cats. Let's have a beer," said Slick. They moved toward the open table. The three seated officers were watching. Alan thought all three looked as if they had had a lot to drink. Durham had a full glass of clear liquor in front of him.

"Well, boys, it's hard get away from the sorry end of the squadron, isn't it?" boomed Durham as Alan and his companions sat down.

There were titters from Featherstone and Simpkin. Jolly was smiling, amused, as usual, at Durham's antics. Alan was facing Durham's table, and Teeth had his back to it, with Slick and Jolly on the other sides. A waitress approached. They ordered a round of beers, and she returned quickly with them. The band struck up with a lively number, which made conversation difficult. Alan was enjoying the music and beer and had almost forgotten about the neighboring table by the time the music stopped. Alan looked around and noticed that Durham had already finished his drink.

Durham spoke up again in a loud voice, "I'm surprised even those guys would allow themselves to be seen with a fairy like Ericsson."

There was a grunt from Teeth. He had an expression as dark as a thunderhead. Alan pointed to himself to show he would answer for their group. Those at Alan's table all stood up.

Alan was not the type to spoil for a fight, because he felt that fighting was usually childish and stupid. On the other hand, he hated bullying, and he felt his adrenaline flowing. He moved toward Durham as Teeth turned around and faced Durham's table. Durham was taller and much heavier than Alan, so he would be hard for Alan to handle if he was sober. Alan was wary, but he thought, *He's too angry and drunk now to handle himself very well.*

Durham sprang up quickly, sending his chair over backward with a bang. Conversation ceased at neighboring tables. Durham had a look of intense hatred, and his eyes were bloodshot. As Alan approached, Durham raised his clenched fists and led with a left hook. Alan easily dodged the hook and was ready for a knockout punch from the right. He stepped nimbly to his right when it came. Durham had thrown himself behind the punch, expecting to connect. The momentum spun him further to his left, and he lost his footing. He fell on the seated Featherstone, whose chair gave way in a splintering crash. Alan began to relax, and he turned back to his companions.

Teeth said with a grin, "Now perhaps we should move along before someone decides to get themselves hurt."

"Agreed," said Alan, and the four filed out of the bar.

Outside Alan felt himself unwinding. He said, "Well, gentlemen, it's been a busy day, and I think it might be hard to get back into a festive mood. I think I might head for the ferry."

"I'm thinkin' along the same lines," said Slick.

Jolly and Teeth nodded agreement, and they headed for the ferry terminal.

Thursday, January 1, 1942

Alan was awakened at 0600 by a general commotion in the BOQ. There were shouts and sounds of running in the hallway. Soon the door to his room burst open and banged against the wall.

"Air raid alert. Squadron muster in the ready room in fifteen minutes," called Bellingham in a loud voice.

"OK, coming," shouted Alan, now wide awake and glad he had not stayed out late the night before.

He dressed quickly, threw on his sheepskin flight jacket, and ran to the hangar. It was an hour before sunrise, but there was light enough to see. He saw pilots from the whole *Yorktown* air group and others he did not recognize all running to their ready rooms in the hangars. It was 0620 before most of the Bombing Five pilots had appeared in their ready room. Armiston and Bellingham looked alert and ready. Alan noticed that quite a few of the pilots did not fit that description. Several seemed to be still waking up, shaking their heads, rubbing their eyes. A few appeared definitely unfit to fly. Durham, Featherstone, and Simpkin were missing.

Armiston stood in front and announced, "The army has picked up some kind of intelligence, and they issued an alert for a Jap air raid here. The navy is asking for confirmation. Meanwhile, we need to be ready to take off at very short notice. Try to make yourselves comfortable. We'll send for coffee and pastries. That is all for now." He and Bellingham left the room.

The pilots relaxed in their chairs and started talking among themselves. *The army probably has the jitters, and this is a false alarm*, Alan thought, *but you never know.*

Jolly was sitting next to Alan. "It's not like Bull to be late," he said to Alan.

"You're right. Not so surprising that Pooh and Slippery are late," replied Alan.

"Is this the army's idea of a joke?" asked Ensign Jacques Lagarde. He and Ensign Becker had joined the squadron two months before Alan.

"After what happened at Pearl Harbor, it's hard to see the humor," said West.

About a half hour later, Bull Durham shuffled into the ready room. He walked slowly and stiffly; his clothing was disheveled, and his eyes were bloodshot. This was the first time he had not appeared tidy and ready for action. The other pilots glanced at each other in surprise. Durham was a pitiful sight, Alan realized. Rather than pity, however, Alan found himself feeling it was another sign that he had no place in a carrier squadron.

At 0700, Bellingham returned, followed closely by orderlies bringing coffee and a variety of baked items. The pilots eagerly began to consume them.

At 0710, Armiston returned and stood at the front of the room, staring at Durham for a moment. Conversation stopped. He glanced at a piece of paper in his hand and announced, "The air raid alert has been cancelled. Apparently the intelligence has been deemed false, and there is no particular threat. Repeat, the air raid alert has been canceled.

"Now I have some other announcements. Admiral Fletcher is flying in from Pearl and is expected around eleven hundred. He will be hoisting his flag in *Yorktown* today, as commander, Task Force Seventeen (TF-17). Task Force Seventeen will be escorting a troop convoy from here to Samoa, departing on the sixth. *Yorktown* will have more aircraft as cargo, in addition to those that we brought from Norfolk. There will be some operating limitations as a result. MacAllester and Ericsson, report to the air officer on the hangar deck at eleven thirty. Others follow previous orders. That is all. You are dismissed."

Alan turned to Jolly and said, "So the scuttlebutt was dead right. Let's get some breakfast, meet in the cafeteria in twenty minutes. Pooh and Slippery never made it."

"Good idea. Pooh and Slippery should get bilged, unless they have one hell of an excuse," said Jolly.

They walked out of the briefing room into a clear, cool day with the sun just above the mountains in the east. Twenty minutes later, after they had sat down with their breakfasts in the cafeteria, Alan said to Jolly, "I thought Admiral Fletcher was a cruiser admiral. I don't think he's even a kiwi."

"Kiwi" was part of the naval aviator's jargon for high ranking officers who had some training in aviation but had never served as pilots. As the aircraft carriers came into the fleet, the navy needed high ranking officers who were familiar with aviation to command them, but all of the trained naval aviators were too junior. Therefore, from the early 1920s until the late 1930s, there was a program, started by aviation pioneer Admiral Moffet of the Bureau of Aeronautics (BuAer), in which selected senior officers were given a short course at Pensacola and qualified as naval aviation observers, receiving wings of silver to wear on their chests. These officers were known among the aviators as "kiwis," after the flightless bird of New Zealand. A few of these officers succeeded in arranging to convert their course into the regular full course for pilots and qualified for their wings of gold. These were known among the aviators as JCLs, jargon for Johnny-Come-Latelies. Naval aviators regarded only pilots who had seen active service as their peers, putting the JCLs and Kiwis in a distinctly lower class.

"That's right, but I heard he commanded a task force built around *Saratoga* recently. I guess there must not be enough flag rank Kiwis available," said Jolly.

After breakfast Alan went to his room and wrote to Jennifer.

> *c/o Fleet Post Office*
> *San Francisco, Calif.*
> *January 1, 1942*

Dear Jennifer,

Happy New Year! I found out yesterday that the mail to Hawaii was running again.

I got your telegram in the evening of December 11, you scalawag. If you try very hard, you might be able to imagine what a huge relief it was. Your choice of words was exquisite. Whatever you had to do to send it, it was well worth it. I will remember it for the rest of my life. I was never so glad to spread good news. I called your parents and mine that night, and wrote some letters, so I got the word out.

It was hectic getting ready to leave our last port in a huge hurry, but the voyage here went well. We have gotten a chance for some practice, and my scores are starting to get better.

We had liberty on New Year's Eve. I had a good time with three friends, and we got back to the BOQ well before midnight. The next morning the army put out an air raid alert at 0600, canceled a short time later. As you can imagine, some of the pilots were not in good shape to respond.

The news from the Philippines sounds extremely grim, although there is little news coverage. As my roommate pointed out, the witch hunt over the attack at Pearl Harbor continues, while nothing is said about the Philippines.

I will not speculate on where we are going next.

I miss you so much. I hope we can get together before too long. You must have had some adventures, and I can't wait to hear all about it.

Write soon. I love you very much.

Tons of love,
Alan

It was a very short letter, but he had trouble thinking of anything more to say without revealing something about *Yorktown's* movements, which she would already know, but others might see the letter. Writing her made him feel close to her, nevertheless, and he missed her a little less afterward.

Around 1050, Alan joined Scottie for the walk over to the pier. Alan became aware of the rumble of an approaching formation of airplanes. He turned to the west toward the sound, and after a few seconds' search, he made out a single large flying boat, flying southeast. As it got closer, he could see that it was a big, plump Consolidated PB2Y Coronado, the first one that Alan had ever seen. Its four engines made it sound like a formation of single engine planes. He thought there was something stately about the Coronado, with its high wing and big twin tail.

Consolidated PB2Y Coronado
(US Navy/PD-USGOV-MILITARY-NAVY)

"That'll be Admiral Fletcher," said Scottie, also watching the Coronado. "They probably took off from Pearl in the early afternoon and flew all night."

"Hmm. That makes sense." Alan had heard that the navy was using the Coronados mostly in the Pacific for fast transportation to Hawaii and points west. They watched as the airplane made a wide 180 degree left turn and flew northwest over the harbor at about 200 feet.

"He's talking to the tower and letting the surface traffic know they should get out of the landing area," said Scottie. The Coronado made another complete circuit and then set down gently in the water with small showers of spray.

Twenty minutes later they walked onto the pier where *Yorktown* was docked. She loomed large as they walked up, dwarfing the big Coronado that was also at the pier. They went aboard and headed for the hangar deck. That space was cleaner and neater than Alan had ever seen it. *Of course*, Alan reminded himself, *there will be the traditional inspection of the ship by the admiral after he hoists his flag. I'm glad I changed to a fresh uniform.* They spotted a group of officers gathering in the middle of the empty hangar. Shortly the engineering and assistant engineering officers of all four squadrons were grouped around the air officers and group commander.

The air officer, in his dress uniform, announced in a loud voice over the general background noise, "The ceremony for Admiral Fletcher hoisting his flag will start on the flight deck at twelve fifteen, with the hoist at twelve thirty. Therefore, there will be quiet on the hangar deck from twelve ten to twelve fifty."

He paused and consulted some notes in his hand. "Now, about the additional aircraft: They want us to find room for a utility group of three Ducks, plus six unassembled floatplanes, in addition to all the Wildcats and Dauntlesses we brought from Norfolk. All the extra planes are going to Pearl, except the six floatplanes, which are a scouting detachment for Samoa, so we'll have a little more room after leaving there." The officers looked at each other with some dismay at the news that crowding on the hangar deck would get worse, and then they began to look around the hangar. Alan thought that using one of the few available carriers as a freighter, to the point where her fighting power was impaired, indicated some poor decision making somewhere.

Alan suddenly realized that the air officer had confirmed that the ship would be going to Pearl Harbor after Samoa. He might really get to see Jennifer. After a few seconds enjoying this news, he forced his mind back to the business at hand.

It took about a half hour of discussion for the officers to evolve a plan for where to put the new cargo. It would mean that

Scouting Five and Bombing Five would only be able to operate ten to twelve planes each. The other Dauntlesses would have their wings removed to enable more compact storage. The air officer promised that both the captain's and the admiral's staff would be made aware of the situation as soon as possible. The officers wanted to get started moving equipment, but the enlisted men were extremely reluctant to touch anything before the admiral's inspection, and there was not much time before the ceremony anyway. Something moving on the pier caught Alan's eye, and he looked out through a side opening to see two big flatbed trucks, loaded with parts of a crated airplane, pull onto the pier.

At 1210 the klaxon sounded, and the bullhorn announced, "Now hear this. Quiet on the hangar and flight decks." The men quietly continued with last minute tidying up, and the officers went to the wardroom for coffee. Alan was glad that, as a member of the air group rather than part of the ship's company, he did not have to interrupt this busy day to appear at the ceremony in dress uniform. Promptly at 1230, the first gun of the thirteen gun salute due a rear admiral boomed out across the harbor.

The engineering officers came back onto the hangar deck at 1250 anxious to get started but knowing that nothing would happen until after the admiral's inspection. They contented themselves with planning the sequence of work to get everything moved and the cargo aircraft stowed. The first truck with a crated airplane was parked on the pier just aft of the carrier's island, where the ship's crane could hoist the crates aboard.

At 1105, the five minute warning was passed through the hangar deck. The officers and men took their places in their normal work areas. In due course, the inspection party rode down to the hangar deck on the forward elevator and gradually made their way aft. Alan recognized the captain, the ship's exec, the air officer, and the ship's first lieutenant.

As the party approached where Alan was standing on the port side amidships, everyone nearby came to attention. The captain promptly called out, "As you were," and the officers and men partially relaxed.

Alan was able to look the members of the party over. He took it as a good sign that Admiral Fletcher smiled occasionally. He also seemed to be taking a genuine interest in what he saw and asking Buckthorn a lot of questions. The ship's exec remained aloof.

Suddenly Alan noticed a tall lieutenant hovering close to the admiral. He recognized Lieutenant Henry Stinson, an old friend from his service on *Pennsylvania*. When Alan came aboard *Pennsylvania* for his two year surface tour, Stinson was a j.g., academy class of 1930, and had been on board two years. Stinson was one of those few who had not let a few years of seniority stand in the way of friendship.

Stinson was standing behind Fletcher when he recognized Alan with a look of surprise. He gave a big wink, and Alan gave a quick wink back. Stinson was wearing aiguillettes, the gold braids around his shoulder that showed he was part of the admiral's staff. Stinson was too junior for most staff positions with a rear admiral, so probably he was the flag lieutenant. Alan was glad to see his old friend. *And he could be a great source of information if he is willing to tell me anything*, Alan realized.

The party continued to make its way aft. A little farther on, it stopped while the air officer explained something, pointing occasionally. It looked as if the air officer was fulfilling his promise to inform the staff about the crowding problem.

Soon the inspection party had gone below. Immediately there were hails back and forth with men on the pier, and the ship's crane swung out to hoist a crate off the truck. It was similar to the loading of disassembled airplanes at Norfolk, except now the overhead storage was full. The dollies with the crates were rolled to the port side amidships, where they were secured to the deck and bulkhead. All six of the crated airplanes had been brought aboard by the end of the day. Alan noticed that each crate was prominently labeled "Scouting Detachment, Naval Station, Tutuila, Samoa." Therefore, everyone working in the vicinity of these crates knew where TF-17 was headed, and probably this information had made, or soon would make, its way to the Japanese. Alan hoped that someone on the admiral's staff was aware of this. *Some parts of the navy are not on a war footing yet*, he thought.

At supper in the officers' club, the word spread among Bombing Five's officers that Featherstone and Simpkin had been dismissed from the squadron, and two new pilots from the Advanced Carrier Training Group (ACTG) located on the naval air station would replace them. All the other Bombing Five pilots, with the exception of Durham, thought that Featherstone and Simpkin had been given plenty of opportunities to shape up and they had not. If the new pilots were any good at all, they would soon learn enough to be more valuable than those two. There was also a rumor that Durham had received another dressing down by Armiston for his late and unready appearance that morning.

Saturday, January 3, 1942

All the air group pilots were ordered to their shore ready rooms at 0800. Alan arrived in the nick of time at 0758. There were photographs and drawings of four unfamiliar airplanes posted on the blackboards. There was a file of papers on each seat. There were two new faces, belonging to the new pilots that had just joined. Armiston was at the lectern, ready to start the briefing.

"Two new pilots have joined us today from the Advanced Carrier Training Group. Please stand when I call your name: Ensign Glen Cobb, Ensign Philip Goodwin." The new pilots stood up. "Welcome to Bombing Five. I hope you're both ready to go to work, because we have a lot to do to get ready to depart in three days." The new pilots sat down.

"Now, you each have a folder of papers. In the Pacific we expect to be in combat with Japanese aircraft, both shore based and carrier based. The Fleet Tactical Unit here in San Diego collects information on enemy aircraft, and they have produced the information in your folders, pertaining to four of their combat aircraft. In addition to these, we may see other types, such as float observation planes and large flying boats for long range patrol. The information comes from various sources, including photos and movies taken during the attack on Pearl Harbor. This briefing is going to provide you with an introduction to what we know about these four aircraft, which is not very complete, due to Japanese secrecy and our peacetime constraints.

"We'll start with their new navy fighter, the Type Zero, usually called the Zero." He pointed to some blurry photographs and a three view drawing that showed the airplane from the top, side, and front. "The Zero's very light weight gives it great maneuverability, high climb rate, and long range, all better than the Wildcat. It's probably slightly faster than the Wildcat. You can recognize it by its low wing, rounded wing tips, and long greenhouse extending behind the cockpit."

Armiston moved to another set of photos and a three view drawing. "Their dive bomber is the Type Ninety-Nine. It has elliptical wings like a Spitfire, fixed main landing gear with large wheel pants, and a long streamlined greenhouse. It is probably slightly slower than the Dauntless. Like the Dauntless, the bomb is carried externally, and we suspect it cannot carry as large a bomb as our one thousand pounder."

Armiston moved again to a third set of pictures. "Their torpedo bomber is the Type Ninety-Seven. Our experts suspect that the design is derived from a Northrop design that we sold them in the early nineteen thirties. It also has rounded wing tips and a long greenhouse, but it has a fully retractable landing gear like the Dauntless. The torpedo is carried externally parallel to the fuselage. It is probably as fast as the Dauntless, although perhaps not when carrying a torpedo, much faster than our Devastator. Like the Devastator, the Type Ninety-Seven can be used for horizontal bombing, as well as for torpedo bombing. Some of these were used for horizontal bombing at Pearl Harbor, but we expect they would not be used that way against ships underway."

Finally, Armiston moved to a fourth set of drawings and pictures, showing a twin engine airplane. "This is the G-Four-M, the principal land based bomber used by their navy. There is an earlier G-Three-M, but this is the one you are most likely to encounter. It is well armed, and be sure to note the tail gun, which makes an attack from straight behind risky. It is fast and has a long range. It can carry bombs or a torpedo internally. This is the type that sank the British ships, the *Repulse* and the *Prince of Wales*, off Malaya a few days after the Pearl Harbor attack. They came from Indochina, some seven hundred miles away, which gives you an idea of their range.

"Study your information packets and memorize the identification features and the principal performance characteristics."

Armiston paused, walked back to the lectern, and smiled as he faced the pilots. "Now I have more welcome news. An AlNav arrived from BuNav today, announcing a navy wide promotion, in which most of you are promoted one rank. Exceptions are those who have been promoted within the last year or those who have unsatisfactory fitness reports."

He proceeded to read out the promotions in the squadron. Armiston was made lieutenant commander, while Bellingham's and MacAllester's promotions to lieutenant were too recent. Alan, Jolly, Teeth, and West made lieutenant. Alan was very pleased. He could now sit at the special tables in the wardroom reserved for officers above lieutenant j.g. Several of the ensigns in the squadron, including Alan's friends Slick and Mike, made lieutenant j.g. Ned Morris was too junior and remained an ensign. *With so many promotions, there will be something of a scramble for the promoted officers to obtain the correct insignia for their uniforms*, Alan thought.

Bull Durham was a very senior lieutenant, but he was not promoted. The reason had to be that his fitness report was unsatisfactory. Alan saw that he was unable to conceal his anger. He heard that Durham had spent a long time in Armiston's office later that day. Most of the pilots thought it was a good sign that the system was working the way it was supposed to. They also thought it was unfortunate that Bellingham was still junior to Durham.

Sunday, January 4, 1942

There was fine weather on January 4, and another session of bombing and gunnery practice was held. When they had arrived at San Diego, the air group had been informed about the new aircraft markings promulgated by CINCPAC. They had resulted from an army-navy conference to try to improve aircraft recognition, which had been poor during and after the Pearl Harbor attack. When the pilots reported for bombing practice, they saw that the roundels, consisting of a white five pointed star on a dark blue circle, with a red circle in the middle, were much larger, and there were two more on each plane. The red and white horizontal stripes on the rudder remained the same. Alan thought it was a handsome and bold scheme, but at some point the advantage of reducing visibility to the enemy with camouflage might outweigh trying to improve recognition.

A session was held at the end of the day in the squadron's shore ready room to go over the bombing and gunnery results. In the bombing practice, Alan got a hit about ten feet in from the edge of the target this time, his best yet. In fixed gunnery, he had the best score. Kidd had improved his technique with the flexible gun in the rear cockpit and was now able to achieve an average score. On the way back, Kidd had another flying lesson, consisting of turns in both directions, while holding altitude. Before ending the session, Armiston announced that the air group airplanes would be hoisted on board the next day, the day before their scheduled departure, rather than have the airplanes fly out to the carrier after departure from San Diego. This would be done to allow more time for careful stowage on the hangar deck and a final determination of exactly how many Dauntlesses could be operated. In order to depart early the following day, all personnel were to be on board by 1730.

Monday, January 5, 1942

The weather was cool and rainy, marking the beginning of the wet season in Southern California, but fortunately no flying had been planned. Scottie and Alan spent a busy day helping to get everything stowed and squared away on the hangar deck. Scottie told Alan when they started that the six disassembled floatplanes on *Yorktown* had been hoisted back ashore. Alan was gratified that apparently somebody higher up appreciated the seriousness of the crowding on the hangar deck. In the end, Scouting Five and Bombing Five could operate fifteen Dauntlesses each, and there would be one more for the CYAG.

When the Wildcats of Fighting Forty-Two were hoisted aboard, Alan saw that they all now had illuminated reflector gunsights installed. These were a big improvement over the telescopic sights that they had had previously, which were similar to those in the Dauntlesses. However, the installation was jury rigged and still presented a hazard to the pilot's face when landing or ditching. He had talked with the engineering officers in Fighting Forty-Two and had heard how they worked hard to scrounge up the sights and get them installed.

By 1715 he had changed for supper and was just leaving his stateroom for the wardroom. As he started up the passageway, he saw the tall figure of Hank Stinson approaching from forward.

"Good evening, Lieutenant Commander, sir," said Alan with a smile, eyeing the new shoulder marks Stinson was wearing.

"Good evening, Lieutenant," answered Stinson, also smiling, as they shook hands.

"It's been four and half years since I last saw you, but it seems like yesterday."

"That's right. You don't seem to have changed too much. Do they still call you Stringy?"

"Yes, they do. Do they still call you Shorty? Say, how about having supper and really getting caught up?" Alan was very pleased that Stinson had looked him up.

"Yes, I'm still Shorty. It would be great to spend some time with you, Alan, but shortly I will have to tag along with the admiral, who is having a last dinner ashore with the commander of the Eleventh Naval District. How about a brief chat in your stateroom? Would I be imposing?"

"Not at all. My roommate may appear, of course, but I think you might enjoy meeting him." Alan turned around and went back into his stateroom, followed by Stinson.

Alan closed the door and sat down on the lower bunk, leaving the single chair for Hank.

Stinson sat and said, "I guess you've figured out I'm the flag lieutenant. It's a great job, but you have to keep politics always in mind. It's perfectly all right for the flag lieutenant to have a friend among the aviators, but it wouldn't do to flaunt it—you know what I mean?"

"I think so. The admiral and his staff should be seen to be evenhanded and not play favorites."

"That's right, but it could hurt you too, if you're seen as having pull in high places."

"Hmm. I see what you mean. Thanks for the advice." Alan paused and said, "I've got some Scotch stowed away. Would you like a nip?"

"Tsk-tsk. Very nice of you to offer, but with this being the admiral's last dinner ashore, there will be plenty to drink."

"That AlNav was a pleasant surprise," said Alan.

"Quite a scramble to find the insignia."

"Yeah, there was a lot of trading in the squadron, which helped, but only one lieutenant was promoted in Bombing Five, so I had to get mine ashore. It took a while for Captain Buckthorn to get through swearing in everybody. I think he barely got through the j.g.'s yesterday. Now tell me how you got to be flag lieutenant."

"Well, in thirty-six, after you left *Pennsylvania*, I thought it was time to start rounding out my experience with duty on other types of ships. I got destroyer duty on *Farragut* for three years and got promoted to lieutenant. Then I applied for cruiser duty and got assigned to *Astoria*. Admiral Fletcher hoisted his flag in her in June 1940 as skipper of Cruiser Division Six. A year later I was the ship's communications officer, and so I had a lot of interaction with the admiral's staff and occasionally with the admiral himself. When his flag lieutenant got reassigned, Admiral Fletcher sent for me and offered me the job. I was flattered and accepted right away."

"You're a rising star I can see. What's it like being flag lieutenant?"

"It's a little tedious sometimes, and you don't get a lot of time to yourself. But mostly I've enjoyed it and learned a lot. Sometimes I feel like I could teach at the War College, even though I haven't been a student there yet. There are discouraging times too. The admiral and his staff recently had a sour experience. He was made commander of a task force to relieve Wake, including *Saratoga*. Somehow this high priority effort got delayed starting and then got stuck with *Neches*, one of the old, slow oilers, which also has obsolete equipment for refueling at sea. We went as fast as we could, but in the end we were still quite a way from Wake when it fell, and there were indications of one or more Jap carriers present. Everyone was mad as hell when we got the recall message, but the level headed men came to realize it made sense. Luckily for the admiral and his staff, the temporary CINCPAC, Admiral Pye, got most of the blame for the moment. Don't repeat any of this, Alan."

"Aye aye, sir. Very interesting."

"Now tell me how you got to be a pilot. Last time I saw you, you said you had decided to go into submarines, rather than aviation."

"After I left *Pennsylvania*, I went to sub school for six months, then served eighteen months on S-Twenty-Four and got my dolphins along the way. Then I was promoted to j.g. and assigned to *Squalus* as engineering officer. All the survivors of the sinking in May of '39 were asked to write reports, and mine was technically correct but a big political mistake. It indicated how the accident could have been avoided and laid the blame squarely where it really belonged, fairly high up. That got me assigned to a cobbled up desk job at the Newport Torpedo Station for nine months as punishment. Because of the damage to my career in subs and the dirty linen I found on our torpedoes, I decided to transfer to aviation. I got my wings at Pensacola last May and joined Bombing Five in June. My first choice was fighters, but dive bombers were a close second. Even though aviation is very different from submarines, I have enjoyed it as much or more so far."

"That is an interesting career path." Stinson smiled and continued, "You and I are opposites, career wise: I have stuck to the surface, and you have gone under and over. Can you tell me anything about the captain and his staff?"

"A little. Buckthorn seems like a capable captain. He's a qualified naval aviator, not just an observer, but he's short on aviation experience. The exec, Josh Clapp, is an old aviator, who must have a lot of useful background. Unfortunately, being the senior aviator seems to make Clapp think that his knowledge is superior to the captain's on most everything. Between that and Clapp's sour disposition, Buckthorn has learned to avoid him as much as possible. Buckthorn bypasses him and consults with the air officer and the air group commander often, and occasionally with the squadron commanders. This seems to have worked to the benefit of the ship and the air group. The air group gets heard, and the captain has no fixed dogma, so the air group has been able to try new ideas. Everything seems to work well as long as no one listens to the exec."

"Very interesting and very unusual. Thanks very much for giving me an inside view."

"How about Admiral Fletcher? He doesn't have much aviation background either, does he?"

"Quite true, but not by choice. You know, a lot of people don't remember that Fletcher tried to become a naval aviator, not an observer, in 1928, but he was rejected because of his eyesight. As I said, I think he did a good job under bad circumstances with the Wake task force. But there he had a staff aviator with him in *Astoria*, and he had his good friend Admiral Fitch, who has quite a bit of aviation experience, in *Saratoga*. Now he has neither. Nimitz has put out a new policy that carrier task force commanders must be embarked in the carrier. He also wants to have two admirals in any carrier task force, so he wanted to find a cruiser admiral to sail in *Louisville* for this mission, but he could not come up with one in time. For aviation knowledge, maybe Admiral Fletcher will have to follow your captain's lead and reach down into the air officers aboard *Yorktown*."

"Thanks very much, Hank, for being so candid with me. I'll do my best not to betray your trust. Closer to my own little role, do you know what caused the unassembled floatplanes to be removed from *Yorktown*? The hangar deck was getting strangled with cargo, and it was really good to see them go."

"I do, Alan. Your air officer did a good job of explaining the crowding problem and its consequences during the admiral's inspection on the first. Then the admiral's operations officer noticed that there is no airport on Tutuila Island, where we are going. To unload the floatplanes, *Yorktown* would have to go into Pago Pago Harbor, with the air group stuck nearly helpless on board. Even the admiral and his staff have enough aviation background to take a very dim view of that situation, so he consulted with Buckthorn and then had the floatplanes removed. Two were assembled and embarked on *St. Louis*, and the other four were loaded on *Jupiter*."

"Good for Admiral Fletcher. I think I like him already. I imagine you know that those crates were prominently labeled with our destination, so everyone around here knows where we're going."

"Those crates weren't the only ones so labeled. It was duly noted and passed upstairs."

"Can you fill me in on the rest of the task force and the convoy?"

"Sure. The task force consists of *Yorktown*, *Louisville*, and *St. Louis*, and the four destroyers that came out with *Yorktown* from Norfolk. The convoy consists of three Matson liners carrying the marines, ammunition ship *Lassen*, oiler *Kaskaskia*, and cargo ship *Jupiter*. *Lassen* and *Jupiter* are the slow ones, around fifteen knots."

"Thanks, Hank. I imagine it will be a little different for Admiral Fletcher to be on a carrier instead of a cruiser."

"Very much so. And not only that, this is the first ship the admiral has been embarked in that has had radar. The carriers have first dibs, for good reason. In fact I gather *Yorktown* was one of the first to get hers in a year and a half ago. It hasn't reached very far into the cruisers yet. *Louisville* has nothing, and *St. Louis* has early fire control radar that has some surface search capability. The cruisers don't even have VHF talk-between-ships."

"Wow. That's something I haven't heard much about."

It seemed to Alan that Stinson was willing to fill him in on quite a bit of what was going on from the admiral's point of view, as he had hoped. *This could potentially give me a whole new window on things.*

Stinson looked at his watch. "Uh-oh, I am supposed to go ashore with the admiral in fifteen minutes. It's been good to catch up, Alan. Sorry to run off, and I hope to talk more with you, but discreetly."

"Looking forward to it, Hank."

They shook hands again, and Stinson hurriedly left.

Alan was about to leave when Jolly appeared.

"Who was that lieutenant commander who was just here?"

"The flag lieutenant, Hank Stinson," said Alan with a grin.

"So how do you know the flag lieutenant, Stringy?"

"He was a j.g. on *Pennsylvania* when I did my surface tour on her. He's a good guy, a friend in spite of the difference in seniority. He reminded me of the perils of flaunting our friendship, under the circumstances."

"Undue influence high up, eh?"

"You got it."

Alan and Jolly went to the wardroom together for supper. For the first time, they sat at the air group table reserved for officers above lieutenant j.g. Teeth Jensen and Jerry West were there. Alan sat next to West. Even though he and Jerry now had the same rank, West's long experience in the squadron had made him seem like a person of higher rank. Even so, Alan felt like he would enjoy getting to know him better.

CHAPTER FIVE

Milk Run to Samoa

Tuesday, January 6, 1942

The task force departed on schedule from San Diego. Alan was at his favorite vantage point on the bow, as the ship left the Coronado Islands to port, heading southwest. Alan had thought the voyage from Panama to San Diego was fairly long, but this voyage would be about 25 percent farther. When they got to Tutuila, Pearl Harbor would only be a little more than half as far away as San Diego, so the voyage there should be much shorter. Alan was starting to get excited about seeing Jennifer.

Sunday, January 11, 1942

The ship received the bad news that a Japanese submarine had torpedoed the carrier *Saratoga*, southwest of Hawaii. She was not sunk, but she was limping back toward Pearl and would probably be out of the war for months. He thought of his friends from Pensacola who were on the *Saratoga*, Wade Buckner in Fighting Three and Les Travis in Scouting Three. They were probably very disappointed, especially after the Wake relief debacle.

Alan thought *Sara*'s torpedoing was likely due to the task force steaming at less than 15 knots, as was common practice to save fuel. Being a former submariner, he was acutely aware of the effect of small differences in a ship's speed on vulnerability to submarine attack, even when escorted. With the navy so dependent on a few carriers to provide the available strategic strength in the Pacific, it seemed like a false economy to slow down carrier task forces to save fuel. Alan thought the vulnerability of a ship was roughly inversely proportional to the difference between the submarine's surface speed and the ship's speed. Modern submarines could go about 20 knots on the surface, so increasing speed from 14 to 18 knots would lessen the ship's vulnerability by a factor of three, while roughly doubling fuel consumption.

A thought struck Alan: *It's only been a week that we've had four fleet carriers in the Pacific, and now we're back to three.* Even with four carriers, Alan thought it would be a while before the navy could consider trying to start taking back any Japanese occupied territory. Raids seemed possible, especially if it could be determined that the Japanese did not have carriers nearby.

Wednesday, January 14, 1942

The task force crossed the equator, well south of Christmas Island. The weather was warm and very humid, producing thunderstorms, which caused flight operations to be canceled.

In peacetime, crossing the equator was commemorated by a rowdy ceremony in which those who had not crossed before, the Pollywogs, would be put through humiliating initiation rites by those who had crossed before, the Shellbacks. Now, in wartime, things were more subdued. It was decided that the individual departments and squadrons could have whatever low key celebration they wanted. The officers of Scouting Five and Bombing Five decided on a small joint party in the afternoon on the flight deck, at which the Pollywogs, including Alan, were required to dress in odd costumes and do silly things, like search the horizon with binoculars made out of two coke bottles taped together. Alan was glad to get off so lightly, compared to what he had heard about the peacetime tradition.

Fighting Forty-Two decided to forgo any celebration because the squadron had had a run of bad luck since leaving San Diego. One fighter went into the barrier after an arresting wire broke, with injuries to the deck crew. Three others went into the water on takeoff. After the third, the squadron felt that wake turbulence left over from the previous airplane's departure was part of the problem. They asked permission to experiment with a new procedure in which the carrier would steam 10 degrees off the wind to the left, and the departing planes would turn left after takeoff, instead of the usual right turn, so the wake turbulence would move off to the left before the next airplane departed. The procedure seemed to work and was adopted.

Saturday, January 17, 1942

TF-17 began refueling from *Kaskaskia*, beginning with the cruisers. Alan took a few minutes occasionally to watch the maneuvers through the open sides of the hangar deck. It seemed to go very slowly.

That day the ship's newsletter said that a German submarine offensive along the East Coast of the United States had begun. The newsletter said that the New York newspapers had reported on January 16 that a ship was sunk within sight of civilians and police in eastern Long Island the previous day, and the coast guard had sent out several rescue vessels. The navy, however, had refused to discuss any of this. The newsletter said that convoys had not been organized and a blackout on the shore had not been started. It sounded to Alan as if the navy was attempting a cover-up, indicating they were acutely embarrassed, having done little to prepare. He wondered how Admiral King could have let this happen. It seemed likely to Alan that this situation of apparent helplessness would soon generate an uproar among civilians and members of Congress, giving the navy another black eye, soon after the one from Pearl Harbor. The navy had had over a month to get ready, so, in Alan's view, this black eye was deserved.

Alan had met briefly with Stinson a couple of times since leaving San Diego, but Stinson was extra busy. The reason was that Stinson had taken over the flag secretary's duties, in addition to those of flag lieutenant. The flag secretary had suddenly been taken ill and had gone to the San Diego Naval Hospital just before the task force departed. Alan and Stinson had kept their meetings discreet, but word got around anyway that they knew each other. Stinson had revealed that the admiral's staff had little detailed information on the facilities at Tutuila, including how many ships could be accommodated in Pago Pago Harbor, so the time required for unloading was unknown. Stinson had also told Alan that Fletcher had been giving himself a crash course on aviation by talking with the air officers, following Buckthorn's lead. He had also talked once to each of the squadron skippers and recently had been talking to the flight officer in each squadron. Alan wondered how the interview between Fletcher and Durham had gone.

Sunday, January 18, 1942

At lunch an orderly had handed Alan an envelope. Inside it was a request from Admiral Fletcher for Alan to meet with Fletcher in his quarters at 1600. This was a surprise. Alan thought Stinson had to have had a hand in selecting him for an interview. At the same time, Alan wondered what had motivated the politically astute Stinson to pick his friend. Alan rushed back to his stateroom, grabbed his best working uniform, and bribed the laundry to have it cleaned and pressed by 1530. He got one of the stewards to put a quick polish on his best brown shoes and then went back on duty on the hangar deck.

Yorktown's turn in the refueling came that afternoon, and Alan saw *Kaskaskia* appear close by to starboard. Fortunately, the swell was small, but Alan was surprised to see that the sea between the ships was very rough indeed. Then he remembered that both ships were making a wake, and the wakes combined in the narrow space between the ships to produce a watery tumult. With her low freeboard, the oiler was taking seas over her main deck on the port side frequently, and the sailors on deck were frequently drenched. This was another difficult aspect of underway refueling, but the oiler sailors seemed to be used to it.

Alan knew that, because of the shorter distances in the Atlantic, underway refueling was unusual there. Thus, unlike the carriers remaining in the Pacific, *Yorktown* had gotten no experience with it there, and the refueling detail was probably rusty. The process did not start off smoothly, with the distance between the ships fluctuating rapidly, and men with megaphones on both ships shouting back and forth, as first lines were passed to link the ships, and then a fueling hose was rigged across.

Yorktown refueling underway
(US Navy/PD-USGOV-MILITARY-NAVY)

At 1550, Alan had showered, changed clothes, and was on his way to the admiral's quarters, known as "flag country." Most heavy cruisers and larger combatant ships had special spaces that could accommodate an admiral and his staff, in addition to special spaces for the ship's captain. Soon after coming on board the previous September, Alan made sure he knew where the admiral's and captain's quarters were, in order to avoid the embarrassment of blundering into them uninvited. The admiral's quarters were on the port side forward on the gallery deck, one level below the flight deck. The captain's quarters were similar, situated on the starboard side opposite flag country. At sea the captain spent much of his time on the navigation bridge, in the island three decks up from the flight deck, or in his sea cabin just aft of the bridge. Similarly, the admiral had his own flag bridge one level below the navigation bridge. Aft of that was the flag plot, where all communications needed by the admiral were centered, and there was a large chart table with positions of nearby ships shown. Next aft was the flag radio room, and aft of that was the admiral's sea cabin.

Alan approached the admiral's quarters on the gallery deck, feeling nervous. He would have been more nervous if he had not spent a couple of days with another admiral almost a year earlier. He showed his invitation to the marine sentry and was told to go on in. A yeoman showed him in to a small waiting area. Fletcher's personal marine orderly was seated outside the admiral's office. He rose and looked over Alan's invitation and then invited Alan to have a seat. Soon the door opened, Admiral Fletcher strode out, and Alan stood to meet him.

"Good afternoon, Lieutenant. I am Admiral Fletcher," said the admiral, smiling.

"I'm honored to meet you, sir," said Alan, also smiling as they shook hands.

Fletcher had thinning dark hair, a tanned and somewhat wrinkled face, and sparkling brown eyes. He was of medium height and looked fit.

"Please come into my office."

Alan followed Fletcher into his office and closed the door. The office was not large or luxurious, and it was lined with shelves containing reports, maps, and books.

"Have a seat. Try to relax; this is not a test," said Fletcher kindly, sitting at his desk.

"Thank you, sir."

"I have not had a chance to get very much experience with aviation, and this is the first time I have been embarked on a carrier. I have been trying to get more aviation background and get acquainted with a few of the aviation officers by talking to the air group and senior squadron officers. Now my staff has selected one junior officer at random from each squadron for me to talk to. I have talked to Lieutenant Crommelin from Fighting Forty-Two, and now you are representing Bombing Five. They have given me your personnel folder, so I know a little bit about you.

"I have a few questions to ask each of you pilots. The first is, how well do you think your squadron is prepared for combat, and what should be done to get it better prepared?"

"Well, sir, I think we're in pretty good shape. We're all pretty green, but only action will cure that. More bombing and gunnery practice would be good. Also, when we flew into San Diego, we practiced a running rendezvous with the other squadrons, instead of a deferred departure. Most of the pilots think it is a good idea, and it seemed to be working, although the flight was too short to be sure. It would be good to try it again on a longer flight."

"Yes, the running rendezvous has come up in my talks with other officers. It seems like a good idea to me and to most of the officers I have talked to, although I would defer to the air department and the air group commander. However, the ship's executive officer and your flight officer, Lieutenant Durham, take a dim view of it." Fletcher consulted his notes. "Any materiel shortages or defects?"

"Shoulder harnesses for the pilots would a blessing, sir. It is difficult to keep your face from hitting the gunsight, particularly in a ditching. Many pilots, including me, have gotten injured that way." Fletcher was making a note. "On the hangar deck, we have a shortage of space with all the cargo, as you know. However, it would be worse if you had not had those six crated floatplanes off loaded. Everyone on the hangar deck is grateful to you for that, sir."

Alan could feel the vibration of the ship's propellers going to maximum speed and then slowing down again, and he had been feeling unusual motions of the ship. He wondered if there were problems with the refueling. He thought there were hints that Fletcher had noticed also.

"How do you know that I was responsible for that?"

"I heard it from your flag lieutenant, who is an old friend from my surface tour, sir."

"Hmm. I did not know that. In that case, some may not believe your selection for this interview was random," said Fletcher, smiling.

"Yes, sir."

"Can't be helped now. I see you were a submariner and worked at the Newport Torpedo Station. Would you have preferred to be in a torpedo squadron?"

"No, sir. May I speak frankly, sir?"

"By all means, Lieutenant. I won't quote you."

"When I was at Newport, I learned a lot, maybe too much, about our torpedoes. I think the testing of torpedoes is far from thorough, and therefore their reliability is questionable. But I want to say also, sir, that I believe torpedo bombing could be very effective. When the navy decided about ten years ago to emphasize dive bombing over torpedo bombing, I think it is possible that it was a mistake. On the other hand, I would not want to give up any of the great progress that we have made in dive bombing. I think the torpedo bombers are inherently more vulnerable than the dive bombers, and I think they should get the bulk of any fighter escort."

"Certainly the Japanese torpedo bombers were very effective at Pearl Harbor."

"I cannot speak to that, sir, having heard very little detail so far about what happened there. However, I know the obsolete British torpedo bombers were very effective at Taranto."

Fletcher's eyebrows jumped up, and then he smiled and said, "That's right; they were. Well, I can see you have given quite a bit of thought to tactics. Keep it up. Any other thoughts?"

"Nothing at the moment, sir."

"Thank you, Lieutenant, for your views and your candidness."

"My pleasure, sir." They both stood up and shook hands again.

"Good luck, Lieutenant."

"Thank you, and good luck to you, sir."

Alan turned and left the admiral's office. As he started down the passageway, he caught sight of Stinson in another office, and they exchanged winks. He was relieved that the interview was over, but he thought it had gone fairly well.

At supper, Alan learned that he had missed some excitement while he had been talking to the admiral. During the refueling, in spite of emergency maneuvering by both the oiler and the carrier, there were two collisions and minor damage to both ships. *Kaskaskia* had had to make unexpected maneuvers to keep parted lines and fuel hoses from fouling her propellers. Clearly underway refueling required a lot of seamanship. Alan guessed that lack of experience explained why it did not go smoothly. It seemed likely that the ship would be underway a lot of the time from now on, and therefore they would gain experience fairly rapidly.

Just as Alan was leaving the wardroom after supper, Stinson came up to him. Stinson was curious about Alan's interview with the admiral, and they agreed to meet in the aft end of the port gallery in half an hour. They met in a relatively secluded spot aft of the five inch antiaircraft guns. There was still a nice breeze this far aft, but most men looking for relief from the tropical heat and humidity went farther forward, so the aft gallery was a place where they could talk in privacy.

"How did your interview with the admiral go?" asked Stinson.

"Pretty well, I think. He seems both competent and pleasant, and I don't think I made any gaffes. But why did you pick me when everyone knows we're friends?"

"I didn't pick you. The yeomen did it at random, and it would upset things if I interfered. Now, what's the story on your flight officer, Lieutenant Durham? His record says he is an excellent pilot, but he did not get promoted even though he is very senior. Admiral Fletcher told me Durham seemed competent, but he spoiled it with excessive brown nosing."

"That sounds like Durham. He joined last August, from Bombing Seven, and there were unfavorable rumors about why he asked for the transfer. He is an excellent pilot and a consistent top scorer in both bombing and gunnery. But he brown noses everyone who is his senior, which in Bombing Five is only the skipper, and has difficulty treating everyone junior to him with respect. I ran afoul of him in October, and now he has worn out his welcome with many of the pilots in the squadron, including the exec. He would be a terrible leader. His days in the squadron may be numbered, in spite of his skills."

"Wow. Difficult combination to deal with, I can see. It's pretty hard to tolerate an openly selfish guy in the navy, no matter what his talents are."

"Exactly." Alan admired how Stinson had captured the situation in a nutshell.

Monday, January 19, 1942

When two opposing aircraft carriers approached each other, the one that found the other first would attack and, because it attacked first, would likely emerge the victor. Therefore, whenever an aircraft carrier approached an area that might contain an enemy carrier, it was standard procedure to conduct air searches, usually once or twice each day. When long range land based search airplanes were too far away, the US Navy used carrier aircraft for searches, rather than cruiser or battleship floatplanes. Each aircraft would be sent out to a given distance, then turn 90 degrees, fly a short distance, and then turn again back toward the carrier. The pilot and gunner would then have visually searched a sector shaped like a very narrow slice of pie. In the US Navy, the distance out was usually 100–250 miles. The width of the sector would be adjusted depending on the local visibility and the distance out, but the angle covered was usually less than 15 degrees. A group of aircraft would be sent out singly or in pairs to cover a fairly wide angular range, sometimes a complete circle if the possible direction of the enemy was completely unknown.

The scouting and bombing squadrons carried out the searches, because the Dauntless had more range than the Wildcat or the Devastator, and they were trained in scouting. These squadrons were capable of searches out to close to 300 miles. However, even if the pilots were skilled and careful, they would be expected to accumulate a navigation error of two to four miles for every 100 miles flown. This would mean that they might be 12 to 24 miles off at the end of such a mission. Unless the visibility was good, they might not be able to see the carrier when they returned. In that case, they would have to fly a search pattern, for which scouting doctrine required a three hour reserve, cutting the search range in half.

Fortunately, the Fleet Problems had uncovered this problem many years earlier. The Naval Research Laboratory started working on the problem in the mid thirties. The solution they developed was a homing transmitter on the carrier, designated model YE (or Yoke Easy, in the military phonetic alphabet), and a homing receiver in each aircraft, designated model ZB (or Zebra Baker). If the aircrew could receive the Morse code signal from the homing transmitter, they could determine which thirty degree compass sector they were in, relative to the carrier. Then, using their compass, they could find which way to go to return. Deliveries of the YE homing transmitters began in late 1940, and all the fleet carriers had them by mid 1941. Bombing Five received their ZB receivers in the fall of 1941. To make it difficult for the enemy to use the system, the code of which Morse code letters corresponded to which compass sectors was changed every day.

That day *Yorktown* sent out two searches at 0830 and 1200, to the south to 150 miles, covering the approach to Tutuila Island. Bombing Five, including Alan, conducted the first. Kidd was again his gunner, and the Zebra Baker was helpful in finding the carrier when they returned. Searches were a boring but necessary exercise for the aircrews. At least here in the tropical Pacific, there was some chance of survival if they ran out of gas and had to ditch. Alan had participated in searches the previous fall in the North Atlantic, where that was not the case, due to exposure to the frigid water. The boredom on this search was relieved on the return leg by another flying lesson for Kidd, consisting of climbs and descents to given altitudes. Alan was glad that Kidd was turning into an enthusiastic student pilot.

Scouting Five made the second search. With the searches revealing no threats, Fletcher released the three Matson liners, with an escort of two destroyers, to go ahead to Tutuila at their 20 knot speed.

Tuesday, January 20, 1942

As *Yorktown* approached Tutuila Island, Scouting Five was ordered to make an early morning search. Alan saw that two of the Grumman J2F-5 Duck amphibian airplanes had been brought on deck for launching after the search departed. They would be used for ship-to-shore communication and to carry mail to and from the task force. Being amphibious, unlike the cruiser float-planes, they could use their retractable wheels to operate off the carrier and their floats to operate in Pago Pago Harbor. Alan thought the Duck was an exceptionally ungainly looking aircraft, but he knew it performed its function well. Like the Seagull, it was a biplane.

Grumman J2F-1 Duck
(US Navy/PD-USGOV-MILITARY-NAVY)

Yorktown could accommodate seaplanes in a way similar to that of cruisers and battleships. She had a crane on the hangar deck on the port side aft that could swing out, pick up a seaplane, and swing it inboard to the hangar deck through the large opening there. Landing amphibians on the flight deck, however, was faster and did not require the ship to stop.

The pilots had been briefed that the task force would remain in the vicinity while the convoy was unloading but would not approach close to Tutuila. Alan wondered if the ship would get any personal mail. Early in the afternoon, one of the Ducks returned but carried only official mail and messages.

Shortly the three remaining ships of the convoy were sent on into Tutuila. Bombing Five sent six planes to escort the ships to the harbor, and Alan flew one of them. He enjoyed the aerial view of Tutuila, a beautiful tropical island under scattered puffy clouds. The harbor at Pago Pago appeared to offer good shelter and deep water, the best in the Samoan Islands, he had heard.

The harbor probably was the reason the United States coveted this island when there were two larger ones to the west, which belonged to France. Stinson later told Alan that the returning Duck had brought news that the harbor could accommodate all the ships of the convoy at once, greatly facilitating rapid unloading.

That evening, Captain Buckthorn announced to the whole ship that TF-17 would not be going directly on to Pearl Harbor after the ships were unloaded at Tutuila. Instead, they would be participating with TF-8 in raids on the Gilberts and the Marshalls. The Marshalls were part of the islands mandated to Japan after World War I, and the Japanese had occupied the Gilberts two days after the attack on Pearl Harbor. They were southeast of the Marshalls and had been administered by the British. TF-17 would be under the overall command of Admiral William "Bull" Halsey, embarked in *Enterprise*, which was the nucleus of TF-8. Alan remembered, *Halsey is the only vice admiral who is a qualified naval aviator, a JCL.*

This news was greeted with great enthusiasm by most of the ship's company and the air group. It would be *Yorktown's* first true combat mission beyond convoy escort, and some shore based enemy air opposition could be expected. They would be participating in the first offensive move made by the United States against Japan. The nonchalance of a convoy escort mission, with little prospect of contacting the enemy, was suddenly gone.

Alan was excited, both eager to try his hand in combat and apprehensive about it. At the same time, he was disappointed not to be going straight to Pearl Harbor and Jennifer. He thought of his friend from his pilot training at Pensacola, Ed Miller, who was in Fighting Six aboard *Enterprise*.

Thursday, January 22, 1942

The previous day, during an unusual period of good visibility, Tutuila could be glimpsed from the task force as a verdant mountain on the southern horizon. The Ducks occasionally went back and forth, but still no personal mail had arrived on *Yorktown*.

Daily searches had continued, with Bombing Five taking the odd numbered days and Scouting Five the even. Kidd got a flying lesson on the return leg of each search. Now the lessons were close enough together that little review of the previous lesson was necessary, and Kidd progressed rapidly.

Today the Duck returning in midmorning brought several large sacks of personal mail. Yeomen did not finish sorting it until midafternoon. When Alan returned to his stateroom at the end of the day, he found what he had been hoping for—a letter from

Jennifer. Other than the six words in her telegram, this was the first time he had heard from her since before the Pearl Harbor attack, and he couldn't wait to read it. He glanced at the date and saw that the letter had taken more than three weeks to reach him.

> *Honolulu, T. H.*
> *December 29, 1941*

Dear Alan,

I just found out that the mail service has been restarted. I hope you got the telegram I sent you on December 11. If not, I was not injured in any way by the Japanese attack, nor was anyone I know. Even so, it was a very frightening experience. It would have made me feel a lot better if you had been here. I had the day off, and I was in my apartment in the Waikiki area. There wasn't a lot of damage or injuries in the city. It was the aftermath with all the bodies being moved to burial that was the worst part. I can tell you all about it much better in person, which I think is quite likely to happen sooner or later.

In case we have trouble reaching each other after this, and you get here, call the navy base headquarters and ask for my unit.

How are you? I assume you are still on board and have not had any serious mishaps. Warmer weather was welcome, I imagine.

I am fine, a little tired from long hours at the office. Things are starting to settle down a little bit here. Having the army running everything makes a lot of things different. There are some shortages, but most people are getting along OK.

You are part of a very small group of service men in the Pacific whose wives have been allowed to stay. The others are mostly those who have been here more than five years, and they are considered permanent residents. Two of the officers in our unit are in that group. One is Jasper Holmes, the officer who helped me with buying my car.

That is about all I can say at the moment. I love you very much and I miss you a lot.

Oodles of love,
Jennifer

It was obvious that the letter was written under censorship. She sounded lonely but OK. When the mail was being sorted, the loudspeaker announced that mail dropped off before midnight would go out via Tutuila. Alan grabbed the opportunity to write to Jennifer and to his parents.

c/o Fleet Post Office
San Francisco, Calif.
January 22, 1942

Dear Jennifer,

I just got your letter of December 29, so I guess the mail got backed up during the time it was shut down. On December 31 I heard the mail was restarted, and I sent you a letter on New Year's Day. I hope you have gotten it by now.

The news says that German submarines have arrived on the East Coast, and the navy is having trouble coping with the situation.

I am fine, and I have not had any serious mishaps since the one you know about last fall. I got promoted to lieutenant in the big promotion on January 3. My bombing scores continue to gradually improve.

There is a senior officer on board, and it turns out that one of his staff is an old friend from my surface tour. I think I

mentioned him to you when I told you about that experience.
We have been able to exchange some gossip, some helpful and
some just entertaining.
    I love you, Jennifer, and miss you every day.

Tons of love,
Alan

It seemed to Alan that short letters would now be the rule, because of so many forbidden topics.

At suppertime, Alan and Stinson had agreed to meet in the starboard gallery aft at 2000. Alan arrived a little early and enjoyed the breeze. Soon the tall silhouette of Stinson appeared from forward.

"Good evening, Hank."

"Good evening, Alan. Well, we heard today that Rabaul fell. Not much could be done about it, I'm afraid. However, it caused an interesting confrontation in flag country, I can tell you."

"Really. How did that happen?"

"Apparently, the exec, Commander Clapp, was upset that everything was falling apart in the Bismarks, and he decided he was the one person in the US Navy who could do something about it. About fifteen hundred, I got a call from an orderly that Clapp wanted to see the admiral right away. I checked with the admiral and shortly Clapp appeared. He spent about thirty minutes with the admiral and then left. Afterward, the admiral called his staff in to tell them what the conversation was about. Clapp wanted to break radio silence to get permission from Nimitz to raid Rabaul!" Stinson put his hands on his temples in a gesture of frustration. "The admiral turned him down. It seemed like a poor idea to all the staff also, with Jap carriers near Rabaul, a shortage of oilers, and Nimitz having a more complete picture than any of us. Clapp accused the admiral of being inflexible. Do you believe it? Apparently he thinks he's a commander who knows more about how to run the Pacific war than two admirals. As expected, Clapp went first to Buckthorn, where he got a very similar reception, we found out later. Obviously that confirms your impression that Clapp doesn't have confidence in Buckthorn either. I get the feeling that some of the headstrong aviators don't respect the leadership of any of the black shoes, like Nimitz or Fletcher. Keep this to yourself, Alan."

"Wow. That is an earful. Headstrong is putting it mildly. Mum's the word."

CHAPTER SIX

First Offense: Marshalls Raid

Wednesday, January 28, 1942

It was early morning on another warm, clear tropical day. TF-17 had recrossed the equator, this time without ceremony, about 100 miles southwest of Baker Island during the night of January 27. The task force had started refueling. *Yorktown*'s turn would come last, as usual, later the next day. Alan had noticed that, since the near fiasco on January 17, the special refueling detail, which consisted of the sailors directly involved in refueling, had been called on the bullhorn a number of times for training sessions and drills. He hoped it would be smoother this time.

Daily searches had continued with the same alternating pattern. Now Alan was letting Kidd fly the cross leg in the middle of the search, with the turns at both ends.

At around noon, a Dauntless from Scouting Six on *Enterprise* had appeared overhead and landed aboard *Yorktown*. The pilot was the exec of Scouting Six, carrying dispatches from Halsey for Fletcher. He waited on *Yorktown* for a half hour for any return messages. He chatted with the air officers and the group commander. He soon took off again to return to TF-8. This was the way coordination between carriers took place under radio silence and out of blinker signal range, Alan realized. Alan heard later that Scouting Six's exec was surprised to hear that the air group and the air office got along well aboard *Yorktown*. He said they did not on *Enterprise*.

Thursday, January 29, 1942

Flight quarters had been advanced to 0530 because of the earlier dawn in the tropics. Alan arrived at the Bombing Five ready room at 0525. The blackboards were blank, but there was a large chart of the Gilbert and southern Marshall Islands posted. He sat down, guessing this might be a preliminary briefing for the raids, with details to be filled in later.

At 0530, Armiston and Bellingham arrived. After quarters sounded, Armiston announced, "Here's the plan for the raids, which will take place day after tomorrow. TF-Seventeen's primary target will be Jaluit in the southern Marshalls"—which he pointed out on the chart—"which intelligence has indicated is the principal location of Japanese activity in the area. TF-Seventeen will also simultaneously attack Makin in the northern Gilberts and Mili in the southern Marshalls." He again pointed to the map. "TF-Eight will be attacking targets in the northern Marshalls simultaneously. Bombing Five and Torpedo Five will go to the primary target, Jaluit, one hundred forty miles from the launch point. Scouting Five will get Makin and Mili. Fighting Forty-Two will be held back for the defense of the task force, so all of the attacks will be unescorted. Bombing Five will borrow one of Scouting Five's airplanes to send sixteen bombers to Jaluit. The Dauntlesses will be armed with a five hundred pound bomb. The Devastators will be armed with three five hundred pound bombs, in the absence of definite ship targets. The launch will be in the predawn darkness.

The Jaluit attack will take off first, at oh five hundred; then the deck will be respotted for the other two raids. Arrival at the targets will be timed for sunrise. There will be another briefing tomorrow afternoon before the strike to fill in all the details."

Alan felt the tension rising in the room as the reality of combat sank in. No fighter escort added to the tension. Alan thought to himself, *This is it, the real thing, action against the enemy. Time to stop practicing and show our stuff.*

Friday, January 30, 1942

The detailed briefing was held in the Bombing Five ready room at 1600. Alan arrived at 1550 and scanned the blackboards. Now on the left, in addition to the map of the Marshalls and Gilberts, there was a detailed map of Jaluit. On the right was the flight roster. There were sixteen airplanes listed, and one was 5-S-14 from Scouting Five. Alan scanned the list of pilots, and his name was not there. He was going to be held back from the squadron's first combat mission. He felt humiliated and angry. *How could Durham have the gall to try it again?* He got himself under control again, feeling that Durham had become a serious nuisance. He would have to take this up once again with Bellingham after the briefing. He looked at Durham and noticed that he seemed to be more jovial than he had been in some time, chatting with his neighbors. In the meantime, Alan assumed he would be going on the raid.

Armiston began the briefing right on time. "The task force will be split, with *Yorktown* and the two cruisers running in to the launch point at twenty-five knots, going west through the middle of the one hundred seventy mile gap between Mili and Makin to minimize the chance of detection," he said, pointing to the map. "Jaluit is here"—pointing to the map again—"and will be one hundred forty miles west-northwest of the launch point, designated Point Bomb, about here. The four destroyers will follow at fifteen knots and join up as the carrier and cruisers continue east after the launch into the easterly trade wind. Therefore, the return trip of the Jaluit raiders will be fifty to seventy-five miles farther. The return trip will also be upwind, adding to the time for that leg. Nevertheless, the Dauntlesses should have plenty of fuel, since the airplanes will be carrying less than the maximum armament. The Devastators will be operating with less reserve."

Armiston moved to the map of Jaluit. "Like many of what we call islands in the central Pacific, Jaluit is actually an atoll, a ring of small islands made of coral that grew on the rim of an extinct volcano as it subsided. You can see the ring is shaped roughly like a pear. There are inhabited islands on the southwest and northeast sides, but most of the population is on the southeastern islands, here," he said, pointing again. "There is a relatively straight section in the island chain here, with a gap in the middle. The military facilities are thought to be located on the southwest side of this gap, here. Final briefing will be at flight quarters tomorrow morning. Lieutenant Durham."

As flight officer, Durham stood up and gave the weather. "The forecast is for low barometric pressure over the area, overcast with occasional heavy clouds and showers."

Good for defense, bad for offense, Alan thought.

After the briefing, as the other pilots left the room, Alan went toward the front to speak to Bellingham. This time he felt he could bypass Durham and speak to the exec first. As Alan approached, Bellingham turned to him and said, "Come to my office in five minutes."

"Aye aye, sir."

Alan went directly to the exec's office to wait for him there. In a few minutes, Bellingham came in and closed the door.

"You want to know why you were not in the roster for the attack, don't you?"

"Yes, sir."

Bellingham continued, "Armiston, Durham, and I were called into the admiral's office at fifteen hundred. The admiral said he had just gotten word that someone on the search on January twenty-seventh had flown over Howland Island. We had the search that day. He wondered how that happened when he had issued strict orders that search aircraft were not to be seen from land. Durham said that your sector in the search was the one that went near Howland, and you told him you had flown over Howland, and nothing was amiss there. He wrote it down in his report on the search, which eventually caught the attention of the admiral's staff. He apologized to the admiral, saying that, since nothing of importance was reported at Howland, he had not called attention to it.

"The admiral said it was very important because it was reported that Howland and Baker were bombed by the Japanese, presumably from Makin, and that had to have happened either that day or the next. The Japanese airplanes on the attack could have seen the search aircraft and then concluded there was a carrier nearby. Naturally, we were embarrassed and chagrined that Bombing Five had apparently disobeyed his orders, and we said we would take care of disciplining the pilot in question.

"We met in Armiston's office after we left flag country. Durham suggested that you be grounded, pending an investigation. Armiston and I reluctantly agreed. By then it was fifteen thirty, and I did not have time to track you down before the briefing."

Alan realized that this was a deliberate scheme of Durham's to get him grounded. He felt his anger rising but tried to remain calm. "Well, I did have the search sector that passed nearest to Howland Island. But I was well aware of the admiral's orders.

When I reached a point forty miles southwest of Howland by dead reckoning, I turned northwest onto my cross leg. The island was off to the right of my outbound course. The search plan called for a left turn, so I was flying away from it after the turn. I reported all this to Durham and to Lowery after the flight. I never said I flew over the island or gave any information about how the island appeared. I looked carefully in the right direction before I turned, but I was not able to see it at all." He did not mention that he had plenty of opportunity to look because Kidd was doing the flying.

"Well, your story and Durham's definitely contradict each other, which is not a complete surprise to me," Bellingham said with a grin. "It is not like you not to follow orders. But that is just my opinion, and it is not enough to get you off the hook. Is there anything you can think of to convince others that your version is the correct one?"

"Hmm." Alan thought for a minute. Then he said, "Remember, during the briefing for that search, the skipper announced the admiral's order not to be seen from land. Knowing Howland was close to my sector, I asked whether we should estimate our position and stay well away or wait until we were just able to see it and turn away. He said use dead reckoning to stay forty miles away. Also Lowery would remember my debrief with him."

"Thank you, Alan, for reminding me. Now I remember you asking that question. It is hard to believe you would casually over-fly the island after that. That clinches it in my mind. Lowery's statement, being your roommate, might not carry much weight, but it would help. There will still need to be a formal inquiry after the raids to determine what happened. I will put you back on flight status and tell the skipper and Durham. You will replace Meyer, flying wing on the skipper."

"Thank you very much, sir. I hope I will continue to earn your confidence."

As he headed toward the wardroom for supper, he came upon Armiston, who gave him a thumbs up in greeting. Alan was gratified that apparently Durham was losing this latest conflict.

After supper, Alan felt the throb as the ship's propellers sped up. They were starting their final run in to the launch point. He felt his tension continuing to rise. Tomorrow had so many unknowns. It would be his first time in real combat, where there was likely to be return fire. Three months earlier, on the other side of the world, he had dropped a depth charge on a German submarine, but the submarine was diving and could not fire back. Like most of the pilots, he felt that the likelihood of being seriously hurt or killed was very small. Nevertheless, he was scared and nervous. In addition, the intelligence about what they would find at Jaluit was very sketchy, letting the imagination run wild.

Saturday, January 31, 1942

Wake up call came at 0230, and breakfast was served in the wardroom at 0300. Alan was ready to get going. He had not slept very well, but he felt reasonably fit. He had a surprisingly good appetite and appreciated the stewards' efforts to produce a hearty and tasty breakfast at this early hour. The other pilots were also nervous, some chatty and some silent, but few seemed to have much appetite. Flight quarters was at 0345, followed by the final briefing. Alan's tension rose as he reported to the Bombing Five ready room. He noticed Durham glaring at him. Heading into combat, Alan was a little surprised that Durham was still publicly nursing his personal grudge.

All the pilots donned red tinted goggles. This would help their eyes to begin to adapt to darkness while the lights remained on for the briefing. Because the weather was far from ideal, the ship's aerologist, rather than the flight officer, gave the weather briefing. "There is a high overcast with occasional showers and thunderstorms, particularly to the west. This is expected to continue through the morning, with some improvement possible in the afternoon. Wind is from one zero zero true, nine zero magnetic, at fifteen knots." Then the aerologist left to brief Torpedo Five. All the pilots were writing down the numbers.

Jolly Lowery, as navigation officer, went to the front and gave the navigation data. "The course to the target is two nine four true, two eight four magnetic, and distance, one hundred forty miles, from Point Bomb to the target. After the launch, the carrier will continue east at twenty-five knots and therefore will be sixty to seventy-five miles east of the launch point when Bombing Five returns, depending on the actual groundspeed of the airplanes and time spent at the target. The return course will be roughly one zero zero true, nine zero magnetic. The wind is close to aligned with the course to and from the target, so course correction for wind can be neglected, but time and distance will be affected. Use of the Zebra Baker homing system may be needed. Today's Yoke Easy sector letters are posted here," he said, pointing to a chart. Jolly returned to his seat.

Next Durham directed the pilots' attention to the ruled blackboard that listed aircraft and pilots. Alan would be flying his usual airplane 5-B-12. He would be flying wing on Armiston with Lowery.

Armiston then stood up and addressed the squadron. "Bombing Five will launch first, led by me, then the air group commander, and then Torpedo Five. There will be four Wildcats spotted at the aft end for CAP after the attack group has launched. We have a launch in the dark in fairly crummy weather. We will try to form up, but it may be difficult. We will use running lights, at least until we have formed up. Even if we do get formed up, the formation could get separated flying through weather on the way to the target. Try to stick together, but if we get separated, I expect every pilot, even if entirely alone, to do his best to get to the target, attack, and return. Good luck, and hit 'em hard. Stand by for orders to man your planes. That is all."

A few minutes later, the bullhorn barked, "Now hear this. Bombing and Torpedo crews, man your planes."

Alan thought, *Finding the target and the ship when we come back may be the hardest part of this mission.*

It was 0415 as Alan stepped onto the flight deck, and he could just make out the airplanes spotted aft for launch in the dim light. He knew it was a new moon, so no help there. He glanced up at the island and was able to see that Vulture's Row, the catwalks high up on the island, were jammed full of spectators, waiting to see *Yorktown's* first combat launch. He felt his excitement mounting.

Alan's airplane was in the second row, behind Armiston's and Lowery's. As he walked up, he noted the five hundred pound bomb in the bomb crutch under the fuselage. He greeted Klein, who had just shut down the engine of 5-B-12 after warming it up. Kidd was standing behind the left wing.

"Good morning, Kidd. All set to go?"

"Good morning, sir. Yes, sir." Alan did a quick walk around the airplane to check it over. He climbed up on the left wing, squeezed past Klein, and climbed into the cockpit. Kidd climbed into the rear cockpit.

"Everything is in good shape, sir; we made sure of that," said Klein, smiling.

"Thank you, Klein. We may be wringing her out today," Alan replied with a grin.

"Good luck, sir. Give 'em hell." He gave a quick salute and Alan returned it. Klein jumped down off the wing and disappeared.

Alan flipped on the master switch and the cockpit lights, so he could see what he was doing. He made sure his charts and notes were carefully stowed away and then fastened his parachute straps and seat belt. He turned on the intercom.

"Everything in order back there, Kidd?"

"Ready to go, sir."

Alan looked up and saw that a deck crewman was shining a portable light on Fly One, who was giving the signal to start engines. Then Alan followed the warm start procedure to get the engine started. The engine had a reassuringly normal rumble. He could see the yellow flames in the exhaust stacks of Armiston's and Lowery's planes ahead. The flames would turn to blue when the engine went to full power for takeoff.

Alan felt a change in the ship's motion and noticed the deck was canting slightly to port. It was 0445, and the ship was turning around to the right to steam eastward into the wind for flight operations. A few minutes later, he watched Armiston and then Lowery take off, and then it was his turn. After Fly One gave him the signal, he accelerated rapidly down the deck. He lifted off with about 200 feet to spare.

As he passed over the bow, he was immediately engulfed in the black night, in instrument flying conditions, with the dim horizon visible only here and there. He looked around hurriedly for Jolly ahead and to his right. He finally saw his lights and blue exhaust flame faintly and moved to close up. After another minute, he was close to Jolly, and he could occasionally make out Armiston's lights beyond Jolly. Jolly and Alan slowly moved into formation, with Jolly on Armiston's left stepped down and back, and Alan on Armiston's right, stepped down and back. Alan was too busy to think about the unlucky weather or his first bombing mission.

Armiston continued to circle near the carrier. After what seemed a very long time, two other sections of three had formed up with them. Armiston rocked his wings as a signal that he was departing for the target. It was 0515.

The nine plane formation climbed to 3,000 feet, just under the overcast, and leveled off. The weather required flying low to try to stay out of the clouds, and particularly out of thunderstorms. However, there was more drag in the denser air at low altitude, so their range was reduced.

It was pitch dark, and it was impossible to detect clouds and showers ahead until all visual cues disappeared. After about fifteen minutes, they were suddenly flying through rain, and the visibility dropped. Alan stayed close to Armiston and was able to keep him in sight. Without running lights, he would have lost the skipper. After a few minutes, they flew out of the rain. Now Alan could see one of the other sections, but the third had disappeared. Suddenly they were flying in clouds, and Alan could barely see Armiston. Armiston began to slowly descend, and Alan followed. The cloud began to have breaks in it at 1,000 feet, and Armiston leveled off. Alan glimpsed the second section occasionally through breaks in the clouds.

They flew on for another twenty minutes. Then the breaks in the clouds became less frequent, and Armiston began another slow descent. Finally he leveled off at 500 feet, where there were few clouds. The weather was worse than forecast. The second section had disappeared. After another twenty minutes, there was dim light. Dawn was approaching behind them, but the sunlight was obscured by heavy clouds. It became possible to see and dodge the clouds and shafts of rain, however.

It continued to get brighter, and they could see about ten miles, except where there were shafts of rain. Suddenly they glimpsed surf ahead and to the left. *Likely the southern tip of Jaluit*, Alan thought. It was 0630. Armiston began to climb, dodging the clouds and rain, circling over the tip.

Alan told Kidd over the intercom, "Island ahead, seems to be Jaluit. Starting to climb for the dive."

"OK, sir. I'll get ready for action."

Alan charged his machine guns and armed his bomb. He could feel an occasional thump as Kidd swiveled his seat to face aft, opened the canopy fully, and mounted the flexible machine gun. Alan pulled down his goggles and slid his canopy back.

They continued to get occasional glimpses of the island as they climbed, finally leveling off at 9,000 feet. There were two very dark clouds with lightning, which they stayed away from. It was much cooler, around 60 degrees. Armiston began flying northeast, looking for a break in the clouds to observe the target.

Suddenly they got a break, and they could see a fair amount of the atoll nearby. They could see the gap in the island chain, with a cluster of buildings on the southwest side and a ship anchored in the lagoon. Armiston hand signaled to prepare to dive. Alan got behind Armiston to follow him in the dive, but Jolly kept circling.

"Ready for the dive?" Alan asked Kidd.

"Yes, sir."

Armiston flew straight for a few moments and then abruptly rolled over and pulled into his dive.

"Here we go." Alan followed when he got to the same position. As expected, Armiston aimed for the ship. Passing through 5,000 feet, the dive seemed to be going well. A few seconds later, the bombsight became fogged with moisture. Alan looked up, and the bulletproof windshield was also fogged. He tried leaning to the left, to look beside the bulletproof windshield. With the slipstream outside the cockpit tugging at his helmet, he could see the target, but there was nothing to align the airplane with the target to achieve accuracy. He did the best he could, dropping at 1,500 feet. He immediately began his pullout and saw a patch of foam where Armiston's bomb had fallen about 100 feet from the side of the ship.

He leveled off at 500 feet over the lagoon, following Armiston. He could detect the smell of the tropical vegetation in the air.

"We missed about one hundred feet astern," reported Kidd.

Dauntless dive bombing
(US Navy/PD-USGOV-MILITARY-NAVY)

"OK," Alan replied. *No surprise*, he thought, but he was very disappointed.

A Japanese floatplane buzzed by, going in the opposite direction. They followed the island chain northeast a few miles to the eastern tip, dodging rain showers. There appeared to be a seaplane base there, with a small ship. Armiston began a strafing run on the ship, and Alan followed him down. They picked up speed, and as he got close to the ship, Alan began firing. He was surprised to see how much damage the ship was taking as it was hit by the heavy slugs. Small objects were flying off under the impact, equipment fell on the deck, and men were diving for cover. The hammering of the .50 caliber machine guns and the smoke swirling in the cockpit added to the excitement. Leaving the ship they continued northwest along the chain for another five miles, seeing nothing larger than thatched huts.

Alan followed Armiston as he turned left and flew south toward their original target. Suddenly they spotted a Dauntless on their left, which turned to join up with them. It was Jolly. Alan wondered if Jolly had gotten a hit. Now there was a thunderstorm directly over their original target area, and they turned right and followed the chain south-southwest about seven miles to the southern tip. There was a larger island there but only thatched huts. They flew back along a small road up the chain to their original target. The thunderstorm had moved west into the lagoon. They saw two Devastators making glide bombing runs on the buildings.

Suddenly Alan saw three airplanes in formation approaching from dead ahead. They looked like Dauntlesses. Armiston was wagging his wings and signaling them to join. The leader passed close by on Alan's left. He could read the number on the aft fuselage, 5-B-5. It was Durham. He and his wingmen continued straight on, not joining up.

They saw no other Dauntlesses. The two other sections that had originally been with them should have arrived at the target around the same time, but they could be easily missed in the clouds and rain. Armiston signaled to return to the ship at 0725.

Lots of bad weather but no return fire, the opposite of what Alan had anticipated the day before. He relaxed a little. With the advantage of daylight, they were able to cruise at 1,000 feet, dodging shafts of rain and only occasionally passing through scud. They kept their formation fairly tight so that they each could make out at least one of the other airplanes in the clouds.

Alan felt the call of nature and reached under his seat for the relief tube. This was a small cone attached to a long rubber tube. The other end of the tube was on the bottom of the fuselage, connected to a venturi that maintained a small suction to make sure any liquid in the tube went overboard. On long flights like this, the relief tube was a necessity.

At 0815, the radio came alive. "This is seven seven victor four four—seven seven victor four four and seven six victor four four are landing at Jaluit, are landing alongside one of the northwestern islands of Jaluit. That is all." Alan was able to interpret the special radio call signs: 77V44 was the exec of Torpedo Five. The Devastators were carrying three man crews, so six men would be stuck on Jaluit, provided they were not hurt in the ditching. *Not much chance of them being rescued by our forces*, Alan thought, so they would probably be captured, a grim prospect that left Alan with a cold feeling in his stomach. There had been many reports that the Japanese had no respect for prisoners and generally mistreated them.

Alan said on the intercom, "Bad news."

"Yes, sir," replied Kidd.

"Fire up the Zebra Baker, and see what we get."

"Zebra Baker coming on," replied Kidd. There was nothing but static. Alan knew that the range of the Yoke Easy transmitter on the ship was less at lower altitudes, because it used ultrahigh frequency. This caused the signal to go strictly line of sight, and it could be blocked by the curvature of the earth. Twenty minutes went by. Then Alan could just make out the faint Morse code: dot dash dot dot, the letter *L*. He consulted the code. They were in the sector that was between 270 and 300 degrees bearing from the ship, or 90 to 120 degrees course to the ship. That was as expected and was very reassuring.

In another half hour, Alan started to hear a faint dash dash, the letter *M*, superimposed on the letter *L*. That meant they were approaching the next sector on their right, and the border in between was 270 degrees from, 90 degrees to, the ship. Armiston continued until the signals were equal and then turned slightly left to keep them equal, so they would fly directly down the 270 degree bearing from the ship.

Ahead there were dark clouds, and the airplanes began to bounce around in the increased turbulence. Now they had to work around shafts of heavy rain. Another fifteen minutes went by, and suddenly there she was, *Yorktown*, headed east. Alan moved to the right into right echelon, with Jolly on Armiston's right wing and Alan on Jolly's right wing. They glimpsed several Dauntlesses orbiting around outside the landing pattern and wondered what they were doing. They needed to change course only slightly to fly upwind on the starboard side of the ship and turn left into the landing pattern.

There were heavy rain shafts all around, so they kept their downwind leg in close. As Alan slowed to pattern speed, the turbulence seemed to get worse. When he opened the canopy, light rain came into the cockpit. On base leg he realized that he would have to stay more than five knots above stall in this gusty wind, to avoid stalling. He slowed to an average of 70 knots, but he could not keep his airspeed from moving up and down. His usual tension before a carrier landing had turned into real fear.

As he turned onto his final approach, he could not see Soupy through the rain. Then he found him and followed his signals. Jolly had landed successfully. The ship was pitching more than he had ever seen it during a landing. He would try to land near the fourth wire and hope his extra speed did not cause the arresting wire to part. Soupy gave him the cut signal, and he closed the throttle. The deck was coming up to meet him, and he landed hard near the third wire, bounced up, and landed again near the fifth wire. The hook caught the seventh wire, which slowed the airplane so fast that Alan was unable to keep his forehead from bumping the gunsight, but the wire held. He let out a long sigh and felt the tension slowly subside. *What a relief to get aboard OK in such lousy weather!* Although the weather was not very hot, he realized there was a lot of sweat mixed with the rain in his damp clothing.

Alan raised his arresting hook, taxied forward, and parked. It was 0930, but it seemed like afternoon. He had been flying for almost five hours in bad weather, requiring constant attention. He had never turned on the autopilot, which he would normally have used for most of the flight out and back. He was tired. He climbed out and found Kidd standing behind the wing.

"That was a long and scary flight," Alan said, "even without any enemy fighters or return fire. How do you feel?"

"I'm fine, sir. Thanks. You're right about the flight. That was pretty crummy weather for a combat mission. I could never see enough of the area around the target to be sure we didn't miss something."

"Well, let's go get some coffee and find out what everyone else did."

"Yes, sir."

They were about halfway to the island when a big gust of wind hit them. They both staggered and fell.

"Dammit all," said Alan.

"Second the motion," said Kidd.

Alan was beginning to appreciate Kidd's gift for words.

They got up and continued, their clothes flapping in the wind. As they approached the island, the bullhorn announced, "Now hear this. One aircraft on anti-torpedo patrol has flown into the water. *Hughes* has the crew in sight. Stand by to recover the anti-torpedo plane patrol and the combat air patrol." Just as they reached the island, a heavy rain squall hit. The visibility in the rain was so poor that Alan thought flight operations would have to stop, at least temporarily.

Alan said to Kidd, "So that was what the Dauntlesses were doing. It seems to me the weather is plenty bad enough to bring everyone back on board." Alan knew that Dauntlesses were sometimes used for anti-torpedo plane patrol because there were not enough fighters to go around. He had heard that many carrier pilots, however, felt that defense of the ship came first, and all the fighters should be used for that if necessary, and the dive bombers used only for offense.

"I agree, sir. I hope that ditched crew is all right."

"Yeah. See you later, Kidd," said Alan as they parted ways in the island.

Alan stopped at the wardroom, downed a cup of coffee, picked up another one, and reported with it to the Bombing Five ready room at 0950. Durham was the senior officer present, and he was standing at the front, attempting to hold court. He couldn't think of much to say, and the other pilots ignored him, continuing to chat with each other. He looked frustrated. Alan thought he was making a fool of himself.

Alan sat down and turned to his neighbor Jolly. "Where's the skipper and the exec?"

"The skipper is debriefing with the captain and the admiral. Nobody has seen Gordie."

"There's still time for him to get back."

"That's right." Their eyes met. Alan knew that Jolly shared his deep respect for the exec.

"Did you get a hit?" Alan asked.

"No, I tried to find a bigger hole to dive through but didn't have much luck. In the dive my windshield and gunsight fogged up. From what I hear, that happened to all the pilots that went high for their dives. How about you?"

"Same thing happened. The skipper missed too, so I think he had the same problem. The windshield and sight got cold at altitude and fogged up in the warm air, which was near the dew point lower down. We'll need some kind of fix for that to have any accuracy when diving in these conditions."

A few minutes later, the ship's bullhorn announced, "Now hear this. The pilot and gunner of the Scouting Five aircraft that flew into the water are safe aboard *Walke*. Stand by to recover the combat air patrol."

The ship's bullhorn came on again, announcing that *Russell* was being sent west to look for ditched aircrews.

"The Devastators must be coming back on fumes," said Ned Morris.

The pilots continued chatting. Fifteen minutes later the strike radio frequency came on, and the chatter in the ready room abruptly stopped. The radio had been piped in to a loudspeaker in the ready room, and the volume was turned up. A Torpedo Five pilot reported sighting a ditched Devastator. A few minutes later, another Torpedo Five pilot reported a ditched Devastator and gave the bearing and distance to the carrier. Shortly there was a conversation between this airplane and the skipper of *Russell*, which the pilot had sighted. The pilot gave *Russell* the course to the ditched Devastator.

The ship's bullhorn announced a minute later that *Hughes* and *Sims* were being sent to assist *Russell* in the search to the west.

Over the radio, there were several conversations between *Russell* and other Devastator pilots needing a steer to the carrier, which *Russell* provided.

Now the remaining Bombing Five pilots, except the exec, came into the ready room, having just landed.

A few minutes later, Armiston walked in and stood at the front, motioning for the pilots to remain seated. Durham sat down. "Anyone see the exec during the mission?" he asked and looked around. The pilots were shaking their heads.

Mike Burke spoke up: "I was flying wing on him in the first section of the second division. I lost him a few minutes after I took off. I never saw him again. I joined up with another section and went to the target."

Ensign Alvis Monroe said, "I was his other wingman. The same thing happened to me."

Armiston looked at the clock and said, "He could still make it back." Alan thought it was possible, but it was getting less likely by the minute. "OK, I'm going to start debriefing now, individually in my office, in the order in which you took off. Each session should go five to ten minutes. Keep track of the guy ahead and wait outside my office when he goes in. After debriefing, you can stand down until called again. That is all."

Jolly and Alan stood up and followed the skipper toward his office. After only a few minutes, Jolly came out and Alan went in.

Armiston had a stack of sheets of paper to make notes for each pilot. He quickly began. "OK, Ericsson, since you were one of my wingmen, this can be very short. That was definitely lousy weather for a combat mission. You did well to just stick with me. In the dive, did your windshield and bombsight fog up?"

"Yes, sir. I leaned to the left, to look past the bullet proof windshield, and was able to see the target, but of course I couldn't align my plane."

"I did the same thing. At the target you saw me signal to a section of Dauntlesses to join up?"

"Yes, sir. It was Lieutenant Durham and his wingmen."

"Correct." Armiston paused. "Coming back was easier, but that was a very difficult landing with the pitching and turbulence. You did well to get aboard without damage."

"Thank you, sir."

Armiston studied his notes. "I think that's about all, Ericsson. Well done."

"Thank you, sir." He stood and left the office.

Ten minutes later, as Alan was going from his debriefing to his stateroom to freshen up, the ship's bullhorn reported that the destroyers and the radar on *Yorktown* detected a snooper airplane nosing around. *Hughes* had sighted the snooper, a big four engine Kawanishi flying boat, and had fired on it. She requested air support, and six Wildcats were sent to investigate. They were not able to find the snooper, who had headed back west.

At lunch Alan talked to some of the Scouting Five pilots about how their missions had gone. The skipper, Lieutenant Commander William Burch, had taken nine Dauntlesses to Makin in the Gilberts, and they set fire to two anchored flying boats and got hits on their tender. Their exec, Lieutenant Warren Stubb, had found no targets at Mili in the Marshalls. Both missions had good weather near the target, and no one reported fogging of windshields or bombsights.

Around 1300, a relief of six more Wildcats for CAP was put up, and the first six came back aboard. Just then the carrier's radar picked up another snooper. The klaxon sounded, and the signal for general quarters blared out. Flight quarters were called on the bullhorn. Alan reported to the Bombing Five ready room and listened to the loudspeaker and radio circuit. He wished he could go topside to watch the action.

The bullhorn reported that the snooper was sighted by *Yorktown* about eight miles away. On the radio, the CAP was given vectors to pursue, and the ship held its fire to avoid hitting the Wildcats. Shortly the bullhorn reported that the snooper was another Kawanishi flying boat, and it was crossing *Yorktown*'s bow, with two Wildcats in hot pursuit.

The radio circuit suddenly came alive with a whoop and "We just shot his ass off."

From the bullhorn a different voice said, "Burn, you son of a bitch—burn!"

Jolly said to Alan, "That's Clapp. Not too eloquent."

"I'll say," said Alan.

Then the bullhorn announced that the Wildcats had gotten the snooper, and the airplane had fallen apart into flaming pieces plummeting toward the ocean. The ship secured from general quarters, flight quarters were canceled, and the two Wildcats landed. Their pilots received a joyous welcome, with Alan joining most of Bombing Five, Scouting Five, and Torpedo Five pilots cheering from the gallery. The Fighting Forty-Two pilots had to stay in their ready room. The two Wildcat pilots were ordered to report to the bridge, where there was a small celebration of the first aerial victory by Fighting Forty-Two and *Yorktown*.

The task force continued east, away from the targets. Then refueling operations for the destroyers got underway. It seemed clear to Alan there were not going to be any more strikes that day. He felt relieved because he was very tired. The weather remained poor for the whole day, although Fighting Forty-Two managed to maintain the CAP until dusk.

In midafternoon, the bullhorn told all Bombing Five pilots to report to the ready room at 1600. Alan was not sure whether the meeting was a briefing for another raid the next day or to announce who would be replacing Bellingham as exec. The word had passed among the pilots in the squadron that no one had seen the exec or his gunner since shortly after they took off. When Alan got to the ready room, he saw that the blackboards were blank, so it would not be a mission briefing. He noticed that Durham had moved to the exec's chair.

"Atten-shun!"

Armiston arrived with just a minute to spare, with Scottie following. Standing behind the lectern, Armiston looked tired, like all the pilots except Durham. It had been a long and busy day. He looked at Durham and frowned. "As you were." The pilots sat down.

"Once it became clear that our executive officer, Lieutenant Gordon Bellingham, was not coming back from the strike, I had to make some new appointments. Let us hope and pray that Gordie and his gunner are safe on land or in their raft and will be rescued." There were nods and murmurs of agreement.

"The new executive officer is Lieutenant Angus MacAllester. Congratulations, Scottie," he said, smiling and looking at MacAllester.

Alan was gratified that his friend Scottie would be the exec, although he was not sure Scottie had Bellingham's sensitivity and discretion.

"The rest of the officers are as follows. The new flight officer is Lieutenant James Lowery. The new engineering officer is Lieutenant Jeremiah West. The new gunnery officer is Lieutenant Alan Ericsson. Now—"

Armiston stopped and stared as Durham rose from Bellingham's seat in the front row and walked deliberately toward the door.

"No one has permission to leave yet," Armiston barked.

Durham did not pause, continuing out the door and down the passageway.

Armiston appeared remarkably unfazed, almost relieved. "Well, Lieutenant Durham has just committed his last act as a member of this squadron. From now on he is a passenger in this ship. He is restricted from entering this room, the hangar deck, or the flight deck." He paused. "Let this be a lesson. Durham is a fine pilot, but it takes a lot more than that to be a fine naval aviator. You have to be able to work closely with all your squadron mates, and he could not do that."

All the pilots had grave expressions after this stern speech.

Armiston paused and his expression brightened. "Now, I will give out the remaining officer assignments in the squadron. Scottie and I have been over this list." He proceeded to read out the list. The new appointments were generally received with satisfaction. Ned Morris was appointed to be assistant gunnery officer, so he would be working closely with Alan. Alan was pleased because, although Ned was pretty junior and much younger than Alan, he was a friend and an eager, diligent officer. Growing up on a cattle ranch in Arizona, Ned naturally had to be familiar with mechanical things and how to maintain them. The new assistant engineering officer was Ensign Goodwin, one of the newer pilots who had joined in San Diego.

"Now, some of you may have noticed that our base course is northeast, rather than east. After getting orders by radio from Admiral Halsey, Admiral Fletcher has decided to refuel tomorrow and then head to Pearl Harbor. That is all."

There were smiles at the thought of going to Pearl. Jennifer's image popped into Alan's mind's eye. He couldn't wait to see her.

As Alan started to leave the ready room, Armiston approached. "Follow me to my office."

"Yes, sir."

When they sat down there, Armiston looked intently at Alan and said, "There will be no inquiry regarding the possibility of you flying over Howland Island. Just now I was able to see the admiral, and I told him that Lieutenant Durham was dismissed from the squadron and what I think really happened. All references to it will be removed from the records. That is all."

"Thank you, sir." Alan was glad to know that the incident was completely over with.

As he started toward his stateroom, he thought of Bellingham again. He was grieved to realize that Bellingham had most likely crashed or ditched somewhere. He was probably either dead, captured, or facing a long ride in his raft, so he would not be heard from for a long time, if ever. Alan thought of how nicely Bellingham had handled the question of Alan flying over Howland Island. He would sorely miss Bellingham's thoughtful leadership.

It had been a very long day. He felt physically and emotionally drained. Fatigue was settling on him like a huge blanket.

CHAPTER SEVEN

Pearl Harbor and Jennifer

Thursday, February 5, 1942

There was very cheerful atmosphere aboard *Yorktown*, as all hands were looking forward to going into Pearl Harbor the next day and having some time to relax. The ship's bullhorn announced that all squadrons should report to their ready rooms at 1600. The pilots were aware that most likely they would fly in from the carrier, so they were expecting a briefing to be announced.

When Alan came into the ready room, he noticed that there was a large map of the whole Pearl Harbor area, with the airfields marked, taped up in the center of the blackboards. On the left was a diagram of an airfield he did not recognize. The flight roster had been filled out on the blackboard to the right. He would be a section leader for the first time, leading the last section.

"Atten-shun!"

Armiston came into the ready room and motioned the pilots to sit down. He began, "We're all looking forward to getting into Pearl. There you will probably hear all sorts of stories about what happened during the air raid and what the casualties were.

The top brass has decided you should hear a true summary, so you will have an idea what not to believe. This is not to be repeated ashore."

He read aloud from a paper on the lectern. "There were two separate attacks, about an hour apart, with well over one hundred aircraft in each. It appears there were at least four large aircraft carriers participating, probably more. The navy lost around two thousand killed and seven hundred wounded. Most of the navy killed were aboard *Arizona*, whose magazine blew up. None of our carriers were near Hawaii. Four battleships were sunk. Some of these are repairable. One battleship had to be beached, and three had light damage. Three destroyers were lost. One cruiser was heavily damaged; most other combat ships had some damage. Around ninety navy and marine aircraft were lost, nearly all on the ground. Army aircraft losses were similar. Fortunately, tankers, oil storage, and repair facilities had only very light damage." He stopped reading and looked up. "Again this is not to be repeated ashore. A lot of the damage has not been cleaned up. Be ready for a depressing scene." Armiston paused and rearranged the papers on the lectern.

There was complete silence. Alan sensed that most had known it was bad, but this sounded worse. He thought of Jennifer. *How much of this did she see? How frightened was she? In her last letter, she mentioned that the aftermath was the most depressing part.*

Alan's attention was drawn back to the briefing. Armiston was saying, "Now, let's turn to the plan for tomorrow's flight into Pearl. *Enterprise* is a day ahead of us, and her air group flew into the Pearl Harbor Naval Air Station on Ford Island today, taking up much of the available space there. Therefore, our air group will fly into the Marine Corps Air Station (MCAS) at Ewa, five miles southwest of Ford Island, near the coast. Ewa was strafed and hit with light bombs during the attack, and most of the air-craft there were destroyed. This is a diagram of the airfield," he said, pointing to the diagram. "It has two runways, both long enough for us, three two one and eight two six. The ramp area and the tower are here on the northwest side of three two one. Shortly after the attack, an expansion project was started there and is continuing. Both existing runways are being extended, and two new runways added. Be on the lookout for construction ac-tivity on runways and taxiways.

"We're going to try a running rendezvous again, this time from one hundred fifty miles out. This time we will follow Torpedo Five; then Scouting Five will follow us. The Dauntlesses will cruise at fifteen thousand feet to make it more realistic. Now, when we get to Ewa, the wind will almost certainly be from the east, and they will be using runway eight. In that case we cannot use a normal squadron break, because it would carry us far up-wind into the army traffic at Hickam here and even the traffic at the former Rodgers Airport, here, which is being converted into a naval air station," he said, pointing to the map. "Therefore, we will execute the break going downwind near the shore, turn left, and fly upwind until we're abeam the east end of the field, then turn left onto a crosswind leg, and then turn onto a left down-wind leg on the north side of the field.

"Tomorrow afternoon buses will take us to the Royal Hawaiian Hotel, where we will have twenty-four hours to un-wind, courtesy of the navy. The hotel is mostly occupied by re-cuperating submariners, so take it easy. Some of our submarines have been attacked by our aircraft, so you will not—repeat, *not*—be regarded as heroes by our submariners. The flight roster is posted here. Pack an overnight duffel and keep it with you for the Royal Hawaiian. Your regular duffel bags and cruise boxes will be delivered to the new BOQ at Ewa. The rest will be covered in a detailed briefing at oh eight hundred tomorrow. That is all."

There were smiles and a buzz of conversation as the news of a stay at the Royal Hawaiian sank in.

Alan got up and approached Scottie. "Scottie, could I see you in your office?"

"Sure, Alan. I'll be there in five minutes."

Alan headed toward the squadron offices. Scottie appeared a few minutes later and closed the door.

Alan said, "I'd like permission to skip the stay at the Royal Hawaiian." Alan knew he did not have to address Scottie as "sir" when they were alone.

"Alan, are you crazy? You won't get a chance like this too often. Gunnery problems can wait. We won't be going right out again, as I understand it."

"That's not it. I'd like to spend the night with my wife at her apartment in Honolulu."

"Your wife? Aaah, I completely forgot she was at Pearl Harbor. That's the kind of thing a good exec should remember. I apologize, Alan. Certainly you can do that. I'll need an address and telephone number in case something unexpected happens. You're very lucky, you know. I guess that makes up a little bit for not having her with you at Norfolk."

Alan wrote down the address and telephone number and thanked Scottie.

Friday, February 6, 1942

The air group was on its way in to MCAS Ewa and was approaching Oahu. It was sunny with a layer of scattered to broken cumulus clouds. Bombing Five was cruising well above the cumulus layer at 15,000 feet, while Torpedo Five was at 1,000 feet, below the layer. Unfortunately, that meant that the uncomfortable oxygen masks had to be used. The cumulus clouds became widely scattered approaching the southwest side of the island, and Alan could see the island in the distance. Alan was keeping a lookout for Torpedo Five, but it was difficult to find them through the small gaps in the clouds. He thought, *This is a much better approximation of a true running rendezvous than the approach to San Diego.*

Then all of sudden he saw them, black dots against the shining water, when the gaps in the clouds got larger. They were ahead, perhaps ten miles. The skipper, leading the first division, had probably seen them earlier. The skipper signaled to begin descent, and they gained faster on the torpedo bombers, as they picked up speed in the descent. Bombing Five had almost caught up to Torpedo Five when they reached 1,000 feet, approaching the coast.

Armiston came on the radio and said they were using runway 8, wind 090 at 15. He signaled a left turn, and they flew west parallel with the shore. Then he signaled the break, and the squadron executed it, ending up spaced apart and flying east, about two miles offshore. As the third-to-last airplane, Alan was almost to Barbers Point, where the coast turns northwest, when he made his break. Now in line astern, they turned north on a crosswind leg, crossing over the shore. Alan glanced over toward the harbor to his right and saw what appeared to be several sunken battleships in Battleship Row on the southeast side of Ford Island. Then he had to turn his attention back to keeping his spacing on the airplane ahead. He followed its left turn onto a left downwind leg, north of the field, and landed. As they taxied into the ramp on the northwest side of the field, Alan could see carcasses of wrecked airplanes that had been cleared from the ramp area and put aside. There were still a lot of broken windows and charred areas on the hangar.

The control tower consisted of a small crow's nest on top of a single mast. Alan remembered hearing that the air station started off as a navy dirigible base, and the single mast was for mooring the dirigibles. The navy dirigibles were lost in crashes in the twenties and thirties before any of them made it out to Hawaii.

Alan shut down and followed the other pilots into the hangar. His mind was filled with thoughts of seeing Jennifer again. He wondered how he would let her know he had arrived. He thought she would at least have found out that *Yorktown* was coming in that day and probably that the air group would fly into Ewa. Would she know when, and that they were headed for the Royal Hawaiian? It was 1110. Armiston announced that they could relax until lunch was served in the cafeteria at 1200. Then he approached Alan.

"There's a message for you, you lucky dog," he said, smiling and handing a sheet of paper to Alan.

"Thank you, sir."

It was a very short typewritten message:

For Lieutenant Alan Ericsson, Squadron VB-5
Call me when you get to the Royal Hawaiian.
Jennifer Ericsson, Combat Intelligence Unit

Alan smiled as he realized that she was right on top of things.

By midafternoon, the pilots from *Yorktown* were aboard buses making their circuitous way around Pearl Harbor from the west side to the east side and on to Honolulu. Torpedo Five and Bombing Five were on the first bus. They passed West Loch, and as they approached North Loch, the stench of fuel oil permeated the bus through the open windows. *There must have been a lot of fuel spilled in the harbor during the attack*, Alan concluded.

As they came around to the northeast side of the harbor and passed by East Loch, he began to get glimpses of the harbor and Ford Island. As they got closer, he could make out a large ship, possibly a battleship, with its keel in the air on the northwest side of Ford Island. There was also a smaller ship, possibly a cruiser, riding very low nearby. A few small boats were gathered around each of them. Large patches of fuel oil were still floating on the surface. He could see the skeletons of two hangars at the Pearl Harbor Naval Air Station on Ford Island.

Starting down the east side of the harbor, he could begin to see Battleship Row, the double row of moorings just off the southeast side of Ford Island. There was the superstructure of what appeared to be a sunken battleship protruding above the water at one of the nearer moorings. Beyond that was a large ship, presumably a battleship, upside down, with most of the bottom of the hull above the water. Further southwest there was another battleship sunk with the turrets awash. Small boats and salvage vessels were working around most of the ships. The damage to buildings on Ford Island was now more apparent. Then suddenly he was looking at buildings on the naval base between them and the harbor, which cut off his view. Alan thought the damage fit the description they had been given, but it was still daunting to view the actual scene.

He even felt a small twinge of sympathy for the Gun Club. Their world was suddenly in a shambles, after fifty years of the battleships being the elite of the navy.

A half hour later, they were on Kalakaua Avenue, with part of the city on the left and Waikiki Beach off to the right. Alan started to fidget with the excitement of seeing Jennifer. The bus turned right, and directly ahead was the Royal Hawaiian Hotel. It was familiar to Alan from a visit to Oahu during his surface tour, although he had never stayed there. It was an impressive pink stucco building, six stories in the center with five story wings, with around four hundred rooms. Many celebrities and very wealthy people had stayed there. Nestled between the two wings was the entrance, with a roof supported by majestic Greek columns over the place where vehicles stopped. The bus eased under the roof and stopped. The pilots filed out and were handed their bags by the driver.

After getting his bag, Alan turned around and was startled to see Jennifer, standing near the doorway. Alan had always thought she was very attractive, and now in person he found her irresistible. Her deep blue eyes and her beautiful face framed by dark wavy hair were just as he remembered them. She certainly did not look any the worse for her hard work.

She saw him at the same time. She rushed forward, opening her arms. Alan took a few quick steps toward her, dropped his bag, and hugged her tight. They had a long kiss, oblivious to the other pilots filing by. The feel of her hair on his face, the smell of her perfume, the strength of her hug combined to give him the most joyful feeling he had had since their last reunion when he had come back from Pensacola eight months earlier.

Armiston, Scottie, and Jolly waited nearby. With tears on their cheeks, Alan and Jennifer separated and pulled themselves together. Alan introduced her to the three pilots, none of whom had had a chance to meet her.

"Enjoy yourselves, and, Alan, you be back here tomorrow by sixteen hundred," said Armiston with a big smile.

"Thank you, sir." It was the first time the skipper had called him by his first name.

Alan picked up his bag, took Jennifer's hand, and started back toward Kalakaua Avenue. "Are we walking or driving?" he asked.

"Walking. Parking is scarce here."

"How far is it?"

"About ten blocks. When I told Joe you were coming in today, he said to leave the office whenever I wanted to meet you. So I guessed when you'd get here, and I wasn't too far off," she said, smiling and looking at him. "I am having trouble believing this is really happening. It's so good to see you and touch you."

"I've been looking forward to this since August. Now that it's happening, it seems unbelievable, as you said. It may be a long time between visits, but it's so much better than not seeing you for years."

"That's right. Even Admiral Nimitz won't see his wife for a long time," she said, smiling.

She paused and gazed at him. "Oh, Alan, I've missed you so much—especially the night after the attack when I wanted to be wrapped in your arms and protected."

"How I wish I could've done just that," he said, stopping and turning toward her. He saw she was blinking back tears. Suddenly he felt overcome by love and empathy for her, and his own eyes filled with tears. He dropped his bag and embraced her. She squeezed him to her. They kissed long and hard, with tears running down their cheeks again. They separated, smiling at each other and pulling out handkerchiefs. Then they started walking again.

Alan resumed, "Right after I heard about the attack on the radio, I was beside myself worrying about you. I thought agreeing to let you come out here was the stupidest thing I'd ever done. And there was absolutely nothing I could do about it but wait to hear from you. Your telegram was a lifesaver. Did you have to pull strings to send one that soon?"

"Joe understands morale. I told him how much it meant to me, and he understood right away. Others with spouses on the mainland spoke to him also. He pulled the strings."

"He sounds like a great guy to work for."

"He is. I'm very lucky and grateful that you agreed to let me come here so I could."

Alan smiled. "I calmed down after I got your telegram. I realized it was wrong for me to try to prevent you from taking risks to do your job, just as you have accepted the risks in my job."

"Thank you, Alan. I'm lucky to have such an understanding husband," she said, smiling at him. Then she changed the subject. "Did you see the harbor on the flight in?"

"We were too far away to get a close view. We had a better view riding past the harbor on the bus. We could see the damaged buildings and sunken battleships, and smell the fuel oil. In our briefing for the flight, they gave us a summary of the casualties and damage, so it was only a mild shock to actually see it. Before that, we had only the civilian news to go by, which has had very little detail. What was it like for you?"

"I figured out what was going on pretty fast, because you and I had talked about the possibility. Many of the civilians thought it was just a noisy exercise until hours later. I felt really frustrated and tried to think of something useful to do. I got out that Leica camera that Dad gave me and took pictures from the roof of our building."

Alan stopped short and turned toward her with a stern expression. "Jennifer, you're crazy! Promise me you will never do that again. That was a huge unnecessary risk!"

She smiled meekly and said, "I promise. Joe made me promise the same thing. I guess it was a little crazy of me. But I could see they weren't attacking the city." She paused and said in a pleading voice, "The navy liked the pictures."

"OK. Would they have still liked them if they cost the loss of a valued member of the Combat Intelligence Unit, educated and prepared at great expense over many years?"

Her face had become very serious. "Aye aye, sir. It won't happen again, sir." Her stern demeanor instantly melted his. She continued, "But what about you? You're a combat pilot, taking huge risks."

He became serious again. "Yes, but I'm expendable. There are plenty of competent dive bomber pilots in the training pipeline."

She stopped short with a fierce expression and a blaze of anger in her eyes and said in a loud commanding voice, "Alan! Promise me you will never talk or think like that again!" She continued at a slightly lower volume, "The expense of your training was probably much greater than the expense of mine. Besides, there's a shortage of officers who have your insight into tactics and strategy. I know from being at the War College."

He was taken aback. He had never seen her truly angry before, and she was formidable. He hung his head and smiled humbly. "How can I argue with a big compliment from a superior officer?"

Her expression softened. "Oh, Alan, you rascal. Do you promise?"

He smiled and said, "OK, I promise, you scalawag."

They started walking again and were silent for a few minutes. Then he asked, "What happened in the city?"

"There were a few fatalities and one serious fire. Most of the damage was in the northern and western parts of the city, not around here in the Waikiki area. There was one crater in the street about three blocks north of the Royal Hawaiian," she said, pointing over her left shoulder. "It's not clear how much was due to random strafing, how much to stray bombs, and how much to our own antiaircraft shells falling back after the fuses were set wrong in the rush to return fire."

"The fog of war. Did you go to your office after the attack?"

"Yes. Right after the attack ended, the army came on the radio and said civilians were to stay off the streets. I decided I was an exception and I should try to get to the office. I thought about just using my car, but a navy officer in our building offered me a ride. I was glad to go with him because I thought the police and the army were much more likely to let us through than a civilian woman alone, even with my credentials. There was heavy traffic, but we got there. There were cars going the other way with obviously wounded people. It was pretty horrible.

"By afternoon most everyone had come in. We got busy fast and have worked long hours ever since. Joe didn't go home for three weeks."

"Three weeks—that's a long time!"

"I don't know how he did it. It's a good thing I was busy because I missed a lot of the aftermath. The little I did see was even worse than the attack for me. While the stench of fuel oil and rotting flesh went all around the harbor, burned and dismembered bodies covered with fuel oil were stacked on boats or towed by boats and then dumped into pine boxes to be buried," she said, looking sad but resolute.

Alan drew her to him and said, "Oh, Jennifer, when they briefed us on the attack, so I had more of a picture, I realized you must have seen some terrible things. I know it will be hard for me when I start to see things like that." He felt her sobbing and continued holding her.

She stopped shaking and got out her handkerchief again and wiped her tears. "Thank you," she said softly.

Alan decided to change the subject. "I heard the army took over pretty soon after the attack."

"That's right. A few hours after the attack, the army took over the government, and martial law was declared in the late afternoon, with a curfew and blackout. The next day the army was everywhere. They'd taken over most of the large organizations and businesses.

"There is an interesting side effect to all this. The politics and economy of the islands is never going to be the same, even after the war is over, I suspect. Up until the attack, all but the smallest parts of the civilian business and government of the territory were ruled by what's called the Big Five. This is a close knit consortium of the five biggest companies, which are owned mainly by descendants of the original missionaries. They controlled almost everything, government and business, like feudal lords. Overnight the army reduced them to running only the pineapple and sugar plantations. Still big business but nothing like previously. When the war is over, I suspect it'll be very hard to bring back the old system. Ordinary people will become used to more responsible politics and a more normal economy, even if it's now run by the military."

"Very interesting. You mentioned the feudal aspects of the economy in your letters last fall. Sounds like you have learned a lot about local affairs pretty fast."

"The people in our unit who've been here a long time gave me the inside story. All of these changes were sudden but not totally unanticipated. Then the army sprang their own surprise. They prohibited all sales of liquor. It was just like Prohibition, and with similar unintended consequences. Anyone with a stash could make a handsome profit. The army took over the distribution of malt, so making beer was cut off. However, they couldn't control the juice of the locally grown pineapples, which can be made into a liquor. It doesn't taste very good but is satisfying to some. The submariners seem to have a plentiful supply of refined torpedo alcohol."

"Some surprise! Is that still in effect?"

"No. The army announced it would end day before yesterday. I think it's because they heard you were coming, you rascal," she said, chuckling.

"Oh c'mon, you scalawag," he said, grinning back at her.

"It's true," she insisted, giggling. "But it's taking a while to set up the new controls. Now you have to have a liquor permit, and each person is limited to a quart a week. Inside the Royal Hawaiian, the submariners probably have their alcohol available at a price."

Now they turned into her street. She led the way to her building, a four story wooden structure. They climbed up to the fourth floor, and she unlocked the door and led him inside. She closed the door, and they embraced and kissed for several minutes. Alan noticed he was breathing hard from the climb up the stairs, and she was not. Then she showed him the apartment. It was small, two rooms with a kitchenette, but sunlit and cheery. He particularly appreciated the little decorative touches she had made: fresh flowers and decorations and pictures on the walls. They went out onto a small balcony on the southwest side with a view of Waikiki Beach.

"This is delightful, Jennifer, small but very pretty and cheerful," he said.

"I'm glad you like it. I think I was lucky to get it, because even then apartments were getting scarce. Now it would be hard to find anything larger than a telephone booth for rent. And I'm getting used to climbing four flights. I think the exercise might be good for me, especially since I spend long hours at a desk.

"Most of the food here comes from the mainland, because the Big Five don't want to grow anything but pineapples and sugar. Since the attack, of course, there has been a shortage of shipping space, and hence shortages of certain foods, particularly butter, meat, and oranges. I've hoarded some things in a friend's freezer downstairs, so we can have a nice dinner."

"Oh, Jennifer, that's very thoughtful of you, but I hope you're not skimping on yourself for me. Our food on the carrier has been pretty good."

"Don't worry. If you're only here once in a blue moon, it's the least I can do," she said, smiling. They embraced and kissed again.

"I imagine you haven't gotten my Christmas present, which I mailed from Norfolk before the attack."

"No, and you probably haven't gotten mine, which I also mailed before the attack."

"No. I guess we'll both have to be patient." Alan noticed a newspaper on the kitchen table and picked it up. On the front page was a picture of *Enterprise* receiving a hero's welcome as she came into Pearl Harbor the previous day. "Did *Yorktown* get a reception anything like this?" he asked.

"No. Halsey arrived first; he's a darling of the press, and he sank more ships," she said with a frown.

"Did he sink more ships? We've heard nothing."

"Yeah. They had a lot of targets. They sank a transport and a subchaser, and damaged a cruiser and other ships. They got a lot of planes too, both in the air and on the ground. *Enterprise* was attacked twice."

"A lot more productive than our struggle with weather and few targets."

"Through no fault of your group. Also Fletcher is not a showman like Halsey. I hear he won't even talk to the press, so he is no friend of theirs. But Halsey is their dream come true. On the other hand, it's probably a good thing that, right after the attack, we thought at first that the Japanese had come from the south, because I think Halsey might've rushed to take on their whole carrier force and would have lost his ship."

"I've heard he's impulsive."

"He is." She changed the subject. "Now, before dinner, how about a walk on the beach?"

"That would be very nice, like old times in Newport. Besides, it would be good to stretch my legs some more. I've been sitting down most of the day."

They walked in silence, hand in hand, to the southeast end of Waikiki Beach. The beach was big and beautiful, as Alan had remembered it, but the effect was largely spoiled by barbed wire running the whole length. They started walking toward the other end. With the wind and sound of the surf, it was easy to get out of earshot of the few others on the beach.

Jennifer asked, "Can you tell me what the raid on the Marshalls was like?"

"Since you're in intelligence, I guess I can." He described it in some detail.

"It sounds very dangerous flying in weather like that, especially starting off at night. And nobody knows what happened to your exec. That makes it very hard."

"That's right. I really miss him. He was a very thoughtful exec, always friendly and helpful to me, as well as a fine pilot. Most likely the weather downed him, not the enemy."

"Sounds grim and unrewarding, but perhaps some lessons were learned."

"Yeah. The reason the skipper and I missed badly is that our windshields and bombsights fogged up completely as we dove into the humid warmer air below. It happened to all the pilots that went high for their dives. We badly need heat on them. There is a defroster for the outer windshield, but that isn't the main problem. It's the thick bulletproof inner windshield and the telescopic bombsight. Dive bombing will be pretty unreliable in the tropics, I expect, until we get that fixed. I'm going to start working on it as soon as I get back to the squadron, but it may take a while."

"That sounds very serious, so don't talk about that to anyone else," she said, looking at him with a serious expression. "Speaking of not talking, I imagine you want to know more about our office, and I want to tell you, but you must not pass on anything."

His manner became serious also, and he said, "I agree completely. Please tell me what you feel you can. Oh, and please say hello to Joe Rochefort, Tom Dyer, and Ham Wright for me."

During Alan's surface tour five years earlier, he had become acquainted with four officers who had experience in intelligence and code breaking, when he was serving on the battleship *Pennsylvania*. Jennifer's boss, Joe Rochefort, was one of those officers. Two of the others, Tom Dyer and Ham Wright, were now working for Rochefort in the Combat Intelligence Unit. The fourth was the Pacific Fleet intelligence officer, Commander Edwin Layton.

"I will. They knew I would be seeing you, and they sent their greetings. OK, where do I start?"

"I imagine the attack was a surprise to your unit, just like everyone else."

"Yes. Everybody made mistakes, including us. But Main Navy made the most. They were reading at least one important code that we could not, but they did not tell us anything they learned from it. Everybody knew war was coming soon but expected it to start somewhere in the western Pacific."

Alan added with a frown, "And the people at Main Navy have a better chance of covering their tracks. Is Turner still head of war plans?"

"Yes. I think he has kept ONI and the Office of Naval Communications distracted, so they may not have realized we were not getting a lot of what they knew."

Jennifer continued, "Here's an example of the lack of preparedness here for the attack. The Communications Act of Nineteen Thirty-Four makes it a federal crime for a communications company to deliver anything in the messages the company handles to anyone but the addressees. The district intelligence officer had been trying long before the attack to tap into the messages being sent out of here by the Japanese consulate but had been thwarted by that act, until last November. Then the president of RCA visited Honolulu. RCA was one of the companies handling the consulate's messages. Admiral Bloch was acquainted with the president and persuaded him to release the consulate's messages. The first package arrived in our office about a week before the attack. Their code was not difficult, but we hadn't got very far before the attack. After the attack it became clear that some of the messages indicated a very high level of interest in the exact location of the ships in Pearl Harbor and such details as torpedo nets and barrage balloons. Obviously those messages would've rung alarm bells if they'd been decoded before the attack."

"The embarrassing clarity of hindsight." Alan shifted to the attack itself. "Did your unit figure out how many carriers they had?"

"Layton found out the same day. A chart was recovered from a crashed Japanese airplane the day of the attack. It showed which carriers were used and where they launched. Layton got the chart late in the day and passed it on to Joe. There were six fleet carriers."

"Six! Our navy is hesitant to put even two fleet carriers together. Besides, nothing we have available could stop six fleet carriers. Even with plenty of warning, the most we could muster would've been four carriers, with *Saratoga* in overhaul at Bremerton and *Hornet* not ready. The Japanese really took Mahan's concentration strategy to heart, didn't they?"

She smiled and said, "They sure did. I wonder how many of the brass understand what you just said."

Alan smiled back at her compliment.

"The carriers were *Akagi*, *Kaga*, *Hiryu*, *Soryu*, *Shokaku*, and *Zuikaku*. This information has not gone outside of our intelligence and the top brass, so not a word to anyone."

"Sure thing. It sure was lucky our carriers were absent and that the Japanese didn't attack tankers or the oil storage facilities. In fact, it's puzzling that they didn't."

"I agree, and it was extremely lucky. One of our fast oilers, *Neosho*, was moored among the battleships, but her captain was aboard and got the ship underway shortly after the attack started, and she got across to the east side of the harbor away from the battleships and didn't have too much damage."

He changed the subject. "Where does your unit fit into the hierarchy? Are you under ONI?"

"No. It's odd. Officially we are under the operational control of OP-Twenty-G, which is the decrypt division of the Office of Naval Communications, run by Joe's friend Lieutenant Commander Laurance Safford. You've probably heard about him. Safford is the one that engineered Joe being put in charge here. But we are under the administrative control of the Fourteenth Naval District, so we answer to Admiral Bloch, and we used to be known as COM Fourteen. Joe would rather report directly to CINCPAC, and through his friend Layton, he was able to report indirectly to Kimmel, and now to Nimitz."

"What do you think of Nimitz?"

"So far, Nimitz has been a pleasant surprise. Within a week of taking over as CINCPAC, he came to our office, which we nicknamed 'the Dungeon,' for a visit. That in itself was a good sign. But at that time, Joe was totally wrapped up in a Japanese message that he was working on, which happens fairly often. I think Nimitz may have wondered why Joe couldn't focus on a high ranking visitor. Not a great start I would say."

"That's unfortunate."

"That aside, Nimitz has impressed everyone. He seems very calm and unflappable. He kept Kimmel's staff, including Layton. That was a relief because there was enough turmoil without big staff changes, and Joe's good relationship with Layton helps a lot. Nimitz does have one quirk. Except for nurses, he doesn't think women have any place in the navy. The few that were here have been transferred. It seems mainly to concern uniformed women, so hopefully it doesn't apply to me. Joe told me not to worry;

he'll insist on keeping all his valuable assets, including me. Even so he had me stay out of sight on the day of Nimitz's visit, so I heard about it secondhand."

Alan said, "It might have something to do with Nimitz's German ancestry. They tend to be very traditional."

"Could be. Fortunately, Joe has developed a good rapport with Admiral Bloch. After the attack, of course, important people were asking why the navy didn't see it coming. Both Safford and Joe came under a cloud in Washington. I'm guessing that, after the attack, Main Navy has woken up to the importance of radio intelligence. So, all of a sudden, OP-Twenty-G is a prestigious group, instead of a backwater, and so command of it has suddenly become a plum. Safford's job could be in danger.

"Before that, right after the attack, Safford made a key change. This is for your ears only. Until then we weren't allowed to work on the Japanese code that has turned out to be the most important for our work. Washington and one other station have been working on it for over a year, and they've made very little progress. As you know, when Safford got Joe to take over here, he let Joe have some of the navy's best code breakers, with the exception of Mrs. Driscoll, of course." Alan knew that Mrs. Driscoll was the very talented woman who had taught all the early navy code breakers their trade.

"After the Pearl Harbor intelligence debacle, Safford decided to let our unit work on that code as well. A month later we were able to read a tiny bit of it, which allowed us to predict the general nature of a recent Japanese operation.

"Then my friend Jasper Holmes, who's a former submariner, asked if he could pass some of our predictions on to the submarine service. Joe was inclined to say no for security reasons, but he went along, provided that nothing was revealed about the source and nothing was put in writing. Jasper says that our predictions have been good enough to be greatly appreciated by the submariners."

"Can you tell me more about your office and your work?"

"I think I gave you some idea of the atmosphere in my letters last fall. It's an extremely dedicated group, partly because Joe himself sets a superb example. Everyone works long hours. Most people work at least eighty hours a week. There is someone in the office working all around the clock, seven days a week. We've been doing that since September, before any other unit. Either Joe or Tom Dyer is almost always there working. Everyone works very hard, but the atmosphere is very informal. Uniforms are often not worn. Rank is irrelevant."

"Amazing and unusual."

"It sure is. It keeps changing because we've been constantly expanding, but our workload has expanded faster. When I joined there were ten officers and twenty-three enlisted men. Now I think we are about four times bigger. We started with a big space in the basement, fifty by one hundred feet, but we had to get more space finished off adjacent to us to handle the expansion.

"The supply of new officers has been fairly adequate, but after the attack we had a shortage of yeomen, and, of course, so did many other units. Admiral Bloch gave us high priority, but it's hard to make people believe you've got an urgent need when you can't say a word about what you're doing. Luckily our top enlisted man, like the 'chief of the boat' in a submarine, Tex Rorie, is a great resource and has brought in a lot of good men. When Bloch heard that the band from the battleship *California* was unemployed, Rorie looked them over and grabbed them. Then the FBI said that some of them had foreign last names and couldn't work in a secret unit like ours. Joe managed to overrule them, and we got the whole band," she said with a chuckle. "They have turned out to be very good men."

Alan laughed and said, "That's a great story. The messages that your group works on—where do they come from?"

"They come from our intercept station in the center of the island. The problem is that there is no direct communication with the station. Messages come on paper by jeep or truck, at least once a day, but on average hours pass between the time a message is intercepted and the time that it arrives in our office. This is an amazingly primitive arrangement. We also have a direction finding station at another location, which is part of a network covering the Pacific. As you know, it takes bearings from at least two stations some distance apart to find where a signal originated. However, our station has no direct communication with the other stations, so a DF fix takes a long time. Joe said it himself, 'It's like having a million dollar organization with a ten cent store communication system.'"

"Whew! Amazingly primitive is an understatement."

Now they were approaching the part of the beach near the Royal Hawaiian, where there was a group holding a party. They turned around and began walking back.

Alan continued asking questions. "With one hundred forty people, you must be divided into groups of some sort. Where do Tom Dyer and Ham Wright fit in?"

"The unit is divided into four groups. First there is Jasper's little group, which plots ship movements and keeps track of all the details we need to refer to, like the names of people, places, and ships. Lately the surface ship plotting has been taken over by other units, but he still keeps track of submarines, the Japanese subs being the main threat around here since the attack.

"The second group does traffic analysis, which consists of sifting as much as possible out of messages without knowing the code. Mainly that consists of the quantity, origins, addressees, and priorities of the messages. When we can't read the code, we have to rely on whatever this group can come up with to figure out what is going on. It can produce a remarkable amount of information, but it can be unreliable.

"The third group is the cryptanalysis group, which unravels the cipher that conceals the actual code words and strips it off before it goes to the Japanese language group. Tom Dyer and Ham Wright are the top men in this group. This is the most difficult job of all. Part of the work is done by putting information on punched cards and sorting and processing them with business machines made by IBM, in a manner similar to the way accounting departments in large firms operate. These machines make a lot of noise and are kept in a separate soundproofed room we call 'the Boiler Room.'

"The fourth group is the Japanese language group, which is where I work. We break the code itself, which requires knowledge of Japanese to make sense of what the code words mean. It also helps to have a vague idea what the message is about ahead of time, which may be just a guess or intuition. If we have enough of the code words, we try to translate the message into Japanese and then into English. We also use the punched card machines sometimes."

Alan shook his head in astonishment and said, "Absolutely amazing. Oh, Jennifer, I knew radio intelligence and code breaking must be intricate work, but now I have some idea of how complicated it is. Thank you for telling me. Your job sounds like the key to the whole thing, although you couldn't do it if the cipher wasn't stripped off first. It sounds like it involves a lot of intuition."

"It does. One of our top language officers is the most intuitive person I have ever met. He has hunches that he can't explain, but they often turn out to be correct. He came to us from the battleship *Tennessee* after she was damaged on December seventh."

"You must be very proud of your work."

"Well, I have to say that I am, although I try not to think about that aspect. Joe has a sign posted near his desk that says, 'We can accomplish *anything*, provided no one cares who gets the credit.' That says a lot about the cooperative spirit of the whole unit."

"It sure does."

"For the officers in the unit that know Japanese, there's an interesting new twist. Before Admiral Halsey left here for the Marshalls, he asked Nimitz for a Japanese speaking officer to listen to the Japanese on the radio. Nimitz was so pleased with what he heard from Halsey about the translations that he ordered Joe to assign a linguist officer to each of the three carrier admirals. Therefore, Joe picked three of the linguists, which leaves us short. They'll listen in on Japanese frequencies and tell the admiral's staff what they are saying right on the spot. Admiral Fletcher will be getting Lieutenant Forrest 'Tex' Biard. Joe told me I'm not eligible because I'm a woman and a civilian, but it does sound like fun."

"I'm very glad you won't be going on a combat ship, Jennifer, where you could get hurt or see more grizzly sights, but I can see your taste for excitement isn't satisfied."

Gravity quickly overtook her lighthearted manner. "Speaking of knowing Japanese, about a week after the Japanese attack, Joe put out a memo to everyone in the unit. He told us to hide the fact that we knew any Japanese when talking to outsiders, particularly people of Japanese descent. He cautioned us that even if we felt we knew them well, they might have a carefully concealed sympathy for the homeland and be open to reporting interesting information. In an extreme case, they might even be motivated to further their cause by killing us, a very scary thought. Naturally I immediately complied. I had one acquaintance in the market who asked me why I never spoke to him in Japanese anymore. I told him I was so busy in my work that I had become rusty and did not have time to practice. He had noticed that I did not come into the market as often, and he seemed to accept my explanation. I suspect there are some people of Japanese descent here who are loyal to Japan, and I also think there are many who are completely loyal to the United States."

"I agree that seems likely. Do you ever practice by speaking Japanese with other people in your unit?"

"Yes, but we're all too busy to do it often."

Now Jennifer and Alan were back at the end of the beach where they started. They walked back to her apartment for a delicious roast ham dinner with pineapples. She also produced a bottle of wine, a gift from Jasper and Izzy Holmes. Afterward they sat on the balcony for a while and then continued enjoying each other's company in bed.

Saturday, February 7, 1942

After a pleasant breakfast on Jennifer's balcony, Alan fished a small envelope out of his bag and handed it to Jennifer.

"I would like to give this to you for safe keeping," he said. "*Yorktown* could be damaged or sunk, and I would hate to lose this."

Jennifer opened the envelope and pulled out her telegram to Alan, the one she sent three days after the attack, and stared at it. She looked up at Alan and smiled in spite of tears in her eyes. "I am so glad you kept it. I will treasure it as you have. Years from now it will be something to remind us of these perilous times and show to our children."

"Just what I was thinking," Alan replied, finding his eyes were moist too. He and Jennifer wanted children, but they had agreed to try very hard to postpone that event until Jennifer could resign from the navy.

As they cleaned up after breakfast, they both felt they had more to talk about. They decided to walk again on the beach, where privacy was assured. When they came out of her building, Jennifer led Alan around to the back and showed him the 1937 Chevrolet she had purchased the previous October.

Sport Sedan

Throughout its twenty-five years' history, Chevrolet has been known for its durability. Sturdiness is built into every model. Skillful design, high quality materials, and precision manufacturing methods are guarantees of long life and service.

The Sport Sedan has a convenient package ledge at the back of the rear seat, and a spacious built-in trunk with a separate tire compartment.

SAFETY PLATE GLASS ALL AROUND AT NO EXTRA COST

1937 Chevrolet Sports Sedan
(from 1937 Chevrolet brochure)

Alan looked it over and said, "Looks like you found a very nice car. I can see why a four door sedan would be nice here, where parked cars get so hot in the sun. Keep me posted on how it works out."

When they were safely alone on the beach, Alan asked, "How has your social life been?"

"OK, considering I don't have much time for it. At the beginning, Joe suggested I not socialize with the men in the unit. I decided that was good advice, unless their wives were around. I keep two pictures of you on my desk, the one you sent me from Pensacola and the one your sister took before our wedding. I think it reminds the men to keep their distance. So I have gotten to know the Dyers and the Holmeses. Edith Dyer and Izzy Holmes could stay because they had been here long enough to be considered residents.

"The Dyers are very nice, but Tom is not as relaxed and approachable as Jasper." She turned to Alan and smiled. "My knowing submariners and having a husband who is also a former submariner gave us a natural connection. He was forced to retire from the submarine service in 1936, the same year you went to submarine school. He was in command of S-Thirty then but had to retire because he had spinal arthritis. He had a master's degree in engineering from Columbia, and he got a job teaching at the University of Hawaii. During the summers he wrote short stories for *The Saturday Evening Post*, some of which have a naval setting. Admiral Bloch knew of Jasper, and when things became more ominous last summer, he asked Jasper to come back out of retirement. He got the doctors to pass him for light duty. Bloch wanted someone who understood navigation and could write readable reports. Jasper knows Swede Momsen, who is on Bloch's staff, and they talk." Momsen had been Alan's CO and mentor during the salvage of the submarine *Squalus*.

"Jasper found that no one was keeping track of the locations of merchant ships, and he started doing that—then later added submarines. When Joe's unit moved into the basement, Bloch told Joe to give Jasper and his yeoman a space, because his work was also secret. Jasper called his operation the Combat Intelligence Unit. Joe came up with idea of giving the same name to his unit also, thereby hiding the radio intelligence operation behind Jasper's. At first Jasper was told to stay away from us, and he came in through a separate entrance. Then when Joe set up a 24 hour watch system, he wanted Jasper to take watches, and so he had to start telling Jasper what we were doing. Gradually Jasper's operation has been absorbed into our unit, and recently it was moved into the center of our space near Joe's desk. Although he has no background in Japanese or code breaking, he has found plenty to do and is very helpful. Since rationing started after the attack, Jasper has been giving me a ride to and from the base when our schedules overlap because he lives on Black Point, east of Honolulu, so he comes right near my place. Jasper and Izzy have done a lot for me.

"Of course I need more friends than two older couples. They have introduced me to some of their younger friends, and gradually I am developing a social network in the little spare time I have. It has been important to get outside the navy."

"I can see how it has been hard for you."

"Yes, but it would have been a lot worse if I was not working so hard. For the time being, I don't need very much social life," Jennifer said with faint smile.

"I guess that's more or less true for me too, and I have friends in the squadron," Alan replied. He paused and changed the subject. "Can you tell me a little about what's going on in the rest of the world? We haven't heard much since we left San Diego."

"Well, our worst fears are being realized in the Philippines. In the end it seems like it will be a greater disaster than the attack here, in terms of losses of both our personnel and materiel, never mind the Filipino losses."

"And they had nine hours' warning. What happened to the B-Seventeens?"

"A lot of them were sitting on the ground when the first raid came in, even though the Japanese had been delayed by bad weather on Formosa. The weather was fine on Luzon, and the B-Seventeens could have been waiting over Formosa for the weather to clear up before the Japanese could take off. Nobody knows why the army squandered the warning. Somebody high up must have really screwed up. Some of the B-Seventeens escaped to Mindanao."

"Much as I guessed. That is a disaster."

"It is. We can blame the army for that one, but now we're working on one of our own. About three weeks ago the *New York Times* had a story about police and civilians on Long Island one night watching a huge fireball and lifeboats from a tanker, which must have been caused by a German submarine torpedo. When the press asked the navy what was going on, they refused to discuss it! Can you believe it? You can imagine what is really happening. Probably there are a lot more sinkings offshore out of sight. No escorts available and therefore no convoys, is what we're hearing."

"We heard a little about that on the carrier. It will be a disaster if it continues. And the navy had over a month to get ready. I wonder what Admiral King has been thinking."

"I do too. And the defense of the East Indies is going badly also. With the Philippines gone, I guess that is not much of a surprise."

"It makes our little raid in the Marshalls seem like a pinprick."

"I'm afraid so. I did not realize until recently how right you were last year about the United States being unprepared for a two ocean war. There could be more disasters before we begin to catch up."

"Can I ask you for any hints about what comes next for *Yorktown*?"

"Well, I think I can tell you all I know, because it isn't very much. She will almost certainly be sent out again soon, probably on another raid. A variety of possibilities are under discussion. No decision has been made as far as I know. I have heard King keeps pushing Nimitz, but Nimitz moves cautiously, because he is well aware of all the practical limitations that King tends to forget."

"That sounds very plausible, from what I have heard."

Their conversation turned back to their own lives. Jennifer asked for a detailed description of life on board the carrier. Jennifer described in some detail what she had done with her spare time, particularly before the attack.

Alan asked about mutual acquaintances in the Submarine Service. Jennifer told him that *Skipjack* had successfully withdrawn from the Philippines to Darwin in Australia. *Sailfish* was still fighting in the East Indies but was expected to withdraw to Darwin. Alan had friends from his submariner days on both of these vessels. *Sailfish* was the new name of the refurbished *Squalus*, the submarine that sank to the bottom out of control when Alan was serving on her. Jennifer also mentioned that the submarine *Tambor* had gone out from Pearl Harbor on a war patrol in December but had been damaged and had to go back to San Francisco for major repairs. Her former fiancé was on *Tambor*, based at Pearl Harbor.

Alan and Jennifer had lunch at a small restaurant on the edge of the beach. In the afternoon they went back to her apartment and made love again before getting ready for Alan's return to the squadron. They walked back to the Royal Hawaiian Hotel, and they had one more long embrace before Jennifer left. They hoped that there would be another chance to see each other before *Yorktown* departed on her next mission.

As Alan walked into the hotel, he was almost in a euphoric trance from his time with Jennifer. Suddenly he became aware of two familiar faces from another time and place. It was Ed Miller and Les "Craggy" Travis, friends from his days as a fledgling naval aviator at Pensacola. Ed was built like a fire hydrant, short and rugged, and he was very outgoing. When Ed left Pensacola, he had orders to join Fighting Six aboard *Enterprise*. Les was tall and thin like Alan, but he had a chiseled face that looked very Scots-Irish to Alan. He was from western North Carolina, and he had felt he had little in common with Alan until he found they had a mutual taste for hillbilly music. After Pensacola, Les had gone to Scouting Three aboard *Saratoga*. Alan snapped out of his euphoria and smiled as his friends approached.

"Well, if it ain't ol' Stringy! How ya doin?" said Les.

"Very nicely, having just spent twenty-four hours with my wife," said Alan, as they all shook hands. Alan noticed they were still ensigns, evidently too junior to get promoted in January.

"We heard Bombing Five was in the hotel, and we asked around and found out you were on your own private vacation," said Ed, grinning.

"We remembered you were going right home after Pensacola to your wedding. Did she get transferred out here?"

"Yeah. She transferred out here in September. At the time I hated to see her go, but we guessed it might work out like this, with me here occasionally and able to see her."

"We saw you two outside just now before she left. She looks like a nice gal," said Ed.

"She is marvelous. I'm a very lucky man. Now, how are you guys?"

"We're fine. We heard that the bus to take you guys back to Ewa has been delayed. Let's go in the bar and get a drink. They have beer at the bar now," said Les.

"Sounds good," said Alan, and they went into the bar. They got a round of beers and sat down.

"Seen any action before *Sara* got torpedoed?" Alan asked Les.

"No. We went to Wake but got recalled just before we got there. Everyone on board was mad as hell. Wade Buckner, the lucky dog—he went with Fighting Three aboard *Lexington* when Fighting Two came ashore to exchange their Buffaloes for Wildcats. So he's gone off on *Lex* with Rudi Fischer in Torpedo Two. Maybe they'll see some action."

Wade and Rudi were also friends from Pensacola. Alan replied, "I've heard a little about the Wake relief turning back. It turns out that Fletcher's flag lieutenant is an old friend from my surface cruise."

Les continued, "The other *Saratoga* squadrons are stuck on the beach. When they asked if any pilots would be interested in transferring to *Hornet*, I immediately volunteered. I guess *Hornet*'s air group is pretty green, and they're looking to transfer in some more experienced pilots."

"That would probably mean going back to the Atlantic for now," Alan said, "but I would probably do the same if I were you. Now, Ed, I hear *Enterprise* had a busy time in the Marshalls."

"Yeah, we sure did. Continuous flight ops from oh four forty-five to nineteen hundred. Twelve of Fighting Six attacked Wotje and Taroa, and I was on the Taroa raid. Dropped two one hundred pounders and strafed. It was a thrill. There were a few Jap fighters with fixed gear, kind of slow but very maneuverable. I didn't score because my guns jammed. Same thing happened on CAP later in the day. Damned frustrating. It looks like the peacetime testing didn't include enough vigorous maneuvers to cover true combat, so the problem wasn't detected. They say BuAer had already heard about it from Fighting Seventy-Two in the Atlantic, and they have a fix in the works. No fighters were lost, but we lost five Dauntlesses. We were attacked during our withdrawal, but there was no significant damage. What happened in the TF-Seventeen raids?"

Alan described the raids as he had for Jennifer. "Did Scouting or Bombing Six have trouble with windshields and sights fogging up in the dive?" he asked Ed.

"Not that I heard about. The weather wasn't crummy like yours, so the humidity must have been less. Also many of the Dauntlesses did not make dives from up high."

A loud voice announced that the buses had come for the air group pilots.

"Have to go. It was great to catch up with you guys, and I hope to see you again soon," said Alan, finishing his beer.

They said good-bye, and Alan boarded the bus to go back to Ewa. Scottie was at the door checking the pilots off his list as they boarded.

Tuesday, February 10, 1942

Dive bombing practice was held. It was good weather, and the sights did not fog up. Alan got a near miss on the first round and a hit 15 feet from the center on the second. He was happy and somewhat relieved but still aspired to be one of the consistent top scorers in the squadron. In the fixed gunnery practice the next day, he continued to be among the top scorers.

Meanwhile, *Yorktown* went into the Pearl Harbor Navy Yard for five days of maintenance.

Thursday, February 12, 1942

The air group learned that Commander Richard "Dickie" Keithley had relieved *Yorktown*'s exec, Commander Clapp. The scuttlebutt was that Keithley was outgoing and positive, as well as having even more aviation experience than Clapp, so he sounded like a much better fit for the exec's job. At about that time, the air officer went on medical leave, and Captain Buckthorn selected Commander Arnham, the assistant air officer, to fleet up to air officer.

There were personnel changes in Bombing Five as well. The exec, Scottie MacAllester, was rotated home. Alan thought Scottie had been a good exec and was sorry that his tenure was so short. Alan felt his absence deeply because Scotty had been Alan's mentor and first friend in the squadron. Lieutenant Percival "Percy" Slack joined the squadron. He was from Bombing Three and had been beached like Les Travis after *Saratoga* was torpedoed. He had been promoted in October, so he was senior to the lieutenants in Bombing Five except West. West fleeted up to exec, and Armiston appointed Slack as engineering officer to relieve West. Slack seemed to be a suave and self-assured person who quickly got to know the officers of the squadron.

The air group held another round of training exercises. There was dive bombing practice for Scouting Five and Bombing Five. Again the sights did not fog up, and Alan got two hits, one about ten feet from the bull's eye and the other near the edge of the bull's eye. He was getting better, and he was very pleased. He was surprised that the senior Slack did poorly in the exercise. Alan guessed that practice for the beached squadrons had not been a high priority for the Pearl Harbor brass.

While not busy with bombing and gunnery practice, Alan worked hard on the fogging problem. He and several mechanics rigged up a crude test apparatus to generate air saturated with moisture and tried a makeshift heating arrangement for the gun sight, with some success. A small electric heater with a fan could be used to keep the bulletproof windshield warm and clear. That would be sort of like the windshield defroster in a car, but the thickness of the windshield meant that it would take a long time to warm it up if it got cold. Therefore, the windshield would have to be kept warm all the time at altitude. All this was written up and sent back to BuAer.

Working in the hangar at Ewa, he noticed that Slack seemed to spend most of his time at his desk, leaving the interaction with the mechanics mainly to his assistant, Goodwin.

Friday, February 13, 1942

Gunnery practice was held, and the unlucky day seemed lucky for the squadron. The other squadron pilots were improving their fixed gunnery, but Alan improved also and remained the top scorer in this exercise. Again Slack did poorly.

After the gunnery practice, the air group landed back at Ewa at midday. The pilots were called to their ready rooms at 1400, and it was announced that TF-17 and Halsey's TF-16 with *Enterprise* would be conducting independent raids in the central Pacific. TF-16 would hit Eniwetok in the western Marshalls, and TF-17 would hit Wake. The Bombing Five pilots relished the thought of getting some revenge at Wake. TF-16 had departed Pearl Harbor that day, and TF-17 would depart three days later.

The pilots heard that Singapore had surrendered, continuing the stream of bad news from Southeast Asia and the East Indies. The "Gibraltar of the Pacific" had proved to be nothing of the sort, falling quickly after an assault from the landward side. After the rapid collapse of the defense of Malaya, the Singapore garrison surrendered to a Japanese force that was much smaller than theirs, revealing remarkable weakness in the British colonial forces.

They were also told that the air group would have a second 24 hour liberty at the Royal Hawaiian, starting at 1400 on Valentine's Day. After they were dismissed, Armiston approached Alan again with another message from Jennifer. She asked him to call her and gave a telephone number he did not recognize. He found a telephone in the squadron office.

"Combat Intelligence Unit," said a deep male voice.

"Could I speak to Mrs. Ericsson, please?"

"Who's calling?"

"Her husband, Lieutenant Ericsson."

"Yes, sir. Just a moment."

A few moments later, she came on. "Hello? Alan?"

"Hello, Jennifer. How do you always know before we do when we will have liberty?"

"Oh, Alan, we're intelligence people—we know everything," she said with a giggle. "I had an idea. I could drive out to Ewa tomorrow and pick you up. How does that sound? The buses for the Royal Hawaiian probably will leave around twelve-thirty, and I could aim to get there around then."

"That sounds great, Jennifer. Can you get past the gate?"

"Yes, my credentials are pretty good."

As she was replying, an idea struck him. *She'll be right here at the base, in plenty of time.* "Let's see…twelve-thirty, OK. Could you wear pants?"

"Yes, I could. Right after the attack, Chief Rorie got me some navy dungarees, in case of a real calamity. But why, Alan? Oh, you rascal, you have something up your sleeve, and I think I know what it is. I hope I'm right."

"Bring a jacket too. Maybe you should wait and get here about thirteen hundred, so we don't have the whole squadron watching us."

"Good idea. Lots of men and too few women around these days. I do get tired of being stared at sometimes."

"I still might hit a snag, but I will start working on it, you scalawag."

"I can't wait. See you at thirteen hundred. I love you."

"I love you too, Jennifer; see you tomorrow."

As soon as he had hung up, Alan started looking for the skipper. The yeoman in the squadron office said he had been called to a meeting with the CYAG and the air officers.

Alan sat down in the ready room and thought about what Jennifer might like to do if he was able to take her for a flight. He remembered that she had told him that she had been up in an airplane only once, when she was twelve. Her father had taken her and her brother David to an air show at Jeffery Field, Boston's main airport, to celebrate the inauguration of scheduled passenger flights by Colonial Air Transport during the summer of 1927, soon after Lindbergh's flight. A pilot was offering rides in a big open cockpit biplane, which could take three passengers in the front cockpit. Alan thought it was probably a New Standard. The three Warrens took an exciting but uneventful ride for thirty minutes.

Saturday, February 14, 1942

It was a beautiful day with bright sunshine. Alan found Armiston in his office at 0815.

"Could I bother you for a moment on a personal matter, sir?"

"Sure, Ericsson, what is it?"

"Sir, my wife is coming out here this afternoon to pick me up, instead of meeting me at the Royal Hawaiian. I would like to get your permission to give her a ride in Five-B-Twelve."

Armiston's face took on a solemn expression and said firmly, "Out of the question, Ericsson; it's strictly against regulations."

Alan's face fell in disappointment. He never expected to be turned down flat.

After a short pause, Armiston's solemnity vanished, and he continued, "Your wife works in the Combat Intelligence Unit, doesn't she?"

"Yes, sir."

"I am prepared to say, if someone presses the matter, that I don't see anything wrong with one of my pilots giving a familiarization ride to a member of the Combat Intelligence Unit."

Alan noticed a faint smile forming on Armiston's face. He said, "I see, sir. Thank you, sir."

Alan went to the Bombing Five hangar to see Klein, who said he would be proud to make 5-B-12 ready for a flight with Mrs. Ericsson. Alan also borrowed a spare parachute, leather flying helmet, and goggles.

Jennifer arrived right on time at 1300, just after the last liberty bus departed. They hugged and kissed, oblivious to whether anyone was watching or not. As they separated he noticed she was wearing a plain blouse and a pair of old tennis shoes, in addition to her dungarees. She was carrying a navy canvas jacket. *Very appropriate*, he thought.

"Well, will we be able to go flying, you rascal?" she asked with an expectant look.

"Yes, you scalawag."

"Yippee! I'm so glad you had the idea," she said as she beamed at him.

"I got permission, sort of, and the plane is all ready. Right this way," he said, taking her hand and going into the hangar.

As they went past the squadron office, they got a surprise when Armiston popped out.

"Good afternoon, Mrs. Ericsson, Alan. Nice to see you here," he said with a smile. "Alan, don't do anything foolish, and you both enjoy yourselves."

"Thank you very much, Commander," said Jennifer in her best navy manner.

"Thank you, sir," said Alan with smile. They continued on out to where the airplane was parked.

Alan climbed on the left wing and gave her a hand to join him. "I will be in the front cockpit, and you will be in the rear. Would you like to sit in the front cockpit for a minute and see what it's like?"

"Definitely."

They moved next to the front cockpit. "What's this?" she asked, pointing to a sturdy structure shaped like a letter *A*, behind the pilot's headrest.

"That's the turnover pylon. It is quite strong and will support the airplane if it ends up upside down on the ground or on the deck so that there is enough clearance to get out of both cockpits and not be trapped."

"That sounds like a very good idea."

Alan had already placed the parachutes in both seats. "OK, push your left foot in here," he said, pointing to a little spring-loaded panel in the side of the fuselage, labeled "STEP." "Now swing your right foot up and over, and step on the seat."

She did and said, "I had visions of scrambling over the edge. That works very well."

"Now pull your left foot in, and stand on the seat. Then sit down."

She did and he leaned in and showed her the more important controls and instruments. He had her move the control stick and the rudder pedals and lean out of the cockpit to watch the ailerons, elevators, and rudder move in response.

"And this is the bombsight and the bulletproof windshield that fog up at awkward moments?" she asked, putting her right eye up to the bombsight.

"Exactly."

She leaned back and said, "Thank you for showing me all this, but I won't be able to remember it all. Do you have an extra pilot's manual you could let me have?"

"I'm sure I can find one," he said, beaming at her interest. "Now let me show you the rear cockpit."

She climbed out, put on her jacket, and climbed into the rear cockpit in a similar way. He explained that the large circular metal ring, surrounding her at chest height, was a track, from which the seat was suspended on rollers, so it could swivel in a complete circle; he showed her how to unlock it, and she swiveled around to face the rear. He showed her the machine gun and its mounting ring. She swiveled around and locked the seat facing forward again.

"I would think the control stick back here would get in the way most of the time, when the gunner isn't flying," she said.

"It's usually pulled out of its socket and stowed over here on the left, but I thought you might want to use it," he said offhandedly.

Her eyebrows shot up, and her eyes got big as she exclaimed, "Whoa, Alan, wait a minute. Me fly the plane? I don't know anything about flying, and I'm afraid I couldn't do it."

Alan smiled and said gently, "It's not very hard to control the plane when it's up in the air. I'm sure you can do it. The hard part is controlling it precisely near the ground, in order to take off and land, but I will do that. We'll go slowly, step by step, and if anything makes you nervous, just tell me, and we'll stop right away."

"OK. I think I can do that."

He could tell she was starting to warm to the idea. He showed her the throttle lever and next to it the tiny instrument panel with just an airspeed indicator, altimeter, and clock. He set the altimeter to the field elevation. Then he showed her the ball instrument and the compass directly in front and the canopy latch on the right. He helped her fasten the parachute harness and seat belt, explaining how to unfasten the belt, jump out, and pull the D ring to open the parachute, if worse came to worst. He described how to adjust the rudder pedals, and, being a tall woman, she had no trouble. He helped her put on her leather helmet. It nicely contained her hair, so it would not be blown into a tangle by the wind, but a few locks hung out below, which he thought was charming. He also had her put her goggles on her head over the helmet and plug in her earphones. He described the intercom between the cockpits and showed her the microphone with the push-to-talk button. He suggested she keep the microphone in her lap so she could reach it easily. Finally he showed her how to turn on the radio and he checked to see that it was tuned to the Ewa tower frequency.

He climbed into the front cockpit and got the engine started. Then he turned on the intercom. "Hi, Jennifer. How do you hear me?"

"Loud and clear, Alan. How do you hear me?"

"Loud and clear, Jennifer. Please turn on the radio. Now I'm going to talk to the tower and find out which runway we should use. You should be able to hear the conversation in your earphones." They were using runway 8 as usual, wind 075 at 10. He went back to the intercom. "Did you hear OK?"

"Yes, runway 8. The engine makes a wonderful rumble, sounds very powerful."

"A thousand horsepower. OK, we'll start taxiing toward the west end of the field."

They got to the west end, and Alan explained the engine run-up and before takeoff checks as he did them.

"All set, Jennifer?"

"Raring to go!"

He got clearance to take off and taxied out onto runway 8.

"Here we go!"

He opened the throttle, and the Dauntless, with its light load, accelerated rapidly, and then they were airborne. He retracted the landing gear and pulled the power back to climb.

"Wheeee! This is terrific, Alan."

He turned right out of the airport traffic pattern and continued in a wide turn to fly west along the coastline. "How about if we take a tour around the island, Jennifer?"

"Good idea."

"OK, it's pretty windy in the cockpit, so let's close our canopies."

"OK, canopy closed," she replied.

He rounded Barbers Point, followed the coast northwest, and continued climbing up to 6,000 feet, where he leveled off and pulled the power back to slow cruise.

He introduced her to the rudiments of flying in the same way he had introduced Kidd. She picked it up just as fast as he had.

After she seemed at home with simple maneuvers, he said, "OK, Jennifer, how is it going?"

"Very nice, Alan, it doesn't seem too hard."

"I think you're getting it already. Now we're coming up to Kaena Point. When we get there, please make another right turn to follow the coast."

"OK, I'll try it." She made the turn quite smoothly, and then they were following the coast east toward Haleiwa.

"Jennifer, you're learning very fast. How about if you keep following the coast, and I'll keep an eye on how you're doing and enjoy the view."

"OK."

He could tell she was focused on flying, not on chatting. She made the slight left turn at Haleiwa and continued northeast. Alan was truly enjoying the view, with the bright green of the vegetation, the blue of the water, and the white of the surf. Soon they approached the north end of Oahu at Kahuku Point. There were scattered clouds on the windward side of the island, and they covered Kahuku Point itself, but the tops were well below six thousand feet. Jennifer rounded the point in a big gentle curve and flew southeast toward Laie Point. Beyond that there were rugged valleys extending inland from the coast. Soon they came to Kaneohe Bay, with the Kaneohe Bay Naval Air Station to the left on the point on the far side. Alan could see planes in the traffic pattern around the very wide single runway. Jennifer flew down the bay and across the peninsula that had the air station on it farther out. She continued southeast toward Makapuu Point.

As they approached the point, he said, "When you finish your turn over the point, look to the left, and you should see Molokai, about twenty-six miles away."

She rolled out of the turn and leveled the wings. "I see it, Alan. What a view!"

She's flying with her right hand and holding the mike with her left—pretty at home already, he thought. She headed southwest toward Hanauma Bay, with Diamond Head in the distance.

"You're flying very nicely, Jennifer."

"Oh, Alan, I've never had so much fun, and I seem to be able to fly, at least a little bit."

"We're almost back to Diamond Head. What else would you like to do?" He was thinking she was doing so well that she might be interested in a little aerial acrobatics.

"Well, I think what I would like to do most is to have you make a dive, like you do when you are dive bombing."

Alan was surprised but pleased. "I had not thought of that, but I think we can do it. I think we better fly over to Molokai, where there's a bombing and gunnery practice area on Ilio Point on the northwest corner. We should go up high, to stay within gliding distance of land in case of engine trouble while we cross over to Molokai, and then we'll be high enough for a nice dive. It'll be quite cold while we're up there. I'm going to start climbing, so I will take over now for a short while to get the climb established." Alan moved the propeller control to increase the rpm and advanced the throttle to get climb power. Then he trimmed for 110 knots.

"OK, the altimeter is going up. Try to keep the airspeed near one hundred ten, by pulling the nose up slightly if it's too fast, and push down if it's too slow. It's all yours."

"OK."

"Now, when we get to Diamond Head, how about a one hundred eighty degree turn to the left? Let's follow the coast back to Makapuu Point."

"OK." She set the left bank and held it nicely. The rate of climb decreased slightly. She rolled to the right, back to wings level, when they were headed parallel to the coast.

"Very nice, Jennifer. I'll hold the stick while you zip up your jacket, because it will get colder higher up. Just wiggle the stick when you're ready to take over again."

He felt the stick wiggle, and he let go. The airplane climbed as the airspeed wandered slightly between 105 and 115. *Very good for a first time student*, he thought. They were nearing 10,000 feet as they approached Makapuu Point again.

"OK, Jennifer, make a right turn, and head toward Molokai while we keep climbing. Let me know if you get too cold or have any trouble breathing in this thin air."

She nailed the turn.

"OK, I'm going to throttle back for a moment and shift the supercharger into high blower." He did so, and they resumed the climb.

By the time they were halfway to Molokai, they were at 14,000 feet. The outside air temperature gauge on the lower instrument panel read twenty-nine. "I'm going to level off here. How are you doing?"

"It's cold, all right, but I'm OK for now."

After twelve minutes they were approaching the shore of Molokai. "OK, I will take over now and get ready for the dive." He turned left toward Ilio Point. "To get into the dive, I will roll the airplane upside down and then pull the nose down until we are going nearly straight down. We dive with both canopies open, and it will be very windy and loud, but it will last only about thirty seconds. Make sure your seat belt is as tight as you can pull it, your helmet is secure, and pull down your goggles over your eyes."

A minute went by.

"OK, belt tight, helmet secure, and goggles on."

"During the dive, use the seat ring to brace yourself, so you don't fall forward. OK, unlatch the canopy, and push it forward."

"Oh, OK," she said with a little waver.

As she slid the rear canopy forward, he slid the forward canopy back. He throttled back, shifted the supercharger to low blower, and adjusted the propeller to coarse pitch. Alan felt tense as he always did before a dive, and he imagined Jennifer did too. Then he opened the dive flaps above and below the trailing edge of the wing. The airplane slowed down rapidly.

"All ready for the dive?"

"Yes, sir." She sounded confident.

He rolled the airplane over to the left and pulled into a near vertical dive and then half rolled again to the right to make the dive toward the north. The wind noise built up to a full roar as the speed stabilized at 240 knots. Ilio Point was rushing up at them at four hundred feet per second. Alan had decided he would start the pullout at three thousand feet and make it as gentle as possible. At three thousand feet, he pulled back on the stick until he thought he was getting pulled down into the seat with about three times the force of gravity, or about three g's. Passing through two thousand feet, the horizon was just coming into view, and he pulled a little harder, getting a little fuzziness at the edge of his vision. At fifteen hundred feet, the pullout was looking good, and he eased the stick slightly. Now he was getting pulled down more than forward. He leveled off at eight hundred feet, and the extra downward pull eased off. Quickly, he closed the dive flaps, set climb power, and began a climb. "Jennifer, how are you doing?"

"Wheeeeeee! That was super exciting. I almost closed my eyes, but I didn't want to miss anything. I knew I would get pressed into my seat in the pullout, but it was quite a sensation. I can see why it would be hard to concentrate on aiming the bomb with everything else going on. Thank you very much for showing me. I will remember that for the rest of my life. I love you, Alan, you rascal."

"I love you too, Jennifer. Very few people, men or women, could do what you just did and feel good about it the first time. You're an amazing person, you scalawag."

"Thank you, Alan."

"I think maybe we should head back now. I think we might go around to the north of Honolulu and Pearl Harbor, to stay away from all the airports and air traffic. Do you want to fly some more?"

"I do, but I think I want to look at the view even more."

"OK, I'll start climbing to cross back to Oahu."

They climbed back up to reach 14,000 feet halfway across and then descended back to 6,000 feet as they flew over the southwestern side of the mountains behind Honolulu. They descended back down over the coast south of Ewa, entered the traffic pattern, and landed. They taxied back in and parked the Dauntless in the same spot.

Alan could feel Jennifer moving around as he went through the shutdown procedure. He thought he would go back and give her a kiss as soon as he climbed out. But as soon as the propeller came to a stop, he noticed she was climbing out first. Alan wondered if she was upset in some way. Before he could climb out to help her, she was standing on the wing beside the front cockpit. She had a huge grin, and she leaned into the cockpit, grabbed his neck, and gave him a big kiss. Then she said, "Oh, Alan, that was marvelous. Do you think we could do it again sometime?"

"I hope so, since you liked it so well. I'm very glad you enjoyed it. You're an intrepid girl, you scalawag."

"I had great confidence in my pilot, you rascal."

"Thank you, Jennifer." He unbuckled and climbed out.

They took the parachutes and helmets and laid them on the wing. He jumped down off the wing and turned to catch her in his arms as she jumped down, and they kissed again. He tied the airplane down and put on the canopy cover. Then they carried the parachutes and helmets into the hangar. Alan found a spare pilot's manual for the SBD-3 and gave it to Jennifer. Then he grabbed his overnight bag, and they walked out to Jennifer's car.

They opened all four doors, and the steady breeze quickly dispersed the hot air inside.

"Could I drive your car?"

"Sure."

"I haven't done any driving since December seventh, about two months. I might be a little rusty."

"I'm sure you'll manage."

As they started driving toward the gate, Jennifer said, "It's only fifteen thirty, so we could take a little side trip on the way back to the city."

"With gas rationing, do you have enough?"

"Being employed by the navy, I can get more than most civilians. And since I am carpooling with Jasper, I have some to spare, which I share with him."

"I like this car. The floor shift is nice and direct, not like the newer ones with the shift on the steering column."

"I agree, and so does Jasper."

With her directions, he drove around Pearl Harbor to the north side and picked up the Pali Highway that led over the mountains toward Kaneohe Bay. It was a narrow winding road that followed the top of a ridge between steep narrow valleys as it ascended to the spine of Oahu northeast of Honolulu. They came to the top of the pass, and Alan found a small place to pull off the road. They got out and were struck by the strong easterly trade wind blowing over the top. They looked down the other side, over the town of Kaneohe to the naval air station on the other side of the bay. They held hands and took in the beautiful view with scattered clouds all along the windward side of the island. Then they turned back and looked down over Honolulu, with the former Rodgers Airport to the right of the city.

Alan said, "This is a dramatic and beautiful spot, Jennifer. Thank you for showing it to me. I can see why it takes some time to drive over to Kaneohe, over that narrow twisty road."

"Yes, they need to improve the road, but it may not be too near the top of the list of construction projects."

He drove back down into Honolulu and back to Jennifer's apartment. Jennifer again produced a fine dinner with a bottle of wine. The next morning they took a hike in the hills north of Honolulu, in a place Jennifer had explored with friends. The tropical vegetation and scenery were a treat for Alan. They succumbed to their urges in a secluded grove under towering trees. They had an emotional farewell kiss in front of the Royal Hawaiian at 1545, and Alan boarded the bus for the ride back to Ewa. Neither of them had any idea how long it would be before they saw each other again.

That evening Alan wrote to Jennifer's parents and to his own, describing his good time visiting Jennifer but leaving out Jennifer's airplane ride.

CHAPTER EIGHT

Loitering and the Southwest Pacific

Monday, February 16, 1942

Yorktown departed Pearl Harbor in the late morning. She was again the nucleus of TF-17, accompanied by the heavy cruisers *Astoria* and *Louisville*, the fast oiler *Guadalupe*, and six destroyers. After lunch, the air group departed Ewa and landed aboard an hour later. The pilots were called into their ready rooms and told that Fletcher had gotten new orders from CINCPAC. TF-16 would raid Wake, and possibly Marcus, because submarine reconnaissance had been unable to detect any military activity at Eniwetok. TF-17 would go to the area southwest of Canton Island, in the Phoenix archipelago, and await further orders.

After the briefing, Alan went to consult the large globe in the wardroom. Looking at the central and south Pacific, he saw that Canton was less than halfway from Hawaii to Australia but more than halfway to the New Hebrides, where the scuttlebutt placed TF-11 with *Lexington*. It was a disappointment not to be going to Wake, but the possibility of joining with *Lexington* was exciting. Everyone knew that the Japanese advance in the area of the Bismarck Archipelago, northeast of the eastern end of New Guinea, was threatening communications between the United States and Australia.

Then Alan headed for the hangar deck to see if anything needed his attention. As he entered the hangar, he was struck by how much more space there was. The cargo aircraft they had brought from Norfolk were gone. A few spare aircraft were stored under the overhead, but the hangar itself had only active aircraft on the deck.

That evening just before supper, Alan ran across Hank Stinson in the wardroom, and they agreed to meet as usual at 2000 in the port gallery aft. Alan looked forward to hearing anything that Hank could tell him about what had been happening in high places during their stay at Pearl Harbor.

As Alan came up into the gallery, the breeze felt very pleasant. With the ship headed southwest, the trade wind was coming in over the port quarter. He made out Hank's long form, sitting on an ammunition box, as he made his way aft in the dim light. "Good evening, Hank," said Alan.

"Hello, Alan. So what have you been up to ashore? Did you get to see your wife?"

"Yes, I got to spend the night with her twice. Of course I had to forgo the pleasures of the Royal Hawaiian, but it was no sacrifice. It was very short but very pleasant, and it helped a lot to make up for not seeing her for six months." He had decided not to mention taking Jennifer for an airplane ride.

"That sounds very nice. What else did you do ashore?"

"We had dive bombing and gunnery practices. In between I worked on the problem of the fogging up of the bombsight, along with the windshield. We were able to determine that heat will solve the problem, but we did not have time to do more than try out a makeshift setup for the sight and the windshield. We reported everything to BuAer, so hopefully they will jump on it."

"Yeah, I hope so, but one occurrence might not be enough to get their attention. It will be interesting to see if it happens again."

"Given the direction we are headed in, I wouldn't be surprised. What can you tell me about events in high places while we were in port? We heard about *Yorktown*'s new exec and air officer, but that's about all. Arnham was the skipper of Bombing Five during the first few months that I was in the squadron, so I know him pretty well. Good officer."

"I haven't gotten to know them yet. There have been a lot of changes in the admiral's staff as well. The admiral finally got the full staff he's supposed to have, which Nimitz and Fletcher were not able to put together in San Diego. That includes a temporary flag secretary, which is a big relief to me. We also got an intelligence officer and a gunnery officer. They all seem like good people. The gunnery officer is also a qualified air observer, so we have a little more aviation background. Your air group has been very helpful in educating the admiral, and the whole staff has come a long way in understanding aviation. And now we have a cruiser admiral in *Astoria*, William 'Poco' Smith, until recently the CINCPAC chief of staff. Fletcher seems to have a lot of respect for him."

"The scuttlebutt says that Smith is a good officer."

"I think you told me your wife works in the Combat Intelligence Unit at Pearl Harbor. We also have a new flag assistant intelligence officer who came directly from there, somewhat reluctantly I gather. He speaks Japanese, and he monitors their radio. He seems a little prickly. Also we were told never to mention the Combat Intelligence Unit to anyone."

"That makes sense, because it's very hush-hush. My wife told me Halsey had someone from her unit on temporary duty for the Marshalls raid. Nimitz was so impressed by Halsey's report on that officer's activities that he requested the same for each of the carrier admirals' staffs."

Hank continued, "We also have a newspaper reporter on board. He works for the Honolulu *Star-Bulletin*, but he is headed to Australia to join the Associated Press there. That indicates we are headed in that direction.

"King keeps pushing for more action, but he tends to forget how few oilers we have. So he seems to think Nimitz is too timid. He also wants to send more carriers to the Anzac area. It takes three oilers to support a task force with one carrier there, because it's so far away. Some say that he wants to do that to get more carriers out of Nimitz's direct control. *Lex*, as well as *Enterprise*, may be headed toward action soon, but sorry, I shouldn't say any more about that."

"Very interesting, especially about the oilers. You know I've been interested in logistics for a long time. What happens next?"

"I don't think they'll let us idle around Canton very long before we get further orders."

Saturday, February 21, 1942

Yorktown had crossed the equator, again with no ceremony, and approached Canton Island. That morning, Alan's friend Teeth Jensen's Dauntless lost power when on final approach to land on the carrier. He went into the water astern. Both he and his gunner were uninjured, and the destroyer *Walke* rescued them. Less fortunate were the pilot and gunner of a Scouting Five Dauntless that crashed on takeoff three days later. The pilot broke his arm, and the gunner received minor injuries. *Walke* also rescued them.

Teeth told Alan that his plane had had a routine inspection, scheduled after one hundred hours of operation, just before the last flight, when the engine lost power. He talked to Slack about it and asked about the carburetor adjustments and magneto inspection. Teeth said that Slack's replies had been vague and evasive. Teeth wondered what was going on. Alan had become aware of a change in the atmosphere on the hangar deck since Slack had taken over engineering. The mechanics seemed uneasy, but he was not sure what was going on either.

The ship's newspaper reported that on February 19, Japanese carrier aircraft had raided Darwin, the principal city and port in northern Australia. Until then it was also the main refuge for ships fleeing the Japanese onslaught in the East Indies. Damage to the ships in the harbor, several of them American, was heavy, with many ships being sunk. *Another demonstration that carrier aviation can show up suddenly and wreak havoc in enemy ports thought to be safe from attack*, thought Alan. He hoped his friends on the submarines *Skipjack* and *Sailfish*, which had withdrawn there from the East Indies, were not hurt.

Thursday, February 26, 1942

They had been idling around Canton now for five days. The weather was hot and humid, with occasional thunderstorms.

It was 1930 on a sultry evening, and Alan was taking a walk in the gallery to cool off. His mind turned again to the atmosphere on the hangar deck. He had come to some understanding of what had changed by talking to several people, mainly Klein and Goodwin. Alan was impressed with Phil Goodwin's knowledge and his handling of his responsibilities.

Most of the carrier pilots had some affinity for machinery before they took up flying. Then through their training and flying experience, they had picked up a fair understanding of airplane mechanics, whether or not they had served in an engineering department. These pilots were capable of learning quickly on the job if they were appointed to engineering, so they could fill that role fairly soon after being appointed. Goodwin was a good example; he shared his generation's love of automobiles, and that provided the necessary background.

Armiston must have assumed that Slack was one of those pilots when he appointed him as engineering officer. Slack had turned out to be remarkably ignorant of physics and all types of mechanics, however, which came as a big surprise to Alan. Slack was also not willing to listen to suggestions from anyone he outranked, including Alan. Slack seemed to feel that the details of airplane mechanics and maintenance were beneath an officer like himself, so he need not concern himself with them. Slack stayed at his desk and did paperwork, rarely going out on the hangar floor, where he might get his hands dirty. He left the details to Goodwin, who worked hard but was struggling to keep up.

Because Slack had little understanding of what the mechanics did, he was not able to distinguish good work from bad. Instead he rewarded speed, which he could easily evaluate. With pressure for faster work, the mechanics were not able to do a careful, thorough job, the sort of work they naturally took pride in. Also they were well aware that Slack did not understand what they were doing. Resentment had begun to build among the mechanics, but nothing really disruptive had happened yet. Goodwin did appreciate what the mechanics were doing, so he was in a difficult position.

Slack was enthusiastic about flying, but Alan thought his lack of understanding of the physics of what was going on probably made it difficult for him to do well. He tried to make up for this by memorizing procedures, but that was of little help.

Alan was aware that he and Slack were opposites, and disdain came easily. Alan tried to tell himself that he shouldn't dislike Slack just because he was a poor fit for engineering officer. He would probably be OK in some other position that did not require knowledge of airplanes or mechanics.

Friday, February 27, 1942
There was more bombing and gunnery practice, and Alan was beginning to feel good about his bombing. Slack's scores had improved also, but he was still near the bottom in the squadron.

As Alan climbed into the cockpit for his last practice flight, Klein leaned into the cockpit and said, "I hope everything's OK, sir. We didn't have time to check her over the way we like to. New management. In the future you might want to do your own preflight."

Alan looked sharply at Klein, who had a disgusted look on his face. Alan knew Klein was a steady hand and not a complainer. *The situation must be becoming difficult to tolerate.* "Thanks for telling me, Klein. I was getting the same impression." Alan resolved to see if he could do a thorough preflight inspection himself in the future.

Saturday, February 28, 1942
In the morning, TF-17 started refueling from *Guadalupe*. The air group was told that Fletcher had received orders from CINCPAC to rendezvous with TF-11, built around *Lexington* and under Admiral Wilson Brown, on March 6, northwest of the New Hebrides Islands, about 1,000 miles short of Australia. When the refueling was completed the following day, there would be no more loitering, and the task force was definitely headed toward a hot spot. Alan thought of his Pensacola friends, Wade Buckner and Rudi Fischer, who were aboard *Lexington*.

Sunday, March 1, 1942

Alan went to supper at 1700, a little earlier than usual. There weren't very many officers at the table for lieutenants and above, and the only one he had met was Lieutenant Commander William "Bill" Burch, the skipper of Scouting Five. He sat down next to Burch and reintroduced himself.

He was surprised that Burch seemed to remember him.

"You're the Bombing Five gunnery officer, right?"

"Yes, sir."

"I try not to let our pilots forget they have fixed guns, and, although the SBD isn't a fighter, it will outmaneuver most other single engine planes except fighters. It's no speed demon either, but it can give a good account of itself if the pilot has some experience with air to air tactics. And since we get assigned to anti-torpedo plane patrol, air to air is an important part of what we do."

"I agree completely. We're fairly good at fixed gunnery, but I think our squadron could use a little more work on air to air tactics."

Burch smiled. "We have some would be fighter pilots in the squadron, and they love it."

"Fighters were my first choice leaving Pensacola, but dive bombers were a close second, so I'm happy where I am. But I too would love some air to air tactics work."

"With the rivalry between the squadrons, advice from Scouting Five might not be welcome. But I will try to mention it casually to Dick Armiston."

"Thank you, sir."

Friday, March 6, 1942

TF-17 had crossed the International Date Line, skipping March 3. During the morning TF-17 approached the rendezvous point in the eastern Coral Sea. Alan was taking a break in the forward gallery in midmorning. Looking around he saw a lot of towering cumulus clouds typical of thunderstorms. He had noticed that thunderstorms and squalls were quite frequent in this tropical area. He saw two Dauntlesses from *Lexington* appear over TF-17 and land aboard *Yorktown*. He noticed packages of papers were delivered. *Probably Brown's orders for Fletcher*, he thought.

Looking out from the hangar deck at noon, Alan saw TF-11 come into view right on schedule, *Lexington* being easy to recognize. As TF-17 continued to approach TF-11, Alan recalled what he knew about the Lexington class ships, consisting of *Lexington* and *Saratoga*. They could be easily distinguished from the other US carriers by their clipper bows and large slab sided funnels. They were older and quite different from the *Yorktown* class ships, consisting of *Yorktown* and *Enterprise*. The new carrier *Hornet*, CV-8, was usually thought of as a member of the *Yorktown* class, but she had enough changes so the navy put her officially in a class of her own. All five had roughly the same overall capability and operated about the same number of aircraft. The *Lexington* class ships were both commissioned in 1927 and were built on battle cruiser hulls and propulsion that could not be completed as battle cruisers because of the limitations of the Washington Treaty of 1922. That made them big, fast, and well armored but less maneuverable than the *Yorktown* class, and it compromised the internal arrangements some. The *Yorktown* class ships were commissioned in the late 1930s and were designed as aircraft carriers from the keel up. The *Lexington* class ships had a standard tonnage of 33,000 tons, while the *Yorktown* class ships were 19,900 tons. In the *Lexington* class ships, the hull extended all the way up to the flight deck, so the hangar deck was not as open. There were four large openings on the port side, but only one on the starboard side, all aft of the island. The *Lexington* class had two elevators, forward and amidships, while the *Yorktown* class had a third elevator near the stern.

USS *Lexington* (CV-2), 1929
(US Navy/PD-USGOV-MILITARY-NAVY)

Saturday, March 7, 1942

After flight quarters, Armiston gave a briefing. "Yesterday afternoon, Admiral Fletcher, with members of his staff, along with Captain Buckthorn and the air officer, took a launch over to *Lexington* for a conference. They discussed and agreed on a plan formulated by Admiral Brown the day before. The plan is to attack Rabaul and Gasmata, on the island of New Britain in the Bismarck Archipelago, on March 10. *Lexington* will attack Rabaul, and *Yorktown* will attack Gasmata, at dawn. Smith's cruisers will later shell Rabaul, and the Anzac Squadron will shell Gasmata.

"The Anzac Squadron is a mixed group, commanded by Rear Admiral John Crace, an Australian in the Royal Navy. The principal ships are the Australian heavy cruiser *Australia*, the flagship, and the American heavy cruiser *Chicago*, and at times they are joined by other Australian, New Zealand, and American ships. That is all."

A buzz of conversation among the pilots began immediately.

Alan said to Jolly, seated next to him, "Sending Smith's cruisers through confined waters without air cover to shell a major Japanese air base like Rabaul seems very risky to me, even after it has been attacked by *Lexington*'s planes."

"You bet. I don't get it."

Alan was very curious about how the plan came to be, and he was glad to run into Hank Stinson in the wardroom at 1300. They planned to meet at 2000 that evening in the gallery aft as usual, but on the starboard side for variety.

Alan and Hank both emerged into the gallery together. Alan turned and went forward for a few minutes, so he and Hank would not be seen as sneaking off together. Then he walked aft to where Hank was seated on a locker, about halfway between the island and the stern, where the stern lookouts were still some distance away.

"Good evening, Hank."

"Good evening, Alan. That fellow Baird from the Combat Intelligence Unit has some balls. The admiral wanted him to give the staff some background on how he does his work. He turned the admiral down flat. Said he didn't have permission to discuss intelligence methods with anyone outside his unit."

"That actually doesn't sound as surprising to me as you might think. Intelligence work has gotten pretty sophisticated, and some officers don't seem to understand how fragile intelligence is. Admiral or not, Fletcher and his staff probably don't really have a need to know in this case. Of course, this fellow may not know how to say no diplomatically."

"Hmm. You might be right. Your wife probably helps you understand these things."

"Definitely. Anyway, I would love to hear any background you can tell me about the operation plan we were briefed on."

"Well, Alan, I think I can tell you something about the command situation. Brown has put Sherman in charge of the air attacks."

Alan knew that Captain Frederick "Ted" Sherman was the captain of *Lexington*. He was a kiwi, with a reputation as smart but headstrong and opinionated.

Hank continued, "Admiral Fletcher is named as second in command, but no one reports to him, and he was not even an addressee on the operations order. Captain Buckthorn gave him a copy as a courtesy."

"Wow. I bet that doesn't sit very well."

"No, it doesn't. The admiral puts up with a lot of slights. A week ago at Canton, when he got the radio message from Pearl to leave and head down here, it was in a different code that we don't have the key to. We had to send a destroyer to Canton to radio to have it sent again in a code we could translate, which caused considerable delay.

"The admiral doesn't think much of this operation plan either. The attack on Gasmata doesn't seem to be worth the effort and risk. Brown seems very lukewarm and tentative about the whole thing. He wanted to attack at night because *Lexington*'s squadrons are night qualified. But ours aren't, so Arnham put the kibosh on that. Brown is allowing only one air attack wave at each target before leaving. Our cruiser admiral, Poco Smith, is very upset about going all the way up the narrow channel to Rabaul without air cover. It seems unlikely that a single air attack will get all the aircraft at Rabaul, so the lack of air cover for the cruisers could be bad."

"I thought that sounded pretty risky."

"The other thing is that Sherman is going to operate both carriers together inside a single screen. I gather that is a radical idea but one that may have merit."

"As I recall, the turning diameter of *Lex* is about twice that of *Yorktown*, so if we come under attack, it could be difficult to keep the two together."

"Exactly. You know your stuff, Alan. These two carriers may not be the best two for the first trial of this idea. But it's all three days away. A lot could happen in that time to change the plan. There is some new intelligence that I can't go into."

"I see. Thanks very much for telling me as much as you can. I guess I don't have any news for you."

CHAPTER NINE

Over the Mountains to Lae and Salamaua

Sunday, March 8, 1942

Early in the morning, Alan had made his usual visit to the bow to get some fresh air and look at the weather. He immediately noticed that the ship had slowed down to less than 15 knots. Something was afoot, because there was no reason to slow down if preparations for the raid were proceeding as planned.

Later in the morning, Alan was on the hangar deck. He looked out through the open sides to see that *Yorktown* was slowing down further, and the escorts were beginning to maneuver to new positions. The bullhorn had announced the plan to put the two carriers together under the protection of a single screen, and now it was being put into effect. The combined two carrier force was referred to as TF-11. Three cruisers stayed near the carriers, and the rest moved out ahead. When the new formation was complete, speed was increased to something like 20 knots, Alan estimated. He thought they were now headed roughly west, instead of northwest toward the launch point in the Solomon Sea.

The task force heard that day the sad news that Java had fallen to the Japanese, completing their conquest of the large islands of the East Indies west of New Guinea. Coming after two months of bad news from the area, it was hardly a surprise. Now only New Guinea stood between the Japanese and Australia, and the amphibious forces they had been using farther west would soon be available for further conquests.

That evening Captain Buckthorn announced to the whole ship that Admiral Brown had changed the target. The Japanese had landed at Lae and Salamaua, less than 20 miles apart in the Gulf of Huon on the north side of Papua, the eastern part of New Guinea, and Rabaul harbor was now nearly empty. The two carriers of TF-11 would attack the invasion sites on March 10. The attack would be from the Gulf of Papua, on the south side of the Papua peninsula west of Port Moresby. Admiral Crace's force of four heavy cruisers would be sent back to loiter near Rossel Island off the eastern tip of New Guinea, where they could intercept any ships that might come from Rabaul toward Port Moresby or New Caledonia.

Alan remembered from his geography studies that there were high mountains on that peninsula, so the strike aircraft would have to climb fairly high to get over them. This was an unusual situation for navy aircraft. It would be a problem mainly for the Devastators, which had difficulty climbing above 8,000 feet when loaded down with a torpedo. Also the density altitude, which is what affected airplane performance, was higher than the true altitude because of the high temperature and humidity. This approach, however, seemed much better to Alan than having the task force steam directly in from the east, following the north side of the Papua peninsula, where the task force would be within range of Japanese air search and attack from Rabaul throughout the day before the raid and could not quickly retreat out of range.

Monday, March 9, 1942

At flight quarters, the pilots were told that each pilot would be provided with a stopgap kit, consisting of a meat cleaver and a bottle of aspirin from the ship's stores, in case of a forced landing in the New Guinea jungle. Alan thought, *The navy has given thought to preparations for many kinds of emergencies but somehow has overlooked the survival of airmen in the event of a forced landing in the wilderness on land.*

At breakfast, the pilots were talking about how wild the interior of New Guinea was. It was said to be very rugged terrain, covered with impenetrable jungle, in which dwelt all kinds of carnivorous predators, poisonous reptiles, headhunters, and cannibals. Unfortunately, Alan's memories from geography class suggested that there was some truth to these stories.

As gunnery officer, Alan was in charge of arming the Bombing Five airplanes for this mission, but this would have to wait until Sherman's operations order was received, specifying which aircraft would participate and how they should be armed. After flight quarters, Alan decided to go with Ned Morris to the hangar deck and see if any word on armament had arrived.

Looking quickly around the hangar, he didn't see anyone. It looked like armament orders were yet to come. Alan realized he and Ned could use the time to do their preflight inspections. He quickly found 5-B-12 among the crowd of planes.

He started on the left side, standing behind the wing, and moved around the airplane clockwise. He had gotten most of the way around when he moved the rudder from side to side to make sure it was free, as he had done with the ailerons and elevators.

The rudder would only move a little bit, and there was a clunking noise coming from the cockpit area. He climbed up on the left wing and looked into the rear cockpit, where he spotted a large screwdriver jamming one of the rudder pedals. He climbed into the rear cockpit, and sliding down through the large seat support ring, he got hold of the screwdriver and pulled it out. He straightened back up in the seat and noticed Slack coming toward him, slipping quickly between the planes, which were parked very close together with overlapping wings.

"What do you think you're doing?" Slack snarled, with an expression of disgust.

"Tomorrow we have a strike mission. We'll be arming the planes as soon as the orders come through. All the airplanes should have had their preflight inspection before now. This airplane sure hasn't. I found this jammed in the rudder pedals," he said, holding up the screwdriver.

"Who are you, the new skipper?" replied Slack, looking surly.

"I can get the skipper if you want, but I guarantee he'll be pissed off," said Alan calmly.

Slack made no reply and turned away, looking annoyed. Luckily Slack hadn't noticed that Ned was also doing his inspection.

Alan put the screwdriver away and returned to continue with the inspection. He found no other squawks until the final item in the inspection. He climbed up on the black wing walk next to the fuselage on the right wing, went forward and opened the little panel on top of the accessory section behind the engine, and checked the engine oil supply in the twenty gallon tank. The oil was a gallon low. This was not crucial, like jammed controls, but still an unforgivable oversight. Knowing where the oil was kept, he got a filler can and pumped a gallon into it. He was walking back to his plane when Slack reappeared.

"Now what're you doing?" Slack almost shouted, getting red in the face.

Alan climbed up on the right wing again. "I'm continuing with the required preflight inspection." Alan hoped he was making an impression, because he was not sure that Slack was even aware of how sloppy the engineering department had become. He started pouring the oil into the tank.

"That's engineering's job. Get off the airplane!"

"That's right, but engineering failed to do it," said Alan as he continued pouring.

"I'm going to tell the exec to get you the hell out of engineering's way."

Alan smiled as he finished pouring and said, "Good idea. I'm sure the exec will want to hear what is going on." He hoped that West was aware of the situation in engineering. He closed the access panel and climbed down off the wing. He put the filler can away, and Ned joined him as he headed back to the ready room.

In midafternoon the operations order was received on *Yorktown*. Pilots were told to report to their ready rooms at 1600. Armiston outlined the plan for the raid. "We're sending seventeen airplanes, and Scouting Five is sending thirteen. Commander Ault, the CLAG, commander of the Lexington air group, flew to Port Moresby today and brought back some very valuable dope about a pass through the Owen Stanley Mountains that we have to fly over. The weather on the pass is usually good in the morning, but it may be obscured by cloud in the afternoon. The pass is at seventy-five hundred feet, much lower than some of the peaks, which we hope will make it possible for the Torpedo Two to get over with torpedoes. Commander Ault will not carry a bomb, and when he gets to the pass with the *Lexington* Dauntlesses, he will orbit there to help the Devastators find the way and monitor the weather.

"*Lexington* will launch a half hour ahead of us, so they should be finishing up at the target when we arrive. We will follow along the same route at sixteen thousand feet, so we should be well above all the mountains. Torpedo Five will be armed with two five hundred pound bombs each, so they should have no trouble getting over. All Dauntlesses will be armed with a five hundred pound bomb and two one hundred pounders." Armiston paused and looked up from his papers with a frown. "Apparently Captain Sherman is one of those who still believes that something can be accomplished with one hundred pound bombs." He looked down again at his notes and continued, "The weather forecast is good. Full details will be given in the morning briefing. Right now launch is scheduled for late morning. Why not earlier—damned if I know. Be prepared for an earlier departure, which could be announced at flight quarters. Try to get some rest. That is all."

Alan thought, *If Ault will be coaching planes over the pass by radio, apparently radio silence is not deemed necessary. That indicates that no opposition by enemy aircraft is expected, which is a relief.*

Alan thought his friend Wade Buckner in Fighting Three might be one of the first pilots to get to the target, unless he was kept back for CAP. He hoped his friend Rudi Fischer in Torpedo Two could make it over the pass with his torpedo.

As soon as the briefing was over, Alan and Ned Morris headed for the hangar deck, to pass the word to the waiting ordnance men on how to arm the airplanes. Sherman's orders said to use instantaneous fuses on the bombs. These were normally preferred for attacking land targets, whereas the alternative, the delayed action fuse, was used for attacking ships because it allowed the bomb to penetrate before detonating. Since the attack was to be mainly against the Japanese invasion fleet, it seemed like the wrong choice.

As Alan was leaving the wardroom after supper, Jerry West approached.

"There you are, Alan. Could I have a word with you?"

"Sure." Alan followed West away from the other officers.

"Slack says you came in the hangar and started working on your plane and telling him what to do."

"Well, sir, I've gotten to know my plane captain pretty well. He's been telling me that Slack rushes the work so much that the mechanics have trouble doing a good job. He suggested I might want to do a preflight inspection myself in the future. So I did one yesterday for the search and this afternoon for the strike tomorrow. This afternoon I found that the rudder was jammed by a screwdriver dropped in the rear cockpit. I also found the engine oil was down a gallon."

"OK. It sounds like you were trying to do the right thing. But you should not be doing engineering's job. I will talk to Slack again. You should try to leave him alone as much as you can."

"Yes, sir, I will try." Alan thought this meant he was being told not to do his own preflight inspections, because Slack would now see that they were done promptly. That seemed highly unlikely, and he decided he would try to do them when Slack was not in the hangar.

Tuesday, March 10, 1942

Alan had breakfast at 0430 and was in the ready room for flight quarters at 0530. He had gotten some sleep and felt ready. The tension of going into combat was building again. Alan scanned the flight listing and saw that he would be flying 5-B-12, and he would be leading the second section in the third division, led by Jolly. His wingmen would be Glen Cobb and Phil Goodwin.

Armiston began, "The start of launch remains at eleven fifteen. I still don't understand why not earlier. Scouting Five and Torpedo Five are the first deck load to go. Then we'll be the second. Fighting Forty-Two's escort of ten is last. We'll use the running rendezvous. The fighters may well arrive first, and, if there is little air opposition, they will strafe the targets. Scouting Five and Torpedo Five will go to Lae, and we'll go to Salamaua. The latest intelligence we've gotten is that there are no aircraft on the landing fields there, so the Japs may not have the fields in shape yet. So unless the Japs have planes on their way in from Rabaul right now, probably we'll only have to contend with floatplanes."

As flight officer, Jolly Lowery went over the weather forecast, which was generally good. He also pointed out that the forecast farther north toward Rabaul was for poor weather. This was good news, because it might hold up any Japanese airplanes that might want to come down from Rabaul. Alan thought, *Good weather should make this very different from the Jaluit raid.*

Teeth Jensen stood up and gave the navigation data, including the bearing and distance to the target from the launch point and the Yoke Easy sector letters for the day. The launch and recovery points were to be the same, simplifying the navigation.

Yorktown had the CAP duty for the task force that morning, and Alan could hear the Wildcats taking off. The briefing concluded at 0615. Armiston was about to dismiss the pilots when suddenly the teletype came to life.

Armiston said, "Stand by—let's see what this is before we break up."

West got up and bent over the teletype machine as it clattered away. After a few minutes, he tore off the paper and handed it to Armiston.

Armiston said, "Now this is more like it. Mighty short notice but better late than never. The start of launch is moved up to oh eight hundred, only fifteen minutes behind *Lexington*. So be ready; report back here at oh seven forty-five. You are dismissed until then."

Alan checked over his notes and charts to make sure he had all the information. The charts showed only the coastline of New Guinea, providing no information on the rugged interior. He was back in the ready room at 0740, and Bombing Five was called to go on deck a half hour later. Torpedo Five had departed, and Scouting Five was taking off. There was a delay while Bombing Five and the fighter escort were brought up from the hangar. Jolly had told him that he was reassigning many of the gunners, so they could get a different experience. Alan found Parker waiting when he found his airplane and greeted him warmly. Parker had flown with Alan many times during the previous autumn.

The mountains of New Guinea loomed over the low haze in the northeast, about 50 miles away. The task force was about as close in as it could get and still have plenty of room for maneuver, Alan thought.

The ship's bullhorn announced quarters for air defense, which included the manning of the ship's antiaircraft guns. Alan noticed that the marines who manned some of the guns were still wearing the old shallow M1917 helmets from the last war. He had heard that the marines were always the last to get new equipment. The sailors were issued the new M1 helmet that provided more protection and could not pivot forward, covering the eyes and injuring the nose.

Alan could see Wildcats landing on *Lexington*, which seemed odd at this point in the operation. He realized that *Lexington's* two slow elevators must make spotting airplanes on her flight deck quite different from the routine on *Yorktown*, and that might explain it.

A half hour later, Alan was off, followed by his wingmen, and they joined up with the rest of the squadron, orbiting nearby. They were the last section, so the squadron departed for the target, heading 013. As they climbed, they rose above the haze, and the tall Owen Stanley Mountains appeared clearly ahead. To Alan, it was an inspiring and beautiful scene, as their Dauntlesses, reduced to tiny objects against the hugeness of the terrain ahead, climbed in the bright sunshine to clear the mountains.

Yorktown Dauntlesses en route to Lae and Salamaua, March 10, 1942
(US Navy/PD-USGOV-MILITARY-NAVY)

They had reached 7000 feet as they crossed the coastline. Looking straight down, Alan could see a small village of thatched roofs and a river coming from the interior. On the radio he could hear Ault giving a weather report at the pass. Listening to the chatter, it sounded like Torpedo Two from *Lexington* was just barely able to make it over the pass by using a nearby thermal updraft to help them gain altitude. So far the radios in the airplanes seemed to be working well, although he had heard from Goodwin that the tropical moisture had been raising hell with them.

Bombing Five continued climbing to 16,000 feet, which necessitated they don their oxygen masks. By then Alan could see the whole ridge of high mountains not far ahead, and they would clear them by a big margin. Here and there were higher summits that rose to 12,000 or 13,000 feet, and those summits were shrouded in clouds.

Near the pass they caught up with Torpedo Five, which had climbed up to 11,000 feet. Carrying only half the weight of a torpedo, they were able to climb high enough to easily clear the pass. Sherman's plan for the torpedo bombers made sense: try to get torpedoes to the target but have a conservative backup in case they couldn't make it over the mountains. The problem was that Torpedo Five had never practiced level bombing, rather than glide bombing or dropping torpedoes, and level bombing was unlikely to be effective against ships. But perhaps Sherman didn't know either of those facts. Also Alan thought that the *Yorktown* Dauntlesses should have been armed with one thousand pound bombs. Once the effort had been made to put dive bombers over a target, it was much more effective to drop one thousand pound bombs.

Once over the pass, Alan could hear the chatter of the *Lexington* pilots, who were having a field day over the target area. Apparently there was very little opposition in the air, because Fighting Three was strafing the ships and shore installations.

After another fifteen minutes, Alan could see the outline of the northern shore through the haze. He said over the intercom to Parker, "Target area in sight." Alan charged his machine guns and armed his bombs. He set the release lever to release the two one hundred pound bombs at the same time as the five hundred pounder. He thought that Sherman was probably unaware that the old tactics of two dives had given way in practice to minimizing exposure to fighters and antiaircraft fire with a single dive.

Meanwhile, he could feel Parker swiveling his seat, opening the canopy, and setting up his machine gun. Alan felt the tension rising, even though the opposition seemed light. Bombing Five came over the coastline at about 0900. Alan could see that they were over Salamaua, and there were ships scattered over the sea between there and Lae, visible off to the north. The last of the *Lexington* planes were leaving the target area headed south.

Armiston turned left to follow the coastline north. Then he came on the radio: "First division will dive on the cruiser directly below. Second division, take the two destroyers behind us. Third division, hold off and dive on the cruiser if it needs more."

The second division, led by West, made a right 180 degree turn to go after the destroyers. Then Alan saw Armiston go into his dive. Alan thought it was inspiring to watch from a distance and see the six airplanes go gracefully into their dives one by one. The cruiser was maneuvering radically. It appeared to Alan that there were some near misses but no hits. There was very little antiaircraft fire. *Maybe the strafing of Fighting Three has scattered the gunners*, thought Alan. On the radio Alan could hear that Fighting Forty-Two was starting to strafe at Lae.

Armiston's voice crackled on the radio: "Third division, follow up on the cruiser."

Then came a garbled radio transmission. He saw Jolly wiggle his wings and hand signal for the dive.

Alan spoke on the intercom, "All set for the dive, Parker?"

"All set, sir."

Alan was the fourth to dive in the third division. With little or no opposition, it seemed a lot like the practice dives on the towed target, so it shouldn't be too hard, he thought, as he started down. As he passed through 6,000 feet, his windshield and gun sight began to fog up. *Not again!* he thought. He had stashed a rag in his parachute harness, and he took his hand off the throttle to give the sight a quick wipe. He had to do it again a few seconds later. After that he had to focus on the target. When he dropped his bombs at 1,500 feet, he could still see the shape of the cruiser vaguely through the sight, but he had lost track of his direction relative to the wind as the cruiser turned sharply. He pulled out at 500 feet, headed north. Parker reported that his bombs hit the water about thirty feet from the side of the cruiser—close enough so there might have been damage. He had seen that the previous two bombers in the dive sequence missed by about the same amount. He was very disappointed, but the fogging made it nearly impossible to do better. It was particularly aggravating that the squadron was struggling when there was no air opposition and antiaircraft fire was light.

Armiston called for Bombing Five to form up again and head back to the ship. Then he radioed *Yorktown*: "Recommend second strike immediately." Armiston's radio seemed to be working fine, but nothing came from others in the squadron, suggesting more radio trouble. The squadron started climbing back to 10,000 feet to easily clear the pass.

As he looked around, he noticed a flight of eight B-17s, high above, and below them eight Lockheed Hudson bombers from the Royal Australian Air Force, heading north. It looked like this Anzac force was on the way to make a contribution to the raid from their bases in Australia.

Around 8,000 feet, Alan felt his engine becoming rough. He felt a cold feeling in his stomach at the thought that his airplane might not get him back. He quickly scanned the engine instruments, and everything was in the green. He checked that the mixture control was in the auto rich position for climb power. He looked sharply again at the big cylinder head temperature gauge in the lower instrument panel; it had moved up to 220 Centigrade, above the green arc. Apparently the mixture was too lean in spite of the control setting.

He radioed: "Ericsson here. Rough engine. Leveling off at eight thousand."

"OK, Ericsson, try to get over the pass; it's all downhill from there," Armiston replied, trying to be encouraging.

At least my radio is working, Alan thought. He slid back the canopy to prepare for a forced landing and felt Parker opening his. He glanced around and saw that Cobb and Goodwin had throttled back to stay with him. Looking back at the engine instruments, the cylinder head temperature was now just at the lower end of the red, 240 Centigrade. He knew 260 was the absolute upper limit. He pulled the throttle back to reduce manifold pressure by three inches and increased the rpm by 200, thereby getting maximum engine cooling while still maintaining altitude.

Now he was approaching the pass, and it looked like he had enough altitude to get through with some to spare. *Whew!* he thought. Just then the engine quit, the propeller windmilling in the heart stopping quiet. The idea of going down in the jungle was terrifying. The engine made no ominous noises as the propeller kept it turning, so the machinery was OK. He glanced at the fuel pressure gauge, and it was still in the green, so using the manual wobble pump wouldn't help. His mind raced, and he thought of one more desperate measure: he operated the fuel primer plunger for one stroke, which squirted fuel directly into the intake manifold, normally used only for starting. The engine coughed and ran momentarily. He pumped again, and again a few seconds later. The engine started and kept running, and he adjusted the rate of pumping to keep it as smooth as possible.

Now he was almost to the pass, and he was at 7,500 feet. It would be close, but he hated the idea of turning back. He went through right on top of the trees, still pumping. Some greenery, cut loose by the propeller, flew past the cockpit. Then he was through, and he could lower the nose and pick up a little speed to help cool the engine. He looked again at the cylinder head temperature gauge, and it had dropped back to the bottom of the red. The engine was running so lean it was actually running cooler. He glanced around and saw that Cobb and Goodwin were still there, but well above his altitude, having gone through the pass at a more comfortable height. At least if he went down, on land or in the ocean, they might be able to summon help to the right place. He became aware he was soaked in sweat and breathing hard.

He had been too busy to say anything to Parker in the back seat. He keyed the intercom: "Was that close enough, or should we go back and try it again?" Alan was surprised by his own giddy sense of humor.

"Jesus Christ, Alan, I think all my hair turned white."

Parker was a little giddy too, or he would never have used Alan's first name, a big offense for an enlisted man addressing an officer.

Alan estimated that his Dauntless would only go about 12 miles gliding from this altitude to sea level with no help from the engine. The coast was about 40 miles ahead, and the ship was another 15 miles off shore. He and Parker closed their canopies to reduce the drag. Alan resumed working the primer pump, changing hands when his hand got sore. The engine continued to run, developing just enough power to keep from descending at more than 100 feet per minute at best glide speed, about 100 knots. The primer was on a small subpanel on the right next to the lower instrument panel. He had to bend forward to reach it, even with his right hand, and he could just barely look over the top of the instrument panel to see ahead. But he kept at it. Finally he saw the coast, and soon he was over the ocean at 5,000 feet. Now if he didn't make it, he would ditch in the ocean, where he and Parker could be picked up by a destroyer, as they had been six months earlier.

He decided to get near the ship before giving up his excess altitude, in case the engine would not restart after he stopped pumping. He keyed the radio transmitter: "Ericsson here. Engine quit, but got it running on the primer. I'm over the coast at five thousand."

Armiston replied, "Good work. Keep your altitude until you're over the ship; then spiral down."

He could see the ship and kept pumping. He listened to the radio chatter as the rest of the squadron landed back aboard. Armiston, landing first, would alert the ship that Alan had a balky engine. He turned on the landing light to make his plane conspicuous. Finally he was over the ship at 3,800 feet, and he radioed that he would spiral down and try to come aboard. He and Parker opened their canopies and Alan put the landing gear, flaps, and arresting hook down. He spiraled down gently counterclockwise, the extra drag allowing him to descend while keeping the engine running. For the last turn, he went out on the port side of the ship and made a circle that would end at the stern of the ship. He followed a fairly normal glide path, but he could barely see Soupy while he was bent forward, pumping. When Soupy gave him the cut, he quickly let go of the primer, sat up, and made the landing, the engine quitting before he hit the deck. He caught the fifth wire and came to the usual abrupt stop. He let out a huge sigh of relief. He felt drained and had to push himself to raise the hook. The barrier went down, releasing a crowd of blue-shirted plane handlers, who had come aft to push his dormant airplane forward to parking.

He felt the tension subsiding further as he climbed out, and he shivered when the wind hit his soaked flight suit. He was shaking as he stood on the wing while Parker climbed out. It was just 1200.

Parker reached back into the rear cockpit and pulled out a big green leaf, almost two feet long. "In case anyone doesn't believe we went over the pass pretty low, I'm going to keep this," he said with a grin.

"Good idea. I'll send any skeptics to you. I think the thought of going down in that jungle was even more frightening than facing Japanese fire."

"Yeah. I was scared shitless when the engine quit."

They climbed down with their parachutes and headed toward the island. Alan went to the wardroom, got some lunch, but decided he was keyed up enough that he didn't need any coffee. Then he took his lunch to the ready room.

Still so shaken by the experience that he forgot to start eating, he described his whole flight to Jolly, ending with, "I don't think I've ever been so scared. I can't wait to find out what went wrong."

"It does sound scary. But carrier flying is a scary business. There's a thousand things that could go wrong and prevent you from getting back, besides enemy fire. You should eat your lunch."

Alan thought Jolly was impressed, but his fatalism toned down his response. Alan started eating his lunch.

Jolly continued, "I took your advice and took a rag for the fogging, and it helped. I think I might have gotten a near miss close enough to do damage, about fifteen feet."

"That ought to do it."

"I heard that the intelligence guy on Fletcher's staff heard the Japs on the radio calling for help during the raid."

"That's good, I guess."

"As you were." Armiston's voice came from the back of the room before anyone could get up. He went to the front and addressed the squadron. "I've been talking to Commander Arnham. The air office and air group want a second strike, and Admiral Fletcher will recommend it to Admiral Brown. Meanwhile, you are to debrief with your division leader. Then you can stand down until further notice. After the debriefing, the division leaders meet with me in my office. That is all."

Alan thought that a second strike could not include torpedo carrying Devastators, because the pass would be obscured with cloud. Also a second strike might find that Japanese fighters had had time to come down from Rabaul. Anyway he might not be selected for a second strike, with 5-B-12 grounded.

Alan had already told Jolly all about the flight, so he did not need to debrief. So he went to the hangar deck to be ready for arming a second strike. As he arrived, the ship's bullhorn announced that Admiral Brown had decided against a second strike, so no arming was necessary. The task force would begin retiring from the area shortly.

Alan looked around the hangar and noticed that Klein was working on 5-B-12. The deck crew had reported to engineering that the engine had quit, and Parker had told him about their flight back. He had already taken off the skin panels on each side of the accessory section behind the engine.

He wasted no time. "Good afternoon, sir. Heard you had a scary flight back. The first thing I want to check is the fuel filter."

Alan could not see past Klein into the accessory section, so he waited. After some minutes Klein said, "Yes, sirree, this filter is plugged up tight." He turned around and showed Alan the filter in his hand. Alan knew the filter material was white, but this filter was a black gooey mess from bad stuff in the fuel. "I think this accounts for your whole adventure," said Klein. "Some of the fuel has been coming through with junk from the bottoms of the tanks in the oilers. The air office is aware of it, and they recommended checking the fuel filters as part of the preflight inspection. The other squadrons are doing it. We started doing it, and it did take a little extra time, but Slack said it took too long and put a stop to it. Goodwin tried to talk him out of it, but he got dressed down in front of us for his trouble."

Suddenly Alan felt anger welling up. He and Parker had almost gone down in the jungle because Slack didn't like taking the time for a simple check, recommended by the air office and being done by the other squadrons. As he thought about it, all his previous tension swelled his anger into a fury. He was quivering with rage and nearly speechless. "That shithead!" was all that came out. He grabbed the filter out of Klein's hand and strode toward the engineering office, leaving Klein staring open-mouthed after him.

Slack barely had time to look up as Alan barged straight into his office. Alan slammed the filter down on the desk in front of

Slack, blackening papers Slack had been working on. "You asshole!" Alan shouted. He grabbed Slack by the collar and yanked him out of his chair. Slack was heavier than Alan, but Alan's rage seemed to give him twice his normal strength. Slack seemed to be taken aback and did little to resist. He shoved Slack against the wall, shouting, "You stupid son of a bitch! You aren't fit to swab the deck here! You can't tell which end of an airplane is which!"

Alan felt strong arms around his chest, pinning his arms and pulling him back. It was Klein. He had two other mechanics with him. As they pulled Alan out of the office, he had a glimpse of Slack staring at the black mess on his uniform where Alan had grabbed him. The image struck Alan as very funny, and his rage subsided rapidly.

"You better clean off your hands before you touch anything else, sir," said Klein.

Alan went to a sink nearby and washed his hands, his breathing slowly returning to normal. As he was doing so, he overheard Slack talking on the telephone, "I've just been assaulted by Ericsson." Noticing that the three men still surrounded him, he said with a faint smile, "I blew my stack, but I'm OK now."

They seemed to relax slightly but didn't move away.

Suddenly Jerry West appeared, looking grim. Apparently West was the person Slack had been talking to. "Follow me to my office." He turned and walked out of the hangar with Alan following. Alan knew that getting angry was only allowed with people you outranked, and only if you didn't lay a finger on them. He was in trouble. West still looked grim when they sat down in his office, and he came right to the point.

"OK, Ericsson, what the hell is going on here?"

Alan described his flight back from Salamaua and how Klein had found the problem and its cause right away. He concluded,

"Slack is a terrible misfit as engineering officer, and the whole squadron is at risk flying planes in his charge. He's got to be relieved."

"Not so fast, Alan. Slack was wrong in this case, but it seems like things have been going OK otherwise. He runs a tight ship: everything is done on time, and the hangar is neat and tidy too."

"You should spend some time on the hangar deck. The men are starting to feel mutinous."

"Is that because Slack is incompetent or because he runs a tight ship?"

Alan stared at West, his anger rising again. He was getting nowhere. He found his respect for the exec ebbing. With great effort, he controlled himself, gave up, and sat silent.

After a pause West resumed, "You've been a good officer and pilot, but losing your temper and manhandling a senior officer is a pretty big offense. Go to your stateroom and stay there until I have a chance to talk this over with the skipper."

When he got to his stateroom, Jolly was there. Alan told Jolly what had happened.

"Throwing a tantrum was dumb. You need to ease up and not take everything so seriously," was Jolly's reaction.

"The prospect of a forced landing in a mountainous jungle will always be serious to me."

"Yeah, but there are a lot of risks on every combat mission, and it's not really anyone's fault."

Alan did not feel like arguing with Jolly.

Jolly left for the squadron office. Alan pulled out a book and started reading, but he couldn't keep his mind on it. He went over the afternoon's events again and again. It was obviously wrong to blow his stack, but he felt very strongly that having Slack as engineering officer was a grave risk to the squadron. As he thought more about it, he realized that by becoming angry he had lost his credibility with West and probably others. That meant that his anger had undermined his effort get Slack out of engineering. It was stupid. It was also reminiscent of his report on the *Squalus* disaster, which had so irritated the brass that it had actually delayed the steps necessary to make it unlikely to happen again. Now he was angry with himself.

His mind turned from what had happened to the immediate future. He was going to be called on the carpet in the squadron office. He tidied himself up and changed into a fresh uniform. His watch said 1430.

A half hour later there was a knock on the door. It was an orderly with a request from West to come to his office. Alan found Armiston and Slack seated in the exec's office when he arrived. He was not invited to sit down.

West did the talking. "We have decided not to take disciplinary action against you, Ericsson, *provided* that you take the following steps: first, you must apologize sincerely to Lieutenant Slack here and now; second, you must confine your activities on the hangar deck entirely to your duties as gunnery officer, and do not interfere in any way with the engineering department."

"Yes, sir." He turned to Slack, who stood up and looked Alan in the eye. Alan looked right back into his eyes and said firmly, "I am very sorry, sir, that I lost my temper with you. It was an extremely stupid thing to do, and I regret it enormously." Alan noticed that Slack was no longer looking him in the eye. He looked bored. Alan continued, "I hope that in the future I may have the opportunity to make up for my behavior and earn your respect." Alan reached forward to shake hands with Slack, but Slack kept his arms at his side. Alan was aware that West couldn't see this, because he was seated behind Alan, but Armiston couldn't miss it.

West said, "OK, Ericsson, now remember the second provision. You are dismissed."

Alan glanced at West and saw the same grim face as earlier. Turning to leave he glanced at Armiston. Armiston looked back with a very thoughtful expression that had no elements of grimness or hostility. Alan wondered what this meant. Evidently the skipper and the exec did not see entirely eye to eye on this matter. To Alan, the fact that they did not discipline him meant that they felt that Slack had made a serious error in stopping the fuel filter checks.

At supper Alan heard that Torpedo Five was disappointed with their results, which were attributed to the lack of training in level bombing. He thought Torpedo Two should take pride in getting their torpedoes over the pass, and he wondered how they had scored. He also heard that Scouting Five did not have their windshields and bombsights fog up, and they had done better than Bombing Five.

It was frustrating that Bombing Five had not done better. They had made two raids with little enemy opposition and didn't have much to show for it, and Scouting Five had done better. The main reason was the fogging problem, in Alan's mind, which Scouting Five had not yet experienced, probably because they had started their dives below 8,000 feet. Alan heard a rumor that some of the Scouting Five pilots were saying that maybe the fogging problem was only in the minds of the Bombing Five pilots. This was irritating but not totally unexpected, given the squadron rivalry. Sooner or later, Bombing Five would get a target with conditions that did not produce fogging, or Scouting Five would experience fogging. Or maybe a fix would come through.

Nevertheless, the task force has put a dent in Japanese shipping. With all the garrisons needed to control their conquests, their shipping must be starting to get spread a little thin, Alan thought, *so perhaps that dent will make a difference*. Also the Japanese now knew there were two American carriers in the Coral Sea, and hence they would need carrier support to continue their advance. *Our next raid could meet with carrier opposition. That would make it far more dangerous*, he thought, his apprehension rising.

Wednesday, March 11, 1942

Alan woke up feeling guilty and depressed about his behavior the previous afternoon. After breakfast he went to the squadron office to look at the armament expenditure records after the raid. Slack came in and ignored Alan, avoiding eye contact, on his way into West's office. Alan then went to the hangar deck to check armament ready inventory.

As he came into the hangar, he noticed the Bombing Five plane captains suddenly leaving their work and converging on the squadron supply area. As Alan walked by, Klein grabbed his arm and pulled him into a supply room. The plane captains were crammed into the small space. Klein closed the door and immediately the captains began to sing, "For He's a Jolly Good Fellow," as Alan stood there dumbfounded. He was even more surprised when he noticed Chief Patterson, standing inconspicuously in the back and singing along. Klein was pouring a glass of clear, yellowish liquid from an unlabeled bottle.

"Just for you, sir, we scrounged up some Scotch," said Klein as he handed the glass to Alan.

Alan beamed, took the glass, and took a good swallow. "That's very good whiskey. Thank you all very much," he said, looking around and smiling at the gathering. "Here's to all of you." He raised his glass and finished the whiskey with a couple more swallows. "I appreciate this very much. It felt good to blow off steam, but now the exec blames me as much as Slack. So it was stupid. I don't want to cut this short, but I had to promise to be on my best behavior and have nothing to do with engineering. So I think we all better get back to work before somebody notices what's going on." He handed the glass back to Klein and left the storeroom, with the plane captains streaming out after him. As he walked toward the armament area, he was pleased that at least they appreciated his efforts.

Later Klein slipped over to the armament area and told Alan what Slack's routine was, and when he was unlikely to be in the hangar, so that Alan could continue to keep an eye on his airplane and do preflight inspections. Klein also said that the whole fuel system on 5-B-12 had been cleaned and checked, and his plane would have a 100 hour routine inspection within the next few days.

CHAPTER TEN

Visiting Lexington

Saturday March 14, 1942

While Alan was enjoying his usual early morning visit to the bow of the ship, he noticed that the heavy cruiser *San Francisco* had slowed down. He watched her leave her position ahead of the carriers and fall back toward them. This was unusual, and he wondered what she was up to. As *Yorktown* passed by, Alan saw that *San Francisco* was stopped, and a Seagull floatplane was drifting next to her stern. The crane on the after deck of the cruiser was already swung out to hoist the plane aboard. It occurred to him that it was odd to have a scout return so soon after dawn, when there could not have been time for more than a very short flight.

The bullhorn announced that the Seagull that was lost on March 7 from *San Francisco* was being hoisted back aboard her. So that was it. The crew must have been relieved to see the task force, Alan thought, instead of having to sit it out for another week or two while the trade wind blew them all the way to Australia. Alan realized that flying a scout off a cruiser could be just as chancy as carrier flying, although it usually did not involve aerial combat.

After flight quarters and breakfast, Alan went on duty on the hangar deck, while keeping an eye on what was happening in the task force. Around midmorning Admiral Crace's Anzac squadron appeared on the horizon ahead. An hour later, he noticed a squadron of Dauntlesses taking off from *Lexington*. They fanned out in a search pattern. Alan wondered, *Were Japanese ships thought to be lurking nearby?*

The bullhorn came on, announcing that five Seagull floatplanes had not returned to the Anzac Squadron and that Scouting Two was making a search. So that was what the search was looking for. Alan wondered how so many had become lost in a short time. Then he remembered that thunderstorms and squalls happened frequently in these waters, and the cruisers did not yet have YE homing transmitters.

At noon, Alan saw two oilers, escorted by a heavy cruiser, heave into sight ahead. He went to lunch. He was just finishing when the bullhorn announced that Scouting Two had no luck searching for the five missing Seagulls.

After lunch Alan was off duty, and he headed for the gallery to relax with some reading material. He ran into Armiston going the other way in the passageway.

"Ericsson, are you off duty?"

"Yes, sir."

"Good. How would you like to take a hop over to *Lexington* and back?" Armiston asked with a smile.

Evidently Armiston did not hold anything against him from the fuel filter incident. "That would be great, sir. What's happening?" Alan asked with a grin.

"I just got the word from the air group commander, very short notice. TF-Seventeen is going to be split off again from TF-Eleven, and TF-Eleven is going back to Pearl. I gather Admiral

Nimitz told Admiral Brown to give us any airplanes we need. *Lex* is letting us have five of their Dauntlesses, two for us and three for Scouting Five. So I need another pilot to go with me to pick them up." He smiled and continued, "We're supposed to be on deck in fifteen minutes to ride over to *Lexington* in a Devastator. Get your flight gear and meet me on the flight deck by the island."

"Yes, sir!" Alan said with gusto and started for the ready room to pick up his flight gear. What a nice break in the routine! He hoped he might get a chance to talk to Wade Buckner or Rudi Fischer. A few minutes later, he stepped out of the island onto the flight deck. Five Devastators were spotted aft, and two Wildcats were in front of them. All the engines were being warmed up. He saw Armiston at the aft end of the island and moved next to him.

Armiston shouted over the wind and engine noise, "Besides the five Dauntlesses, Fighting Forty-Two is getting six of their Wildcats, and we're sending them two of our oldest. Torpedo Five gets one of their Devastators. So five Devastators are taking two pilots each, plus the two in the Wildcats, to bring back the twelve airplanes." Alan nodded.

The history of the Devastator type came to Alan's mind. He enjoyed trying to understand the engineering behind the design of the airplanes and their engines. He remembered that, while the Devastator was obsolescent now, when it first appeared in 1935, it was a very advanced, pioneering airplane. It had a number of firsts for a US Navy carrier airplane: first monoplane, first all metal airplane, and first with powered folding wings. The Devastator was powered by one of the newest and most powerful engines available at the time of the airplane's design in the mid thirties, the fourteen cylinder Pratt & Whitney R-1830 Twin Wasp.

The forces on the parts of an engine were so complex that they were hard to predict. The engineers had to restrict the power in the early models of any engine to prevent parts from breaking. Therefore the Twin Wasp for the Devastator was limited to only 900 horsepower. At the same time, the smaller but older Twin Wasp Junior in the BT-1 had almost as much power. As experience revealed which parts were weak and wore out first, they could be replaced with strengthened parts, and the power of the engine increased. The Twin Wasp in the newer F4F-3 Wildcats that Fighting Forty-Two was flying had 1,100 horsepower, and the one in the brand new F4F-4 Wildcat had 1,200 horsepower.

"Ferry pilots, man your planes!" blared the bullhorn, bringing Alan's attention abruptly back to the flight deck. Alan followed Armiston toward the Devastators, along with the other pilots. Armiston jumped up on the left wing of the second Devastator and climbed into the middle seat. Alan followed and climbed into the gunner's seat at the rear.

By now Alan was quite familiar with the Devastator from working around them on the hangar deck. For torpedo and glide bombing missions, the Devastator carried two men: the pilot and a gunner/radioman. For horizontal bombing, which Torpedo Five did on the Salamaua raid, they carried three men. The third man, the bombardier, sat where Armiston was now sitting, in the middle seat. Before each plane started its bombing run, the bombardier slipped down into the fuselage below his seat and squeezed forward into the little bombardier's compartment, lying prone under the pilot's feet. He then opened a set of doors on the bottom of the fuselage, which exposed a window for the Norden bombsight. The bombardier used the bombsight to aim the bombs, and he dropped them with the controls there. The bombardiers at Salamaua did the best they could with no practice.

Alan knew the Norden bombsight was thought to be a technical marvel—and hence was top secret. This required extreme security measures, such as having armed guards present when it was being moved to or from an airplane for a mission. The sight was developed by the army for their heavy bomber program and promoted by the army air force as part of that program. Alan thought that the sight might be overrated, like the heavy bombers.

Alan's mind returned to his surroundings. The gunner's seat was similar to the one in the Dauntless. As Alan sat in the gunner's seat, he swiveled around to face aft for a moment. He thought of what it must be like to sit there, flying low and slow over the water on a torpedo run, with fighters coming down at him with guns blazing. Like the gunner in the Dauntless, the gunner had only a little bit of armor plate to protect him from machine gun fire, whereas the pilot had the engine in front and a full sheet of armor plate behind his seat. He shuddered. It would be unnerving at best, no matter how good a gunner he was. He quickly swiveled around to face forward again as the airplane in front went to full power for takeoff. Now the pilot of this Devastator used the hydraulic system to unfold the wings from overhead down into position.

It felt strange to be just riding along, instead of being the pilot, on a carrier flight. The Devastator was light and lifted off easily. Alan knew *Lexington* was about two miles in front of *Yorktown*. The Devastator pilot leveled off at about 1,000 feet and headed straight for *Lexington*. Alan enjoyed the breeze with all the canopies open. The pilot flew down the starboard side and turned left into the landing pattern. Now Alan got his first close up view of *Lexington*. She did seem a little bigger than *Yorktown*, and the flight deck seemed a little lower, closer to the water. Alan noticed that the flight deck tapered slightly toward the bow, like that of *Yorktown*. He remembered that when originally built, the flight decks of the Lexington class carriers were very tapered at the bow, to minimize overhang from the narrow hull. It must have been very scary trying to stay on that narrow deck in gusty conditions, Alan thought. Evidently the navy agreed, and *Lexington*'s flight deck was modified in 1936, and he had heard that her sister, *Saratoga*, would finally get hers modified while she was being repaired at Bremerton. Some of the planes to be sent to *Yorktown* were parked at the bow now. *Lexington* had two islands: a smaller forward one for the various conning functions and a big slab sided one about 50 feet aft for the funnels. In *Yorktown*, these functions were combined in a single, larger island.

The landing felt similar to the ones he had made as a pilot. Alan had braced himself against the steel ring, which provided good support when he was thrown forward by the arrested landing. The Devastator taxied forward, and the pilot used the hydraulic system to fold the wings upward, so the tips were close together over the fuselage. Then he shut down the engine. The three *Yorktown* pilots climbed out and made their way toward the forward island, the first to arrive.

Alan immediately noticed the big eight inch guns housed in two turrets of two guns each forward and aft of the islands. These were relics of the thinking of the 1920s, when a gun armament was still deemed necessary for combat against surface ships. Alan could see that the big guns took up a lot of valuable space. He had heard that their weight required unsymmetrical ballast to keep the ship from listing to starboard. He also had heard that if they were not trained to starboard, their muzzle blast would damage any airplanes nearby on the flight deck. He also spotted the air control station, located on the forward end of the aft island, not near the navigation bridge as on *Yorktown*.

Alan followed Armiston as he walked up to the forward end of the forward island, saluted, and greeted a commander, whom he introduced to Alan as William Ault, the Lexington air group commander (CLAG). Ault told Armiston and Alan to relax, because it would be at least an hour before everything was ready for their return to *Yorktown*. He introduced Armiston and Alan to Lieutenant Commander Weldon Hamilton, the skipper of Bombing Two.

Ault turned to greet more of the *Yorktown* pilots who had just landed. Hamilton asked Armiston, "Did your squadron have trouble with the windshields and gunsights fogging up in the dives on Salamaua?"

"We sure did. It really threw us off. We had the same trouble at Jaluit a month earlier, but there the weather was so bad we might not have scored well anyway."

"It threw us off too. These were our first combat dives, and we got hardly any hits. Scouting Two had the same problem."

"When we were at Pearl after the Jaluit raid, Ericsson here sent a detailed report on it, with my endorsement, to BuAer, but we don't know if they're working on it. I'm sure they have a lot of pressing matters."

"Well, we'll sure try to light a fire under BuAer when we get back to Pearl. Say, while you're waiting, come on down to our ready room and meet some of our pilots."

"Sure." Armiston and Alan followed Hamilton toward a door in the island. Before they got there, the door opened and a big j.g. stepped out. Alan recognized his friend Rudi Fischer and grinned. Greetings and introductions were made. Armiston told Alan to meet him at the forward island in an hour and followed Hamilton into the island.

Alan asked Rudi, "Well, did you make it over the pass with your torpedo?"

Rudi grinned. "I sure did. But I have to admit: at first I had my doubts. Somewhere along the line our skipper had some glider training. Near the top of the pass, he found a thermal up-draft over an opening in the trees. That updraft gave us just the boost we needed to get over."

"I heard something about a thermal updraft on the radio and gathered it was helping. Did you get a hit?"

"No, I dropped on one of the transports at Lae, but my tor-pedo ran deep and went under, I think. How about you—did you get a hit?"

"No, we dropped on a light cruiser north of Salamaua. But our windshields and gunsights fogged up as we dived down into the warmer humid air. Since it happened before at Jaluit in the Marshalls, I had a rag and wiped it off, but it still threw me off. At Jaluit it was a surprise, and we had to guess our aim. It's a big problem if we dive from up high in humid conditions. We need a fix badly."

"It looks like our torpedoes do too. I'm beginning to realize that back at Pensacola you might've been trying to give me a hint. I remember you worked at the Newport Torpedo Station before you went to Pensacola. You probably knew there were problems with our torpedoes."

"I didn't know of any problems, but I was suspicious. They are dedicated people there, but it is so expensive to test torpedoes that they don't do nearly enough of it, especially in peacetime."

"Well, maybe they will now. And we should get the new Avenger before too long."

"That's right. It's supposed be great. I like the Dauntless so well that I'm not sure the Helldiver is going to be an improve-ment, if and when it ever gets to the fleet."

"Yeah, it got off to a bad start," Rudi said and then noted the time. "It's been great to catch up with you, but I have to report to the hangar deck. You probably would like to say hello to Wade

Buckner, too. Let's drop by the Fighting Three ready room and see if we can find him." As Alan followed Rudi into the island, they found they were in the midst of the Fighting Forty-Two pilots who were headed to the same place.

Outside the ready room, Rudi said good-bye and headed for the hangar deck. Alan went into the ready room and spotted the cherubic face of Wade Buckner on the far side. Most of the Fighting Three pilots were there, so the room was crowded. The Fighting Forty-Two pilots clustered around a tall, thin lieutenant commander at the front, who Alan gathered was Jimmie Thach. His reputation as an excellent fighter squadron commander had gotten around. Alan also knew that Thach's real name was John, but his classmates at the academy thought it would be good fun to call him by the name of his older brother, who had graduated only days before the younger Thach arrived. The name stuck, causing some confusion.

Thach was describing the squadron's encounter with Japanese G4M twin engine bombers from Rabaul on February 20. Alan stopped to listen. Thach was saying, "We managed to shoot down most of them. One of our pilots, Lieutenant O'Hare here, is already an ace with five kills." He smiled and pointed to a dark haired pilot in the front row. O'Hare stood up and received congratulations from the Fighting Forty-Two pilots. Then they began swapping stories about the Lae-Salamaua raid.

By then Wade had spotted Alan and had worked his way over to him. They exchanged greetings, and Wade suggested they step outside to talk.

"Wow, that Lieutenant O'Hare must be hot, to get five kills," said Alan.

"He is, and he did it all in about four minutes! Then he ran out of ammunition," said Wade with a big grin.

"Holy smoke! He must be really good. How about you—how've you been doing?"

"Pretty well. I got one Betty in that same attack. We were expecting that we might get some attention because we continued our approach after a snooper spotted us that morning. There were only a couple of floatplanes to shoot at on the Lae raid, and I wasn't that far east. I strafed the ships at Lae."

"Good for you!" Alan felt a pang of jealousy, not to be flying a fighter. "Have you seen any of that hot Japanese fighter, the Zero?"

"No, we haven't. How about you, Stringy—have you gotten any hits? Our dive bombers had trouble with fogging bombsights and windshields at Lae and Salamaua."

"No hits. We've had the same fogging problem both times we've dropped. Scouting Five hasn't had the problem, and they've done better, because they haven't dived from high up."

"That fogging problem is serious."

"That's right. I worked on it while we were at Pearl, but I didn't get very far in that short time. I hope BuAer realizes it's serious. Speaking of Pearl, I saw Ed Miller and Les Travis there. Ed saw some action in the Marshalls on February first. *Enterprise* was attacked as they pulled away after the raid. The weather was really crummy where we were farther south. Fighting Forty-Two shot down one flying boat, and no attack came. Since then Ed may have seen some action at Wake or Marcus. Les was going to try to transfer to *Hornet*."

"Yeah, Fighting Three was very lucky to get back aboard a carrier so soon after the *Sara* was torpedoed. The rest of the air group was screwed. Up until then Fighting Two was flying Buffaloes. You know it was a good thing none of our carriers got close to the Jap carriers at Pearl Harbor. Only *Enterprise* had Wildcats on board, and only fourteen of them!"

"Wow. Fighting Forty-Two had had their Wildcats for nine months by then. I didn't realize how few Wildcats had made it out to the Pacific."

Wade suggested they get Cokes at the wardroom and go up to the flight deck where it was cooler in the breeze. Alan noticed that *Lexington* seemed a little hotter below decks than *Yorktown*. Her older ventilation systems probably explained it, he thought. They found refuge from the heat in the shade aft of the forward island.

Alan asked, "Have you heard anything about the newer fighters coming along? I hear that Grumman is working on the new XF-Six-F Hellcat and hopes to fly it in a few months. They got behind because they spent so much time on that odd two engine XF-Five-F Skyrocket. The Hellcat has a single R-Twenty-Eight-Hundred."

"We've heard that too. It'll be a big improvement on the Wildcat, with much more power and should still have nice handling. The Vought Corsair sounds more exciting, but they're still trying to get all the wrinkles out of it, even though it's about to start production. I think the Vought design has superior performance, even though it's a lot older. I guess that by leaping ahead with a radical new design, which Grumman never does, Vought ended up with a lot of problems to iron out."

"Yeah, I agree. That North American Mustang ordered by the British looks like a nice design, and I think they're about ready to try it out in combat. I know the US Navy doesn't want a liquid cooled engine, but I'm surprised the US Army isn't more interested in it."

"That's right, it's very promising, but it needs a better supercharger to fight at altitude."

"Yeah, that's true."

They continued filling each other in on everything that had happened in their lives since Pensacola. Wade said he was very fond of the Wildcat and was very comfortable with the narrow landing gear and hand crank. Meanwhile, the twelve airplanes to go to *Yorktown* were spotted aft, and the rest were struck below. The six Wildcats were in front and then the Dauntlesses, with the one Devastator in the last row.

Suddenly the bullhorn barked, "*Yorktown* pilots, stand by to man your planes."

Alan said good-bye to Wade and then joined the group of *Yorktown* pilots gathering next to the island. Armiston soon appeared. "There is no assignment of planes, so take any one of the Dauntlesses, Ericsson."

"Yes, sir."

"*Yorktown* pilots, man your planes," came from the bullhorn. Alan walked aft, following Armiston, and he and Alan climbed into the first two Dauntlesses. Everything in Alan's Dauntless looked a little less worn than in 5-B-12, so apparently it was newer. Soon they took off, following the last Wildcat in an elongated circuit to the left. Suddenly Alan noticed that this Wildcat had started descending. He was dismayed to see it turn into the wind and ditch in the sea. He hoped the pilot was OK. Apparently the engine lost power. *Maybe Fighting Three did not pick their best Wildcats to give to Fighting Forty-Two*, he thought. He scanned his own engine instruments. Everything was normal, and he continued into the landing pattern. Soon he and Armiston had landed back aboard *Yorktown*.

Later Alan asked the Fighting Forty-Two engineering officer if he knew anything about the ditching. He told Alan that the engine lost power, but they did not know why yet.

CHAPTER ELEVEN

Lonely Vigil

Wednesday, April 1, 1942

Task Force Seventeen had been watching the Coral Sea now for two weeks, staying out of the northern part, where it would be within the range of search planes from Rabaul. For its own search needs, TF-17 relied on Anzac planes. Most were land planes, including some US Army planes, operating out of north-east Australia. There were also Australian land planes from Port Moresby in New Guinea and Australian flying boats from Tulagi in the southeastern Solomon Islands. This tactic allowed the task force to remain hidden.

The task force had been at sea for six weeks, and after four weeks the food had become much less appealing, as Alan had been told it would. The fresh food had long since disappeared. There had been a plan to provision the ships at Noumea, on the south end of New Caledonia, that day, but that had been abruptly canceled without explanation.

Alan gathered TF-17 was being kept in the southwest Pacific because the other carriers were occupied elsewhere. *Saratoga* was in the middle of her repairs in Bremerton, Washington, and

Lexington was undergoing refit at Pearl Harbor. *Enterprise* had completed her raids in the central Pacific some time ago. The scuttlebutt said *Hornet* had arrived in the Pacific, returning the US carrier strength facing the Japanese to four. It seemed that *Enterprise* and *Hornet* were available to help out in the southwest, but they must be doing something else. The scuttlebutt had a variety of conflicting explanations, indicating nobody knew anything.

There had been a few notable events. All five of the long lost Seagull observation planes had been discovered by the Australians at Rossel Island in the Louisiade Islands off the eastern tip of New Guinea. The heavy cruiser *Astoria* had gone and picked them all up a few days earlier, little the worse for wear.

This day another Wildcat had a sudden loss of engine power and had to ditch. The pilot's face was badly cut when he banged into the jury rigged gun sight in the ditching. Alan wondered again why the navy was not moving to install shoulder harnesses.

It was announced that the task force would be refueling from *Platte*, one of the fast oilers, the following day. Before refueling each ship, she would be delivering mail and accepting mail as well. He would have to write a letter to Jennifer before finding out if he got anything from her. When Alan went off duty, he wrote a letter to Jennifer, and dropped it off for the censors and the mail before going to supper.

> *c/o Fleet Post Office*
> *San Francisco, Calif.*
> *April 1, 1942*

Dear Jennifer,

Happy April Fool's Day! I am finishing this letter in hopes that it will be picked up shortly by a visiting ship, which might also have a letter from you.

I had a big scare on our last mission, which I will tell you about when I see you.

The problem I told you about is still with us, with the same effect, so we need to get it fixed soon.

I had a chance to visit another ship like ours and was able to talk with two classmates from school in Florida. They had interesting news, including that they have been experiencing the same problem I mentioned.

I hope you are finding more friends and enjoying your work. I am fine and have had no more mishaps.

I love you, Jennifer, and miss you every day.

Tons of love,
Alan

Alan thought the censors would be satisfied, and it was a very short letter.

Thursday, April 2, 1942

In the late afternoon, Alan spotted *Platte* coming up from astern. By now *Yorktown* had refueled underway many times, and it had become a smooth operation unless the seas were quite rough. When *Platte* had gotten into position alongside *Yorktown* around 1600, Alan noticed that a big parcel came across to *Yorktown* first. Maybe it included the mail.

When Alan returned to his stateroom after supper, he found not only a letter, but also a small package, from Jennifer. In addition there was a note from Hank Stinson.

He picked up the package first. It was postmarked December 5, 1941. It must be her Christmas present, which had been chasing him almost halfway around the world for four months. He found it was a beautifully made gold tie clip in the shape of a two bladed airplane propeller. Although Alan usually preferred silver, only gold could be worn with his uniforms, a very thoughtful gift. He thought of his present to her, a silver necklace, and he hoped she would get it soon.

He turned to her letter.

Honolulu, T. H.
March 11, 1942

Dear Alan,

It's been three weeks since you left, and I miss you very much already.

You should have recently had some excitement, and I held off writing to get what news I could. I hope everything went well.

I continue to work long hours, but it is not so difficult when working with such a dedicated group. It is starting to get hot here, so I am swimming more, sometimes with friends. My car is working out well, and it does come in handy.

The way things are going I imagine you won't be back here for a while. Please be very careful and come back in one piece.

That is about all I can say at the moment. I love you very much, and I miss you a lot.

Oodles of love,
Jennifer

Hers was a short letter also, although it contained a tantalizing hint about the future.

He picked up Stinson's note. It suggested meeting in the gallery at 2000, as Alan had hoped. They had met once right after the Salamaua raid. Alan had confessed his tantrum over the fuel filter, and Stinson had been surprised but knew how important engineering was to Alan. Since then Stinson had appeared to be very busy, although things were quiet around the task force. Not wanting to badger him, Alan had waited for him to suggest a meeting.

They greeted each other in the gallery, and Alan remarked, "You seem very busy."

"I have been. Hopefully that will end now, because *Platte* brought back the regular flag secretary. He's fully recovered, and he will help a lot, because he knows the admiral well. The Japanese have gone ahead and consolidated their base at Rabaul and their foothold in New Guinea, but they haven't gone beyond that. They should have forces available for their next move after finishing up in Java. Perhaps our appearance at Salamaua and Lae did set them back a bit. They could be a little short of transport."

"So we're watching nervously."

"Exactly—TF-Seventeen in particular. *Lexington* had to go in for refit, but nobody's telling us why *Enterprise* or *Hornet* couldn't relieve us. Of course, we can't ask. Could be that *Hornet* is still a little too inexperienced to go out by herself," he said, smiling at the metaphor. "They had to cut short her shakedown to bring her out to the Pacific."

"I've been wondering about that too." *With* Hornet's *shakedown cruise cut short, a green crew and air group, and only her voyage to the Pacific as further experience, her combat effectiveness has to be much less than that of the other three carriers in the Pacific,* Alan thought.

"We're depending on Anzac for reconnaissance, but the coverage varies unpredictably from day to day, and it's not always reliable about ship types. The biggest problem is that their reports seldom reach TF-Seventeen within twenty-four hours, often longer."

"I bet that makes everyone nervous."

"It does. As you know, out here we're directly under King, not Nimitz. King's been getting even more abrasive than usual. He's very anxious to stop the Japanese in this area, to keep them from interfering with our traffic to Australia. Reading between the lines, I'm guessing our carriers may be spread pretty thin, and it's making him nervous and testy."

"How's he been more abrasive?"

"The worst was a couple of days ago. With no Japanese moves toward the south, Admiral Fletcher thought this would be a good time to go into Noumea for provisions, and he notified the brass. Then he got a message from King saying, quote, your message not understood if it means you are retiring from enemy vicinity in order to provision, unquote."

"Jesus! What a slap in the face!"

"The admiral didn't take it that way. He's pretty hard to perturb. It turned out that King's message was probably based on two erroneous reconnaissance reports that were later corrected, but the corrections had not reached Washington at the time. The first one said that Rabaul was full of shipping, which I am sure alarmed King. The other reported TF-Seventeen within two hundred fifty miles of Rabaul, so King thought we were close to striking range. It is likely the reconnaissance mistook some Jap ships for our task force, which is pretty sloppy work, most likely US Army. King sent a much more conciliatory message the next day, so I guess he was at least somewhat satisfied. He wants aggressive action, but he wants us to attack only definite ship targets. In short, he's hard to please. The admiral's staff is looking at a possible raid."

"Very interesting. It fits with King's reputation."

"Yeah, it does. He also tends to forget how slow the communications are here. Besides our reconnaissance being stale, our messages to Washington have to be sent ashore for transmission and then it can take another twenty-four hours for them to get there. It's frustrating at times."

"I bet."

"Now he says not to provision in Noumea; it's too exposed. MacArthur arrived in Australia on March seventeenth, and he's busy trying to set up a new empire. I imagine he is jousting with King, with some help from Marshall, about where the boundary between his empire and the navy is going to be. Apparently he has successfully wooed the Australian government. King ruled out our going to Sidney for provisions, apparently because he's afraid we might get hijacked by MacArthur, with the help of the Australians."

"It's wonderful how smoothly the army works with the navy," Alan said with a grin.

Stinson laughed. "At King's request, Nimitz sent instructions yesterday to all his subordinates, including Fletcher, to read an article by Charles Kettering, the VP of research at GM, in the latest *Saturday Evening Post* with the title, 'There Is Only One Mistake, to Do Nothing.' It will be a while before we see that magazine, but we gather the article validates King's strategy of keeping up raids, even if some mistakes are made. Apparently even the imperious King welcomes support wherever he can find it."

"Wonders will never cease."

"King wants us to go to Tongatabu, but not right away. So Fletcher has sent all the supply vessels there. It's certainly farther from the enemy than Noumea, but it's also a long way there and back. The admiral's staff figures we'll have to be there by the twenty-fourth at the latest."

"The menu should be very short by then."

"Yeah. Any news from the air group?"

"Not much. There is one thing I might mention that could eventually turn out to be a serious problem. A few of the Wildcats have developed leaky fuel tanks, and the two they sent to *Lexington* had that problem. The airplanes with leaky tanks show more dirt when the mechanics drain out a small amount of fuel to check for dirt and water before each flight. So there is a suspicion that the bulletproof rubber bladders inside the tanks are deteriorating from the inside. The Fighting Forty-Two pilots that went to *Lexington* reported that Fighting Three had been experiencing the same problem, but they had selected airplanes with no history of that to go to *Yorktown*. Even so, one had to ditch right away, as you probably know. And yesterday there was another unexplained loss of power in a Wildcat, which caused a ditching. The particles from the bladder could have clogged the fuel system. If the bladders are defective, then the problem could grow, and we might be faced with a dangerous loss of fighter strength."

"I see. Thanks for the heads up, Alan. I don't want to be an alarmist, so I'll keep this to myself for the moment. Please keep me informed."

"Sure thing, Hank."

Monday, April 13, 1942

Task Force Seventeen had continued its monotonous vigil in the Coral Sea for another eleven days, punctuated by refueling days. When *Yorktown* was refueled, Alan usually had a moment to look out from the starboard side of the hangar and watch the operation. The usual watery tumult developed between the ships, and salty spray even came into the hangar sometimes. The weather remained hot and sultry, with occasional thunderstorms. Alan was glad he was spending a lot of time on the hangar deck.

The combination of shade and the breeze coming in the sides made it one of the coolest places on the ship.

Even powdered eggs had run out before Easter arrived. One pleasant distraction was a jamboree held on board *Yorktown* on April 10. Although Alan was not religious, he admired the chaplain for coming up with the idea and pushing it through. *The chaplain definitely has an understanding of morale.* A raffle was held for the last five T-bone steaks on board. The steaks were paraded down the flight deck, escorted by armed marines. A party was held on the hangar deck, with the ship's band playing lively music on the midships elevator. A sailor dressed as a waitress served the steaks up to the lucky winners. Now the scuttlebutt was that the ship was finally headed for port and supplies.

Dancing on *Yorktown*'s midships elevator, April 10, 1942
(US Navy/PD-USGOV-MILITARY-NAVY)

During the previous week, the ship's newspaper had described a rampage by the Japanese Navy in the Indian Ocean. Several carriers attacked Ceylon and the east coast of India, while cruisers sank shipping in the Bay of Bengal. The British lost a small carrier at Ceylon, but most of their navy had withdrawn to East Africa. This diversion explained why the Japanese had not started an offensive in the southwest Pacific. Alan felt that any delay tended to work to the advantage of the United States, which was rapidly building its defenses. *But we can expect big trouble somewhere when they've had a chance to get back and refit, say in about two weeks, the beginning of May.*

The ship's newspaper also reported the fall of Bataan in the Philippines on April 9. The tiny island of Corregidor in Manila harbor still held out, but to what purpose? Alan thought the battle had been lost on December 8, and all the fighting since then had accomplished little.

Alan had noticed that many of the Bombing Five pilots were now doing their own preflight inspections, and Slack had given up protesting when they did. He thought that the skipper and the exec were probably becoming more aware of the shortcuts being taken by the engineering department and resulting risks. Alan continued to carefully conceal his own inspections of his airplane.

It was 1930 on another hot evening, and there was speculation that there would be a search the next day. Alan knew that Slack seldom appeared on the hangar deck after 1800. Alan was starting his preflight inspection, and he remembered feeling a slight vibration in the control stick on his last flight. He reached into the cockpit and moved the stick forward and back. There was a slight grating noise coming from the tail.

He got a screwdriver and removed several inspection plates on the tail cone under the horizontal stabilizer. He could see that the plates had been painted over since the last time they were removed for an inspection. Alan knew from his time as assistant engineering officer that the plates were supposed to be removed during the routine inspection that was done every 100 hours of operating time. He thought back to when his airplane had last been repainted. It was in January, when various changes were made in response to the poor recognition during and after the Pearl Harbor raid. The airplane must have accumulated much more than 100 hours since then, and Alan remembered that Klein had said a 100 hour inspection would be done on his airplane shortly after the Salamaua raid. Probably the inspection had been done, but they had skipped inspection of the area inside the tail cone.

He got a flashlight and looked inside the tail cone at the elevator control cable and crank. He found a wire for the light on the tail had come loose, and the elevator control was rubbing on it, causing the noise and vibration. Not a big problem, easily fixed. He continued to carefully examine everything he could see inside the tail cone. Then he noticed that a crack had started at the base of the elevator crank arm and had lengthened to about a third of the width of the crank. The crank was very close to failing, causing a complete loss of elevator control and making Alan and his gunner passengers in an out of control airplane!

He left everything as it was and went to look for the exec. He found Jerry West in his stateroom, which was a single, a perk of being the exec.

"May I have a word with you, sir?"

"Sure, Alan, close the door and have a seat."

"Sir, I plead guilty to disobeying your order to do only gunnery business on the hangar deck. I have continued to do my own preflight inspections. Just now I was doing that." Alan explained what he had found and that the paint showed the inspection of the tail cone had been skipped.

"OK, Alan, let's go to the hangar deck and you show me."

There West immediately grasped the significance of what he was looking at. "This is really bad. This area is included in the inspection for good reason. Let's go to my office."

On the way, they each got a Coke and then sat down with them in the exec's office.

"Well, Alan, I owe you an apology. Although it is never acceptable to lose your temper with a senior officer, I now believe you were completely correct in recommending that Slack be relieved, and in continuing to do your own inspections. I know that many of the pilots are doing their own inspections now also. Those inspections have turned up a number of other indications of rushed and sloppy work in engineering, but I think what you found tonight takes the cake. I am very glad you came straight to me with this, even though you probably thought there was still a chance I still might disagree with you.

"The skipper and I talked about this yesterday, and we decided that if there were any further indications of trouble in engineering, Slack would be relieved. Then we considered who might relieve Slack. We agreed that you were the best man for the job," he said with a smile.

"Thank you very much, sir."

"Do you think Ensign Goodwin should stay on as assistant engineering officer?"

"Yes, sir. I think he has done an excellent job under the circumstances."

"OK, good." West reached for the telephone. "Hello, Skipper—West here. Could you come to my office? Ericsson is here, and I think the time has come for a change in engineering." He paused for the reply and hung up the phone. "He's on his way."

Armiston listened to Alan's description of what he found with his plane, which was confirmed by West. He had no hesitation about approving Alan's relief of Slack. "OK, Alan, get a good night's sleep; I am sure you will be a busy man tomorrow. We'll have a briefing right after flight quarters and announce the changes. Now you are dismissed while Jerry and I figure out where to put Slack and who will relieve you in gunnery."

As Alan left the office, his watch said 2030, so he decided to turn in. Tomorrow would likely be tiring, just as the skipper said. As he walked back to his room, he thought, *Better late than never*, but it probably would have happened sooner if he hadn't been so stupid as to lose his temper. As he was getting ready to hit the sack, Jolly came in. Alan described what had happened.

"I hate to admit it, but I too realize that you were right all along, and I'm sorry I tried to get you to drop it."

"Thanks, Jolly. But you were absolutely right about losing my temper. It delayed getting a change in engineering, and I regret it very much."

"I guess we both learned a lesson."

Tuesday, April 14, 1942

The briefing on the changes in squadron officer positions was held as planned right after flight quarters. Alan was the new engineering officer, Teeth Jensen was the new gunnery officer, Slick Davis was the new navigation officer, and Percy Slack relieved Davis as communications officer. There was an undercurrent of approval in the room, with grins briefly appearing. Alan noticed that Slack remained impassive at the announcement of what was generally perceived as a demotion for him, so probably he had been alerted to the changes ahead of time. *He probably has come to realize that he was out of his depth in engineering and would be better off elsewhere.* Slack continued his policy of ignoring Alan and avoiding eye contact.

As soon as the pilots were dismissed from the briefing, Alan and Phil Goodwin headed for the hangar deck. Phil mentioned along the way that he had heard about the mechanics celebrating Alan's ruckus over the filter incident, and he thought they would like the new engineering officer. Alan told Phil that he thought Phil had been doing an excellent job as assistant engineering officer under difficult circumstances.

As Alan and Phil walked in, the Bombing Five mechanics stopped work immediately. Somehow they already had heard about the new engineering officer. They gathered, and Alan made the formal announcement. There was a spontaneous round of applause, which was highly irregular, but Alan showed his pleasure with a smile.

"Thank you. OK, men, we've got a lot of leeway to make up, as you know. Ensign Goodwin and I are going to draw up a schedule right away of how to do that. I am sure that we'll all be very busy, but we're not going to skip over anything or cut any corners. Carry on."

The men smiled and went back to work, with cheerful comments and jokes showing their new mood. In a couple of hours, the new schedule was ready. It was ambitious, calling for catching up in a week. Alan called a meeting of the plane captains, and went over the schedule to get their view on whether it was feasible.

Several captains expressed doubts.

Alan suggested, "I have a feeling that around a week from now we might finally get into port for replenishment and rest. I think we would all be happier if we could get caught up around that time, so we can relax."

The men were aware that Alan was a friend of the flag lieutenant, and he could have inside information about going into port.

Chief Patterson said with a smile, "In that case, sir, I think we should do our best to get it done by then."

There were nods and smiles of agreement among the captains.

"OK, let's get at it," said Alan.

Klein was working on 5-B-12, which had top priority because it was grounded. An hour later, Alan was busy explaining something to two mechanics starting an overdue inspection. As he finished, Klein deftly inserted himself in front of Alan.

"I thought you might like to see this, sir," he said, holding out the cracked elevator crank from 5-B-12. "And compare it to this"—now holding out in his other hand the new replacement crank, with its identification tag.

Alan looked closely at the new crank and then back at the old one. He saw that the crank had been redesigned to be much sturdier. "The Douglas guys knew there was a problem with the old crank, and they fixed it. Thanks for showing me, Klein."

Klein grinned and went back to work.

Wednesday, April 15, 1942

Being on the hangar deck every day, Alan was well aware that the problem with the leaky fuel tanks in the Wildcats had been getting worse. Over a third of them were grounded. At least

Fighting Forty-Two's engineering department had come up with an explanation. The aviation gasoline now coming to the fleet had a chemical content that was slightly different from previous supplies, and it was slowly dissolving the self-sealing rubber bladders. Improved bladders were available at Pearl Harbor. Alan found he was getting to know the Fighting Forty-Two engineering officer, whom he held in high respect.

Alan knew that news of this deficiency had been passed up through channels, but he was not certain that it had gotten all the way up to Fletcher, as it should. He put a note in Hank Stinson's stateroom, asking for a meeting at 2100, since he would be working late in the hangar, and Hank accepted at supper.

Alan greeted Hank as his tall figure approached along the gallery. Alan asked, "Is the admiral fully informed on the Wildcat fuel tank problem? A third of them are grounded, and the trend is for it to get worse."

"He is, but thanks for checking, Alan. Buckthorn told the admiral about it on April tenth, and the admiral sent a message on to Nimitz. Yesterday the admiral sent a message to Nimitz saying he would have to go to Tongatabu right away if it got any worse, and to send replacement tank bladders there."

"Good."

"There's more news. Today the admiral got a message that crossed his to Nimitz, saying he is back under Nimitz's orders, effective immediately—a relief to all. The Joint Chiefs finally settled the boundary between MacArthur and the navy as running roughly north and south and going between the New Hebrides and the Solomons. So New Zealand is in the navy area, which is why King offered Auckland for provisioning, even though it's farther from the Coral Sea than Sidney. Nimitz is temporarily in command of the southwest Pacific area until the arrival of Admiral Ghormley, the new southwest Pacific commander."

"All very interesting. So most of the Coral Sea is in MacArthur's fief."

"Yes, but for the time being, MacArthur has no navy and needs us to defend it just as much as King does. So there's no conflict."

"I see."

"Nimitz also told Fletcher to head for Tongatabu, so that's where we're going, arriving on the twentieth. Today the admiral repeated his request by radio for the replacement fuel tank bladders for the Wildcats to be sent to Tongatabu and got a reply right away that they are on their way to Suva, where a destroyer can pick them up."

"That's good news. Well, everyone will be glad to hear we're headed for port at last. After that we should be in better shape to meet the enemy. How long will we be there?"

"I would guess about a week. I expect Buckthorn will announce that we're going there any time now."

"Also there are starting to be signs that the Japanese are getting ready for an offensive down here. It's got everybody jumpy. On April eleventh, Anzac told the admiral there was a carrier at Rabaul. The army bombed Rabaul the next day and claimed damage to what they called the *Kaga*. You have to give the army aircrews credit for their long flights over enemy territory, but their record on ship identification is pretty poor. You know they mistook Japanese ships for our task force, which is why King thought we were near Rabaul that time. After they bombed Rabaul, this possible carrier was last seen headed northwest at high speed. Some of our staff think it was an aircraft transport bringing planes to Rabaul."

"Sounds logical. Now, you remember I lost my temper with our engineering officer?"

Stinson nodded.

"Well, the skipper and the exec eventually saw the light, and yesterday they had me relieve him."

"You probably feel better about the whole thing, but I bet a lot of overdue work just fell in your lap."

"You're right. That's why I couldn't meet until later than usual," Alan said with a smile.

As he walked back to his stateroom, Alan's thoughts returned to what Stinson had said about a Japanese offensive coming their way. *Earlier today I was thinking about the Japanese being prepared to cause big trouble somewhere around the beginning of May. Now it looks like that big trouble is going to be around here.* The thought gave him a cold feeling in the pit of his stomach.

Sunday, April 19, 1942

During the day, word spread through the ship that American aircraft had bombed Tokyo the previous day. Everyone was astounded, Alan included. How did they get there? It seemed very unlikely that they had been allowed to use a Russian base, and most of China was occupied by Japan. If they came from a carrier, how had they gotten within the range without being detected? If it couldn't be done at Rabaul, how could it possibly be done at Tokyo? The ship's newspaper reported that Roosevelt said the planes came from Shangri-La, the fictional secret paradise from the popular novel *Lost Horizon*. It was all very mysterious. Alan could not resist the temptation to ask Hank Stinson if he would be willing to shed any light on it.

When they met in the port gallery aft, Alan asked, "I have no need to know, but can you tell me anything about the Tokyo raid?"

Stinson laughed. "Baird, the officer from the Combat Intelligence Unit, really came out of his shell, bursting out of the radio room, shouting the news. He was listening in to their radio traffic after the raid. It really stirred up a hornets' nest." He paused and said, "About all I can tell you about the raid itself is what the Japanese already know. The raid was executed by B-Twenty-Fives, which came from the east and departed to the west."

"They flew B-Twenty-Fives off a carrier?" Alan asked, inadvertently raising voice. He knew the B-25 didn't have nearly enough range to get to Tokyo from any US held territory to the east. They could replace some of the bombs with a bomb bay fuel tank, but even that wouldn't do it.

Stinson put his finger to his lips.

Acutely embarrassed by his outburst, Alan knew that more questions would be very much out of order. He simply said quietly, "Sorry." *Even if they could get off a carrier, the B-25s would never be able to land back aboard. That was why they continued west to the mainland,* he thought. *I wonder how they're going to stay out of Japanese hands in occupied China or Korea.*

Stinson changed the subject. "I think we're going to get some help down here, but I can't say more. I gather King even suggested to Nimitz that he send Task Force One, the old battleships, down here. Nimitz balked, knowing the slow, vulnerable battleships are worse than useless down here, using up huge amounts of precious fuel. There have also been some more annoying messages from King. Today he suggested to Nimitz that we provision at Noumea—do you believe it? He's denied all Nimitz's requests that we do so, and then, when it's far too late to change, he says go ahead."

"Rank hath its privileges," said Alan.

Alan and Hank said goodnight, and Alan headed for the wardroom. His mind was abuzz, thinking about the Tokyo raid. In the wardroom he spotted Jolly reading and took a seat next to him. Alan usually talked to Jolly about interesting things he had heard from Stinson. He knew that Jolly also enjoyed having this source information and thus he could count on Jolly to be discreet.

Jolly seemed to sense that Alan wanted to talk and he put down his book.

Alan began. "I hear it was B-twenty fives they sent over Tokyo. Apparently they came from the east and departed to the west."

Jolly's eyebrows went up. "Very interesting. Hmm. I suppose they might have been able to get to the mainland, but there would be a big risk of capture, since it's occupied. And if they came from the east they must have come from a carrier."

"I think the wing loading of the B-twenty-five is up in the mid forties. That seems awfully high to operate off a carrier."

"What about the F-four-U? I think it's getting up there."

Alan replied, "I think you're right. Maybe that's why it's taking so long to get them into the fleet. So which carrier was it?"

Jolly squinted in thought. "I don't think *Lex* got back to Pearl in time to replenish and go on this raid. And we've been wondering why *Enterprise* and *Hornet* haven't come down to relieve us. It must have been one of them."

"You know, the B-twenty-five is much too big to fit on an elevator. So they must have been carried on deck, making the carrier defenseless. So they would want that carrier to be escorted by another carrier."

Jolly grinned. "Good thinking. So both *Enterprise* and *Hornet* went. They would put the B-twenty-fives on *Hornet* to have the experienced *Enterprise* for defense."

Alan grinned too. This was the kind of discussion he used to have with Jennifer, and he was grateful that Jolly enjoyed it as much as he did. "Yup, that's right. That means they won't be back at Pearl much before the end of the month. Then they can't get down here by early May, in time to help us if the Japanese mount an offensive then, unless they come here without stopping at Pearl, which might be a tall order."

"In that case it'll be *Lex* that comes back to help us."

"King must have at least approved this raid, if he didn't initiate it, and that would have been quite a while ago. Now that he is so concerned about the connection to Australia, he may be wishing he hadn't sent half his carrier strength off on publicity stunt. Maybe that's why he's been so testy."

"Yeah. Roosevelt must have approved it too. Maybe he put pressure on King."

"True. That would also make King testy."

Jolly chuckled. "I think we're in danger of starting to feel sorry for King."

"Oh no, not that," Alan replied, laughing.

CHAPTER TWELVE

Tongatabu

Monday, April 20, 1942

Alan visited the bow of the ship to look around as usual at 0545, after flight quarters. The air group had been briefed that the task force would reach Tongatabu that morning, and two Scouting Five Dauntlesses and two Devastators would check out the airstrip there. They were taking off as he reached the bow. It was a crystal clear day with a few cumulus clouds. Everyone on *Yorktown* was looking forward eagerly to a brief period of rest and relaxation in a beautiful tropical setting.

The Bombing Five engineering department was only about a day short of catching up with the maintenance backlog, so they would not miss much of the shore opportunities.

Alan got to the hangar deck at 0630. He soon noticed that two Wildcats were being spotted on the hangar deck catapults, which ran athwartships at the forward end of the hangar. The catapults enabled aircraft to be launched while the ship was in harbor. The Wildcats would be useful in the unlikely event that any Japanese aircraft showed up.

Around 1000, the task force turned out of the easterly trade wind toward the south, to feel its way through the channel into Nukualofa Roads at Tongatabu Island. Considerable maneuvering was necessary to get into a line astern formation to navigate the narrow channel. The trade wind, now coming from the port side, blew through the open sides of the hangar right across the hangar deck, a very pleasant change in the tropical heat. This island was in the Tonga group, about 500 miles south-southwest of Samoa, 400 miles southeast of Fiji, and only about 100 miles north of the Tropic of Capricorn. The atlas in the ship's library said that it was about where Melanesia ran into Polynesia. Alan had been studying the crude map of the Tonga group issued to Bombing Five. Tongatabu was not an atoll but was a triangular island, about fifteen miles east to west and about ten miles north to south. The harbor, Nukualofa Roads, was on the north side of the island. Ten miles off to the southeast there was another populated island about one third as big, called 'Eua, and many small islands were in two lines to the north, with the channel in between. The islands were a British Commonwealth protectorate, with their own monarchy.

Yorktown dropped her anchor shortly after noon. Alan was surprised to see that Nukualofa was a not a small village but a real town. The sailors aboard *Yorktown* gazed longingly at the shore, expecting to see the sort of idyllic south Pacific island romantically described in many stories they had heard. Binoculars were focused in hopes of catching a glimpse of beguiling South Seas maidens, but none were seen. Later the word circulated that the queen had hidden them to protect them from the sudden onslaught of young males starved for female company.

Already in the harbor were the provision ship *Bridge*, the repair ship *Dobbin*, and the hospital ship *Solace*. Word soon circulated that *Bridge* carried mail, as well as fresh food.

When Alan left the hangar in the late afternoon, he went to his stateroom and found a letter from Jennifer.

Honolulu, T. H.
April 6, 1942

Dear Alan,

We are very lucky that we get to see each other occasionally, but I still miss you very much.

You are probably bored, and your food is probably not so good now. I have the impression both will change. Please be careful and don't take any unnecessary risks.

I am fine. Our office is gradually learning our business, and we are starting to get more productive. There is a new sense of accomplishment.

Hopefully you will get to come back here before too long, and I look forward to it every day.

That is about all I can say right now. I love you very much.

Oodles of love,
Jennifer

She sure is on top of what Yorktown *is doing,* he thought. It was another very short letter, but it was full of fascinating hints. *Saying that the boredom will change must mean she is expecting action for* Yorktown, *which means a Japanese advance around the Coral Sea somewhere. That seems to fit in with her office being more productive, meaning they are making progress breaking that important code and reading more Japanese messages. That could turn out to be a major advantage.*

From the four intelligence officers he had gotten to know during his surface tour, Alan had learned that once even a small part of a code had been broken, diligent analysts could extract useful intelligence. Also, like the growth of a leak in a dam, once a small part had been broken, progress in breaking rest of the code accelerated.

After supper Alan wrote a short reply.

> *c/o Fleet Post Office*
> *San Francisco, Calif.*
> *April 20, 1942*

Dear Jennifer,

I just got your letter of April 6. I hope you are well and your office is continuing to make progress.

The menu on the ship got very short recently. About ten days ago, the ship's chaplain organized a party on the ship. The last five steaks were raffled off and then very ceremoniously served up to the winners on a platform on a spacious deck, with music and dancing. It was a great idea and a very nice hiatus from the boredom.

Now we are starting a real break. It will be very nice to relax a bit and get fresh food. I have a new job on board, and we have been very busy catching up with things my predecessor neglected. We have a little more to do before we can relax. I am looking forward to getting some exercise ashore. It is very pretty here, but many feel it would be much prettier if the queen had not put all the young ladies away for safe keeping. Actually I think it was a very smart move on her part.

I love you, Jennifer, and I can't wait to see you again.

> *Tons of love,*
> *Alan*

Tuesday, April 21, 1942

Late in the afternoon, the Bombing Five engineering department had finally caught up with its backlog. Anticipating the moment, Alan had commissioned Jolly to find some whiskey ashore. Jolly produced a quart of Scotch, which Alan noticed was an imperial quart, 20 percent larger than a US quart. Alan asked Chief Patterson to get the eighteen plane captains to stay after the other mechanics were dismissed. They retreated to a quiet corner, where he and Phil Goodwin served out the Scotch in generous shots. They all left the hangar in a celebratory mood.

Wednesday, April 22, 1942

It was 1330, and Alan was sitting in a launch at the ship's accommodation ladder with many of the squadron pilots, waiting to go ashore. A softball game had been organized ashore, with a cookout and beer afterward. It was a beautiful, warm sunny day, with the temperature around 85.

He asked Mike Burke, who was sitting next to him, "Where are all the newer guys, the ensigns?"

"I heard a bunch of them planning their own trip ashore. They were going to see if there is some kind of taxi for hire in town so that they might be able to cover the whole island and find out where the young women are hidden."

"Mostly the unmarried guys, I hope."

"Yeah, they were. But Bombing Five won't be able to field a great team without them."

Jolly spoke up with a chuckle: "I have a feeling that a taxi won't be much help."

Most of the other pilots in the boat were now paying attention to the conversation.

Alan grinned and said, "No doubt about it."

A voice at the other end of the launch piped up: "You know where they are?"

Another voice broke in, "Hey, how come you guys are sittin' on valuable intelligence?"

Jolly said with an impish grin, "I don't know where they are. I do know where I'd put them if I were the queen."

There were some grumbles from other end of the launch.

"No beer for Lowery," said a pilot.

"Or Ericsson either," said another.

Jolly spoke to the other end of the launch: "You know, in this part of the world, the people can get pretty angry if they think their leaders are doing a lousy job. If you were the queen and you knew you could actually get eaten for breakfast if a lot of the girls got pregnant by foreigners, what would you do?"

There was a long pause while there was a mumbled conference at the other end.

Finally one word came out, said too softly to be understood. Then it was repeated much louder, "'Eua! That big island off to the southeast."

Jolly said, "You got it. And you would put out the word that it's off limits to foreigners. No boat rides."

The mumbling at the other end of the launch took on a more satisfied tone.

The sailors operating the launch appeared, jumped in, and they got underway.

Three hours later, the softball game was over. Scouting Five beat Bombing Five, 5–3, not a bad showing while Bombing Five was missing five of its more promising players. Both were looking forward to cold beer.

Just then a battered touring car appeared. Alan didn't recognize the make, but he thought it was English. The five ensigns from Bombing Five piled out.

"Gee, sorry, guys, the beer's all gone. We didn't think you were going to show up," said Jerry West, putting on a serious face.

Their faces fell. Alan thought the five ensigns looked like they had been on a forced march with the marines. They were dusty, sunburned, and sweaty.

"Well, did you find the girls?" asked West.

"We looked everywhere. Not a sign of them."

Some sailors from the *Bridge* had gotten a grill going. Just then they gave a whistle and invited everyone to have a beer from an ice chest they had brought. Then they started cooking hot dogs and hamburgers.

Thursday, April 23, 1942

Today, Alan went to the hangar deck at 0630 to check on supplies and spare parts delivered from *Dobbin*. The replacement fuel tank bladders for the Wildcats had arrived in two batches via destroyer from Suva in the Fiji Islands. He noticed the Fighting Forty-Two engineering officers and some mechanics were starting on another tank bladder replacement.

The main tank was in the fuselage directly underneath the cockpit. The mechanics got at it from above through the cockpit by removing the pilot's seat, the control stick, and the channels for the pilot's feet. The metal tank was disconnected and removed up through the cockpit. Then it could be opened up and the fuel bladder replaced. It was a tedious job. It turned out to take twenty man hours per airplane, so the Fighting Forty-Two engineering officers and mechanics had a lot less time off than even Alan's men. Alan was grateful that the Dauntless had escaped this problem so far.

Alan had been ashore a few times and found that it was hot, but the steady trade wind and the swaying palms made for a pleasant atmosphere. He hoped he might be able to take a real break and spend more than a few hours there. He wanted to take a walk and have a swim in the ocean. Tomorrow would be the day, because he was able to get the whole day off.

In the late afternoon he went ashore to find out more about the geography. He quickly found out that his vision of a broad beach did not exist. Most of the shore of the island was rocky, and the best beaches were on the east and west coasts, which were beyond walking distance from Nukualofa. The north coast near Nukualofa was low and there were no beaches. Nukualofa was in an indentation in the north coast, so the south coast was only about six miles away, straight across the island, so a round trip on foot could be done in a day. The south coast was high, but there were a few places where it was possible to climb down to small beaches. There was a reef a hundred yards offshore with heavy surf, with tidal flats behind it. Some swimming was possible on the flats at high tide. He was able to get detailed directions to one of these beaches.

He planned to walk across the island to the south shore, take a swim in the ocean, and return. He talked to Teeth, who also had the day off, and persuaded him to come along. He bribed a mess attendant with a few bottles of beer from on shore to pack lunches for them. Teeth had a look at a tide table in the ship's navigation office, and found that high tide would be at 1210.

Friday, April 24, 1942

They had an early breakfast and got ashore at 0745 on a beautiful day with just a few puffy cumulus clouds. They bought straw hats to ward off the sun at a little shop they passed. Then they started south-southwest on a main road, and the pavement ended at the edge of the town. The terrain was nearly flat and the walking was easy. After about a mile, Fanga 'ula Lagoon, a large, shallow inlet in the center of the island, was visible through mangroves on their left. They were already sweating, and the trade wind off the lagoon felt very pleasant. On their right large fields had been cleared and cultivated. A few houses showed signs of local architecture, with wooden porches and steep roofs, but most were plain European style structures with metal roofs. Continuing to follow the directions, they passed through a small village, apparently populated with farm workers, and then came more farming country.

At about 1045 they were overlooking the beach from a bluff about a hundred feet above. Here the rich dark volcanic topsoil gave way to the underlying gray coral limestone in the form of cliffs, which had been eroded into rough, pock marked shapes. They found a steep path that led down to a small white beach. They found themselves alone in a beautiful setting, with the surf pounding on the reef beyond the flat, sending up geysers of spray.

"Doesn't look like Minnesota at all," said Teeth, grinning.

"Or the New England coast either," said Alan with a smile, "We have very few reefs like this."

Quickly changing into swimming trunks, they waded into the calm azure water on the tidal flat. It was warm but refreshing. Exploring around, they found the deepest spot was only about five feet, but the were able to enjoy a good swim.

Alan spoke up, "Looks like the tide is already starting to ebb, and it's only about 1130, I think."

"The tide table was for Nukualofa. It's possible all those islands and shallows to the north hold the tide back," replied Teeth.

"That makes sense."

They ate their lunches and had one more quick dip before putting their shirts, pants, and shoes back on to limit sunburn. They climbed back up the cliff and were hot and sweaty again when they reached the top. By now the cumulus clouds had thickened to cover more than half the sky, and some were dark. Never having a chance to walk far on the ship, they began to notice some soreness as they walked back. The clouds thickened and darkened, and they found the lack of sun welcome in the heat. As they neared Nukualofa, suddenly the heavens opened in a tropical downpour. They became thoroughly soaked, but all the salt from the ocean and there own sweat was washed away by the time they reached to the pier.

As they neared the ship on the navy shuttle launch, Teeth said, "That was a great break, Alan, thanks for talking me into it."

"Glad you enjoyed it as much as I did," replied Alan.

Once on board *Yorktown*, they headed straight for their staterooms to change.

Saturday, April 25, 1942

Yorktown's stay at Tongatabu was a wonderful break in the routine. Everyone knew their departure was planned for April 27, and the task force would probably go back to playing cat and mouse in the Coral Sea, so they tried to make the most of the short respite. There was plenty of fresh food available, both ashore and on the ships.

The Fighting Forty-Two engineering department put all their mechanics to work and had gotten all the fuel tank bladders replaced in three days, making all the Wildcats airworthy again.

It no longer looked like the ship would be going to Australia, so the newspaper reporter left the ship to find another way to get there. While they were at Tongatabu, the CYAG received orders rotating him home, requiring some personnel changes in the air group. Buckthorn appointed Lieutenant Commander Oscar "Pete" Pederson, skipper of Fighting Forty-Two, to be the new air group commander. Pederson nominated his exec, Lieutenant Commander Charles Fenton, to succeed him as skipper of Fighting Forty-Two, and Buckthorn approved. This all seemed logical to most of the pilots in the air group, including Alan. However, the previous day, a Coronado flying boat sat down in the harbor. One of the passengers was Lieutenant Commander James Flatley, bearing orders to become skipper of Fighting Forty-Two. Apparently the foul up had something to do with the fact that Fighting Forty-Two was only "temporarily" assigned to *Yorktown*, while the squadron was still administratively attached to *Ranger*, CV-4, on the other side of the world. After some head scratching, Fenton was given command of the squadron, and Flatley graciously accepted the exec position for the time being. Alan had heard of Flatley, who had a reputation as a fighter tactics expert, like Jimmie Thach.

Bombing Five's skipper, Lieutenant Commander Armiston, was also rotated home. To the surprise of the Bombing Five pilots, Buckthorn appointed Lieutenant Warren Stubb, the exec of Scouting Five, to replace Armiston. Alan knew Stubb and respected him. After a conference with Armiston, Stubb decided to keep the squadron officer appointments as they were, especially since the most recent shuffle had been only a little over a week earlier.

Stubb went right to work, interviewing all the Bombing Five pilots. Alan's turn came quickly. After Stubb had introduced himself, he jumped right in. "While you were gunnery officer, you probably thought about this problem of fogging of the windshield and bombsight during the dive."

"Yes, sir. I started thinking about it right after we ran into it on the Jaluit raid, and I started work on a fix while we were at Pearl Harbor. I wrote it all up for BuAer, and there are copies of the report in the squadron office."

"Why is Bombing Five the only squadron that has this problem?"

Stubb's assumption that no other squadron has the problem shows a bias against Bombing Five. This is where the rivalry between the Scouting and Bombing squadrons could be a bad thing, Alan thought. "We're not the only squadron that has had the problem, sir. Bombing Two and Scouting Two had the same problem at Lae and Salamaua."

"How do you know that?"

"Commander Armiston and I talked to the skipper of Bombing Two, Commander Hamilton, when we went over to *Lexington* to ferry planes back before she headed back to Pearl."

Stubb's manner softened a bit. "Oh, I didn't hear anything about that from the Scouting Five pilots that went over to *Lexington*, but I didn't ask them. Scouting Five hasn't had the problem, so it probably was not on their minds. If lots of squadrons are having the problem, why hasn't it happened to Scouting Five?"

"As far as I can tell, it's because Scouting Five has happened to start their dives lower, or they have had less humid conditions, or both."

"Hmm. That could be. I'll have to think about that."

Monday, April 27, 1942

Task Force Seventeen had finished its brief rest period and departed Tongatabu. That day a Scouting Five Dauntless had to ditch, and the crew was rescued by *Walke*. There was more excitement when Fighting Forty-Two scrambled four Wildcats to chase a snooper, which turned out to be another Coronado headed for Tongatabu.

In Tongatabu the scuttlebutt had picked up word that the long awaited Japanese offensive in the Coral Sea area, including some carriers, was expected to start soon. Port Moresby seemed like the most likely objective, although a position in the Solomon Islands was also a possibility. TF-17 was headed back to the Coral Sea to oppose this move.

Tuesday, April 28, 1942

As the squadron settled back into the underway routine, Alan noticed that Slack seemed more cheerful. He still would not make eye contact with Alan, which now seemed almost like an expression of deference, rather than hostility.

Buckthorn made an announcement, confirming that their destination was the Coral Sea. He also revealed that before they got to the Coral Sea they would rendezvous with TF-11 again, now with Rear Admiral Aubrey "Jake" Fitch in command in *Lexington*. Alan remembered that Fitch was junior to Fletcher, unlike Admiral Brown, and hence Fletcher would be in command of the combined force. Alan thought of Rudi Fischer in Torpedo Two and wondered if Fighting Three, including his friend Wade Buckner, was still aboard *Lexington*.

Suddenly he was struck with the implications of meeting a Japanese carrier offensive. *This will be a big fight for our carriers, unlike all the action so far. More than a few people will get hurt*, he thought with a shudder.

Fortunately, the interlude at Tongatabu had refreshed everyone. However, Alan realized that it had been about seven weeks since the Salamaua raid, and there had been no chance for bombing or gunnery practice due to the proximity of the enemy and the need for a break at Tongatabu. They were starting to get rusty.

Wednesday, April 29, 1942

That morning Alan felt the ship slow down and saw one of the ship's launches headed toward the destroyer *Sims*, which had just rejoined the task force. The word spread fast that the destroyer had brought nine ensign replacement pilots out from Suva, of which five were dive bomber pilots for Scouting Two and Bombing Two on *Lexington*. The four new pilots for *Yorktown* were to go to Fighting Forty-Two and Torpedo Five. Alan thought, Lex *just came from Pearl, so she should have a full complement of pilots. But Bombing Five and Scouting Five are both short of pilots.*

Friday, May 1, 1942

At dawn Alan was up on the bow, watching the other ships and taking in the fresh air. Suddenly he noticed a large group of ships in the distance to the west. As the task force converged with this group, he recognized the *Lexington*'s familiar shape among them. It was TF-11, which had been expected to meet TF-17 in the afternoon. As the two task forces converged, Alan could see that the eight inch heavy guns on *Lexington* had been removed and replaced by a lot of antiaircraft guns, which were much more useful armament. Later TF-17 started to refuel from the fast oiler *Neosho*, which had joined the task force a few days earlier. Refueling had been planned for the previous day, but the seas were too rough. Today was better, but it was still slow, difficult work. As this was getting underway, Alan was surprised to see TF-11 head off to the northwest and disappear.

Alan saw Hank Stinson in the wardroom after supper, and they agreed to meet at 2000 in the gallery. Alan arrived in the gallery late at 2010.

"Greetings, Hank, sorry I'm late. The squadron was called to the ready room at nineteen thirty, and I came straight from there."

"Greetings, Alan. No problem. What was the briefing about?"

"Buckthorn transferred two of our newer pilots to Scouting Five and gave us four of the dive bomber pilots that were supposed to go to *Lexington*. So Stubb called us in to introduce the new pilots and give out assignments. The other pilot headed for *Lexington* went to Scouting Five, so Buckthorn hijacked all five of them. The other four that came out from Fiji were fighter and torpedo pilots assigned to our air group, so all the squadrons have enough pilots for a change."

"That's interesting about the new pilots. There was almost a further shuffle of a few old pilots also. Arnham told us about the orders that came through from Main Navy to clear up the mess about the command of Fighting Forty-Two. Lieutenant Commander Flatley was given command of Fighting Ten at San Diego. Buckthorn told him to go aboard *Neosho*, because she would be heading back to Pearl, with stops where he might be able to catch a Coronado. Flatley was very disappointed to be missing the expected action in the Coral Sea. He managed to talk Buckthorn out of it, and he will stay as exec of Fighting Forty-Two for the time being. There were a couple of other pilots in Scouting Five that also got orders for San Diego, and they're also staying aboard."

"Can you say anything about TF-Eleven appearing and disappearing?"

"Their appearance this morning was a surprise to everyone. Admiral Fletcher didn't like the idea of two carrier task forces refueling simultaneously in sight of each other, in case of submarine attack, so he sent TF-Eleven on ahead. We'll meet them again tomorrow."

"Admiral Fitch has his gold wings, I think."

"That's right; he is a naval aviator, not an observer. He also has a lot of aviation background, and his staff has a lot of aviators. He's a classmate and friend of Fletcher. He was embarked in *Saratoga* for the Wake relief mission, so they've worked together before."

"Is Sherman still the skipper of *Lexington*?"

"Yes, Fletcher might delegate the combined aviation command to Fitch, but Fitch will not let Sherman run the show like Brown did."

"Do you know if Fighting Three is still aboard *Lexington*? A friend from Pensacola is in that squadron."

"No, Fighting Two is back aboard."

"Oh, they used to be mostly enlisted pilots, Naval Aviation Pilots, but they were good, experienced men and I've heard most of them were grabbed by other squadrons who needed experienced guys."

"That's right. And now that you mention it, we did hear that because Fighting Two had lost most of its pilots, they had to take a lot of pilots from Fighting Three on temporary assignment, more than half of the squadron. So your friend might be among them aboard *Lexington*."

"That's interesting. I'm sure he'd be pleased to be aboard."

"Another bit of news is that the seaplane tender *Tangier* and her Catalinas at Noumea have been placed under Nimitz's command. Maybe the navy can provide better reconnaissance. At least they should be able to recognize ship types and whether they are friend or foe."

"Good news." Alan was familiar with the Consolidated PBY Catalina, a graceful but rugged two engine flying boat. The Catalina had an interesting wing position relative to the fuselage: the wing was above the top of the fuselage, connected by a pylon. This arrangement was called a parasol monoplane. Although slow, it was capable of searching out to nearly one thousand miles.

Consolidated PBY-5 Catalina, 1940
(US Navy/PD-USGOV-MILITARY-NAVY)

Saturday May 2, 1942

In the morning, TF-17 had rendezvoused again with TF-11, and with TF-44, as the Anzac Squadron had been designated. In midafternoon, a search by Scouting Five discovered a Japanese submarine only 32 miles from the task force, reporting back by message drop under radio silence, as reported by the loudspeaker. A half hour later, the carrier turned into the wind, and three Devastators were launched, armed with bombs. They found the submarine on the surface, but it dove before they could drop their bombs. Even so, the pilots thought their bombs had fallen close enough to sink the submarine. Alan kept his doubts to himself. To make sure, eleven Dauntlesses from Bombing Five, armed with depth charges, were sent to follow up, not including Alan, who was kept busy on the hangar deck. They did not find the submarine.

In the late afternoon, Alan was surprised when TF-17 sped up and departed to the west, leaving TF-11 and TF-44 behind. He heard later that TF-11 had been delayed completing its refueling, and a rendezvous had been set for the morning of May 4.

CHAPTER THIRTEEN

Over the Island to Tulagi

Sunday, May 3, 1942

On May 3, twice daily searches were mounted to the north and west, with Scouting Five and Bombing Five alternating morning and afternoon. The skipper had a preference for Parker as his gunner, so Kidd flew with Alan. He gave Kidd a review of his flying lessons. By this time Kidd was very enthusiastic about flying, and he had started to talk about trying to become a navy pilot. Kidd got back up to speed again fast, and they progressed on to turns combined with climbs and descents. As they returned to the task force, Alan noticed that *Neosho* was refueling the short legged destroyers. This time, as a sort of test, he let Kidd fly the entry into the landing pattern when they returned to *Yorktown*. Alan could tell Kidd was nervous, performing in view of everyone topside and possibly making Alan's flying look bad, but he did fine.

That evening around 1930, Alan was cooling off in the gallery. He felt the vibration of the ship's propellers speeding up. He watched as the wake grew steadily. He guessed they were doing more than 25 knots when the speed leveled off. By looking at the stars, Alan could see the ship was headed north, toward the Solomon Islands. Something was definitely afoot. He went below to the wardroom to relax and hoped to hear more about what was happening.

At 2000, Buckthorn announced over the bullhorn to the ship that TF-17 would attack the Japanese invading Tulagi, in the Solomon Islands, the following morning. Alan saw that everyone was pleased, even the stewards. It had been a long wait, almost two months.

Shortly after this announcement, another voice called for all pilots to report to their ready rooms at 2015. Alan headed for the Bombing Five ready room right away. When he got there, many of the pilots were already there. There was a buzz of conversation, speculating about the upcoming raid. There was large, crude map of the Solomon Islands taped to one of the blackboards, a map of a harbor on another, and a map of the Coral Sea on another. Alan knew the Solomon Islands were on the north side of the Coral Sea, east of New Guinea and the Bismarck Islands, but he was not familiar with the names of the islands or how they were laid out. He delighted in maps and eagerly perused these.

"As you were." Stubb's voice came from the back of the room at 2015. He strode to the lectern and put down a sheaf of papers. He looked out over the pilots and grinned. "We finally got the search report that we've been waiting two months for. The Japanese have come out to play. They're invading Tulagi Harbor, right here on the south side of Florida Island," he said, pointing to the map of the Solomon Islands.

"Our intelligence says their attack on Tulagi is probably a secondary to the main show, which hasn't started quite yet. The main show is to send an invasion force from Rabaul down around the east end of New Guinea to Port Moresby," he said, pointing out the route on the map covering the whole Coral Sea. "When that happens, several enemy carriers that are coming down from Truk will probably escort the invasion force. We will probably try to attack them and stop the invasion force before it gets to Port Moresby."

Alan noted that this intelligence included ship movements and intentions that were well beyond what could be learned from the Anzac reconnaissance. It seemed likely to Alan that the Combat Intelligence Unit at Pearl Harbor was providing at least some of the additional information. Jennifer had written that they were getting better at their work. He was proud that she was part of that group.

"Back to Tulagi, which is shown on this map. The harbor is named for this small island in the western part of the harbor, which has been the Australian district capital. There is a small town with a hospital and golf course on the island. There are also some facilities on these two smaller connected islands in the eastern part of the harbor, called Gavutu and Tanambogo, including the Australian seaplane base, which has been providing some of our reconnaissance. The Australians mostly evacuated some time ago, and they just abandoned their seaplane base today, after the Japs bombed it several times. The nearest Jap air base is at Rabaul, where they have brought in a lot of airplanes. We expect to achieve surprise. If they send planes from Rabaul because Tulagi calls for help, it will take four hours for them to get to Tulagi.

"Launch and recovery will be somewhere south of this big island, called Guadalcanal," he said pointing to the Solomon Islands map again. "We'll fly over Guadalcanal to the target, which is about twenty miles farther north. The ship is making copies of a map for each pilot. There is a front stalled south of

Guadalcanal, but the weather is supposed to be good at the target. Commander Arnham is figuring out the details of the raid now. Probably all available Bombing Five airplanes will be going. Breakfast at oh four thirty, flight quarters at oh five thirty. That is all."

Alan remembered it was late autumn in the Southern Hemisphere, so fronts could be coming farther north into the tropics, and maybe that was the source of the weather.

It sounded fairly similar to the Lae and Salamaua raid, except there were not high mountains to get over, and it had been almost two months, rather than one, since the last raid. And this time the maintenance on their airplanes was up to date.

It was another hit and run raid against probable light opposition, the third such operation for *Yorktown*. Alan knew that these raids probably disturbed Japanese operations somewhat, provided much needed practice for the air group, and involved little risk. Practice was especially needed now, when they had been idle so long. That left Alan feeling surprisingly keyed up.

It's another matter entirely, however, to stop a major Japanese advance, like an invasion of Port Moresby. It'll be a much larger and riskier operation, including combat with their carriers. If Fletcher sees such a larger operation coming, he'll want TF-11 close enough to communicate by blinker light. Under radio silence, that can't happen now until the next rendezvous, which will have to be after the Tulagi attack. Alan headed for a quick shower and his bunk.

Monday, May 4, 1942

Alan woke up at 0430, had breakfast, and was in the ready room at 0525. It had been a short night, but he had slept well. There was a copy of an old British admiralty chart on each seat. Stubb began the briefing right after flight quarters. "Thirteen from Scouting Five and twelve from Torpedo Five will take off at oh seven hundred, right after the CAP is launched. We'll be sending fifteen, kept in the hangar until the others are off." A grin flickered over his face. "In the absence of Captain Sherman, all Dauntlesses will be armed with one thousand pound bombs, and Torpedo Five will be carrying torpedoes. Captain Buckthorn has ordered the CYAG to stay behind as the FDO. Commander Burch is in overall charge, but the squadrons will proceed to the target independently, so I will lead our squadron. Enemy air opposition is expected to be very light, a few floatplanes at worst, but there could be Jap carriers within range of the ship, so all the fighters will stay behind."

Since this was the first time there was a threat of an attack from enemy carriers, Stubb reviewed radar fighter direction. The FDO remained aboard and directed the aircraft defending the task force by radio. He sat in a special compartment, watching a radar display, which gave a plan view of all the airplanes near the carrier. He tried to deploy his planes in positions and altitudes where they were best able to attack incoming enemy aircraft before they reached the task force. He and all the defending airplanes talked on the same radio frequency. Unfortunately, there was no way to distinguish enemy planes from friendly ones on the radar display. There was a new device for that purpose, called IFF gear, for "identification friend or foe." It consisted of a radio receiver in the airplane, which received the radar transmission from the ship and responded with a special code to identify the airplane as friendly. Unfortunately none of the *Yorktown* airplanes had this device yet. If strike aircraft returned to find the task force under attack, they were expected to orbit some distance away, where they would not be confused on radar with the enemy or defending fighters.

Alan felt his tension increasing. *They're taking the possibility of an attack on* Yorktown *by enemy carriers very seriously*, Alan thought. *That would be the start of a much bigger fight.*

Alan knew this was the first time in a year that Torpedo Five had carried torpedoes. It seemed ridiculous to Alan to expect pilots to perform a difficult maneuver in combat if they only practiced it once a year. It was part of the weak sister status of the torpedo bombers, which Alan thought was extremely unfair to the torpedo plane crews.

Jolly stood up and went over the flight roster. Limited to fifteen airplanes, the squadron was divided into three divisions of five. Alan was leading the second section, consisting of two airplanes, in the first division, which was led by the skipper. Jolly had told Alan that he had assigned Kidd, whose gunnery had improved steadily, to fly with Alan.

Jolly assigned AMM1c Curt Allison, who had been his gunner since they left Norfolk, to be his own gunner. Allison was a tough, wiry young man from Kentucky, and another top scorer in flexible gunnery. Alan had come to realize that Allison shared Jolly's fatalistic streak.

Slick Davis stood up and gave the navigation data. "Course zero one zero true, zero zero one magnetic, one hundred fifty miles to the target. Return course one eight five true, one seven six magnetic, one hundred forty miles. When flying over Guadalcanal, we should stay out of any showers and clouds, so we can see and avoid the mountains in the middle of the island. The height of the mountains is not known, but we think they are probably less than eight thousand feet. We may not be able to climb for the dive until we are clear of the weather and nearing the northern side of Guadalcanal. We are taking 225 gallons of fuel, in case we have to chase around the area for targets, so we will be at maximum gross weight of ten thousand four hundred pounds. Yoke Easy sector letters are posted here." Slick returned to his seat.

Alan remembered that added equipment had increased the empty weight of the Dauntless since it was originally ordered by the navy. After the SBD-3 model was introduced to the fleet in the spring of 1941, the squadrons began to experiment with increasing the fuel load and gradually worked their way up to a gross weight of 10,400 pounds, which allowed 225 gallons with the one thousand pound bomb, or full fuel with a five hundred pound bomb. Bombing Five had practiced with that load from shore, but they had never taken off from a carrier at that weight.

Then the ship's aerologist appeared, having briefed Scouting Five and Torpedo Five on the weather. He would give the weather briefing, rather than the flight officer. The ship was on the south edge of an east-west cold front with showers, which was between the ship and Guadalcanal. Near or over Guadalcanal, the showers should taper off, and there should be good weather at the target. Wind was from 110 at 15 knots. Alan realized that the weather associated with the front might be a problem for the raiders, but at least it would be daylight, unlike the Jaluit raid. The weather also would probably make it more difficult for enemy snoopers to find *Yorktown*.

The Bombing Five pilots and gunners were called to the flight deck at 0710. Alan stepped out of the island and scanned the sky. Nearby to the north, there was an overcast with showers, but clear sky could be seen to the south. There was plenty of light, and it would be easy to avoid the rain shafts. The last of the Bombing Five planes came up on the midship elevator. With only fifteen airplanes to launch, they were spotted well aft. *That is just as well, with the airplanes at maximum weight*, thought Alan.

Alan did a quick walk around inspection. Then he and Kidd got settled in the cockpits. A few minutes went by, and then Fly One gave the signal to start engines. Alan soon had his engine idling smoothly. He looked up and saw that Fly One was signaling with his flag while looking at the skipper, who would be the first to launch. Alan would be fourth, and soon he was roaring down the deck.

Alan got off with about 200 feet to spare, but he could feel the heaviness of the airplane. He reduced power to the climb setting and waited until his wingman caught up. Then he raised the gear and flaps and turned left to cut inside and catch up to Stubb's section ahead. The squadron circled until all were off and then headed north for the target at 0755. They stayed around 1,000 feet above the water, just under the overcast.

After about thirty minutes, they could see the south coast of Guadalcanal ahead. The ceiling had risen to 3,000 feet and the showers became more scattered. They could see the mountain backbone of the island as they approached, although the highest terrain toward the center of the island was in the clouds. Stubb turned slightly left to lead the squadron around the west end of the high terrain. To Alan it appeared to be another very lush green tropical island. Breaks in the jungle canopy were few and small. The overcast had become scattered clouds as they crossed the north coast of Guadalcanal, and Stubb started a climb to 11,000 feet, anticipating the dive on the target. Alan closed his canopy.

Radio calls of the planes at the target indicated that the raid was a complete surprise to the Japanese. Soon they passed beyond the clouds, and Tulagi Harbor, containing a variety of ships, came into view. They leveled off at 11,000 feet. Alan could feel thumps and bumps as Kidd swiveled his seat around to face aft, opened the rear cockpit canopy, and mounted the flexible machine gun. Alan pulled down his goggles and opened the front canopy. The air felt very cool after the tropical heat; a glance at the outside air temperature gauge showed 51 degrees.

Stubb parceled out targets to each division. Alan was fourth in Stubb's division, which attacked a cargo ship. Passing through 7,000 feet, Alan noticed the fog beginning to form again on his sight and windshield. He wiped with his rag, and he did his best, but Kidd said he missed by about thirty feet. Alan had seen that the three planes ahead of him had also missed.

As he completed his pullout, following the others in trail, Alan noticed that Stubb suddenly descended toward the water. Alan hoped Stubb and his airplane were OK. Then he saw that Stubb was chasing a small floatplane that had just taken off from the harbor. He saw Stubb's tracers stream out, and soon the floatplane flew into the water. "Bravo!" called Alan on the radio, joining others congratulating Stubb. "The skipper just bagged a floatplane, right down on the water," he told Kidd on the intercom.

The second and third divisions claimed hits on a large seaplane tender in the harbor. The squadron rendezvoused south of the harbor and started back for *Yorktown*. Stubb climbed to 3,000 feet for the return flight, clearing the west end of the mountain range on Guadalcanal. Then he descended to 1,000 feet to get under the overcast, which had hardly moved. Stubb brought the squadron neatly back to the ship, which had moved northeast as planned. As the squadron entered the landing pattern, Alan could see only Devastators parked on the deck forward. The forward elevator was in use, and apparently all the Scouting Five airplanes were already in the hangar.

The wind was gusty, and Alan carried five knots of extra speed on the final approach. He landed near the fourth wire and caught the seventh, which stopped his plane very quickly. He had made enough landings now that he was only slightly perturbed by the greater jerk, and he avoided hitting the gunsight. He stopped just short of the midships elevator, the farthest down the deck yet. As he taxied forward and parked, he could see a Devastator starting down on the forward elevator. It was 0945.

Alan had a feeling the squadron might be going out again soon, so he grabbed a cup of coffee in the wardroom and headed for the ready room. When he arrived, he saw that Stubb was there, talking to Jerry West. Jerry had landed after Alan, so he must have rushed to the ready room right away.

Stubb announced that there would be a second attack right away, with Bombing Five sending 14, as soon as the planes were rearmed. Alan would be going. Bombing Five would launch first this time and was ordered to scout the waters west of Florida Island before turning east for Tulagi. The situation had hardly changed, except for the ship's movement. Slick Davis gave the navigation data. The initial course would be 350 true, 341 magnetic, to arrive over the same point on the south coast of Guadalcanal and continue north over the west end of the island from there.

As the pilots filed out after the briefing, Stubb approached Alan. "My apologies for having doubts about the fogging problem, Ericsson. Personal experience has made me a true believer in a hurry. Give Jensen any support he might need."

"Yes, sir. Thank you, sir." He admired Stubb's willingness to admit to a junior that he had been mistaken, and his down to earth manner.

Launch started at 1045, and Bombing Five started for the target at 1100. Nearing the north coast of Guadalcanal they again climbed to 11,000 feet. They continued north and spotted the distinctive cone of tiny volcanic Savo Island to the west.

Suddenly the radio came alive with Stubb's voice, "Tallyho! Three gunboats down there, east of Savo. Each division take one, west to east." Stubb signaled for line astern and shortly went into his dive.

Shortly it was Alan's turn, and he rolled into his dive. As soon as he got settled onto the target, he could see it had been hit, but it continued moving in a tight evasive turn. He could see two Dauntlesses still in their dives, so the skipper must have gotten the hit. Maybe he didn't have the fogging problem! Even though one 1000 pound bomb should finish a vessel of that size, Alan wanted to make the most of the opportunity. The setup looked good, but with nothing but ocean in view and the sun nearly overhead, he was having trouble keeping track of the direction of the wind. There was no fogging, and he dropped at 1500 feet.

Kidd shouted over the intercom, "Very close, about ten feet off the port side!"

Close enough for certain damage, thought Alan. Considering it was a small target, and very maneuverable, that was not too bad. Alan's wingman, Ned Morris, got another close one, and as the division reformed, the ship was going down fast. Alan looked around and saw that the second gunboat had also been hit and was sinking. The third looked like it had sustained damage, but it was still underway.

Bombing Five formed up as a squadron and headed back to the carrier. During the return trip, there was a lot of chatter on the radio about Japanese floatplanes harassing the Americans attacking Tulagi. As they approached the carrier, they saw a loose formation of four Wildcats heading out toward the target, apparently to deal with the floatplanes. The returning pilots found that while the weather north of Guadalcanal had been improving, the ceiling had lowered, and there were more showers near the carrier.

Back aboard, the pilots recommended a third strike. Enough squawks had accumulated to reduce Bombing Five to nine planes. Alan remained in 5-B-12. Throughout the air group, there was sporadic trouble with the aircraft radios. Stubb's radio certainly worked on the second strike, but several others said theirs were not. Alan made a mental note to meet with his radiomen right after the raid.

The carrier had moved east since the launch for the second strike, so they flew over the east end of Guadalcanal, leaving the mountains on their left. Soon they were back near Savo Island at 11,000 feet, looking for targets. They saw a transport picking up survivors from their previous attacks. Then Stubb spotted an oil slick leading west and led the squadron that way. Soon they found a large minelayer, as they approached the Russell Islands, a group of small islands between Guadalcanal and New Georgia, the next group of large islands to the northwest. The slick indicated damage from one of the previous attacks by the other squadrons. They dove on the minelayer. To Alan's dismay, the fogging returned, and they made no hits. They landed back aboard starting at 1655, with the sun peeking between the rain shafts from low in the west.

Back in the ready room, the word circulated that, between the bad radios and the deteriorating weather south of Guadalcanal, one Devastator and two Wildcats had become lost. The Devastator had apparently ditched somewhere, and the two Wildcats had landed on the beach on the south side of Guadalcanal. This was only about 50 miles away, and Fletcher sent the destroyer *Hammann* to attempt to rescue the two Wildcat pilots. All the other aircraft had returned safely. TF-17 began to withdraw at high speed southwest toward the rendezvous with TF-11.

Morale was high aboard *Yorktown* after the raids that day. Alan had a feeling, however, that many of the damage claims were inflated, and they should have done better—at least the Dauntlesses should have done better if their sights had not fogged. *This is our third raid with little opposition and not much to show for it, albeit against mostly small targets. Nevertheless, the activity was just what the air group needed, a very full day of exercises after a long spell with no chance to practice. I'm not feeling rusty anymore.*

All the pilots recognized that this practice came at the cost of clearly revealing to the Japanese that there was an American carrier within range of Tulagi. It was hard to say what all the Japanese snooping had told them, but the raid left no doubt: the Americans were close by in force. The army search reports said there were three Japanese carriers near Bougainville, about 250 miles northwest of Guadalcanal, but these reports had a history of unreliability. If there were Japanese carriers anywhere around, they were almost certainly making plans to attack. Alan thought, *We've stirred up a hornets' nest, and now it remains to be seen if we get stung.*

CHAPTER FOURTEEN

Scratch One Flattop

Tuesday, May 5, 1942

Yorktown was back in good weather, and Alan was up on the bow when Scouting Five sent out a dawn search to the north. He started his duty on the hangar deck at 0700. There were nine airplanes with squawks, so the engineering department was busy. Fortunately, it appeared that none of the squawks would require lengthy repairs. He also checked on the radiomen. They had squawks on five radios, so almost a third of the squadron had problems. They had removed the two worst and were testing them on the radio bench. A little while later, the bullhorn reported a bogey on radar 30 miles west-southwest. Soon after that, Alan heard four Wildcats taking off on the flight deck above. Next the bullhorn announced that one of the search planes had reported a Japanese submarine, 150 miles northwest.

Alan was working on the starboard side of the hangar deck, and he was able to keep an eye out in the direction of the bogey. He didn't have long to wait; a big airplane on fire and disintegrating appeared in the distance, and the pieces plunged into the sea. The bullhorn reported the destruction of another big four engine flying boat. Then the departure of three Devastators to go after the reported submarine was announced. After hearing them take off, Alan saw that TF-11 had come into view at the rendezvous and the destroyer *Hammann* rejoined. The bullhorn reported that she had successfully rescued, through heavy surf, the two Fighting Forty-Two pilots beached at Guadalcanal. The bullhorn also reported the return of the Scouting Five search and the three Devastators, which had found nothing. TF-17 began refueling from *Neosho*, starting with *Astoria* and *Yorktown*, proceeding southeast into the wind.

That afternoon, while Alan was taking a break in the gallery, he saw Admiral Fitch arrive aboard *Yorktown* in a Dauntless. The bullhorn announced his visit for a conference with Fletcher.

In the evening Alan and Hank Stinson met in the gallery aft as usual. The task forces had turned around and headed northwest, reducing the wind over the deck to a zephyr, but it still felt cooler than below decks.

Alan started the conversation. "We've been hearing about Japanese carriers in the area. After revealing ourselves with the Tulagi raid, I wonder where they are and why they haven't hit us."

"You might be surprised to hear that the admiral's staff has been wondering about exactly the same thing. Our reconnaissance is pretty patchy. It seems possible that the Japanese are also having trouble with their reconnaissance, so we're both groping around. But it seems likely we'll find each other soon."

"I saw that Scouting Two Dauntless come in this afternoon. I happened to be taking a break in the gallery then, right near where it parked. I didn't recognize Admiral Fitch when he climbed out of the back seat. Neither did the nearest yellow shirt." Alan chuckled as he said, "The yellow shirt said to the admiral, 'Well, chief, you guys kinda missed out on some fun yesterday.'"

Hank erupted in laughter.

"Admiral Fitch laughed and said, 'Yes, son, I guess we did.' Then he pulled off his Mae West, so his two stars showed. I knew right away then who he was. The yellow shirt was stuttering apologies a mile a minute."

"That would've been great fun to see. I thought Admiral Fitch seemed to be amused about something when he arrived in flag country."

"If we do fight, is Admiral Fitch going to be in charge?"

"Of air operations, yes."

"And Sherman?"

"Well, it appears that Fitch treats Sherman like one of his staff. So Fitch will listen to Sherman."

"Two of Sherman's favorite tactics are very unpopular with the *Yorktown* Dauntless pilots and with our air group and air office as well. One is using a substantial fraction of the Dauntlesses as fighters for anti-torpedo plane defense. They would rather do without fighter escort and attack with full strength, which makes sense to me. The other unpopular idea is arming the Dauntlesses with one five hundred and two one hundred pound bombs. The one hundred pound bombs are supposed to suppress antiaircraft fire, but in fact they're too small to accomplish much. Few Dauntless squadrons are willing to make an extra dive to drop them separately. That was the prewar doctrine, but it has proven unworkable in practice. The pilots feel that one 1000 pound bomb does a lot more damage than seven hundred pounds split between smaller bombs."

"That's very interesting. I'll remember that."

Wednesday, May 6, 1942

Alan was again on the bow at dawn, watching clouds move in and a sea start to build up. It was *Lexington*'s turn for the search duty, and Alan saw twelve Dauntlesses head off to the north. They must have gone out pretty far, because they did not come back for four hours, but word soon passed that they did not find anything. The Japanese seemed to have better luck. Snoopers were seen on radar around 1000 and 1300. Both times Wildcats were sent after them but could not find them in the clouds.

While the search was out, the two task forces were merged, as they had been before the Lae and Salamaua raid. The two carriers were in the center, but now all the cruisers were inside the destroyer screen as well. The combined force, now called TF-17, headed southeast to allow fueling of the cruisers. It was slow work in the heavy sea.

In the afternoon, *Lexington* put out another search to the north and northwest, which again found nothing. A little after 1500, *Neosho* had finished fueling *Portland*. Alan soon noticed that the task force was turning around to head northwest, toward where the Japanese carriers were thought to be.

At 1600 Alan and Goodwin were supervising repairs on the last two airplanes with squawks from the Tulagi raids. Commander Arnham appeared and started talking with Teeth Jensen and the Scouting Five gunnery officer. Alan was curious and listened in on the armament orders.

"We have the search duty tomorrow, and we'll be sending ten from Bombing Five. We are also going to have a strike ready in case the search turns something up, seventeen from Scouting Five and eight from Bombing Five. No armament orders from Admiral Fitch as yet, but I doubt if he will want anything but one thousand pounders to go after ships, so we'll use them. All the strike Dauntlesses are to be armed and spotted on deck, ready for a strike at dawn, and the search airplanes will be in front. We'll start right now, so we have enough time to get it all done before our light is gone and not show any lights after dark. Carry on."

Alan knew that if ten Bombing Five airplanes were going on the search, his would be one of them, and he was disappointed not to be going on the strike. Recently Jolly had shown Alan a list of the squadron pilots and airplanes, which he had put in the order of the probability of that pilot making a hit, based on his judgment. He then gave the list to Teeth so that he could determine which airplanes would be armed for a partial strike, in the event that armament orders were received before the flight roster had been given to the pilots. Alan's name was ninth, in the middle of the list. He understood that Jolly was the flight officer and his judgment, which surely had been confirmed with Stubb and West, should not be questioned. Alan also knew that, when the squadron was split between search and strike, the exec would normally go on the search, and the skipper on the strike.

At 1730, Alan felt the throb of the ship's propellers as speed was increased to 21 knots, confirming that action was likely the next day. By then all the squawks had been taken care of, and he and Phil left the hangar. Alan went to supper via the bow and saw *Neosho* depart to the south, escorted by *Sims*. It was standard procedure to send oilers away to a safe place out of enemy search range when there was the possibility of an attack on the task force. Alan thought, *Looks like Admiral Fletcher is getting ready for action tomorrow. This is it—we are facing real aerial opposition for the first time. I hope I don't screw up.*

It was announced at supper that all pilots should report to their ready rooms at 1900. When Alan arrived, he studied the flight roster on the blackboard. He found his name assigned to the search. Stubb would lead the strike. There was a blank column where the assigned outbound headings of the search planes could be added. There was also a large chart of the northeastern part of the Coral Sea posted in front.

Stubb arrived and started the briefing. "It looks like the main event is starting. The Port Moresby invasion force is coming south from Rabaul and is expected to be traversing the Louisiade Archipelago, off the eastern tip of New Guinea, tomorrow, escorted by up to three aircraft carriers," he said, pointing to the map. "TF-Seventeen is expected to be south of Rossel Island at the east end of the Louisiades at dawn, here. Flight quarters will be at oh five hundred, when there will be a final briefing for the search. The plan for the strike will wait for the search results. That is all. You are dismissed."

Alan had been thinking about the fact that this would be the first battle in history between aircraft carriers. In his mind, the Japanese sinking of a small British carrier near Ceylon didn't count because she was helpless against five large carriers. The Japanese carrier force had a lot of experience, but they had not faced capable carrier opposition. Of course neither had the US Navy carriers. He felt the tension rising among the pilots as the likelihood of confronting enemy carrier planes sank in.

One possibility that he and Jolly had discussed was that the two sides would detect each other at about the same time. They would launch roughly simultaneous air strikes, and each would seriously damage the opposing carriers. Unlike surface combat, in carrier combat the results of an offensive strike were achieved after a delay, during which the enemy's offensive could have disabled your carriers. Thus the carriers could possibly neutralize each other, and the battle could become a surface battle, augmented with whatever land based aircraft each side had available.

After the pilots had been dismissed from the briefing and were getting up to leave, the phone rang and Stubb answered. Alan could see that Stubb was looking at Teeth Jensen, seated behind Alan. Stubb hung up and told Teeth to report right away to the air control station, something about armament. Teeth left immediately. Alan was relaxing in the wardroom about a half hour later when Teeth walked in. Teeth had a faint grin and sat down next to Alan to speak to him.

"I just had an interesting session in the air control station. Buckthorn, Arnham, and the Scouting Five gunnery officer were there. Buckthorn said Admiral Fitch wants the Scouting Five strike bombers armed with five hundred and one hundred pounders, instead of one thousand pound bombs. He wanted to know if we could help out with the changeover. I said sure."

"Sherman was insisting on getting his way."

"You bet. But by then it was pretty late. How was the change-over going to happen, with all the airplanes on deck, without showing any lights? Buckthorn turned to Arnham and told him that Admiral Fletcher suggested we should question the order, which was done, but Admiral Fitch insisted. So Buckthorn said he couldn't go against the order.

"But then Arnham shot back that arming and spotting on deck had been done in daylight to avoid showing lights after dark. Now they'd have to use lights on the flight deck to change the armament, or even to move the airplanes to the hangar deck to be rearmed. Buckthorn glared at Arnham, then stared out the window at the flight deck. Finally he turned back to Arnham and said to leave the bomb loads as they were, and he would try to explain it to Admiral Fletcher. After a pause, he added that he thought Arnham had done the right thing to begin with."

"So Sherman didn't get his way."

"Right. But we may not have heard the last of it."

Alan turned in early, but he kept wondering how he would handle real aerial combat, and sleep did not come quickly.

Thursday May 7, 1942

Alan and Jolly rose together at 0400, had breakfast, and reported to the ready room at 0450.

Stubb began the briefing right after flight quarters. "This search is of crucial importance. We think that up to three Jap carriers are likely to be either with the invasion force near the Louisiades, here, or coming down from the Bougainville area, here," he said pointing to the map. "They are likely to be within the search area. Everything depends on us finding their carriers before they find us. Report by radio in code if you find combat ships larger than destroyers. Do not attack but return immediately to the ship for a message drop to confirm." He paused. "Lieutenant Lowery."

Jolly gave the weather briefing. "The frontal weather that we passed on the way to Tulagi has followed us to the southwest and is now off to the north of us again, still moving slowly toward us. It looks like most of the search will run into it and probably need to stay low enough to be in the clear underneath."

Slick Davis stood and went to the front to give the navigation data. "We'll be sending ten single planes covering one hundred twenty degrees from three two five degrees true to oh eight five, out to two hundred fifty miles. Your outbound true headings are listed here," he said, pointing to the flight roster. He motioned to the next blackboard, saying, "The wind is one zero zero at sixteen, and the magnetic variation is eight degrees east, as shown here, correct for both. After two hundred fifty miles, turn right ninety degrees and fly twenty-six miles, then turn inbound. Yoke Easy sector letters are posted here."

Alan noticed that Teeth was assigned to the left end of the search, going out on a heading of 325 true. Since Teeth was in the search, maybe bombing results were not the only criterion. Alan himself was assigned in the middle at 025, so he would probably encounter the weather early in the flight. Slick returned to his seat.

Stubb smiled and said, "OK, launch is scheduled for oh six fifteen, a half hour before sunrise. Get busy and make a table for your three legs with corrected headings and distances. Keep a sharp eye out. That is all."

Alan plunged into correcting the headings for variation and then correcting the headings and speeds for drift due to the wind, using his E6B flight computer, a kind of specialized circular slide rule, also known as a "whiz wheel." When he finished, he looked around at the other pilots. A few were still not adept at these calculations and were getting help from their neighbors, merely copying not being useful when each pilot was assigned a different set of headings.

At 0555 the bullhorn called for the search pilots to man their planes. As Alan stepped out of the island, he saw that there was light coming from the east, off the starboard quarter. His plane was in the third row. The roar of many engines being warmed up was gradually subsiding as the plane captains shut them down. As he worked his way up close, while staying away from propellers, he could see Klein's face in the cockpit, lit by the glow of the cockpit lighting. The engine coasted to a stop, the cockpit lights went out, and Klein climbed out.

Alan climbed on the left wing next to the fuselage and greeted Klein, "Good morning, Klein. Any squawks?"

"No, sir." Klein jumped down and hurried away aft.

"Good morning, sir. Permission to come aboard, sir?" It was Kidd, standing behind the wing.

"Good morning, Kidd. Welcome aboard."

Kidd climbed up, after Klein jumped down. Alan slid his chart board under the instrument panel, put on his parachute, and climbed into the front seat. Kidd climbed in. Alan flicked on the master switch and the cockpit lights and got settled. It was 0610. Outside it was getting light enough that he would be able to see and avoid the other airplanes even without their marker lights.

Suddenly Fly One was signaling to start engines. Alan got the engine started. All the engine gauges were in the green. Then Alan felt the ship heel to port as she turned to the right into the wind for the launch.

West was in the front row and launched first. Soon it was Alan's turn. He was a little farther forward than he had ever been before for a launch. He checked that he had the landing flaps down 15 degrees for the shortest takeoff roll. Then, following the signals from Fly One, he went to full power and roared down the deck. With full fuel but no bomb load, the airplane was about five hundred pounds below normal maximum weight. He lifted off with about 100 feet to spare, still leaving room for improvement, he thought.

He turned left toward his assigned heading and raised the landing gear and the flaps. As the airplanes fanned out on their headings, he looked around and noticed that Crace's cruiser task force had taken up a course westbound, away from TF-17. *Maybe they've been sent out on a separate mission.* As he climbed, the sun came into view, although the task force was still in shadow below.

Now he could see the frontal zone ahead, and he leveled off. As the lower edge of the clouds became clearer, he gently descended back down to 1,000 feet, which allowed him to pass in and out of the bottoms of the clouds. Most of the outbound leg was uneventful. Then at 0735 Alan heard an airplane on the radio. He recognized the Morse code for West's airplane. His gunner was reporting a sighting of ships in the code they had been taught to use. It used a simple encoding device involving sliding tables.

Alan keyed the intercom to relieve Kidd's boredom. "That's West's gunner reporting. He must have found something. He went out on three one three, I think."

"That should put him over the islands somewhere, I think, sir," replied Kidd.

"I agree. Very good, Kidd. You must be good with maps."

"Yes, sir. My father taught me on camping trips."

Suddenly they were in the clear on the north side of the front. They had only ten minutes more before turning on their cross leg, so it was not worthwhile to climb when they would be heading back under the overcast so soon. Alan turned the flying over to Kidd for the cross leg, and they turned right onto the cross leg about 0805. When they turned inbound ten minutes later, they were still close to the frontal clouds. Just then Alan heard another radio transmission, more faint this time. It was Teeth Jensen's gunner, giving his search results.

"That's Jensen's gunner. He had the most westerly sector, three two five heading, next to the exec."

"Thanks."

Alan took over the flying again for the inbound leg. Those two transmissions were the only excitement on the mission. The Zebra Baker brought them directly back, arriving at about 1020. Alan saw that the deck was clear aft, so either the strike airplanes had been struck below, or they had departed on the strike.

He landed, parked and climbed out. He was surprised to see Arnham come out of the island and walk briskly toward him and Kidd. Another Dauntless landed right afterward, and it was taxiing forward. Arnham shouted, "Good morning, Ericsson," as he approached, but did not slow his pace.

"Good morning, sir," Alan quickly replied.

It looked like Arnham was in a hurry to talk to whoever had just landed. Alan turned to see who that was and saw it was 5-B-9, Teeth's airplane. It looked like Arnham wanted more detail on Teeth's search report, but Alan did not feel he could stay to listen without an invitation. He went to the wardroom for coffee and then to the ready room.

The two pilots from the search who took off just ahead of him were the only ones there, so the strike must have already left. That meant that one or both of the sighting reports must have included carriers! That in turn meant the Jap carriers were near the Louisiades, closely covering the invasion force. That started him thinking about the overall situation. Since the Tulagi raid, the Japs had known there was at least one US carrier in the area. The invasion force would have to consist of many ships and thus would be relatively easy to find. Keeping the carriers close by would make them also easier to find. From his study of the Fleet Problems, Alan was aware of the value of keeping carrier forces separate, not tied to a fleet, so they could move independently and not be easily discovered. He was surprised that the Japanese seemed to think differently.

Alan's mind was brought abruptly back to the ready room as the exec walked in. West's usually cheerful expression had turned somber.

He spoke to the small group. "Things seem to be going to hell. Jensen's radio report said there were two carriers and four cruisers. Based on that, Admiral Fitch released the strike about an hour later, when the ships had cut down the distance to the target enough so the Devastators could go.

"Then, when Jensen got back, his gunner dropped a message that reported four cruisers and two destroyers. No mention of carriers. When he landed and confirmed, he got an icy reception and was hauled up to flag plot. They figured out that the coding device had slipped out of alignment while his radioman was coding the message. That device is probably a little too fussy to use reliably when you're keyed up close to the enemy. If all that isn't enough, there've been snoopers around, and they're pretty sure the Japs have our position." He sat down.

Poor Teeth, getting hauled up before the admiral when it was not his fault, thought Alan.

The other pilots in the search came in one by one, and the grim news was passed to them. About half an hour later, the teletype clattered. West jumped up and stood over it.

"Hey, this is better," he said. The machine stopped, and he tore off the message and turned around to face the group. "A search out of Port Moresby has located a carrier about thirty miles south of the position reported by Jensen. The strike is being redirected by radio in the clear." He looked up, smiling. "One carrier in the target area is a hell of lot better than none!"

"Amen!" said one of the pilots.

Teeth walked in, looking discouraged.

The bullhorn announced, "Bombing Five crews, stand by to go on deck at eleven ten for anti-torpedo patrol."

Four hours of boredom, circling around the task force. Fitch is pretty conventional, or he is letting Sherman call the shots, thought Alan. *Even if the Dauntlesses could make it rough for the enemy torpedo planes, radar should give enough warning, so they could stand by spotted on deck and not wear out the pilots and airplanes, who might be needed for a strike later.* He rushed to the wardroom, grabbed two sandwiches, and returned. He ate one and planned to take the other to eat during the patrol.

Alan's plane was in the middle of the anti-torpedo patrol launch at about 1130. As far as he knew, nothing had come from his brief conversation with the Scouting Five skipper, Burch, back in early March, about putting more emphasis on air-to-air tactics work. Therefore, the Scouting Five guys were probably better than Bombing Five at anti-torpedo plane combat in the event of an actual attack on the ship.

About a half hour later, the radio came alive, and he heard one of the strike pilots say something like, "We got that carrier good. What about the other one?" Alan thought that pilot had not gotten the word that there was probably only one carrier. Ten minutes later another voice came through loud and clear on the radio: "Scratch one flattop, signed Bob."

Alan keyed the intercom for Kidd's benefit. "I think that must be Commander Dixon, the skipper of Scouting Two."

"Great news, sir!" shouted Kidd.

Alan wondered if his friends Wade Buckner and Rudi Fischer had gone on the strike from *Lexington* and, if so, how they had made out. Another half hour went by; then another voice came on the frequency: "Returning strike aircraft are fifty to sixty miles out on radar." Alan recognized the voice of *Lexington*'s FDO, who would be orchestrating the defense if the Japanese attacked.

"That's the FDO on *Lex*," Alan told Kidd.

"Good to know, sir," replied Kidd.

Soon the whole task force turned around into the southeast trade wind to take the strike airplanes aboard. By 1315 all the strike aircraft had returned and landed aboard the two carriers.

Alan counted them as they landed, and he thought there were one or two missing, but he was thankful that the losses were few. Soon he needed to use the relief tube and did. Then he retrieved his sandwich and ate it.

As the afternoon wore on, the frontal cloud band moved south, and the weather around the task force gradually worsened. Occasional rain showers appeared. Alan and Kidd closed their canopies and bounced around in the turbulence. In the rain shafts, visibility was less than one-quarter mile. When these passed over the carriers, the ships were not visible to the anti-torpedo patrol or to each other. It seemed unlikely to Alan that a Japanese strike would be able to find the task force in this weather, even if their snoopers had given them the rough position. At around 1500, Arnham came on the radio and called in the anti-torpedo plane patrol.

"About time," said Alan on the intercom.

"Right, sir," replied Kidd.

Alan maneuvered to get in the traffic pattern for landing aboard the *Yorktown*. He noticed some cruiser floatplanes on antisubmarine patrol were also maneuvering to land next to their ships, apparently because of the weather. Fortunately the swell had not had time to get up since the weather moved in, and Alan landed uneventfully. His watch said 1530.

He went first to the head and then to the wardroom for coffee. He was anxious to hear about the strike, so he took his coffee to the ready room. There the atmosphere seemed to be relaxed. He took his seat next to Jolly.

Jolly filled him in. "We're on standby for another search or strike, in spite of the weather, but I think it's too late now. We'd have trouble finding the other two Jap carriers, which are now thought to be somewhere east of us, instead of northwest."

"Yeah, it's late and the weather's pretty poor. It got to the point on anti-torpedo patrol where we kept losing the ships in the rain, so they called us in. Tell me about the strike. From what I heard on the radio, that carrier got pasted."

"It did. Nobody is sure which carrier it was. I'm convinced it was some kind of small carrier, probably a conversion of a transport, not one of their fleet carriers. It was hard to tell how many planes it could operate, because a lot of them could have been off on a search or strike. Still it seemed unlikely they would leave only the few fighters we saw for defense, unless she really couldn't carry many.

"The weather was clear, and there was no windshield fogging. We had a field day. Lex's planes arrived first, as planned, and they attacked. We got there in time to see that Torpedo Two was nicely coordinated with their later part of their dive bombers. They got at least a couple of bomb hits and several torpedo hits. There were a few enemy fighters, including Zeroes, but the fighter escort easily handled them."

Alan thought Rudi Fischer was probably there, and maybe he had gotten a hit. Wade Buckner could have been in the escort.

"Burch was leading our group, and he decided not to switch targets, which now seems like a mistake. We got several more hits. Burch got one near the middle of the flight deck. I got a hit, but it was up near the bow, not as effective as some of the others. The last guy in my division, Briggs, switched to a cruiser and got a hit. Some said it rolled over and sank, but I did not see that. Torpedo Five got more hits on the carrier, and she only stayed afloat a few more minutes after that. She was a goner before that, and more planes should have switched targets. She was part of a task force, and they all turned around and started hightailing it back north. We started back without Meyer. He was last seen chasing a Jap plane toward Deboyne. He was the only *Yorktown* pilot who didn't return.

"Most of the guys were ecstatic when they got back, but I was pretty sure we weren't playing against the first team. And even so, I didn't get a real solid hit. If I ever get another chance to drop on a carrier, I'm going to do whatever it takes to get a solid hit."

This sounded like Jolly's fearless fatalistic side coming through again, and Alan looked sharply into his eyes. Jolly looked back with an expression of fierce determination. It was a look that Alan had only seen once before, when Bull Durham had stood up to fight in the bar in San Diego on New Year's Eve.

The bullhorn suddenly came alive. "Standby for search and strike crews is canceled. All pilots report to ready rooms at seventeen thirty."

"Orders from Fitch must have come through," said Jolly.

"Yeah, I'm going with Phil to the hangar to make sure all the squawks are taken care of."

Alan and Phil got back to the ready room right at 1730.

Stubb was standing at the lectern, ready to start the briefing. "Well, I guess we're pretty lucky the Japs never came visiting today. Part of the reason could be that they may have been busy giving hell to *Neosho* and *Sims*. They radioed they were being attacked by enemy airplanes but said nothing more."

Sims and Neosho *under air attack.* Alan immediately thought of *Sims's* imperturbable crewmen, who had fished Alan and Parker out of frigid water seven months earlier in the north Atlantic and had taken excellent care of them. *If the ship was hit by a big air attack, probably many of them are injured or dead.*

He didn't have as close a feeling for *Neosho*, but he knew they were a hardworking bunch also. He remembered that seven enlisted men from *Yorktown* had gone aboard her two days earlier for rotation back to Pearl, including one he knew from Bombing Five. Jimmy Flatley and a couple of other pilots almost went aboard her too. He also remembered that Jennifer had told him that *Neosho* was in the middle of the Pearl Harbor attack but had handled herself well and escaped serious damage. Oilers were supposed to be kept out of harm's way, instead of sitting defenseless while being pounded. *Not knowing where the Jap carriers were, Fletcher may have sent those ships to an unlucky place. Or maybe the Japanese have gotten the seaplane base at Tulagi operational, in spite of our raid, and they were in search range from there.* His attention was hauled back to the ready room as Stubb continued the briefing.

"We think the Japs have two carriers remaining in this area, which are operating independently from their invasion fleet, which has gone back north of the Louisiades. Their carriers are probably somewhere east of us at the moment. The top brass are considering all options, including a night search and strike this evening, which seems to me like a long shot with this weather. If that does not happen, tomorrow there will probably be a dawn search by *Lexington*, followed by a strike with airplanes from both ships. You are dismissed, but be prepared to come back here on short notice. That is all."

A few pilots stood up and left.

Jolly got up and addressed the pilots: "Today I got a hit on the carrier, but it was up near the bow, not a solid hit. If I get to drop on a carrier tomorrow, I am going to do my best to get a solid hit. The way to do that is to stay straight on the target, keep the ball centered, and keep the point of aim upwind. Then you have to go low, below fifteen hundred feet, before dropping. Then start your pullout right away, or you'll hit the water. Most likely we'll be using delayed fuses and armor piercing bombs, so the blast shouldn't damage your plane."

There was silence as he went back to his seat. The pilots had been trained to drop at 2,000 feet or above, even though many went lower. What Jolly was advocating seemed nearly suicidal. Jolly's fearless side was stronger than Alan had realized. Suddenly he thought of his promise to Jennifer not to consider himself expendable. He might go lower than ever before but not that low.

His thoughts were interrupted by the klaxon and bullhorn announcing, "General quarters. Several large bogies on radar southeast eighteen to forty-eight miles, inbound. Stand by to launch relief CAP." Tension filled the ready room again at the prospect of the long awaited attack on the ship.

"Maybe we didn't get away without a visit after all," said Alan to Jolly.

Jolly glanced at his watch, "It's almost sunset, pretty late for them to be showing up. They must be trained for night landings."

The pilots all glanced at each other as they noticed the throb of the ship's propellers and the ship heeling to port as she speeded up and turned into the wind. Five minutes went by, and the pilots who had left returned.

Another voice announced on the bullhorn, "Radar targets now appear to be passing to our south, east to west. CAP aloft will intercept." Then the fighter frequency came on with the FDO on *Lexington* vectoring the fighters aloft out to intercept, while the relief CAP was launched. Another ten minutes passed, and then there was rapid fire chatter among the fighter pilots as they found the Japanese airplanes and attacked. It sounded like they were having good luck shooting down the intruders. Then the frequency went quiet.

After about twenty minutes, the radio talk with the CAP fighters to be relieved indicated they had returned to the task force. The Bombing Five pilots began to relax. Alan's watch said

1805. "The enemy aren't the only ones that are going to be landing in the dark," he said to Jolly.

Jolly nodded as they heard the first Wildcat thumping down on the flight deck immediately above. There were two more landings and then a pause.

"Who are the airplanes circling off to starboard in right hand traffic with running lights on?" asked a voice on the radio circuit.

"They're signaling with a lamp in Morse code!" said another excited voice. Suddenly there was the sound of antiaircraft guns.

"Cease fire!" said an authoritative voice on the bullhorn.

"Watch out, boys—they've got meatballs and round wing tips!" said another voice on the radio. Alan realized the only American planes aloft were Wildcats, and they had square wing tips. "Meatball" was the nickname for the Japanese rising sun insignia.

Suddenly a tremendous boom echoed through the ship.

"Jesus, what the hell was that?" said a pilot. None of the pilots had experienced a bomb or torpedo hit on a ship, and they wondered if this was what it felt like.

"The whole starboard antiaircraft battery went off all at once, I think," said West. Several pilots nodded. Alan thought this was a plausible, and much more welcome, explanation. He knew that the location of the ready room near the island on the starboard side made the starboard antiaircraft guns sound louder. Then came the sound of continuing sporadic fire by antiaircraft guns. Alan decided that West was right.

"What are you shooting at me for? What have I done now?" came a plaintive voice on the radio circuit, a tone so strange for a fighter pilot that Alan thought he must be trying to inject a little humor into the situation. Several pilots smiled.

The ship heeled hard to starboard, as if maneuvering radically to avoid air attack while the antiaircraft fire continued. After a few minutes, the antiaircraft fire wound down rapidly, and the ship heeled gently to port as it turned back.

"Now here this. After a hot reception, the Jap airplanes have turned off their lights and departed. That is all," said a calm voice on the bullhorn.

"It sounds like their pilots thought we were one of their carriers. I guess they don't really have a much better idea of our location than we do of theirs, thank goodness," said Jolly.

"True, but they can't be too far away, if they mistook us for one of their carriers," said Alan.

"Could be, but maybe they haven't heard we sunk one, and they thought we were that one."

"Yeah, that could be."

The normal radio chatter returned, coming from the FDO and the CAP aircraft remaining in the landing pattern. The Bombing Five pilots gradually relaxed.

"Secure from general quarters," came from the bullhorn.

The teletype began to clatter. West got up and stood over the machine, and the pilots stopped chatting. When it was finished, he tore off the paper and handed it to Stubb at the lectern.

Stubb announced, "Flight quarters at oh five forty tomorrow. Jensen and Morris, report to the hangar for arming; others are dismissed."

It was 1930, well after the normal supper hour, but most of the pilots departed for the wardroom to see what remained. Alan and Jolly joined them and found that the stewards had managed to keep some supper warm for them, and they were hungry.

Alan sat down with Jolly and Teeth. Alan said to Teeth, "That was lousy luck, getting hauled up before the admiral."

"Yeah, I was upset at first. Then I began to feel the strain the admiral and his staff were under. It's a hair trigger situation, with both sides looking for each other and ready to strike. I couldn't blame them for being angry, so I just tried to stay calm. I thought to myself that I was screwed by my gunner's carelessness. Then I remembered looking over one of those coding devices. It was kind of clever, as long as you're sitting still on the ground. But bouncing in and out of clouds to stay undetected or hide from CAP, it could easily slip out of alignment, so I couldn't blame my gunner. They need something solid that you can lock in place, so it can't slip. That device is actually worse than useless."

Thank heavens for steady, sensible guys like Teeth, Alan thought.

About a half hour later, they had had their fill. They adjourned to the wardroom. It had been a long day and tomorrow promised to be another. He had been very keyed up the evening before at the prospect of combat the next day. Now Alan was very tired after eight hours of flying plus the other excitement that day and was much less keyed up, in spite of the same situation looming for the next day. After a half hour of chatting, he found it was hard to keep his eyes open. He and Jolly headed for their stateroom.

CHAPTER FIFTEEN

Carrier Battle in the Coral Sea

Friday, May 8, 1942

Alan and Jolly rose at 0430. Alan felt well rested but groggy after sleeping quite soundly. They had breakfast and took a quick walk up to the bow to look around before reporting to the ready room. In the predawn light, with the help of a half moon, they could just make out that the front had moved off to the north but was still visible 20 to 30 miles away, making it good cover for enemy snoopers tracking the task force. The task force was in the clear, with good visibility—good for attack, that is, but bad for defense. They arrived at the ready room at 0535.

Stubb appeared just as flight quarters sounded a few minutes later. He went to the lectern and arranged his notes. After the alarm stopped, he started the briefing. "The front we were in yesterday afternoon has drifted north again, so we are in the clear. The Jap carriers could be in most any direction, so a three hundred sixty degree search is going out from *Lexington* shortly. The enemy may not be far away, so the search could be short, and we need to be ready to launch the strike immediately after we hear from the search. Both carriers will send airplanes on the strike, and the *Yorktown* group will depart first, the opposite of yesterday.

"Our CAP, anti-torpedo patrol, and Torpedo Five with four escort fighters will be the first deck load and will be launched in that order. Then the other strike aircraft will be brought on deck: our two fighter escort farthest aft, then us, then Scouting Five in front. Commander Burch will be leading all the *Yorktown* Dauntlesses. Scouting Five is sending seven airplanes, including their exec with Commander Schindler, the flag gunnery officer, in the back seat. All seventeen available Bombing Five aircraft will be included in the strike, as shown on the roster here, armed with one thousand pound bombs." He glanced at Teeth, who nodded. "Final briefing will be after the search results are known and the mission ordered. You are dismissed until called back for standby."

Having had mostly boredom on his missions the day before, Alan was ready for some excitement. Attacking enemy carriers, however, went far beyond excitement. It was the ultimate mission, the one he had been training for over the last 20 months. But since this was a new type of combat that had never happened before, there was the fear of the unknown. This was added to the known dangers of dive bombing and air to air combat with enemy fighters. He was determined to do his best, but he was scared. He thought again of Rudi Fischer, who might also be facing heavy fighter defense in today's attack, and Wade Buckner, who might be in the escort.

He had noted from the roster that he would be leading the second section in the second division, led by West. His wingmen would be Morris and Monroe. As flight officer, Jolly was leading the third division, so Jolly would be three planes behind Alan.

He decided to make one last visit to the hangar. While Alan was there, he felt the ship heel to starboard as the ship turned into the southeast trade wind. This was the Point Option course, the course to be followed by the task force and given to the search pilots to help them find the task force on their return. *With that course, flight operations, such as rotating the CAP, could take place without changing course.* "Now here this. All pilots report to ready rooms—Condition One," came from the bullhorn. "Condition One" for the air group meant full readiness to launch the strike.

A few more pilots appeared, and they were all there except the skipper. Alan knew that Condition One did not necessarily mean that anything would happen very soon. He had a book stashed under his seat for standby sessions, and he pulled it out and started reading. He noticed that Jolly followed suit.

Thirty minutes later came the subdued roar and rumble of an airplane taking off on the flight deck above. Alan stopped reading and looked at Jolly. His watch said 0730.

"They're probably launching the CAP and anti-torpedo patrol," said Jolly.

Alan nodded and went back to reading, as more airplanes took off. Another half hour went by.

The radio came on with orders from the Lexington FDO to the CAP to pursue a bogey 22 miles northwest. A few minutes later, the chatter from the fighters indicated they were having trouble finding it.

"That snooper might be in and out of that front, hard to find," Alan said to Jolly.

"You're right. It might have been a good idea to get the task force under that front before dawn, so we'd be harder to find."

"But then the search would have trouble finding us too."

"Yeah. Now I hope our search finds the Japs pretty soon, so we can launch our strike before theirs shows up here." Jolly went back to reading.

The radio chatter between the fighters and the FDO continued for another ten minutes—then silence. Alan went back to reading, but he was pretty excited and kept stopping to think about what was going on.

Their hopes for the search were fulfilled fifteen minutes later. Suddenly the bullhorn barked, "Now hear this. Search has located two enemy carriers roughly two hundred miles north-northeast. Stand by for strike orders." Alan checked his watch, which said 0820.

"Thank goodness," said Jolly.

"That sounds like what we've been waiting for. But we'll have to cut down the distance for the Wildcats and Devastators to make it."

"It all depends on the courses of the two task forces. If we both steam toward each other, they could make it even now."

"I think we're on the course given to the search pilots, southeast, close to ninety degrees from the course to the Japs. It'll be hard for the search guys to find the task force if it changes course before they get back. They'll probably have to wait for the search to return before they can change course toward the Japs."

"You're right. It's the kind of prickly situation that makes it nice not to be the admiral," said Jolly with a grin.

Stubb strode hurriedly into the ready room, saying, "As you were." Stubb had a brief conference at the front with West and Slick Davis, and then they returned to their seats.

Stubb put some papers on the lectern and immediately began the strike briefing. "We'll be launching soon, so listen carefully and write the numbers down. No changes in the roster. Fitch has ordered a deferred departure, so the whole group leaves together. We will cruise at one hundred thirty knots at seventeen thousand feet. CYAG's orders to Commander Burch were to proceed to the target independently but coordinate our attack by radio with Torpedo Five, which will be cruising at one hundred five knots right on the water. There will be two Wildcats with us and four with Torpedo Five. Lieutenant Davis."

Apparently Fitch and Sherman are either ignorant of, or disagree with, our air group's experience with the running rendezvous, which would be much better than a deferred departure.

Slick hurried to the front. The sense of urgency continued to come through as he spoke rapidly, "Course to the target zero two eight, distance one hundred seventy-five. Wind one two zero at twelve. All the pilots were writing rapidly. We should be above most of the frontal weather at seventeen thousand. The frontal weather could extend all the way to the target. Yoke Easy sector letters posted here." He returned to his seat.

Stubb spoke again: "If the Japs are under the clouds, we might have to do some hunting, but the frontal weather has been patchy, so we should be able to find a whole task force with two carriers. We'll have time while we wait for the torpedo planes to arrive."

Alan thought, *Without radar, the Japanese have to do all their fighter direction visually. As long as we are able to locate their carriers and make our dives, the frontal weather at the target could be an advantage for us.*

Stubb continued, "TF-Seventeen will have to maintain the present course of one two five until the search is recovered, probably around an hour from now. Then it will be turning and heading directly for the enemy to shorten our return. On the way back, we will have to use our Zebra Bakers. At launch we will be at max gross weight with 225 gallons of fuel and a one thousand pound bomb."

He had hardly stopped speaking when the first plane could be heard taking off on the deck above. *Probably one of the antitorpedo Dauntlesses*, Alan thought. The later planes sounded a little heavier and louder, so Alan thought they were Devastators. The first deck load launch took about ten minutes. Another fifteen minutes went by as the strike Dauntlesses were brought up on deck.

Then the bullhorn announced, "Now hear this. Scouting and Bombing strike crews and escort, man your planes."

Stubb turned to the pilots and, raising his voice, said, "Good luck and hit 'em hard!"

As the pilots stood up, Jolly shouted, "The folks back home are depending on us. I am going to get a hit if I have to lay it on their flight deck."

Alan found this side of his roommate disconcerting. He grabbed his heavy sheepskin lined flight jacket along with his parachute and plotting board. It would be cold at 17,000 feet, probably in the thirties.

All the pilots were heading for the flight deck. Alan looked at his watch, which said 0900. It had only been about forty minutes since the search results were announced.

Alan emerged from the island into a hot, sunny day on the flight deck. The plane captains were warming up the last few planes to be brought up. The Bombing Five pilots quickened their pace so as not to hold up the launch when their turn came.

From his position on the roster, Alan knew his plane should be in the fifth row from the aft end of the Dauntlesses, and, watching for spinning propellers, he soon found 5-B-12. He saw Kidd approaching as he skirted around the tail to the left side. After his walk around, Alan climbed on the wing as Klein was climbing out of the cockpit.

"Good luck, sir!" said Klein. He gave a snappy salute, which Alan returned, and jumped off the wing.

"All aboard," said Alan, as Kidd climbed on the wing. Alan donned his flight jacket and parachute, grabbed his plotting board, while Kidd donned his, and they climbed in. He got settled pretty fast and got the engine started, just as the roar of the first Dauntless going to full power drowned out the other noise on the flight deck. He looked up to see Fly One drop his flag, and the launch was underway. Alan's watch said it was 0915. By the time he had gotten through his checklist, Scouting Five was gone, and the skipper of Bombing Five was next. He quickly rehearsed the takeoff in his mind.

Yorktown Dauntlesses ready for launch at the
Battle of the Coral Sea, May 8, 1942
(US Navy/PD-USGOV-MILITARY-NAVY)

A few minutes later, it was Alan's turn. Fly One swung his flag down, and Alan started down the deck. When the bow looked to be about two hundred feet ahead, he eased the stick back and lifted off. This time he was a little farther forward than on the Tulagi strikes. He would have to keep working on his technique, because he could be spotted farther forward at maximum weight.

He followed West's section as they turned left and began to circle to wait for the third division and the two escort Wildcats to get off. He throttled back to climb power as his wingmen cut inside his turn to close up on his plane; he then raised the landing gear and flaps. He could see Torpedo Five circling nearby. At 0921 the two escorts had taken off, and the whole strike group departed.

He could see Stubb's division ahead clearly and just make out the Scouting Five Dauntlesses farther ahead. Torpedo Five was below close to the water. They preferred it that way because they gained little speed by climbing, and at least they could not be attacked from underneath, where they had no defensive armament.

In fifteen minutes they were entering the frontal weather. There were cumulus clouds, some fairly dark, but there was a lot of space between them, and they could maintain their cruising formation, only occasionally flying through small clouds. About a half hour after departure they leveled off at 17,000 feet, still below the tops of the highest towers of clouds. Alan looked around for some time before finally locating the two escorting Wildcats. They were still at five o'clock low, struggling to get into escort position above.

After another twenty minutes, as Alan scanned the sky, he spotted a large formation of airplanes headed south. "Two o'clock, looks like an enemy strike group heading south," he told Kidd over the intercom.

"Yeah, I see them too."

Now, on top of the risks of their mission, Alan knew their ships would be attacked before they got back, possibly disabled or sunk. He had a cold feeling in his stomach.

They droned on. Another three quarters of an hour went by. They passed over many small openings in the overcast but saw no ships. Then Alan could see a large opening in the overcast ahead and to the right of their course.

Suddenly there was a crackling in Alan's earphones. "Burch here. Tallyho! Directly below." Alan glanced down at the clock on the lower instrument panel, which read 1032.

Alan also looked at the outside air temperature on the gauge in the lower panel, which read 36. He keyed the intercom. "It's mighty cold out there. Keep your canopy closed until I open mine."

"Yes, sir."

Burch led the formation around in a shallow turn to the right, circling clockwise around the opening, staying over the clouds mostly out of sight from below. Now Alan came up to the opening, and he could see many ships below, including two carriers, all heading south. He led his section slightly to the left to get out of sight again over the clouds and then followed the planes ahead in a shallow right turn. His tension increased, but they were lucky to find no Japanese CAP up high.

The formation continued in a large circle around the opening. Now they were northwest of the opening in the clouds and could see that the Japanese task force was headed for a black squall with heavy rain on the south side of the opening. If they had to wait a long time for the torpedo planes, the enemy carriers might disappear into that squall. Alan glimpsed the leading carrier through the clouds. She had turned into the wind and was launching fighters. Others that had taken off earlier were climbing toward their formation. They were very lucky to be out of sight while they waited, but they would get a hot reception when they made their dives, and the fighters might keep climbing and find them. *It was stupid to use the deferred departure!*

When Burch had made a full circle, reaching the southwest side of the clearing, he began a smaller circle to the left to stay southwest of the Japanese ships, and Scouting Five followed. Alan could see that the leading carrier was approaching the rain squall.

Burch came on the radio again: "Joe, bear a hand because time's a-wastin'!"

Joe was Lieutenant Commander Joe Taylor, skipper of Torpedo Five. There was no reply from Taylor. Stubb, with Bombing Five, began his own circle to the left on the northeast side of the opening in the clouds. This was good for concealment, because the Japanese were closer to the northeast side of the opening. Alan wondered, however, if they would be able to dive from that side, because the ships seemed almost under the clouds. Alan felt his adrenaline flowing as he got ready for the dive.

About eight minutes later, the radio crackled: "OK, Bill, I'm starting in." That must be Taylor, meaning he had the Japanese task force in sight and was starting his run in to the target. Burch did not waste any time. He abruptly rolled into his dive, and the Scouting Five pilots began to follow. It was 1058.

Stubb waggled his wings and began to continue the large circle around the cloud opening toward the southwest side. Alan pulled down his goggles, opened the front canopy, and felt the icy wind. Then he could feel the thumps and more wind as Kidd folded the rear canopy forward, pulled out and mounted the machine gun, and set up the ammunition feed. About five minutes went by as they continued around to the southwest side, and

Alan's tension continued to increase. Then Stubb waggled his rudder again and rolled into his dive.

Now Alan could see Stubb and his division below and the Japanese carrier beyond. The carrier had her island on the starboard side, so she was not *Akagi* or *Hiryu*. Alan was too busy to study the details that distinguished the other four Japanese fleet carriers. She was making vigorous evasive maneuvers, leaving a snakelike wake, and the Scouting Five airplanes had disappeared, probably into the clouds. Alan could see no signs of a hit on the carrier. The leading carrier had vanished, and he realized she must have disappeared under the rain squall.

As the first division followed Stubb, two Japanese fighters swooped in, but they hardly had time to fire before they passed the Dauntlesses in their dives. They looked like the vaunted Zero that he had been hearing about. As he had been warned, they were easy to mistake for bombers because they had long canopies. They were very maneuverable and able to zoom back up for further attacks, but they had not fired yet. Alan's wingmen got in trail behind him.

"Zeros ahead. All set for the dive?" asked Alan over the intercom.

"All set, gun charged," replied Kidd.

Now West rolled into his dive. Alan put out the dive flaps and went through the routine: supercharger low speed, propeller low rpm, mixture rich, and carburetor heat on. As he slowed he noticed Jolly coming up on his right. He looked over and was amazed to see that Jolly was making a monkey face. He smiled but had no time to think about it. West's wingmen followed, and it was Alan's turn. More Zeros were coming up fast.

"Here we go," Alan said to Kidd, and he closed the throttle and rolled into his dive. As he steadied in the dive, the carrier appeared in his windshield with West's section diving ahead of him. There were towering splashes next to the carrier from near misses made by the last two planes in Stubb's division. Suddenly he saw a few tracers, and he heard a few rounds from Kidd's gun; a Zero zoomed by and then immediately pulled up. *Luckily they're too clean to stay with us very long*, he thought.

Passing through 10,000 feet, antiaircraft bursts appeared ahead. *That should make the Zeros back off.* He was not very afraid of the antiaircraft fire because he was coming down so fast that there was only a small chance that the gunners would get the range right. That was a big advantage of dive bombing.

He put his right eye on the bombsight. A few seconds later, he saw the dreaded fog beginning to form on the sight and the windshield. He could still see the blurred outline of the carrier in the windshield. The wind was from the southeast, so he rolled ninety degrees to fly northwest and tried to aim to the southeast of the carrier as it twisted and turned. He had brought along a rag again, and he reached for it. Passing through 3,000 feet, he gave the sight a quick wipe and put his eye up to it again. It was momentarily clear, and he adjusted his aim and centered the ball. He dropped the rag and put his left hand on the bomb release lever. The mist was rapidly reforming as he was passing through 2,000 feet. He held steady another long second and released at 1,400 feet.

He started his pullout quickly and adjusted the g-force, so his vision did not quite disappear. His vision began to come back in time to see the water was coming up rapidly. He got the airplane close to level at 100 feet. He eased the stick forward to level off at 50 feet, which he thought was probably so low that some of the antiaircraft guns would not depress enough to fire at him.

"A hit! A hit! You got a hit!" Kidd yelled over the intercom. "On the port side near the bow."

Alan was too busy to reply, although he felt a glow of satisfaction. Now there was a cruiser looming close ahead. He pushed the propeller and throttle levers gently but firmly forward for full power and retracted the dive flaps. He pulled up suddenly and passed very low over the cruiser amidships, giving her gunners a very fast moving target; he then jinked left and right with the rudder to spoil their aim as he flew away.

He made a hard left turn to fly south and looked back to try to try to see Jolly's dive. All of a sudden, he saw a Dauntless in its dive. Flames and smoke were streaming out, so it had been hit, but it was steady in the dive. It continued until it was awfully low, less than one length of the carrier above the water. He saw the bomb separate, and the pullout looked steady. Then there was a huge explosion on the carrier, just abaft the island. Instantly there was a giant cloud of smoke, which obscured the airplane. No airplane emerged from the cloud. It must have gone into the water.

Alan's heart sank. It had to have been Jolly. No one else would drop that low. He did exactly what he said he would do. He felt tears coming. *Jennifer told me I am not expendable. Jolly wasn't either,* he thought, anger overcoming his grief.

Suddenly he heard Kidd's gun hammering and saw tracers go by. His anger turned into a fierce survival instinct. He chopped the throttle and jinked left. A Zero zoomed by on his right, trailing smoke. Alan wanted to jab the throttle wide open again, but he had trained himself never to do that because the engine would quit for several seconds. He pushed the throttle lever slowly right forward to the stop and made a very hard climbing turn to the right to head northwest for the nearest cloud, his tunnel vision returning momentarily as he sank into his seat. Now Kidd's gun was hammering again. Alan jinked right and left, as he felt bullets striking his plane. Then a Zero appeared on his left going away, having passed over him after a side attack. A few more seconds went by, and then they were in the cloud.

He saw no Zeros in the cloud, so they had escaped for the moment. Alan throttled back to climb power and began a gentle left turn to head south. He found he was breathing hard, and he was sweaty, even though he had been in the warm air down low only a few minutes. He scanned the instrument panel and looked over what he could see of his airplane. He could see some bullet holes, and doubtless there were more. *Nevertheless, everything seems to be working normally, at least for the moment.*

He keyed the intercom: "Are you OK, Kidd? Did you get hit?"

"No, I'm all right," Kidd replied, his voice high and wavering.

"Looked like you hit that one that went by on the right. Great shooting!"

"Thanks. I think I might've hit another, but I'm not sure," Kidd replied.

Kidd just went through the wringer too. Alan wanted to review all that had just happened, but he forced himself to focus on making it back to the task force. They were in and out as they passed through breaks in the clouds. In the breaks Alan could occasionally see other Dauntlesses ahead, but no Zeros. He had lost his wingmen in all the violent maneuvering. He started to slowly unwind. He leveled off but kept climb power to catch up with the planes ahead, and after a few minutes, he was in loose formation with four others. Morris and Monroe were there with two others. They managed to stay together and began a slow climb.

Above 3,000 feet, the breaks became larger, and Alan spotted another formation of four Dauntlesses ahead. Slowly they caught up with the formation ahead and became a formation of nine. They continued a slow climb. The air cooled as he climbed, and he closed his canopy. He felt Kidd stowing the flexible gun and closing his canopy. Alan looked around in the cloud breaks to try to recognize the other airplanes in the formation. He saw that West was leading, and gradually he was able to determine that West's wingmen were there too, so the second division was intact. One had the rear canopy still open and the gun mounted. *The gunner must be wounded*, he thought. *It's Becker's airplane, the one immediately ahead of me in the dive sequence. The other three are from the third division, which had five on this mission. There's Teeth Jensen and his wingman Mike Burke, who is flying a little erratically. Jolly is down, so one other plane is missing from the third division, as well as the whole first division. Most likely the first division, including the skipper, has gathered into a separate formation, which is far enough ahead to be hard to see through the breaks in the clouds.*

West leveled off at 8,000 feet. At this altitude the clouds had become scattered, and Alan was a little surprised that he was not able to see any other Dauntlesses. After ten minutes, Alan was startled to see a plane on fire in a steep dive off to the left of their formation. He recognized right away that it was not American. He could see it had fixed landing gear, with large streamlined fairings around the wheels, called wheel pants. He remembered the descriptions of Japanese airplanes the pilots had been given in San Diego. *That's a Type 99, their dive bomber.* The plane disappeared into the clouds below, evidently doomed. *It must be one of their strike airplanes, and maybe it was attacked by one of our fighter escort up high.*

After another few minutes, Alan spotted a large formation of airplanes ahead, off to the left and lower. It quickly became apparent that this formation was going in the opposite direction, and therefore was probably Japanese also. *It must be their strike returning.* Then he saw that they were also Type 99s. He had an overwhelming urge to try to get some revenge for the death of Jolly and his gunner, Allison. *It's a V formation, stepped down, and there's a big cloud that'll conceal my approach. It's a perfect setup, and I've got enough fuel.*

"I can see some of the enemy strike returning ahead," Alan told Kidd. "I'm going to try and nail one." He felt Kidd open his canopy and start to mount his gun. He turned abruptly out of the formation, going well to the left to stay ahead of the Japanese, so he could maintain his lead angle as he made a high side run on the leader. When attacking from the side, a lead angle was necessary because the target would move forward in the time it took the bullets to get there, and he did not want to get behind his target, where the enemy gunners could shoot back. He test fired his twin .50 caliber machine guns in the nose.

Then he set full power and dove into his firing run. The setup was looking good as he entered the cloud. He held his course and rate of descent, suddenly emerging from the cloud only about half a mile from the target. His lead angle was a little too much, so he corrected to the right. The rear gunners had stowed their guns and closed their canopies, removing that threat. When the range got close enough, he opened fire. He turned slightly to bring the stream of tracers to the junction of the wings and fuselage. He glimpsed the Japanese gunner opening his canopy, but he would never be ready to fire in time. Now smoke was showing. Suddenly the 99 pitched down. Alan flashed by above, then pulled up, and turned right. The formation being stepped down, the fixed forward firing guns of the 99s could not bear without breaking formation, and Alan passed rapidly out of range.

"You got him! He's on fire and headed down!" shouted Kidd on the intercom.

Alan turned and looked back. The other planes held their formation, realizing it was hopeless to try and follow him. The smoking 99 was in a very steep dive. Alan realized he had probably killed the pilot, and he had slumped forward against the control stick. Luckily there was a break in the clouds below, and he was able to follow the 99 until it struck the water with a splash. This made it a confirmed aerial victory. By this time he was crossing behind the Japanese formation, headed back toward his own formation, climbing back to their altitude. He pulled the power back to climb and very gradually caught up, easing into his former position behind Becker.

After about ten minutes, they heard Commander Burch on the radio, saying he was running into Zeros and requesting fighter escort. Presumably Burch was somewhere ahead. Alan had no appetite for taking on more Zeros in aerial combat. The FDO radioed that Burch was still thirty miles out, and he did not have enough fighters to send them more than ten miles out. Then Burch replied that the Zeros were actually Wildcats, apparently one of the fighter escort groups. *Even the senior, steady Burch has gotten a little jumpy*, thought Alan. West's formation reached the southern edge of the cloudy weather safely.

Then Alan began to see some ships ahead. Soon he saw the unmistakable outline of *Lexington*, so it was the American task force. As he got closer he could see *Yorktown* beyond. The ships were scattered around apparently at random, definitely not in their usual neat formation. Alan realized that the last Japanese strike airplanes had departed only recently. With the carriers under attack and maneuvering radically at high speed, the formation had broken up.

As he got closer still, he saw that both carriers were underway, not down much in the water, with no smoke showing.

There's no sign that either carrier has sustained substantial damage from their strike. Alan felt relief flooding into him. He might spend the night in his own bunk after all. *Whew! What a lucky break!* As West's formation approached *Yorktown*, Alan could see that another formation of Dauntlesses, which had arrived back ahead of theirs, was orbiting nearby. Getting closer, Alan could see that this formation consisted of Burch, leading his seven from Scouting Five and five from the first division of Bombing Five, including the skipper. So there were two missing from Bombing Five, in addition to Jolly. *Sad, but it could have been much worse.*

Alan began to watch the operations around the *Yorktown* intently. The Dauntlesses had to wait while three CAP Wildcats took off. Then Burch's formation went into the landing pattern. One of the Scouting Five airplanes turned out of the pattern and ditched nearby. *Probably because combat damage prevented landing aboard.* Then one of the Bombing Five airplanes in Burch's formation made a fast approach, cleared the wires and the barrier, and flew into the aft end of the island. The pilot and gunner were rescued, and the airplane was pushed over the side.

West's formation of nine followed Burch's. As Alan followed in the landing sequence, he noticed a formation of Devastators approaching. The three Dauntlesses ahead of him all landed safely. In spite of his fatigue, he was able to concentrate for the landing, and he caught the fifth wire. He felt relief flooding into him as he taxied forward and shut down, noticing it was 1256. He climbed out and met Kidd on the deck. Overjoyed at making it back, he shook hands with Kidd and said with a grin, "Thank goodness you're OK. You really gave it to those Zeros. Well done."

"Congratulations should go to you, sir," said Kidd, also grinning. "You got a hit on that carrier, and you shot down a plane in an SBD."

"Thank you, Kidd. But my roommate, Lieutenant Lowery, got a perfect hit and died doing it. He was a very good friend."

"That was him that hit amidships, was it? I'm very sorry, sir. His gunner, Allison, was a friend of mine, also."

"I'm sorry, Kidd. I'm afraid that they aren't the only ones who are gone."

"Yes, sir."

Then Alan noticed two pharmacist's mates on the left wing of Becker's Dauntless. They and Becker were working to extract the gunner from the rear cockpit. There were many bullet holes in the aft fuselage.

They lifted the gunner out, and he was on his back in the arms of the three men on the wing, with his feet still in the cockpit. There was a lot of blood on his flight suit. Kidd had noticed too, and they glanced at each other and went over to offer their help. As they approached, two other pharmacist's mates came around the tail and rushed up to support the gunner's legs. Seeing that the men did not need help, Alan and Kidd stopped short and stayed out of the way. The gunner was eased onto a stretcher on the deck. Alan could see that he was unconscious, and there was large wound in his abdomen, revealing his guts. *He'll be lucky to survive*, he thought, the feeling of elation at getting back in one piece now severely damped. He and Kidd turned back toward their plane.

"Let's look over our airplane," Alan said. They walked around the airplane. They counted ten bullet holes in the aft fuselage and four in the wings. They looked like they were around .30 caliber.

"The Zeros are supposed to have twenty millimeter cannon also. We're awful lucky we didn't get hit with those," said Alan.

"I mean and how, sir," said Kidd, nodding. They started for the island.

"Looks like the ship came through OK," said Alan, "but I see a steel plate over there, which may be covering some damage." He was pointing slightly inboard of the aft end of the island.

"Yes, sir."

Alan looked across at *Lexington*, a few miles to the north. "*Lex* looks a little down by the bow, but otherwise she seems OK."

"That's right, sir. Neither carrier seriously damaged is almost a miracle."

As they neared the island, Alan noticed another stray Bombing Five Dauntless in the landing pattern with the Devastators of Torpedo Five, leaving only one unaccounted for. Considering the tough mission, they had gotten off pretty lightly, but it was still hard to accept that Jolly was gone. He and Kidd separated in the island. Alan noticed that the ship had stood down from Condition Affirm to Condition Baker. This meant that ventilation could be started up again, and men could leave their battle stations temporarily. Alan went to the head and then to the wardroom. He grabbed a cup of coffee and a sandwich and left for the ready room. The crew of the ship seemed to be easing down from the tension of being under attack.

Alan had been so preoccupied with the mission that he given no thought to what came next. Now he was dismayed to realize, *There's a possibility of second strikes by both sides, so the battle might not be over.*

Most of the other pilots were in the ready room when he entered, including the exec, but not the skipper. Animated chatter filled the room, as each pilot tried to find out what had happened beyond his own view. As Alan scanned the room, the sight of Jolly's empty seat struck him.

Teeth looked up and boomed out, "Congratulations, Stringy, you got a hit!" Conversation stopped, and approvals were echoed all around.

Alan looked around and smiled. "It was up near the bow, not amidships like Jolly's, but I think it added to the damage."

"A hit is a hit," said Slick Davis, "and we only got two, with that damned fogging."

"There was already a big fire on the bow from your hit when I dropped," said Teeth.

Teeth was next to last to drop, Alan realized as he smiled at Teeth.

"And Stringy shot down a Type Ninety-Nine on the way back!" blurted out Ned Morris.

"Jesus, Stringy, you hit the jackpot!" said Slick Davis with a big smile.

Alan grinned briefly at Slick; then his face fell. "But we lost Jolly."

"Bryant didn't come back either," said Ensign Briggs. The atmosphere turned abruptly from jubilant to somber. Ensign Bryant was one of the new men who had come out by destroyer from Fiji.

"I think I saw enough of our planes, so everyone else should have made it back," said Alan, looking around the room. "But I saw one of our planes fly into the island. Who was that?"

West replied, "Young hit the island. His airplane was badly shot up, and he had no flaps. He and his gunner survived and are in sick bay. Burke and Hill were wounded in the attack, so they're also in sick bay. We hope to hear soon how they're doing."

Alan wondered if his friend Mike Burke was badly wounded. *That was why he was flying erratically.* Then his mind turned to other losses. "I guess some of the gunners were also hurt. Becker's gunner was in a bad way."

Becker was just coming into the ready room, looking haggard. "That's right. I just came from sick bay. They're giving him a fifty-fifty chance."

Several other pilots said their gunners were hit but were expected to come through.

Alan wondered what had happened to the other squadrons, but it would be a while before they heard about that. Then he thought about *Yorktown*. "What about the ship? I noticed a steel plate on the flight deck near the island, but she seems OK."

West replied, "That's where she took a bomb hit. It went a couple of decks below the hangar before it detonated. There were a lot of casualties, some unrecognizable. I hear it's a real mess down there, but the damage is limited. Some boilers went out temporarily, but the ship can still operate OK. There were some near misses, which also caused some damage below the waterline, but no torpedo hits, thank goodness."

Alan nodded and sighed. *West is right on top of things, as usual.* "It looks like *Lexington* is not too bad off either. Seems like we did a lot more damage to the carrier we hit." He took his seat.

Just then the telephone at the front rang. West went forward and picked it up, and there was a hush. "Bombing Five, Lieutenant West." There was a brief pause. "Yes, sir. I am the exec." There was long pause, and West was making notes. "Thank you, sir, for letting us know." He hung up and faced the other pilots. "That was sick bay letting us know how our men are doing. Young has a concussion and broken leg, which will take a few months to heal. Amazing he was not hurt worse in that crash." He glanced down at his notes. "Burke was shot in the right ankle and left elbow. He will be out of action for some time, weeks at least, but should fully recover. Hill took shrapnel in one leg, but it is not broken. He should be the first to be ready for action, maybe less than a month. Thank heaven they will all come out of this OK. It could have been much worse."

"Amen," said a pilot.

Mike Burke had painful injuries. It was amazing he was able to land safely, Alan thought.

West went to his seat. The pilots' chatter resumed. Alan's seat was at the end of the row next to Jolly's empty seat, so he turned around to talk to Slick Davis and Teeth Jensen in the row behind. He looked at his watch, which said 1410, and asked, "It's getting late for a second strike, which is just as well; all the pilots are tired."

"And a lot of planes are too shot up," said Teeth.

Slick asked for a description of Jolly's dive, which he had not been able to see, because he was in the first division. Teeth didn't have a clear view of it either, being three planes after Jolly in the attack. Alan gave it, having trouble mastering his grief at the end.

Changing the subject, Alan asked, "What happened to Bryant?"

Slick replied, "The first division pushed over before all but a couple of the high Zeros were ready. He made his dive OK, but two of the low Zeros were on him in the departure. They had to have hit him with their cannon, because his airplane suddenly came apart in flames. He was too low for a chute to open, even if he survived the cannon."

"They weren't using their cannon on me and Kidd later. Maybe they'd used up their cannon ammo on Scouting Five and the first division."

"Probably. I didn't have a great view of your shootdown because of the clouds, so tell us about it," said Teeth.

Alan did so, and they continued talking about the mission for a while.

The bullhorn suddenly interrupted, "Now hear this: there has been a large explosion on *Lexington*. Smoke and flames are visible. That is all."

Alan glanced at his watch, which said 1445. "The attack ended a couple of hours ago. There must have been a fire that was not out."

"Could also be fuel oil or gasoline leaks," said Slick.

Teeth added, "I talked to one of the Scouting Five guys coming off anti-torpedo plane patrol. He said Scouting Five lost four of the eight on the patrol. He was bitter to say the least."

More evidence that the Dauntlesses should have been used for what they were designed for—offense, thought Alan.

"He also said *Lexington* took a lot more damage than *Yorktown,* including several torpedo hits, because more planes of both types attacked her, and she's a lot less maneuverable than *Yorktown.*"

"Anyway, the fact that this is happening now means the damage is not under control, and it could get worse," said Alan.

"Definitely," said Teeth.

Our troubles are minor compared to those of the battered Lexington, thought Alan. *If we lose* Lexington, *then the Japanese will have won the carrier battle, because that carrier we sank yesterday does not compare with her.*

"As you were," sounded from the back of the room. Stubb strode to the front and listened as West passed on the condition of the three wounded pilots. West sat down, and Stubb faced the pilots.

"The bad weather actually helped us because we could still find them, but we could use the clouds to hide beforehand and escape afterward. But the second carrier slid under a squall, so it is undamaged, as far as we know. We might have had a shot at her too, if we hadn't wasted so much time with that damned deferred departure," he said, grimacing.

Damn right, thought Alan.

Stubb's grave expression brightened. "Of the three bomb hits on their carrier that we're sure of, two were ours!" he proclaimed. "Lowery hit square amidships, and"—nodding at Alan—"Ericsson got one up near the bow. The *Lex* guys got one more thousand pound hit near the island after we left. There might have been others, but we're not sure." He paused and his expression became resolute. "Lieutenant Lowery did exactly what he said he was going to do and dropped so low that the explosion could have damaged his plane, but he hit dead center. I gather his plane was also on fire in the dive, from the antiaircraft or fighters, and he may have been wounded, so there were a number of reasons why he might have been unable to complete his pullout." He became forceful and formal as he continued, "In any case, his conduct was in the highest tradition of the US Navy, and I will do my best to see that it is duly recognized." He paused in complete silence.

Alan was in total agreement, and he was sure that most, if not all, the squadron pilots were also.

"The new flight officer is Lieutenant Jensen," Stubb announced, smiling and nodding at Teeth. "The new gunnery officer is Lieutenant j.g. Davis, and the new navigation officer is Lieutenant j.g. Briggs." He paused to let these changes sink in.

Then Stubb continued, "The torpedo guys think they got hits, but that carrier was last seen heading north at high speed, so she can't have had a lot of damage below the waterline. The undamaged carrier probably took some of the other carrier's planes aboard, but we aren't sure what else she might be doing." He paused. "*Yorktown* took one bomb hit and a few near misses that caused leaks but no torpedo hits. The damage is under control. She is leaking fuel, leaving a slick that is easy to follow. *Lexington* took a lot more hits, both bombs and torpedoes, and, as you just heard, she is in bad shape. So the upshot of today's battle is unclear.

"In regard to a possible second strike, flight operations on *Lexington* are probably not possible, so the planes aboard her are out. The *Lex* planes in the air can land aboard our ship, but they would need to be refueled and maybe rearmed. Not counting them, we are down to roughly seven Wildcats, eleven Dauntlesses, and eight TBDs with seven torpedoes currently operational. Also there are some indications of a third Japanese carrier joining. So a second strike is very unlikely."

There was an audible sigh of relief from the pilots, including Alan.

CHAPTER SIXTEEN

Coral Sea Aftermath

May 8, 1942 (continued), Time 1530

Stubb turned to the immediate future. "We need to relieve the CAP and anti-torpedo. We will land six of *Lex*'s Wildcats and ten of her Dauntlesses. We have three of their Dauntlesses on board already. In hindsight they should have had all of her returning strike land on our ship too. Many of the *Lex* planes have not been in combat, so they are undamaged and will be a significant addition to our strength. For the relief of anti-torpedo, Scouting Five will send eight, and we will send two, Ross and Schultz." They were the two reserve pilots who had not flown so far that day. Stubb paused and rearranged the papers on the lectern.

Just then the bullhorn came on. "Now hear this. Combat air patrol and anti-torpedo patrol pilots, man your planes."

Ross and Schultz gathered their gear and left.

Stubb continued, "Now I would like to have each of you debrief with both the exec and me in my office, in order of takeoff. After that come back here for standby."

Alan glanced at his watch, which said 1544. He would be sixth to debrief, following Becker, so he had about half an hour to wait. He wanted to check on airplane repairs in the hangar, but half an hour was not enough time. Alan suggested to his wingmen that, while they were waiting, they make a quick visit topside to take a look at *Lexington*. They went up to the port gallery and looked across the water at *Lexington*. A column of smoke rose from her, and flames were visible in the hangar, but she was underway. A few minutes later, more smoke shot up, followed a few seconds after by a deep boom. The three pilots groaned. Now they could see that she was slowing and venting steam. She was clearly in a bad way.

Soon Alan made out lines being thrown over the side. "Looks like they're getting ready to abandon ship."

"You're right. A very sad sight," replied Monroe.

On *Lexington*, men were gathering on the flight deck, and several destroyers were hovering nearby. Alan hoped Rudi Fischer had returned from the strike and would get off the ship with no injuries. He thought it would be a long time before he would find out what happened to Rudi Fischer, as well as whether Wade Buckner had participated.

"OK, we better get back to the ready room," cautioned Alan.

Coming into the ready room, he saw that Becker was still there, but Phil Goodwin was not. *Having more time to wait, he probably went to the hangar. Good man*, thought Alan. When Becker left for the skipper's office, Alan followed shortly after.

When Becker came out of the skipper's office, Alan stepped in. West and Stubb each had a pile of papers in front of them, with notes for each pilot. Before Alan sat down, Stubb began, "Well, Ericsson, you've had one hell of a fine day: a hit on the carrier and an aerial victory. Congratulations!" He stood up beaming and shook Alan's hand, followed by West. They all sat down again, West and Stubb poised to make notes.

"Did you push over before the Zeros got to you?"

"Yes, sir. But I think I might have been the last."

"Did the low ones bother you on the way out?"

"Oh yes, sir. Several of them. There are fourteen holes in my plane, but luckily Kidd and I weren't hit, and nothing vital in the plane either, apparently. I'm pretty sure Kidd hit at least one; it was smoking when it went by."

"Good for him! Any sign of our escort fighters?"

"Not in the target area, sir."

"Tell us about the shooting down of that Type Ninety-Nine on the way back."

Alan described it as factually as he could.

"You went for the leader, so no rear gunners could get you?"

"Yes, sir."

"Well done, Ericsson," Stubb said, beaming. He continued, "I'm going to recommend you for the Navy Cross."

Alan was taken aback. He knew he had done well, but the Navy Cross was the highest navy medal short of the Medal of Honor. He recovered quickly and said, also beaming, "Thank you very much, sir." *The Navy Cross! Back in January I wasn't really sure I could cut the mustard in the squadron.* He had come a long way.

Stubb changed the subject: "We're a little unclear about Lowery's dive. Did you see it?"

Alan's face fell. "Yes, sir. I turned south after I got away from the carrier, before the Zeros got on to us. I picked him up when he was around two thousand feet and saw the rest very clearly." Alan described it for Stubb and West. Although talking about it seemed to ease his grief a little, he broke down in tears at the end.

West rose and put his arm around Alan's shoulders. "That's OK, Alan; let it out."

Alan put his head down and followed orders, pulling out a handkerchief.

After a long pause, Stubb said, "There's a medal higher than the Navy Cross, Ericsson. Do you think Lowery earned it today?"

He's talking about the Medal of Honor, the highest military decoration there is! He looked up quickly at Stubb, smiling and blinking through his tears. "Oh yes, sir!"

"We do too. OK, Ericsson, try to relax—no telling what tomorrow might bring. I know there is a lot of work to do repairing planes, but having you rested and able to fly is more important. Get the men started on repairs and then hit the sack no later than twenty-one hundred. That is an order," said Stubb with a friendly smile.

"Yes, sir." Alan rose to leave, wiping his face.

"Again, you did a terrific job today. I'd like to make you flight officer, but there's no one who can do as good a job in engineering, and frankly that's more important right now."

"Thank you, sir." He turned and left, wishing he could bask in the feelings of accomplishment, but Jolly's loss made that impossible.

He went to the hangar next, to see how many planes were flyable and whether any more could be repaired in time to fly tomorrow. There would certainly be at least a search, and every flyable Dauntless would be needed. Goodwin was there and reported three airplanes immediately ready, but four more had minor damage and would probably be repaired by tomorrow morning, including 5-B-12. The plane captains were assessing the repairs needed by the remaining planes. There were two more planes in the air, being flown by Ross and Schultz. No further supervision or decisions were needed for the moment, and he returned to the ready room, while Phil went directly to the skipper's office to debrief.

Stubb and West returned to the ready room at 1720. Stubb came to Alan's seat and asked, "How many airplanes available, Ericsson?"

"Three now, plus the two on anti-torpedo, and probably four more for tomorrow morning."

"OK." Returning to the lectern, he addressed the squadron. "Flight quarters at oh five thirty tomorrow. There will be a dawn search, and the rest of you will be standing by for a strike in case they find anything. All squadrons will report the number of aircraft operational to the air office before flight quarters, and we will base the search and strike on those numbers. We want to send twelve planes in pairs between Scouting Five and us. Any left over will join the *Lexington* Dauntlesses for the strike, armed with one thousand pounders. Jensen, we will need a flexible roster for both groups for flight quarters tomorrow. Davis, after flight quarters, go to the hangar and get your men to help out with arming the *Lex* airplanes. No dress for supper. You are dismissed, but be ready to return here on short notice."

Teeth said to Alan, "I'm hungry. I'll make up the roster after supper. How about a quick look at the bomb damage on the way to supper?"

They wandered around on the third deck, under the hangar deck, neither of them being very familiar with that part of the ship. They became aware of odors of burned paint and flesh, and suddenly they came to a door that had charred paint. It stood open, and they saw that there was no deck on the other side. Alan wondered why it was left open, and then he saw that it was bent and could not close.

They looked through the doorway and saw that the deck in the next compartment had been split and bent upward against the bulkheads by an explosion in the compartment below, which was a complete shambles. At the doorway, they looked down on three sailors working to remove the remaining bodies and body parts from the tangled wreckage. Alan felt his stomach heave, and he thought this might not have been a good idea just before supper. Then he noticed that the men had the insignia showing they were rated as musicians, so they were members of the ship's band. He knew they were also rated as stretcher bearers, explaining how they got pressed into this duty.

The sailors had noticed the two pilots looking down and continued talking as they worked, probably to relieve the stress. "Damn pilots, they just have a good time zooming around and leave the dirty work to somebody else."

Alan had told Teeth he did not want his accomplishments on the strike trumpeted around the ship, but Teeth couldn't restrain himself. "Easy, sailor, today this pilot"—pointing at Alan—"got one of our few solid hits on a Jap carrier and used the forward guns in his bomber to shoot down one of their bombers on the way back."

The sailors abruptly stopped and looked up. One said, "I'm very sorry, sir. I guess I let this mess get my goat."

"That's OK, sailor; I don't blame you. You're doing the hardest work of all and getting no glory," Alan replied.

"Thank you, sir." A grateful smile flickered across the sailor's face, and they went back to work.

As Teeth and Alan started toward the wardroom for supper, Alan thought about how much worse the scene on *Lexington* must be. He found his feelings about the loss of Jolly were easing. Seeing the human remains in that compartment had made him realize that a lot of other men had suffered and died that day, and he shouldn't let his personal loss overwhelm him.

Meanwhile, Teeth had been quiet as they walked along the passageway, but suddenly he stopped, and, looking Alan in the eye, he blurted out, "You know, Jolly would be very proud of what you did today."

Alan smiled, looked Teeth in the eye, and said, "Thank you, Teeth. That means a lot to me." Alan knew that Teeth was grieving over the loss of Jolly also, and that made his statement stronger.

As they approached the wardroom, they became aware that it was filled with activity. Officers were coming out, and one said, "Wardroom's filled with the overflow from sick bay. You have to get sandwiches and coffee and take them back to your duty station."

Teeth and Alan got their sandwiches and coffee and returned to the ready room. As they came in, they noticed several strange faces. They turned out to be five pilots from Bombing Two. With five missing from Bombing Five, there were just enough seats. As the Bombing Five pilots settled into their regular seats, the Bombing Two pilots took the remaining seats, a lieutenant taking Jolly's seat.

Alan reached out to shake hands. "Alan Ericsson, Bombing Five."

The lieutenant shook his hand, saying, "Bill Moore, Bombing Two flight officer."

They both started to eat their sandwiches.

"And I'm the Bombing Five engineering officer. Our flight officer was my roommate, and he sat where you are. He went real low before he dropped on that Japanese carrier, and he got a hit square in the middle of the flight deck, but he wasn't able to complete his pullout. Einar Jensen, sitting next to the exec in the front row, is our new flight officer."

Bill looked glum and said, "Very sorry to hear your roommate didn't come back. It sounds like he was a genuine hero. I went on the strike, but we weren't fully fueled due to some snafu. We couldn't search very long, and we never found their ships. So we had to jettison our bombs and come back. We got back OK, and later I went on anti-torpedo patrol, before being told to land on *Yorktown*. We *Lex* pilots watched our ship being abandoned, and then we gathered in one corner of your wardroom, feeling pretty low. Then your Commander Keithley showed up with four bottles of Red Roses. The timing couldn't have been better," he said with a smile.

"He's a great exec, with a real understanding of morale."

At 1840, as they were finishing their makeshift supper, the bullhorn came on. "Now hear this. All personnel are off *Lexington* and have been picked up by Admiral Kinkaid's ships. Admiral Fitch and Captain Sherman are safe aboard *Minneapolis*. *Phelps* has been ordered to sink *Lexington* with torpedoes. That is all." There was a collective groan, although they had all known something like this was coming.

The pilots speculated about what would come next. The consensus was that with *Lexington* out of action, *Yorktown* alone did not have a lot of striking power left, even with the *Lexington* planes added, because so many needed repair. Alan guessed that only about half the airplanes on board were flyable. In addition to the airplanes needing repair, there were one or two from each *Yorktown* squadron that were stored disassembled, with the fuselages under the overhead in the hangar, but those would also require time and manpower to make operational. Until that was done and some airplanes were repaired, a strike would be too small to be very effective. Without *Neosho*, they had little choice but to leave the Coral Sea and head for a source of fuel. *Enterprise* and *Hornet* were rumored to be on their way to help, but they were still at least several days away. *If King hadn't sent them on a publicity stunt, they could've been here for the battle,* thought Alan. Alan thought of his friend Ed Miller in VF-6 on *Enterprise* and wondered if Les Travis had gotten into the *Hornet* air group.

Now West came in and addressed the pilots: "You've all noticed that we have five Bombing Two pilots here with us. Please make them welcome. Two of our pilots didn't come back, and three are in sick bay. If your roommate is one of those five, then your new temporary roommate is the Bombing Two pilot who is now sitting in your old roommate's seat. Any questions?" He paused and looked over the group. "Good. As you know, the wardroom is pretty well occupied with wounded men and medical people. Those who have a new roommate, on your way to your stateroom, take him down to the commissary for some uniforms and a toilet kit."

Alan turned to Bill with a grin. "Well, I guess we're now roommates. Welcome."

Bill smiled and said, "Thank you. I don't know which of us is senior, and I don't care."

"Fine with me, let's just forget about that for now. Do you know Rudi Fischer in Torpedo Two? He's an old friend from Pensacola."

"A big guy, full of enthusiasm?"

Alan smiled and nodded. "That's him."

"Don't know him real well. But he has a good reputation in the air group. I think he went on the strike."

"How about a fighter pilot named Wade Buckner?"

"Don't know most of the fighter pilots. A lot of them in Fighting Two came from Fighting Three, which was the squadron aboard at the Lae raid."

"You know I almost met your squadron back in March. I was waiting on *Lexington* to ferry a Dauntless back, when we took some of your planes before *Lex* headed back to Pearl. I ran into those same two Pensacola friends and chatted with them instead."

It was nearly 2000 when the ship suddenly shuddered. "What the hell was that?" Alan exclaimed.

"Damned if I know," said Bill.

"Never felt anything like that," said Teeth.

"I hope it isn't a sub torpedo," said Slick.

The conversation gradually resumed. After about fifteen minutes, the bullhorn came on. "This is the captain speaking. All ships have reported a shockwave from an underwater explosion, but no torpedoes or depth charges have detonated around the task force. We have learned it came from an explosion aboard *Lexington* when she went down. That is all."

Around 2030 Alan was feeling very tired and rose to go back to his stateroom. "It's been a long day. I think I'm ready to hit the sack."

"Me too," said Bill.

"OK, let's head for the commissary and get you fixed up. Follow me."

Alan and Bill went to the commissary and on to Alan's stateroom. As they approached, they were surprised to see that orderlies were carrying a wounded man on a stretcher into Alan's stateroom. Alan came up behind them and told them to take the man somewhere else, because he and Bill would be flying tomorrow, and they needed both bunks. The orderlies mumbled something and complied.

As they walked away, Alan was startled to see that another man occupied Jolly's bunk. Alan's exhausted mind was having trouble digesting all this. As he stared at this man, he noticed that he did not seem to be breathing. Alan approached and grasped the man's wrist. It was cold, and there was no pulse.

He straightened up and said to Bill, "This man is dead. Everybody is so busy; we won't be able to find anyone to move him."

"Let's get him out of here," said Bill.

"We'll park him in the passageway, and then they'll have to take him away."

Alan and Bill gently picked up the dead man and moved him to the passageway.

"I don't like asking you to take the bottom bunk after all this, but the top is mine."

"That's OK; don't worry about it." Bill started hanging up his new uniforms.

"You're lucky you weren't on the anti-torpedo patrol during the attack. Scouting Five lost four out of eight planes with their crews."

"Whew! That is bad."

"Yeah, they need to put more fighters on the carriers, so they won't have to use Dauntlesses as fighters. The new F-Four-F-Four Wildcat with folding wings should be a big help."

"You're right. I feel pretty frustrated. Most of you fought a big battle, but the Bombing Two pilots that went on the strike never saw the enemy all day long. You were on the strike?"

"Yeah."

Bill stopped and turned to face Alan. "Did you have any luck?"

"I got a hit on the carrier too, but it was up toward the bow. I also got one of their dive bombers on the way back."

Bill's eyebrows shot up. "What? You two guys got two of the three sure hits? I didn't know I would be staying in the dive bombing capital of the fleet! And an aerial victory too—congratulations!" He shook Alan's hand.

Alan smiled and said, "Thanks very much. On that note, I think it's time for a drink." He turned and began rummaging in a desk drawer. Soon he straightened up with a bottle of Scotch in his hand. "Would you like to join me?"

"Certainly. Much appreciated."

Alan took a good swallow from the bottle and handed it to Bill, who did likewise. Alan sat down on the one chair in the room, and Bill sat on the lower bunk. They each took several more swallows from the bottle as they chatted and wound down further from an extremely hectic day. Around 2100 they were both ready to hit the sack.

Alan went right to sleep but woke up later as his mind replayed the scene of Jolly's last dive over and over. Eventually he dozed off again but slept fitfully.

Saturday, May 9, 1942

Alan and Bill got up at 0415. The corpse had been moved away. Alan felt OK, but he knew he needed more sleep. Bill joined Alan for his usual walk up to the bow, and then they got breakfast to go in the wardroom. They could see that one corner of the dining area in the wardroom had been cleared, but there was not room for more than a few to sit down for breakfast. For flight quarters the six Fighting Two pilots had been told to meet with Fighting Five in their ready room. The seven from Scouting Two and the five from Bombing Two had been told to meet with the Scouting Two skipper, Dixon, in the cleared corner of the dining area in the wardroom.

Alan left Bill and headed for the hangar deck. Chief Patterson reported that they had completed the repairs on four airplanes, for a total of nine operational, and were getting ready to assemble their one stored airplane. Alan's airplane, 5-B-12, was one of those repaired during the night. The remaining unrepaired planes were thought to need more work than the work of assembling the stored one. They had also been able to repair three Bombing Two airplanes, which had minor problems. Still toting his breakfast, Alan went to the air office and reported the number of airplanes operational. Then he left for the Bombing Five ready room.

There Alan started munching his lukewarm breakfast at 0525. Stubb arrived just before flight quarters. When the alarm stopped, he had a brief conversation with Teeth, who went to the blackboards and began filling in names on two rosters of pilots.

Stubb went to the lectern, put down his papers, and looked out over the pilots with a resolute expression. "The undamaged enemy carrier and a possible additional carrier could be coming after us, but we don't know. Engineering reports they have repaired four planes, so we now have nine of our fifteen remaining Dauntlesses available for duty. There will be a dawn search of the northern semicircle with twelve Dauntlesses in pairs. We will send five, and Scouting Five will send all seven they have available. Lieutenant Jensen is putting up the roster now, and he will fill in the four on the list over here, which will be our contribution to the strike, if it happens. The rest of you will be on standby. The dive bombers on the strike will be mainly composed of the twelve airplanes from Scouting Two and Bombing Two. Stand by for the rosters to be posted."

Teeth was writing the names and consulting a sheet he had in his hand. Soon he was finished, and Alan looked over the two lists. He saw that he was not one of the five pilots on the search roster. The roster for the strike was Stubb, West, Jensen, and Ericsson. He looked around the room and noticed that all the uninjured pilots were present, so there were four more if needed. Tired as he was, Alan was gratified the he was one the four assigned to the strike, which might not be needed, rather than the boring search, which would definitely happen. He was particularly pleased as he realized that his bombing hit had apparently elevated his bombing status in the squadron.

Stubb continued, "Our ship's radar is out, so we are depending on *Chester*'s radar. *Russell* has been ordered to trail twenty miles behind to act as a radar picket. That is all for now." He sat down and started chatting with West.

As dawn approached, the bullhorn gave orders for the search crews to man their planes, and the five pilots gathered their gear and departed.

Alan had been hoping to visit Mike Burke in sick bay and perhaps have time to start writing letters to Jolly's wife and family. He couldn't go to sick bay under standby, but he started a draft letter to Irene, Jolly's wife.

Suddenly the teletype at the front came to life. West went over, tore off a message, and handed it to Stubb. Conversation stopped.

Stubb read it quickly and looked up at the pilots. "Admiral Leary in Australia reports that reconnaissance has confirmed that the Japanese invasion convoy has continued north. That's good news and indicates that, in spite of heavy losses, Task Force Seventeen accomplished its mission. The invasion of Port Moresby was stopped."

Maybe the Japanese are not the victors after all. They caused more damage, but in the end we got what we wanted, and they did not, Alan thought. *But then again, maybe it's not over yet.* He resumed writing his draft, fervently hoping that it was indeed over.

The men in the ready room relaxed as best they could for the next two and a half hours. Alan's eyelids drooped after a few minutes, and he fell soundly asleep.

He woke up with a start when the bullhorn suddenly barked, "Now hear this. Search has found a carrier force. Stand by for strike." Alan groaned along with most of the other pilots. His watch said 0912. The teletype gave the details: bearing 310, distance 175, course 110, speed 25.

Apparently the battle is not over, thought Alan with a heavy heart. *They're headed into the wind for flight operations. If they're launching a strike, it should be here within two hours.*

The phone rang, and Stubb answered. He listened briefly and said, "Yes, sir." Then he quickly left the ready room, apparently called to a meeting. A few minutes went by. Then the klaxon sounded, and the ship went to general quarters.

Alan felt the throb of the ship's propellers as she picked up speed. He thought fuel must be a concern. *The big ships probably have a fair amount of oil left, and, if there was no enemy threat, they would refuel the destroyers. The destroyers must be getting very low on oil, with so much high speed steaming and no chance to refuel. I'm surprised they don't wait to increase speed until an incoming enemy strike shows up on radar.*

The bullhorn announced, "Now here this. *Chester* has seen bogeys on radar, so the enemy may know our location. That is all."

Stubb returned about twenty minutes later and announced, "Admiral Fletcher has been considering a strike. With us steaming away, it would be a very long mission for the Dauntlesses, and the Devastators would have to hope they could get close to

Australia. The Wildcats would all be needed to defend the ship. So it would be a desperate move, only justified if an enemy attack was close and certain. Commander Dixon, the skipper of Scouting Two, volunteered to lead three of his pilots on a search and strike mission, to be sure of what we're up against, a very courageous proposal. The admiral took him up on it, and they'll take off shortly. *Aylwin* is being sent back as another radar picket and to help Dixon's men find us when they get back. Also we might learn something more when the dawn search returns, a couple of hours from now. So for now we wait."

Soon Alan heard the roar of each engine and the rumbling on the flight deck above as the four Dauntlesses took off. He wondered if Bill Moore was one of the three with Dixon. Quiet descended on the ready room again.

Having napped, Alan was no longer sleepy. An hour went by, and he completed his draft.

> *c/o Fleet Post Office*
> *San Francisco, Calif.*
> *May 9, 1942*

Dear Irene,

    Yesterday our ship was in combat with the Japanese, and I am deeply grieved to tell you that your husband, Jim, lost his life as a result. I am not allowed to tell you the details now, but I saw what happened. His actions were in the highest tradition of the US Navy, and I believe that he will be duly recognized, and you will be informed.

    As you know, Jim and I have shared a stateroom for many months, and we became close friends. Jim was a mentor to me in all his flying, and we shared an appreciation of all that was going on around us. His loss has left a deep void in my life, as I am sure it will in the lives of all who knew him.

Please accept my most sincere condolences. I hope that at some time in the future there will be an opportunity for me to visit you and answer any questions you may have about what happened.

Sincerely,
Alan Ericsson

Then the bullhorn announced that *Chester* could see the dawn search returning on radar.

Or is it their incoming strike? No, our search planes will be coming in on various headings, not in formation, so Chester should be able to tell. Whew!

About twenty minutes later, the Dauntlesses began thumping down on the flight deck one by one. Alan counted eleven, so one was missing. His watch said 1142. The bullhorn reported that one of the search planes had ditched, and *Morris* was picking up the crew.

One less Dauntless. Why hasn't a Japanese strike shown up on radar by now? Alan wondered.

Another half hour went by, and the teletype came to life. West tore off the message and handed it to Stubb, who read it and announced, "The search pilot confirmed the sighting. Admiral Fletcher has decided to request help from the army in Australia. He is sending the flag gunnery officer, Commander Schindler, to Rockhampton in the back seat of a Scouting Five Dauntless." A half hour later there came the sound of the lone Dauntless taking off.

A long, one way mission, thought Alan. *This long wait in the ready room is getting very tiresome, and I'm getting hungry.*

"Now hear this. Stand down from condition one to condition two," came from the bullhorn a few minutes later.

Stubb stood up and addressed the pilots. "OK, you're free to go, but be ready to get back here fast."

This was the longest time by far that most of the pilots, including Alan, had ever been confined to the ready room. They were glad to take a walk, and they headed for the wardroom for some food. Alan was always a bit surprised that his appetite seemed to grow faster when he was sitting still than when he was getting exercise.

The pilots brought sandwiches and coffee back to the ready room and ate their lunches there.

Alan looked over his letter to Irene and decided it was OK, and copied most of it into his letter to Jolly's parents. Some of the pilots were asleep. He pulled out his book and began to read.

The bullhorn came on again. "Now hear this. Four scouts returning on radar." Alan checked his watch; it was 1504. They were gone five hours, so they must have made a thorough search, but there had been no announcements. *Two searches have gone out and returned in good weather without seeing any Japanese airplanes, and the last one would have reported any ships right away. Now it seems unlikely that the Japanese are coming after us. Maybe they turned back north, or the sighting was some kind of mistake.* Soon the four had thumped down on the flight deck.

A half hour later, the bullhorn announced, "Now hear this. The second search did not find any ships in the position reported for the enemy force by the dawn search. That is all."

The tension in the ready room slackened considerably, but no orders to stand down from condition two arrived.

Alan went up to the front and asked Stubb, "Could I get permission to visit Mike Burke in sick bay?"

"Unnecessary absence from the ready room under condition two? Out of the question," said Stubb, looking grim. Then his expression softened. "But I won't notice unless you don't come back fast if anything happens. Give him my best."

Sick bay was down low in the ship toward the bow. Alan had only been there a few times, and it took him a while to find it again. He decided to check there first, and they would tell him if Mike had been moved to the wardroom. As he walked in, he noticed a talker standing near the central supply area with earphones and a microphone. Alan realized he was there to quietly relay messages and ship announcements to the staff, instead of having a bullhorn disturbing the patients. Alan stopped and told the talker to let him know if there were any alerts.

Alan spotted Mike's red hair and turned toward his bed. Mike looked up as Alan approached and asked, "Stringy, what the hell are you doing here? Aren't we being pursued by a Jap carrier force?"

Apparently some word had leaked in to the patients about what had been happening. Alan replied, "The dawn search reported a force headed our way. Then a second search right around the reported location couldn't find anything. Radar has seen some bogeys, but no one, including the search pilots, has seen an enemy airplane, carrier type or otherwise, and the weather is good. Most people are beginning to doubt the one crew that says they saw anything. The skipper said he would take no notice if I left the ready room and sent his best."

Mike's smile broke through. "Thanks, Alan. We get only bits and pieces of news down here, and it's worse than getting the whole hard truth. I heard *Lexington* went down, but I have heard almost nothing about our strike or *Lexington*'s yesterday. I was tail end Charlie yesterday, flying wing on Jensen. I came close, but no hit. There seemed to have been two areas hit, slightly aft of the island and up near bow on the port side. I was very sorry to hear Jolly didn't come back. What happened?"

Alan described both strikes and gave a detailed description of Jolly's dive, his own dive, and his victory on the way back. "I'd be much happier if someone else got a hit and a victory, instead of me, but Jolly survived."

"Yeah, he was such a great guy, a great pilot and never overburdened with the gravity. We'll all miss him terribly."

Alan asked, "Now what about you? I heard the Zeros were on the third division before the dive. Is that when you got hit?"

"No. Although they might've gotten Jolly. They tried to get us, but we were so slow even before we pushed over that they didn't have long to fire. I got hit after the pullout, when they were all over us."

"What about your flight back? You must have had a lot of pain in your elbow and ankle. I don't see how you landed safely."

"It was hard, but I was determined to get back aboard. I worked out a system on the way back. I used my right hand for the throttle as well as the stick. I used rudder trim on the way back, so I wouldn't have to use my feet. Then when I got into the landing pattern, I put in a lot of right rudder trim and then pushed only the left rudder pedal, so I wouldn't have to use my right foot. It worked."

"Pretty damn clever," said Alan with a smile. "Did your gunner get hit?"

"Yeah, he got hit in the upper left arm. It wasn't too bad, and he was able to climb out on his own when we got back."

"Do you have any pain now?"

"Not much. Mostly I'm bored. Stubb stopped by briefly last night, but you're the first one that's given me any real news. Keep it coming."

Alan grinned. "OK. Now I better get back. See you soon." He quickly returned to the ready room. Nothing had changed, and Alan settled into his book again.

After another hour and a half, the bullhorn came on. "Now hear this. Stand down from condition baker and condition two. Set normal watches. That is all."

Alan looked up and realized he was hungry again.

A little while later, the teletype came to life. West tore off the message and gave it to Stubb, who stood up to address the pilots. "Commander Schindler made it to Australia and got in touch with Admiral Leary. The army sent out a big search/strike mission. It's now almost dark, and there has been no word that the searches turned up anything. I would say it looks like this enemy force turned around and went north after the first sighting, or perhaps it was a mistaken sighting. Supper in the wardroom is delayed to nineteen hundred, dress not required. Flight quarters at oh five forty tomorrow. You are dismissed."

There was a buzz of conversation among the pilots, making all sorts of speculations, as they got up and started to disperse.

Arriving at the wardroom for supper, Alan saw that most of the dining area had been cleared of wounded men. He sat down at the higher officers table next to Bill Moore. Stubb was a few seats away down the table. Burch and Pederson were also there. There were more new faces, which he quickly realized were those of the other higher ranking *Lexington* pilots that had landed on *Yorktown*. Burch introduced his opposite number on *Lexington*, Lieutenant Commander Dixon, skipper of Scouting

Two, sitting across from Stubb. Then introductions went around the table, including three lieutenants, one each from Fighting Two, Scouting Two, and Bombing Two, the last being Bill.

Alan asked Bill, "Did you go on the search with Commander Dixon?"

"Yeah, it was long." Alan was aware that nearby conversation at the table had stopped.

Just then Stubb said to Dixon, "Bob, hats off to you guys for volunteering for a search and strike mission. You didn't find any trace of an enemy force?" Now the whole table was listening.

"Thanks, Warren. The only thing we saw was a reef. Part of it had a flattop, kind of rectangular. The surf made a pattern pretty similar to the wakes of ships. It would have been possible to mistake the reef for a carrier task force, especially if you stayed away so you wouldn't be spotted."

"So maybe that's what the crew that reported the carrier force actually saw," added Stubb.

"That is what they saw. A little while ago, when Admiral Fletcher had gotten no word of the army finding anything, he sent for the pilot, Falconer. When the admiral questioned him, Falconer admitted he might have seen a reef instead of ships. I was in the air office when the admiral called and gave us the word. So I think the mystery is solved."

"Falconer is a great pilot, but he can be a little overeager at times," said Burch.

Stubb nodded and said, "Wow. Everybody's been on edge the whole day over a reef."

Dixon replied, "That's right."

There were grins and contented comments around the table.

Alan hoped he would be able to meet before long with Hank Stinson to get an idea of the admiral's staff view of the battle and aftermath.

This was the first time since the battle that the pilots had a chance to talk to pilots outside their own squadron. The discussion turned to the momentous battle of the previous day. Dixon described the search for the enemy carriers, which had departed shortly after dawn. With the location of the enemy carriers completely unknown, it was a full 360 degree search, consisting of twelve from Scouting Two covering the northern arc to 200 miles and six from Bombing Two covering the southern arc to 150 miles. The enemy turned out to be in the search sector next to Dixon's, so he flew over and corrected the location given in the first report and gave the course and speed, which had been left out of the first report. He then shadowed the enemy force for a full hour before returning to *Lexington*.

Alan was impressed. *And he volunteered to lead the search today. A brave and diligent officer.*

Then the conversation turned to hashing over the strikes against the Japanese carriers.

Dixon asked, "Have you guys heard anything about how the *Lexington* strike went? We haven't been back aboard her since the strike returned, so we've heard nothing."

Pederson said that he was the *Yorktown* FDO, so he heard a lot of the strike planes on the radio. He said that apparently Bombing Two never found the target. "There was some foul up, so they were not fully fueled. They couldn't search very long before they had to jettison their bombs and come back. They made it back to *Lexington* OK."

"I was in that group, and that is correct," said Bill.

"Besides the fogging, maybe that helps to explain why we only got three sure hits," said West.

Pederson continued, "Anyway, your air group commander, Commander Ault, got to the target with three from Scouting Two. By then Bombing Five had gotten two hits and departed. One of Ault's group got the third hit on the carrier, a solid hit amidships. Sorry, I don't know the names of Scouting Two pilots."

Dixon grinned and gave a thumbs up at the news that one of his men got the third hit.

Pederson continued, "One of those Scouting Two planes came back alone and landed safely on *Lexington*. Ault and the other two stayed together, but they got disoriented and low on fuel. Both Ault and his gunner were wounded. Ault called your FDO, but he couldn't help because the *Lex* had to shut her radar down. Then I talked to Ault, but I couldn't find him on radar because he was still too far away. Ault said he didn't have much fuel left and signed off. I was really upset, because there was nothing I could do to help. All of our air group remember Commander Ault with respect because of what he did at the Lae raid."

Alan remembered meeting Commander Ault when he visited *Lexington* seven weeks earlier. He probably became disoriented because he was disabled or distracted by his wounds.

The *Lexington* men seemed gratified that the *Yorktown* men appreciated the situation.

As the officers were finishing supper, the ship's exec, Commander Keithley, appeared and called for quiet to make an announcement. "We went through a battle yesterday and then had a long and anxious day today. I think you all deserve something to relax with, so we are serving good old fashioned navy grog at these two tables. Help yourself."

"Hear, hear," shouted one officer, and there was a standing round of applause, followed quickly by the officers clustering around the two tables. Alan got his mug of grog, and they all went back to their seats.

Pederson stood up and raised his mug. "I would just like to salute the gallant ship *Lexington*, Lady Lex, and all her officers and men, some of whom are here aboard with us."

The *Yorktown* officers stood and gave an emotional toast to *Lexington*, which was appreciated by the little group of *Lexington* officers, some of whom wiped their eyes.

Sunday, May 10, 1942

Bill and Alan had breakfast and reported to their ready rooms at 0540.

The flight and general quarters alert came over the bullhorn, followed immediately by a stand down to normal watches.

Stubb addressed the pilots: "We're still not sure yet that we're out of danger. Ericsson and Ross, stand by. The rest of you are dismissed, but be ready to return here on short notice. Regular duty schedule. That is all." As the rest of the pilots dispersed, Alan and Ross went up to the front.

Stubb looked grim. "As the roommates of the two men who didn't come back, I have to ask you to gather up their personal belongings today. Bring them to the squadron office, and give them to the yeoman for safe keeping. I hope you will write letters to any close relatives that you know about and bring those to the squadron office also, where I will put them with the letters I have to write."

"Yes, sir," they each said.

Stubb looked both of them in the eye and said, "Thanks."

Alan decided to get that duty done right away. He went to the commissary and got some empty cardboard boxes and then went to his stateroom. He packed up Jolly's uniforms and clothes and turned to the desk and shelves above it. He had shared the desk with Jolly, each having a shelf and a couple of drawers. There were two photos of Irene and letters from her. Alan remembered that they had seemed like a compatible and happy couple when he had socialized with them at Norfolk. There were also letters from Jolly's parents in New York.

Just then the klaxon sounded general and flight quarters, and the bullhorn announced, "Radar has a formation of bogeys approaching from the east, about fifty miles out. That is all."

That doesn't sound good. Alan left quickly and reported to the ready room. Soon all the uninjured pilots were there. Stubb had no more information, and Alan resigned himself to waiting.

About fifteen minutes went by, and then the bullhorn announced, "Lookouts have spotted the bogeys. They are B-Seventeens. Possibly they are being ferried from Noumea to Townsville. Stand down from general and flight quarters; resume regular watches. That is all."

That's better. Alan returned to his stateroom and continued collecting Jolly's things. As he searched further, he found an unopened bottle of Scotch that he had not been aware of. *Tricky devil*, thought Alan with a smile. He put the Scotch with his own, knowing that if he passed it on with Jolly's other belongings, it would not get far. The only other things were a few knickknacks whose significance was unknown to Alan. *It all amounts to just a shadow of the Jolly I knew*, he thought sadly. He put his two letters in envelopes and addressed them. He collected the boxes and his letters and carried them all to the squadron office.

Then he went to the hangar to supervise the ongoing repair of the squadron's airplanes. Goodwin was there, and Alan knew he had been working very hard on the repairs. Alan took him aside and let him know how much Alan appreciated his efforts. Then he rolled up his sleeves and went to work. For Alan and Phil, supervision included helping directly in the repair work and getting their hands dirty. Alan knew that this was irregular in the navy, but he knew that the men appreciated the assistance and knowing that the officers knew firsthand what was going on. Of course they had chosen the planes needing the easiest repairs to work on first. The remaining unrepaired airplanes had much more extensive damage.

Throughout the day there were further scares from bogeys on radar. Alan knew that no refueling was possible while this was going on.

At 1705 the bullhorn announced, "Now hear this. *Yorktown* and her escorts are turning east to pass south of New Caledonia and head directly for Tongatabu. Officers dress for the evening meal. That is all."

There was a cheer throughout the hangar. Alan thought it most likely was echoed throughout the ship. Everyone, including the enlisted men, knew that officers dressing for supper meant that they were out of danger. As a relaxed feeling flooded into him, Alan realized how keyed up he had been for the whole last week. Now the battle was really over. At Tongatabu, he might get a letter from Jennifer. It seemed like a long time since he had gotten her last letter, even though it had only been three weeks.

Suddenly he realized that by now she would know every-thing about the battle, except that she might not have been able to find out whether he had been killed or injured. She might be very worried. He thought about it, but there was no way to let her know, except by writing a letter. He was sure that with her connections she would get ahold of a casualty list before the letter arrived. Anyway, with no oilers coming, no mail could leave the ship before they reached Tongatabu, and he could write her then.

As he came into the wardroom for supper, he saw that the eating area had been cleared of wounded men, but they still occupied the lounging area. The *Lexington* officers were excused from dress uniforms, since they didn't have any. Alan thought the return to the normal routine, however, helped everyone to relax and put the battle behind them.

After supper Alan spotted Hank Stinson leaving the wardroom. He was dragging himself along, looking completely worn out. Alan hastily dropped the idea of meeting with Hank that evening.

CHAPTER SEVENTEEN

Rest and Relief

Monday, May 11, 1942

Bill Moore went with Alan to the hangar deck at 0600, to check on the maintenance of the Bombing Two airplanes, which were being serviced by Alan's men.

Around 0900 the bullhorn announced, "Now here this. All the *Lexington* survivors, except those on this ship, have been transferred to *Portland* and *Chester*. Admiral Kinkaid, with *Minneapolis, New Orleans*, and two destroyers, is departing for Noumea to provision and then join Admiral Halsey and Task Force Sixteen with *Enterprise* and *Hornet*, which is nearing the New Hebrides. Admiral Smith with *Astoria* and a destroyer will accompany Admiral Kinkaid to Noumea, then rejoin Task Force Seventeen at Tongatabu. The rest of Task Force Seventeen is continuing direct to Tongatabu. That is all."

So Halsey is relieving us at last. Since Kinkaid has not been out here very long, it makes sense for him to join Halsey. Alan saw Bill Moore nearby, and he went over and said to him, "It's good to hear your squadron mates are off the destroyers. They must have been awfully crowded. And that would have severely limited the destroyers' combat capability also."

"That's right. I'm sure it's a little cozy on the cruisers too, but far better than the destroyers and not all that rolling motion."

It was a peaceful day, and Alan was on the hangar deck for most of it. After supper, Hank Stinson approached Alan. He looked well rested, and he proposed meeting aft in the port gallery at 1930.

Alan got to the gallery a little early and enjoyed the steady wind as the ship cruised along at 15 knots. As they were going east, almost directly into the trade wind, the wind over the deck was almost 30 knots. Right on time Hank emerged out of the darkness.

"Good evening, Hank. Well, we have a lot to catch up on."

"Damn right, Alan, greetings. Last night I was a basket case. It was all I could do to dress for supper. I had slept about six hours in the previous three days. I'm certainly not ready to go through that again right away. It really started on the seventh, when we went into action against the invasion force. As soon as the admiral got the scouting report, he shot the bolt, which is what I would have done. Then *Neosho* radioed that she was under air attack, but she didn't say whether it was carrier aircraft or flying boats. Later we decided it was probably carrier aircraft, coming from the carriers we fought the next day. Then a short time later the search returned, and we found out the report was miscoded, so no carriers. Then a little later, we got the report from Australia that there was a carrier in that vicinity after all. It was like riding an emotional roller coaster."

"It was for the whole air group too. So was it really just bad luck that their carrier search found *Neosho* and *Sims*?"

"Well, yes, but we later realized it was a big mistake not to send them farther south, since the enemy carriers could have been almost anywhere in the northern Coral Sea. Also they were within search range of Shortland and Tulagi, which may be operational as seaplane bases. We were too focused on the invasion convoy. So anyway, our strike sank the carrier, but all indications were that she was some kind of light carrier.

"It was quite a scene on the flag bridge when Burch and Taylor came up after the attack. The admiral quizzed them about the attack, and Taylor said he would have pictures of the carrier in just a few minutes. The admiral thought he was joking. Sure enough Taylor's gunner came up, with photos still dripping from the darkroom. When Buckthorn and Fletcher saw them, they bounced up and down like they had hit the jackpot!" Hank was grinning.

Alan laughed, "That would have been fun to see."

"It was. But we all had to come back down to earth and face the lack of location of the enemy fleet carriers. Then at suppertime an enemy strike shows up on radar, but it's going past us to the south, not knowing we're there. Our CAP shot down a bunch, and then the rest of them come over and hover around like they want to land aboard. It was one unbelievably bizarre event after another."

"You bet. Were you on the flag bridge?"

"Mostly right behind in flag plot. But by then it was too dark to see much from the bridge. After that a night air strike and night surface action were considered but rejected because we only had Baird's direction for their carriers, with distance unknown, and the weather was lousy. Finally around midnight Fitch and Fletcher made plans for the eighth, and we all turned in around oh one hundred.

"On the eighth, an orderly woke me up at oh four hundred. The dawn search found them at extreme range, and they found us. We couldn't turn toward them because of the point option course for the returning search. After that it was a long and busy day, as you well know.

"I finally got to turn in around midnight and had to get up at oh four hundred on the ninth again. It was very gratifying to hear from Admiral Leary that the invasion force was continuing north, so we accomplished what we came to do. But we lost *Lexington*, and *Yorktown* had taken a beating. We didn't have very much striking power, even with the planes from *Lex*. Then Falconer's mistaken report came in, and we were all on edge again. Dixon should get a medal for volunteering to lead that search; it was just what was needed. When he got back and reported that reef, we began to put two and two together, and finally in the late afternoon Falconer confessed his honest mistake. It must have been an anxious day for you pilots also."

"It was."

"That evening, when Keithley was serving grog to the pilots, the admiral's staff got some too. It was most welcome. But it was another short night, with the threat of pursuit still there.

"Yesterday the admiral planned to fuel the destroyers, but we kept having scares, so it couldn't happen. Nimitz and King didn't get the word that *Lexington* had been sunk until that morning. Our report on the eighth apparently did not get through, but it was routinely retransmitted. We assume that King was not pleased to hear about the loss of his favorite ship.

"Finally in the afternoon, the admiral decided we were out of the woods. I imagine the whole ship was glad to hear we were headed straight to Tongatabu. Nimitz had arranged for an oiler and transports for the *Lexington* personnel to meet us there. It was good to get back to the normal routine. Last night I finally got to sleep for ten hours straight, and I felt like a new man this morning. Now let's hear your side of it."

Alan proceeded to tell how the search and anti-torpedo patrol made most of the seventh a boring day for him. The Japanese strike coming by at suppertime made for excitement. Then he told Hank about the *Yorktown* dive bomber strike on the eighth, including his hit, his roommate's heroic performance, and his aerial victory on the way back.

"Alan, I hope you are very proud of what you did—you should be."

"Thanks very much, Hank."

"I was very sorry to hear about Lowery. Keep this to yourself, Alan, but there is some talk among the staff about a Medal of Honor for him. Did you see his dive?"

"Thanks, Hank. Our skipper is considering making that recommendation also. And yes, I saw the last part of his dive very clearly."

"Good. I think Lowery definitely earned it. The admiral might like to hear your eye witness account. What happened after you got back?"

"We waited in the ready room. None of us were looking forward to a second strike, so we began to relax in midafternoon when it no longer seemed likely. The skipper briefed us on the big picture, and then we went back to routine duties. The five Bombing Two pilots joined us in our ready room for a sandwich supper.

"We had two pilots lost and three in sick bay, so the Bombing Two pilots got their seats in the ready room and slept in their bunks. The Bombing Two flight officer got Lowery's bunk. Nice guy. He had a frustrating day, never sighting the enemy. The

Bombing Two strike never found the target, and then he had anti-torpedo patrol after the Japanese had gone home. Looking back I think his presence helped me not to dwell on Jim's absence."

"That makes sense, Alan."

"I didn't sleep too well that night. On the ninth it was the longest wait in the ready room I've experienced. I fell asleep in the morning until the search report came in, and that helped. Around lunchtime they eased up, so we could leave and get lunch. I really began to relax when Dixon's search was returning on radar with no reports of finding anything."

"I did too."

"At supper we heard about the reef and Falconer's mistake. Yesterday we knew the enemy might still be in pursuit. I listened to the various scares on the bullhorn and gathered up my roommate's clothes and personal effects. The Tongatabu announcement was great news. There was loud cheering through the whole ship. We're going to rest and replenish there, and then what?"

"We're going on to Pearl. Two days ago Nimitz told us to go direct from Tongatabu to Bremerton, but yesterday he changed it to Pearl. It seems a little odd, since I'm fairly sure that Pearl Harbor does not have as good facilities for major repairs as Bremerton."

"Bremerton would probably have been much more welcome to all hands except me."

"Probably. Maybe *Yorktown* is going to make a brief stop at Pearl and then go on to the West Coast, because Nimitz needs our pilots and planes. If not, and *Yorktown* is going to be repaired at Pearl, then it must be because Nimitz doesn't want *Yorktown* to be tied up in repair on the West Coast for a long time, like *Saratoga* has been. He has our damage report, and maybe he thinks she could be made serviceable at Pearl under his direct supervision, so she would be available much sooner than if she went to the West Coast. Anyway, if that is the case, it suggests that Nimitz thinks *Yorktown* can't be spared.

"It has only been about a month since *Hornet* became available, giving us four carriers in the Pacific until we lost *Lexington. Saratoga*, the Dry Dock Queen, is planned to leave the West Coast sometime in early June, and *Wasp* is expected to arrive from the Atlantic around the same time. Until then we're back to three carriers, counting *Yorktown*. So maybe she can't be spared.

"You're probably aware that, until this battle, most of the navy brass thought we were better than the Japanese, and we could accept numerical inferiority in a head to head carrier battle and still win. The tone seems to have changed now."

"I guess I'm one of the skeptics that thought the Japanese were as good as us, or close to it, all along, so my feelings about their capability haven't changed. Your logic seems very sound to me, Hank. They must be feeling the pinch if they're bringing *Wasp* out to the Pacific. The only reason to deny complete overhaul to a worn and battered ship is that she can't be spared. In that case Nimitz might want to use *Yorktown* with her air group, or he might replace her air group with squadrons available at Pearl Harbor. It also sounds like there is some kind of threat that may come to a head before mid June."

"You know, Alan, you would fit right in on the admiral's staff. Too bad there isn't an opening."

Alan smiled and replied, "You'd have to fleet up to Senior Sage, so I could have your job."

Stinson laughed. "Senior Sage, I like the sound of that."

Alan knew that nearly all hands were looking forward to continuing on from Tongatabu to a West Coast port for a well deserved rest. He decided that, except for his good friends Teeth Jensen and Slick Davis, he would not cast a shadow over anyone's dreams by mentioning his and Hank's speculations to the contrary.

Tuesday, May 12, 1942

Around 0930 an orderly found Alan on the hangar deck and gave him a request from Admiral Fletcher to meet him at 1100. At 1050 Alan was hurrying to flag country in a fresh uniform. He was admitted and waited a few minutes before Fletcher came out of his office. Alan thought he looked tired and worn.

"Lieutenant Ericsson, nice to see you again."

They shook hands while Alan said, "My pleasure, sir; thank you, sir."

"Come into my office," said Fletcher, turning, and Alan followed.

"Have a seat," said Fletcher as he took his seat. He smiled and said, "You brought great credit to your ship and your squadron, making a hit on their carrier and shooting down a dive bomber—well done!"

"Thank you very much, sir."

"Now my flag lieutenant tells me that you had a clear view of what happened when Lieutenant Lowery dove on the carrier. We have been considering how to properly recognize his heroic conduct, and I would like to hear an eye witness account."

"Yes, sir." Alan proceeded to tell the story again. Being in the presence of the admiral seemed to heighten his emotions, and Alan had moist eyes once more at the end of his account.

"Thank you very much, Ericsson. That was very helpful. I can see that his loss weighs on you."

"Yes, sir. He was my mentor and best friend, as well as my roommate."

"I see. Well, his sacrifice was not in vain. For the first time, we were able to stop the Japanese and turn them back, although it was very costly." Fletcher's grim expression gave way to a formal smile. "And you should be very proud of your part in it."

"Yes, sir. Thank you, sir," replied Alan, faintly smiling also.

Fletcher stood and said, "Thank you for your account, and good luck to you."

Alan was on his feet and replied, "Thank you, sir. It has been a pleasure serving under you. Good luck to you."

Fletcher smiled and said, "Thank you, Ericsson."

Friday, May 15, 1942

TF-17 was nearing the Tonga Islands once again, this time after a fast moving battle, instead of weeks of boredom. At 0530, as Alan and Bill were finishing breakfast in the wardroom, they heard the sound of airplanes taking off. They had been briefed that most of the flyable airplanes would be flying into the airstrip on Tongatabu. The pilots and plane captains, riding in the back seat, would remain ashore. The remaining pilots and enlisted men would be living on board *Yorktown*. The task force would be at Tongatabu several days, and all hands would have a chance for liberty ashore. Both Alan and Bill were in the group staying aboard, because they both had work to do in the ongoing aircraft repairs. *Yorktown* now had 55 planes operational, including those from *Lexington*, seven more than their strength the day after the battle. Fourteen remained to be repaired.

Alan was on the hangar deck later in the morning when he felt the wind start to blow in from the port side of the open hangar. He looked up and could see from the new direction of the sun that the ship had turned right onto a southerly heading to pick up the channel into Nukualofa Roads.

Just before lunch Alan went up to the bow and saw that the ship was entering the harbor. He saw several transports in the anchorage but no oilers. The ship was steaming slowly west, following the channel, so the trade wind was blowing from aft forward along the flight deck. Alan got a strong whiff of the stack gas coming from the funnel and was struck by its unusual odor. The odor normally varied some, depending on how the boilers were being fired, but this was quite different. Alan wondered why it should suddenly change.

As Alan approached the wardroom for lunch, he recognized a lieutenant from the ship's engineering department. "Hi, Vern. Say, what's going on in the fire rooms? The stack gas smells really different."

"Oh, hi, Alan. It should smell different. We got so low on bunker oil early this morning that we had to switch to diesel oil from the auxiliary generator tank. The admiral was told to expect oil here, so he cut it awfully close."

"Wow. That is cutting it close. I was up on the bow just now, and I didn't see an oiler."

"*Kanawha* was supposed to be here, but I heard she hasn't come in yet."

"Thanks for the dope, Vern."

"Sure thing, Alan." Alan knew *Kanawha* was the navy's first oiler, AO-1, commissioned in 1915, a slow ship with around half the capacity of the modern fast oilers.

Alan did not get to go ashore that day. The word circulated that mail was coming aboard. When Alan went to shower and change for supper, he found a letter from Jennifer in his room.

Bill Moore was there, and he said, "I wonder if any mail will catch up with me."

"Wherever they send it, somebody there will know where you are, so I wouldn't give up hope yet. Please excuse me while I read this letter."

"Sure."

> *Honolulu, T. H.*
> *April 27, 1942*
>
> *Dear Alan,*
>
> *How are you? I miss you a lot, even though my friends do a great job trying to keep my mind off you. I got your letter of April 20. Who knows where this letter might find you.*
>
> *I gather your boredom will probably end soon. Please be very careful, and remember you are not expendable. I hope you are proud of what you are doing—you should be.*
>
> *We continue to get better at what we are doing. The office is extremely busy now, for reasons that will become clear, but morale is holding up well.*
>
> *Maybe we will get to see each other again soon. I can't wait, you rascal. I love you very much.*
>
> *Oodles of love,*
> *Jennifer*

Her letter set his mind in a whirl. *What a lot has happened since she wrote this! And she hints that she saw it coming. A week before the battle started, I bet her office was busy!*

This letter also made him feel close to her, as they always did. He couldn't wait to see her, and that should happen soon. So soon that he would see her before anything he wrote could reach her.

He said to Bill, "It's a letter from my wife. I'm very lucky because she's a civilian working for the navy at Pearl, and I should get to see her soon."

"She works for the navy? What does she do?"

Alan knew he should have seen this coming. "She's in something called the Combat Intelligence Unit. They keep track of ship movements, things like that."

"Oh, sounds interesting."

On the bow with Bill just before supper, Alan noticed that the cruiser *Astoria* and her escorts, with Admiral Smith, had rejoined the task force from Noumea.

At supper he learned that the *Lexington* pilots aboard *Yorktown* would be riding her back to Pearl Harbor, unlike those on the cruisers, who were going to the West Coast. So Bill would be his roommate for a while longer.

After supper, Alan joined most of the officers and men in attending a movie on the hangar deck. Just before the scheduled start time, a loud voice boomed out, "Attention!" All the men stood, realizing Captain Buckthorn was joining them, as he often did for movies. Then, contrary to normal etiquette, cheers broke out among the men, and they gave the captain a standing ovation. *Well deserved*, thought Alan, realizing that, apart from all the captain's other duties, his conning of the ship during evasive maneuvering while she was under attack was a crucial part of her defense.

Saturday, May 16, 1942

Ashore in the morning, Alan tried to find out where all the other *Lexington* survivors were, in hopes of finding out if Rudi Fischer and Wade Buckner were among them. Eventually he learned that the survivors had already been transferred to two transports in the harbor, which were ready to depart for San Diego. He had been briefed that the transports would be escorted by TF-17, however, which he knew was not going anywhere until it was refueled. He was disappointed not to be able to find out more, but there was nothing he could do about it. Back at Pearl Harbor, maybe Jennifer could find out who the surviving *Lexington* air group members were.

Back aboard at lunchtime, Alan noticed an Australian convoy had come in, led by the armed merchant cruiser *Kanimbla*. In the afternoon, he watched as *Kanimbla* came alongside *Yorktown* and transferred oil to her. *I guess we are pretty desperate for oil, but I doubt if she could give us enough to take us very far.*

Sunday, May 17, 1942

Around the middle of the morning, Alan became aware of a conversation coming in through the open side of the hangar. Leaning out, about halfway between the flight deck and the water, he saw a party of men on an accommodation platform. These platforms floated on the water below a long retractable accommodation ladder, actually a stairway, which came down from the hangar deck. Normally these were used to get in and out of launches, but no launch was present. Soon he saw that two men had diving suits on. *What are they doing? Inspecting the outside of the hull to assess the battle damage, I bet.*

Alan had the afternoon off, and he went ashore. By way of celebration, he stopped in for a beer in a sort of temporary officers' club that the navy had set up. Coming in from the brilliant sunshine, it took a moment for his eyes to adjust, and he became aware that there was a group of US Navy officers with brown shoes seated on the far side of the establishment, and none of their faces were familiar. *I know most of the pilots at Tongatabu, except the* Lex *pilots that were not on* Yorktown, *so they must be on liberty from one of the transports.*

Then he recognized Rudi Fischer among them. *They must be from Torpedo Two.*

Rudi spotted Alan and left the group to come over, grin big as ever, beer in hand. "Alan, how are you? You're looking pretty chipper. We have a lot to catch up on. Get a beer and let's sit down."

"I'm fine. How are you? You don't look too much the worse for wear. You're right; we have a whole battle to hash over. I heard all the *Lex* pilots that were on the cruisers had been embarked on the transports to go to San Diego. I imagine you're looking forward to that."

Rudi's usual jovial expression vanished. "No, Alan. Bad news. The Torpedo Two people have been assigned to shore duty to try to help defend Noumea and Suva. It stinks, but we have to stay here to await transport. The rest of the air group goes to San Diego, minus the crews on *Yorktown*."

"That does stink." Alan got a beer from the bar and sat down with Rudi. "Before I hear your story, I have been wondering if Wade Buckner was among the Fighting Three pilots that joined Fighting Two."

Rudi's face became glummer, and he began speaking, in what was for him a strangely somber tone. "He was. He was flying one of the four Wildcats escorting our squadron on the strike on the eighth. On the way to the target, they throttled way back to our speed—I guess to save gas. Suddenly we came out of the clouds into the clear space around that one carrier, and we started our approach. There were several Zeros nearby, and they pounced on the escort before the Wildcats could accelerate, so they were sitting ducks. Two went down, no parachutes. Wade was one of them."

That news hit Alan very hard, and he blinked back tears. "Oh, Rudi, I never expected to hear that. He always seemed like such a competent pilot, and a fighter pilot at heart. After I talked to you on board *Lexington*, I had a nice chat with him. He's the second good friend I lost that day." Alan had never seen the perennially cheerful Rudi look so morose.

"He was an excellent pilot. He was in the strike escort on the seventh, and he got a confirmed Zero."

"That sounds more like Wade."

"He happened not to be on CAP at dusk when that enemy strike showed up on radar. He didn't really have a chance on the eighth, going so slow."

"I guess not. Very sad news. In hindsight, the fighter escort wasn't able to do a lot for the strike. They only had seventeen Wildcats total to defend the carriers, so they should have kept back the fifteen that went on the escort. And they should have not held back the eighteen Dauntlesses for anti-torpedo defense and sent them on the strike, where they would have made a real difference."

"I think you're right."

Alan asked, "Now how about you? Let's hear your story."

Rudi's enthusiasm showed through again. "Well, us torpedo guys went on the strike both days. On the seventh, Bombing Two attacked just before we did, distracting their fighters and anti-aircraft crews. Our escort handled the few remaining fighters, and we got to make a classic anvil attack. I attacked on the port side and got a hit for sure—I saw the explosion. Our squadron claimed nine hits, but I think we actually got five or six. Bombing Two got some hits also, and the carrier was doomed."

"Congratulations on getting a hit! That's great!"

"Thanks, Alan."

"I went on the search, so not on the strike, but some of our pilots thought that the *Yorktown* strike should have gone after other ships, because the carrier was already a goner when they got there. At dusk that day, did the Japanese circle around *Lexington*, the way they did around *Yorktown*?"

Rudi replied, smiling, "Yeah, when the Japanese airplanes came around the ship, it was unbelievable. Finally our CAP backed away, and our antiaircraft opened up, so the Japanese hightailed it away."

"Yeah, the same thing happened around *Yorktown*."

They both had finished their beers, and they went to the bar for refills.

They sat down again, and Rudi continued, "On the eighth, we were up against the first team, and we had weather that both helped us and hurt us, so it was very different. The weather made it impossible for our air group to stay in visual contact on the way to the target. Bombing Two at eighteen thousand feet became completely separated and couldn't find the target, so the weather put them out of the game, although they got back OK. None of our strike attacked the second carrier to the south because she was hidden by the weather, but we're pretty sure that some of her CAP came over to help defend the northern carrier. Having that second carrier hidden enabled them to concentrate their defense. Once we popped out of the clouds, we too were under attack by Zeros, so we didn't have time to maneuver around into an anvil attack. Our air group commander, Ault, had just attacked with the command section of four Dauntlesses, which helped a little to divide the CAP in the absence of Bombing Two, but there were plenty of Zeros available to go after us. As we approached from the south, the carrier made a one-eighty to the right, so we were coming up from astern at a closure speed of all of seventy knots. My gunner was shooting, and we got hit, but luckily nothing important was knocked out. The carrier continued the turn to the right, so then we were glad to see we could attack from abeam on the starboard side. But just as we dropped, she turned to port to comb our torpedoes. The closure speed of our torpedoes, with her at flank speed and going away, was less than five knots. I had my hands full and couldn't watch, but my gunner was able to follow our torpedo's wake. He said it was erratic and never caught up with the carrier. What a letdown. But we were lucky in that, while everyone else was getting chewed up, us torpedo guys all got away with the help of the clouds, and we all made it back, although many had damage. Our squadron claimed five hits, but between us, Alan, I suspect we didn't get any."

"I heard later she was last seen headed north at high speed, which makes it sound like Torpedo Five didn't get any hits either, although they claimed three. You know, on the eighth the Devastators didn't seem to accomplish much, but I think they all came back, in spite of being the most vulnerable type on the carriers. It was the fighters and dive bombers that suffered the losses."

"Yeah. We need those Avengers, but even with them, we're not likely to be very effective without better torpedoes. They're unreliable, as you suspected a long time ago. But they're also too slow, and they have to be dropped too low and slow. From what the guys on the ship said about the Japanese torpedo attack, the Japanese torpedoes have none of those problems."

Wow, our torpedoes are too slow and too fragile, as well as unreliable.

"So you got back OK. What was it like abandoning ship?"

"Well, we kept hoping that *Lexington* would make it through, until we had a big explosion around fourteen forty. After that it just got worse, with occasional further explosions. A little after seventeen hundred, we got the word to abandon ship. No sharks, no depth charge explosions, so we had it much better than some other ships that have had to be abandoned. It went about as well as it could, under the circumstances. It was just in time, too. By eighteen hundred the ship was uninhabitable. The hurt men went first, but still they were the ones who suffered. I went down a line hand over hand into the water. I got picked up by a launch from *Morris* and went aboard her. It was very crowded. I slept on deck under the stars. Late the next day, I got transferred to *Chester*, which was not so badly crowded. We were still allowed to sleep on deck, so I did."

"Sounds like it could have been a lot worse."

"Definitely. Now I want to hear your story."

Alan recounted how the seventh was mostly boring, except for the Japanese wandering by at suppertime. Then he told Rudi about the *Yorktown* dive-bomber strike on the eighth, including his hit, his roommate's heroic but fatal dive, and his aerial victory on the way back.

"I bet you were very proud of what you did, and rightfully so, but the loss of your best friend took all the joy out of it."

"Exactly right." Alan admired how quickly Rudi had understood his emotional conflict.

"I remember fighters were your first choice at Pensacola, and it sounds like you haven't lost your knack for grab-ass."

"Yeah. After I joined the squadron, I got to be one of the top pilots in fixed gunnery, long before I was any good at dive bombing on a target moving evasively.

"Well, Rudi, I am very glad I ran into you. It's been great to catch up, even with the very sad news about Wade. Now I need to get back to the ship. I hope you get reassigned aboard a carrier soon. Good luck!"

"Thanks, Alan. Good luck to you too. Who knows what will happen next or where we might run into each other again. So long."

They shook hands, and Alan left to find his way back to *Yorktown*. That day a small package of mail came aboard for the *Lexington* men, having gone to *Portland* and *Chester* first. Bill was very pleased to have a letter from his wife.

CHAPTER EIGHTEEN

Expedite Return

Monday, May 18, 1942

Alan reported to the hangar deck at 0800. A short time later, he glanced out across the harbor and saw *Kanawha* coming in at last. She immediately went to work refueling the task force, and the work continued after dark.

That evening Alan met with Hank Stinson, up in the gallery aft as usual, well after dark at 2100. Hank was already there when Alan appeared, enjoying the light breeze coming aft. "Good evening, Hank. I imagine you've been busy with all the reports on the battle."

"You're right. Meeting you is a nice break from that. I remember you said the air office and air group do not like using Dauntlesses for defense of the carriers. After the way Scouting Five was mauled in the battle, the admiral and his staff are in that camp also. The admiral will endorse an air group recommendation for new doctrine on that score."

"Well, that's progress. The reverse seems to be true of the fighters. At least in this battle, the escort fighters would have been more effective on defense."

"The staff has been talking about that too. Now, what have you been up to?"

"Well, yesterday I noticed divers going off an accommodation platform. Were they looking at the hull, and if so, what did they see?"

"That's right. They said the damage was minor."

"Good. Later I went ashore and ran into a Pensacola friend who is in Torpedo Two. He gave me the dope on the two *Lexington* strikes during the battle. Another Pensacola friend of ours was among the Fighting Three men who were assigned to Fighting Two. He went down, no parachute, escorting Torpedo Two on the eighth."

"I'm very sorry to hear that. So two of your good friends did not come back."

"That's right. My Torpedo Two friend described getting off *Lexington* just in time and a hectic trip here in *Morris* and *Chester*. He also told me that the Torpedo Two people are going to be sent ashore to defend Suva and Noumea. Do you know anything about that?"

"A little. We know that King has been fixated on defending the southwest Pacific, which is why all three of our carriers are down here, leaving the central Pacific wide open. Reading between the lines, we're pretty sure that the loss of *Lexington*, his former command, was quite a blow. Now it's six to three in fleet carriers remaining, although we know one of theirs has got to be out of action for a few months. So now he seems to have turned suddenly cautious and wants to put carrier squadron personnel ashore to defend the southwest Pacific and keep the carriers themselves out of harm's way. Nimitz must not agree, or he would put the whole *Lex* air group ashore, except possibly the pilots with planes aboard *Yorktown*. Putting just Torpedo Two ashore may be Nimitz's way of making a gesture in the direction advocated by King.

"Speaking of Nimitz, this afternoon we got orders from him to expedite our return to Pearl. That could still mean he wants just our planes and pilots. But since he has no ship for them, it seems likely he wants *Yorktown*, and possibly her air group, for an urgent threat, probably nearer Pearl than here, so Midway or Hawaii or both. There's a lot of ifs, but that's the way it looks to the staff."

"What about *Enterprise* and *Hornet*?"

"If he needs us near Pearl, either he'll call them back to Pearl too, or he has two threats, one here and one there. But so far we haven't heard."

"When do we leave?"

"After we've got every drop of oil out of *Kanawha*, which we expect to be sometime tomorrow morning. We estimate we'll arrive at Pearl on May 27. *Kanawha* is too small to fill us up, so we couldn't make it direct to Bremerton anyway unless Nimitz sent another oiler meet us."

Tuesday, May 19, 1942

Early in the morning, the bullhorn announced that the task force would depart at 1300. Then Alan noticed the oiler *Kaskaskia* coming into the harbor, the same oiler that had accompanied *Yorktown* and TF-17 from San Diego to Samoa in January. *She should have plenty of oil, but more refueling would delay our departure.*

Soon he noticed that *Kaskaskia* had come alongside *Portland* to refuel her. At lunch time the bullhorn announced that *Portland* would remain in harbor to complete her refueling and then catch up with TF-17. Departure time for the rest of the task force would be 1500.

The task force departed on that schedule and maneuvered into cruising formation after passing through the channel to the open sea.

During the night the task force crossed the International Date Line, so a second May 19 started at midnight.

Thursday, May 21, 1942

Alan was up on the bow at dawn and saw the maneuvering as *Chester*, with Admiral Fitch, and the two transports bound for San Diego, parted company with the task force. TF-17 was now northeast of American Samoa. Thus the departing ships would be steaming back to San Diego along the same route that *Yorktown* had followed when she came out to Samoa in January.

Sunday, May 24, 1942

Alan remembered it was his and Jennifer's first anniversary. What a lot had happened since then. He was glad he would probably be able to have a brief visit with her when he got to Pearl Harbor.

Tuesday, May 26, 1942

All hands were aware that their arrival in Pearl Harbor was planned for the following day.

Around mid morning the bullhorn came on to announce, "Now hear this. Stand by for a message from Admiral Fletcher." There was a pause, and then, "This is Admiral Fletcher. On this the one hundredth day since our departure from Pearl, I wish to congratulate all hands upon the successful operations, the splendid seamanship, the remarkable engineering performance, and the fine spirit which has marked each of the hundred days."

An appropriate and appreciated gesture on the part of the admiral, but it is unfortunate that it could be interpreted as leaving out aviation.

Airplane repairs continued, and Alan thought Bombing Five would have fourteen operational when they reached Pearl, four more than when they arrived at Tongatabu. Alan was proud of the engineering department's effort to get so many repaired at sea.

In the afternoon, Alan was threading his way to the starboard gallery, to take a break and enjoy the 22 knot wind over the deck. The bullhorn came on to announce quarters for flight operations. It had been a peaceful voyage with very little in the way of flight operations, so Alan wondered what was going on. He emerged into the gallery and noted that the ship was headed into the wind, and flight deck personnel were taking their places. About ten minutes went by, and then he heard the sound of distant aircraft engines to the north. He spotted two Grumman Ducks, which flew directly into the pattern and landed aboard. *We're supposed to be about 24 hours out from Pearl Harbor, so the only place that might be closer is Johnston Island, an unlikely place for them to come from. They must be from Pearl, the only other place that is within range for the Duck.* He watched as the pilot and two passengers got out of each Duck. Captain Buckthorn himself greeted the passengers. They were not in uniform, so they must be civilians. They disappeared into the island. *What is going on now?* he wondered.

Meeting with Hank Stinson that evening, he got his answer.

"Nimitz had the navy yard repair superintendent and three engineers from the yard flown out to us to inspect and assess the damage. They're going to ride the ship into Pearl. That makes it obvious that Nimitz wants this ship repaired and back in action as fast as possible. We won't hear why until we get into Pearl, but it must be something coming up very soon."

"Wow. Are *Enterprise* and *Hornet* coming back also?"

"They arrived at Pearl today."

"Wow again. They too must have expedited their return. Sounds like our biggest speculations are coming true, only faster than we thought."

"Exactly."

CHAPTER NINETEEN

No Rest for Yorktown or Bombing Five

Wednesday, May 27, 1942

It was announced at flight quarters that there would be a briefing of the air group for the flight into Pearl Harbor at 0830. Alan took his seat in the ready room at 0820. After nearly living in that room for many hours during the battle, the squadron had only met once for a short session since leaving Tongatabu a week earlier. Alan scanned the blackboards. On the left was a large diagram of the Pearl Harbor Naval Air Station on Ford Island. In the center was a chart of Pearl Harbor, showing the location of the various airports. On the right the roster showed fourteen airplanes and pilots. He would be flying 5-B-12, leading the second section in the first division.

Stubb began, "This morning the operational airplanes, including the *Lex* airplanes, will be flying into the Pearl Harbor Naval Air Station on Ford Island. Admiral Halsey with *Enterprise* and *Hornet* arrived yesterday. Air Group Six is at Ford Island, and Air Group Eight is at Ewa.

"We now have fourteen planes flyable, matching our fourteen pilots. The roster is posted. Launch is scheduled for ten thirty. The first deck load will be the fighters in front, including the *Lex* Wildcats, and then Torpedo Five. The second deck load will be Scouting Five, then us, then the *Lex* Dauntlesses. We will cruise at five thousand feet for the sixty mile flight.

"Here is the layout of the Pearl Harbor Naval Air Station at Ford Island. There is a single runway that is four hundred fifty feet wide, so it is divided into two runways by a stripe down the middle, and operations can be conducted simultaneously on both sides. We expect to be using runway four left. We will descend to one thousand feet and follow the harbor entrance in to Ford Island, to stay away from Ewa and Hickam, and then make a slight right turn to make the break over the threshold of runway four left."

Slick Davis gave the navigation information, and Teeth Jensen went over the weather, which was good.

The launch went off on schedule, and the short flight in was uneventful. As they approached Oahu, Alan felt like he was coming home. He had never spent much time there, but being away at war for three months made it seem very welcoming, and now his home was Jennifer's apartment in Honolulu.

The squadron flying low over the harbor entrance made a beautiful sight, he felt. He touched down on the wide runway at 1115 and followed the skipper and his wingmen in a left turn off the runway to the parking area on the northwest side. The *Enterprise* airplanes were all lined up nearby.

Alan shut down, climbed out, and looked around. He could see *Enterprise* docked on the other side of Ford Island. The Bombing Five pilots went into the hangar, where they were directed to a ready room. The pilots sat down and waited for the skipper.

"As you were," barked Stubb as he strode to the podium. "There was some foul up, so we weren't expected until tomorrow, so I don't have any orders. Stand by and try to relax. There's a cafeteria in the next hangar. I'll let you know when I hear anything. That is all."

The pilots stood and began to talk among themselves. Stubb motioned to Alan to come up to the podium.

Stubb smiled and said to Alan in a low voice, "You earned it, you lucky dog," as he handed Alan a note.

For Lieutenant Alan Ericsson, Squadron VB-5
I cannot leave the office until 1700. I hope to meet you in the Officers' Club at the Pearl Harbor Naval Air Station at 1800. Call if that will not work.
Jennifer Ericsson, Combat Intelligence Unit

He was a little disappointed to have to wait to see her, but Alan remembered that she had said in her letter that her office was extremely busy. *No wonder she can't leave until 1700.*

Alan chatted with Teeth and Slick and then went with them to the cafeteria for lunch. The cafeteria was very busy, and it became clear that most of the other people there were pilots from Air Group Six on *Enterprise*. Alan looked around for his Pensacola friend Ed Miller of Fighting Six, and spotted him in a far corner. When he had gotten his food, he went over to sit with Ed.

Ed was chatting with two other pilots. Suddenly he looked up and said with a big grin, "Stringy Ericsson, how are you doing? We thought you guys were coming in tomorrow. You survived the Battle of the Coral Sea, I see. Sit down and tell us about it. Meet Roger and Martin from Fighting Six; this is Alan, an old friend from Pensacola, who went to Bombing Five."

"I'm fine, Ed; how are you? Nice to meet you," he said, shaking hands with the two other pilots. "I'll tell you about Coral Sea, but not until you tell me what's going on. Why were three carriers called back here in a hurry?"

"Haven't you heard? The Japs are fixing to come after Midway. We haven't heard when, but it sounds like early June, maybe only a week away."

"Holy smoke! No wonder. We knew something was up, because of the hurry. *Yorktown* took a bomb hit and some damaging near misses at Coral Sea, but she can still operate, and they can probably patch her up." He began eating his lunch. "But the Japanese still have five fleet carriers operational. Are we going to stop them with three?"

Ed replied, "Well, we know they're coming, and hopefully they don't know we know. Both our carriers were spotted by one of the routine Japanese searches, down near the Santa Cruz Islands, north of the New Hebrides. Then right away we skedaddled back here. We figured there was something fishy about it, since we've had no trouble staying out of search range when we want to. Maybe Nimitz wanted us to be spotted, so the Japs might think we're still down there."

"They might think they sank both *Yorktown* and *Lexington* at Coral Sea too. Who knows? Say, do you know if Les Travis made it into the *Hornet* air group?"

"He did. He's in Bombing Eight on *Hornet*, but of course all the *Hornet* air group have yet to see any combat because the only mission they've had is to take the B-Twenty-Fives on the Tokyo raid. I'd like to tell you about that, but we've been told not to talk to anyone about it. I saw him here after that, and he says most of the air group, including the commander, is green as hell. Our little trip to the southwest couldn't have changed that too much. OK, let's hear about Coral Sea."

Alan told the story, starting with Tulagi and going right through the battle and having a roommate from *Lexington*. The pilots congratulated him and were sorry to hear about his former roommate. Then he told Ed about seeing Rudi Fischer at Tongatabu. "He got a hit on that smaller carrier the first day, but his torpedo couldn't catch up to that big carrier the next day. He said our torpedoes are very inferior. He also said Wade Buckner was on temporary assignment to Fighting Two. Wade got a Zero the first day. The second day he was in the torpedo escort. They slowed way down to stay with the torpedo planes. Near the target they popped out of the clouds and were jumped by Zeros, with no chance to accelerate. He didn't have a chance."

Ed's smile vanished. "Oh shit." He sighed and looked down, blinking back tears. "He was one of my best friends, as you know. I'll sure miss him."

Alan ate in silence for a couple of minutes. Then he asked, "Now you've been to Wake and Marcus. How did that go?"

"Bad weather at both, and not many airplanes or ships at either, so only land targets. It was kind of disappointing, but I guess it was good practice."

Alan had finished his lunch and sat back to relax. Suddenly there was the sound of whistles and sirens coming from the harbor through the open windows. The pilots quickly went outside to see what was happening. Looking northeast over the runway to the ship channel, there was *Yorktown*, going clockwise around

Ford Island to the Repair Basin, her sailors mustered on the flight deck in their dress whites. Alan's watch said 1350.

"A rousing welcome well deserved," said Ed, standing beside Alan. "Our reception was pretty routine."

"Yeah, it was the other way around after the Marshall and Gilbert raids; *Enterprise* got a big welcome, and we got nothing."

"That seems like years ago, doesn't it?"

"It sure does."

The *Enterprise* pilots began to drift back to their hangar, and Alan said good-bye to Ed and his two friends and wished them good hunting, which they returned. Alan got back to the ready room in time to find that his squadron was starting to walk over to the BOQ to get their rooms for the night. He joined them and found his room. He chatted with West and Briggs until the duffels and cruise boxes arrived from *Yorktown* around 1700. He showered and changed for supper, fidgety but filled with pleasant anticipation at the prospect of being with Jennifer again.

Alan went to the officer's club and took a seat in the lobby near the door at 1750. Only a few minutes later, he heard a roar from outside. He turned to see a topless gray navy jeep slide to a stop at the door. He saw that Jennifer, in the front passenger's seat, had been thrown forward by the sudden stop, even though she had her hand on the dashboard to brace herself. She settled back into the seat and straightened her hair before climbing out. Hardly had she done so, when the navy driver ground the gears, dropped the clutch, and roared off.

She turned and saw him coming toward her and opened her arms. They embraced and had a long kiss. Feeling her was just as exhilarating as the last time and transported him away from the war like nothing else. Tears were running down both sets of cheeks before they were through. They separated with huge smiles on their faces.

"Your driver seemed to be in an awful hurry."

Jennifer laughed and replied, "I think he was a little flustered by having a female passenger, probably the first time. Also I made the mistake of telling him to step on it."

Alan chuckled. "It's so good to see you again, and you look great. I thought you might be worn out by your work."

"I was last night. Joe knew you were coming today. About eighteen hundred, he came to me and gave me strict orders to go home and not to come back until ten hundred at the earliest. I slept twelve hours straight. We've been working all out, all of us in the office, but it was well worth it, as you'll see when I give you an idea of what is going on. Just seeing you is plenty of reward in itself."

He took her hand and said, "Let's have dinner, and you can tell me all about it, you scalawag."

As they walked into the club, she said, "I want to hear all about your adventures too, you rascal. This will be our only time together this visit, so we better make the best of it."

They found a table away from where others were seated and sat down. Alan said, "I wanted to let you know I was all right, but the first chance to send mail was at Tongatabu, after we lost our oiler. I'm sorry I didn't have quite enough pull to send a message to you by radio through Pacific Fleet headquarters."

Jennifer laughed. "You'd need quite a promotion to pull that off, you rascal."

"By the time we got to Tongatabu, I thought I would get here at least as fast as a letter."

A waiter took their orders for dinner and a bottle of Beaujolais. Alan noticed some friends coming in, who took one look and moved away to let them have their time alone. *Just as well, given what we want to talk about.*

Jennifer smiled and said, "After the battle, everyone in the office knew there were a lot of casualties and that my husband could be one of them. They were very kind to me. Jasper was pretty quiet about it until the tenth, when he came to my desk and handed me the Air Group Five casualty list. He has his own remarkable connections. He smiled and said, 'He's not on there.' I burst into tears and said, 'You're a life saver, Jasper.' He said with a chuckle, 'Thank Izzy. Her orders were very firm.' I wrote a note to her, thanking her, although I think Jasper would have done it anyway."

"You're working with wonderful people, Jennifer."

The waiter served their wine.

Alan raised his glass, smiled and said, "Happy Anniversary, you scalawag!"

Jennifer smiled as she raised her glass, "Happy Anniversary, you rascal!" After a pause she said, "What a lot has happened since then."

"We should remember this occasion and tell our children about it."

"Good idea."

Alan resumed. "Now please tell me what is going on."

"Before that, I did look at the casualty list, and I was very sorry to see Jim Lowery's name. I know how close you two were. It must have been terrible."

"I was devastated at first, but I will tell you about it. But first I can't wait to hear what's next. I did hear they plan to take Midway sometime in early June."

Jennifer's eyebrows shot up. "Whoa, Alan, that's top secret. How did you hear that?"

"I ran into my Pensacola friend Ed Miller, who's in Fighting Six. He told me. He didn't say anything about secrecy."

"Oh boy. This place leaks like a sieve. OK, even so, keep these details to yourself, Alan. You'll hear most of it soon, so pretend it's all new when you hear it again. They are coming to take Midway. We're wondering why they want it, but it looks like they want to get our carriers to come out and fight. At the same time, they're going to take a couple of the western Aleutian Islands, which is relatively unimportant, so we'll put up a defense, but we're not going to get distracted from the main event down here.

"Since they won't be far away from here, Pearl Harbor won't be a safe place. Nimitz has sent away ships that are not going out to Midway. He sent the battleships back to San Francisco.

"There will be three separate fleets converging on Midway: the invasion fleet, a heavy surface force with battleships, and the carrier force with four, or possibly five, big carriers. *Zuikaku* is the one that was not damaged in the Coral Sea, so she should be able to come, but we think she is not. The carrier force will attack Midway on the fourth."

"Wow. You people must have made a lot of progress with... uh...your business," said Alan.

Jennifer smiled and said, "Nice catch, Alan. We have, and working to exhaustion is the least any of us can do."

"I understand now."

"King was pretty skeptical at first, because he's so focused on the link to Australia. Also we think ONC and Turner were telling him what they thought he wanted to hear, that we were wrong. Main Navy wanted confirmation that we correctly identified the target, which had a particular Japanese code word. Jasper came up with a great idea for doing that. He knew that fresh water was a problem at Midway, and he suggested that we get Midway to send a fake radio message in the clear that their desalinization plant had broken down. The Japanese would pick that up and re-broadcast it, using their code word. Rochefort persuaded Nimitz and Bloch. It worked like a charm, and the skepticism is quashed for the moment."

"When did you get all this figured out?"

Jennifer smiled and said, "That's another good story. Late yesterday we still didn't have it all. I went home on Joe's orders, but I heard all about what happened when I came in this morning. Joe Finnegan, one of our best language officers, was stuck because some messages had an extra layer of enciphering. Ham Wright was about to go home after twelve hours, when Finnegan asked for help. Ham and Joe worked all night, and by this morning they had it put together. Joe Rochefort waited to get their confirmed results before he rushed off to a big meeting with Nimitz and his staff and two generals. Getting that made him a half hour late for that meeting, but that's Joe—getting good information trumps everything else."

"Holy smoke, he kept Nimitz and the brass waiting for half an hour?"

"He sure did, and he looked like he had slept in his uniform, because he had. He told us afterward that he got a frosty reception at first." Jennifer chuckled and continued, "But it gradually melted when he handed papers to Nimitz that told them how many carriers were coming, then when and even from what direction."

Alan said with a grin, "It would take a lot to melt the ice among all that brass, but I can see how that would do it. That is spectacular. What a coup!"

Jennifer broke into a big smile. "It really is." She paused and then exclaimed, "I almost forgot. Did you know Pearl Harbor was attacked again?"

"No. You're kidding, you scalawag."

"No, it's true, but it didn't amount to much. Two of their big flying boats flew over at night and dropped bombs. There was an overcast, so they couldn't see anything, and there was no damage. We're pretty sure that they refueled from a submarine at French Frigate Shoals, to make the round trip from the Marshalls with bombs."

"Amazing." Alan knew that there was an underwater mountain range of old volcanoes between Hawaii and Midway, and French Frigate Shoals was the top of one, which formed a protected harbor of sorts.

"There is an amazing coincidence involved also. I think I told you that, while Jasper was out of the navy, he wrote short stories for the *Saturday Evening Post* as a side job. He was still doing that last summer until Bloch brought him back into the navy. One appeared last September that was about the Japanese attacking Pearl Harbor with flying boats after refueling from a submarine at French Frigate Shoals."

"That is unbelievable. I wonder if the Japanese read his story."

"We think not, but if he could think of it, so could they."

They were quiet while the waiter served their dinner.

Alan resumed, "But the fourth is only a week away. They'll have hardly any time to patch up *Yorktown*. She can operate OK now but might be vulnerable to further damage. So we'll be opposing four or five with three. But I've heard *Hornet* is very green. At least all three are Yorktown class. Part of what made *Lexington* vulnerable was her lack of maneuverability. And they won't have all the land based reconnaissance they had in the Coral Sea."

"Exactly. Even so, we'll have to try to even the odds by ambushing them. *Enterprise* and *Hornet* will be ready to go in plenty of time, but Nimitz had to put Halsey on the sick list. He's worn out and has extreme dermatitis. Halsey nominated Spruance, his cruiser admiral, to stand in for him, and, to everyone's surprise, Nimitz accepted it.

"Nimitz hopes to get *Yorktown* patched up as much as possible in a very short time, a few days at most. And there are going to be major changes in the air group. Fighting Forty-Two, Scouting Five, and Torpedo Five are all going ashore, to be replaced by the former Saratoga squadrons: Fighting Three, Bombing Three, and Torpedo Three. Only Bombing Five will be kept on board."

"So our squadron goes right back into the fray. I can't say I'm looking forward to that."

"Me either. You guys earned the chance for rest, like the other squadrons."

"I don't think anyone, from Admiral Fletcher on down, is going to like switching most of the air group, although Scouting Five did get hit pretty hard. Whose idea was all this?"

"Admiral Noyes, who was first in line to replace Halsey— he was head of the Office of Naval Communications before December seventh, so he got sent out here under a cloud as part of the housecleaning after the attack. Nobody seems to have a lot of respect for him, but Nimitz more or less agrees with Noyes in this case, so Nimitz won't publicly rebuke Noyes by overruling him on that. *Yorktown*'s new air group is assembling at Kaneohe, where the *Saratoga* squadrons are based, so I think Bombing Five will be sent there, probably tomorrow. That and my hours are why we won't be able to see each other after tonight."

"I see." He paused and asked, "Can you tell me anything about the Tokyo raid? I heard it was B-Twenty-Fives that came to Tokyo from the east and left to the west."

"Don't tell anyone about this, Alan. They were on *Hornet*, escorted by *Enterprise*. They were planning to launch four hundred miles east of Japan, but Japanese fishermen, acting as pickets, spotted them six hundred fifty miles out. They had to launch there, and then the B-Twenty-Fives could barely make it to the mainland west of Japan. We've heard that some got through.

"When they got to Japan, the Japanese went wild on the radio. Unfortunately the whole mission was so secret that they didn't tell us until the last moment. There was a marvelous burst of radio traffic, but we missed a lot at first because we couldn't staff up the intercept station that quickly. Therefore, we couldn't have helped Halsey if he ran into any heavy Japanese forces. Even so, we caught up eventually, and that helped us a lot in determining where their carriers were. They chased Halsey for several days afterward, but they were way behind. Now tell me about your adventures."

"Slack, the new pilot we got from Bombing Three when we were here in February, was appointed engineering officer. It gradually became clear that he had no understanding of mechanics and was totally unfit for that position. He got away with it because he let his assistant do most of the work. He measured the mechanics' performance by speed, rather than the quality of their work. I couldn't mention it in my letters. Being sort of the opposite of me, I found it easy to dislike him."

"I see."

"Then there was the Lae-Salamaua raid. With no air opposition to speak of, it was frustrating to have our windshields and bombsights fog up again. Then on the way back, I had the big scare I mentioned in my letter. You know we had to cross a big mountain range to make the raid?"

She nodded.

"Before I got to the ridge on the way back, my engine got rough. I was barely high enough to get through the pass, the one that the torpedo planes used on the way over. I headed for it, but then my engine quit. Going down in that mountainous jungle full of scary people and animals was a worse prospect than anything that had happened before then."

Jennifer's eyes had been getting bigger and her breathing faster as he talked. Now she grasped his forearm.

"The propeller was still windmilling, turning the engine over, so the machinery wasn't broken. It seemed like the engine was starved for fuel, but the fuel pressure was normal. Then I thought of using the primer, which squirts extra fuel in for starting. It worked. But by then I was right at the pass. We went through so low that were skimming through the tops of the trees. My gunner had a great big green leaf in his cockpit when we got back."

"Oh, Alan, that's the scariest thing I've ever heard," she said, pressing his arm. "But how did you make it back?"

"I had to pump the primer until both my hands were sore, but we got back to the ship and made a fairly normal landing, thank goodness."

"I'm glad I wasn't there. I would have died of a heart attack."

"I was so keyed up afterward; I didn't need a drop of coffee. A couple of hours later I was in the hangar, and my plane captain was working on my plane to find out what went wrong. He found it right away—a clogged fuel filter. The air department recommended checking the filters because of increased contamination from the oilers, but Slack wouldn't do it because it took extra time.

"When I saw the fuel filter, I completely lost my temper. I went straight into Slack's office and blew my stack. I grabbed him and yelled at him. My plane captain and some mechanics pulled me out of the office, and I calmed down. But I knew I was in big trouble. I was hauled into the exec's office with the skipper and Slack. I was required to apologize, which I did, and stay away from engineering, which I mostly did. That's pretty light punishment, so I think the skipper and the exec weren't too happy with Slack either."

She put her hand on his. "Oh, Alan, I've never seen you lose your temper. I would be terribly upset if I did."

"I know. I quickly realized how stupid it was. I lost my credibility, and that delayed any change in engineering. Only the mechanics were pleased. The plane captains gave me a glass of Scotch as a reward. I did keep on doing preflight inspections on my plane because engineering was too rushed to do it right. About a month later, I found there was a part in the controls that was cracked and about to fail. There was an inspection that should have found it, but they skipped opening up that part of the plane during the inspection. If the part failed, the airplane would have been completely out of control.

"I went to the exec, half expecting to be dismissed. But by then he and the skipper had tuned into what was going on. They were waiting for one more slip on Slack's part, before relieving him. When they saw what I found, they were ready. They had already decided who would relieve him—me!"

She smiled and said, "You must have felt very gratified."

He grinned. "I did, but then there was a big backlog of work dumped in my lap. But we got it done."

"I remember you mentioned it in one of your letters."

"We got to rest at Tongatabu, as you know, and then the Tulagi raid came up shortly after. When they were briefing us for that, they were talking about ship movements that were beyond the search range of our reconnaissance. And they knew something about enemy intentions. I realized that your unit must have been at least partly responsible."

She smiled and said, "Definitely."

Alan described the whole battle, starting with the Tulagi raid.

When he got to his hit on the carrier, Jennifer interrupted, "You got the first hit? With a fogged windshield? I heard there were only a few bomb hits, and the fogging explains why, but it was enough to disable flight operations. You're a hero, Alan!"

"Well, maybe. But Jim Lowery got a better hit right near the island. Let me tell you about that."

When he had finished, Jennifer said, "Now I think I am starting to see what you went through. You were a hero, but you watched your best friend die being even more of a hero."

"That's the gist of it. But there's more." He told her about the flight back and shooting down a dive bomber.

"Oh, Alan, I think Jim would have been very proud of what you did. I hope you get a medal."

"The skipper said he would recommend the Navy Cross."

She beamed. "I'm so proud of you. I want permission to brag about you a little at the office."

Alan smiled and said, "Permission granted reluctantly, and only inside the office. There's a move to put Jim up for the Medal of Honor."

"He definitely earned it."

"I agree. Speaking of the fogging problem, we never had it happen outside the tropics, including around here, and Midway is north of here. So it seems likely it won't happen there, unless the weather is very wet."

"I hadn't thought of that, but you're right. We hear BuAer has a solution to the problem, some kind of a coating, but it hasn't gotten out here yet."

"That's good news." Alan went back to the aftermath of the battle and described the anxious wait in the afternoon, the loss of *Lexington*, and having a *Lexington* pilot as a new roommate. He left out viewing the bomb damage and the corpse in his stateroom.

"I would think he might have helped to take your mind off the loss of Jim."

"It took me a while to realize it, but you're right."

She continued, "We heard that Admiral Crace's Anzac Squadron was sent to guard the exit of the Jomard Passage through the Louisiades, to stop the invasion fleet if the carriers were not able to. While they were there, they were bombed by the Japanese *and* by the US Army. Fortunately there was no significant damage."

"Wow. We didn't hear about that. The army's lack of training in ship recognition is a menace."

"Very true. When did you finally get the feeling the battle was over and you were not being pursued?"

"We had a big scare on the ninth when a scout reported an enemy fleet, but it turned out to be a reef that looked like a fleet from a distance. There were more scares from radar sightings on the tenth. Late in the afternoon, there was an announcement for the officers to dress for supper. That's when we knew."

"By then you must have been mentally exhausted."

"We were. Sort of like you must have been last night."

Jennifer sighed and smiled. "You're right."

Alan told her about seeing Rudi Fischer at Tongatabu and the loss of Wade Buckner.

She said, "That is very sad too. Your friend the fighter pilot got shot down, and your friend the torpedo pilot came through without a scratch—not what you would expect."

"That's right."

"Speaking of torpedo bombing, everybody is disappointed that only a handful of the new Avenger torpedo bombers have gotten out here yet, with a big battle coming up. Not too many know that the Avenger is heavy, and only *Saratoga* and *Hornet* have the newer arresting gear that will handle them."

"You're right. I keep my ears open, but I haven't heard that."

The waiter came and cleared away the dishes. Alan poured another glass of wine for each of them.

Jennifer began again. "Now let me tell you about the big changes at Main Navy. It seems that Turner finally wore out his welcome. The rumor is that Marshall got fed up with him. Anyway he was suddenly replaced, and he is coming out here to be in command of amphibious forces. At first that sounded like good news for us, because Turner was continually attacking our conclusions. Remember when I saw you in February I told you Safford was in trouble?"

Alan nodded. General George Marshall was the chief of staff of the army, equivalent to Admiral King.

"Well, he was replaced as head of OP-Twenty-G by Commander John Redman, who is now nominally Joe Rochefort's boss. Now he *also* has been attacking our conclusions. By the way, Redman's only discernable qualification for that office was that his older brother was deputy director of naval communications. Fortunately, until now the Redmans have been kept fairly busy fighting Turner, but now they are free to direct all their energy against us. So Turner is not the only rotten apple in the barrel."

Alan was surprised at her strong language. *The endless destructive behavior at Main Navy is enough to make anyone angry,* he thought. "It sounds like the infighting, which you hoped to escape when you came out here, is spreading this way."

"I'm afraid it is."

Alan paused for a moment. Then he said, "It's really very fortunate that Nimitz trusts Rochefort and discounts the stuff coming from Main Navy."

"Absolutely. Nimitz used to be the chief of personnel for the navy, so he knows something about all the top brass. He must know something about Safford's and Joe Rochefort's background, and he's probably aware that the Redmans and Turner don't know much about intelligence."

"That makes a lot of sense." Alan noticed the dining room was nearly empty. He changed the subject. "What's happening in the Atlantic?"

"The navy is finally starting to cope with the U-boats along the coast and in the Caribbean. Rainbow Five, giving Germany top priority, is logical, but it's not going over well at home. The public wants revenge for Pearl Harbor. Roosevelt is struggling to keep the focus on Europe."

"That makes sense."

She paused and continued, "You have a much better understanding of strategy than most lieutenants. Remember you are not expendable."

"I won't forget. I am starting to feel more vulnerable than I used to. I guess it comes from getting shot at."

"That sounds like a healthy attitude."

"It makes me think I might be safer, and perhaps more valuable, in a fighter, in spite of what happened to Wade."

"I don't know. You did try to get into fighters originally. With your record, I would think they might be willing to let you transfer."

"Maybe after this battle, I'll have a better idea."

They stood up and moved into the lobby. Alan asked a yeoman to send for a jeep to take Jennifer back to the ferry.

They embraced and shared a long kiss. Jennifer's smile softened into sadness as she said, "I love you very much, Alan, and personally I think it's unfair that you have to go off into a major battle for the second time in a month."

"I suppose it is. But after that they'll have to give the squadron a rest."

"True. But you have to come back in one piece so we can enjoy it."

"I'll do my best, Jennifer."

A squeal of brakes announced the arrival of the jeep. They had a quick embrace and then Jennifer walked resolutely out of the club. Alan stood watching with moist eyes as she climbed into the jeep and disappeared.

Glossary

abeam	in a position off to one side, ninety degrees from straight ahead
aft	adverb meaning farther toward the back or stern of a vessel or vehicle
after	adjective meaning farther toward the back or stern of a vessel or vehicle
ailerons	panels on the outer wing trailing edge that can be angled up and down; those on opposite wings move in opposite directions when the control stick is moved sideways, causing the airplane to roll
AlNav	a dispatch from naval headquarters to the entire navy
amidships	adverb meaning in or toward the middle of a ship
Anzac	Originally ANZAC, for Australian New Zealand American Command, a combined naval squadron with ships from those countries, later extended to mean a US naval command area in the southwest Pacific, which had command over some Australian and New Zealand forces

astern	the backward direction from a ship
athwart his hawse	literally "across his bow"; used to mean "at cross purposes"
athwartships	in a crosswise direction on a ship
attitude	the orientation of an airplane relative to the horizon
AvCad	Aviation Cadet, a student in, or graduate of, a navy program which took in college men and gave them military training to become officers while they were getting their flight training
beam	the maximum width of a ship or boat
bilge	noun meaning the inside of the bottom of a ship, which usually has some water and refuse in it, and, hence, anything disgusting; or, in US Navy slang, verb for failing a test or for a superior to rate an inferior as a failure, and also to expel that person from the unit under the superior's command
black shoe	a navy officer who is not an aviator
BOQ	bachelor officers' quarters, accommodations on a naval base for officers whose wives live elsewhere or are unmarried
brown shoe	a navy officer who is an aviator
BuAer	Bureau of Aeronautics: oversees the development and production of naval aircraft
buffet	strong vibration of part of an airplane due to turbulent airflow passing over it
bulkhead	the wall of a ship's compartment, separating it from the adjacent compartment

BuOrd	Bureau of Ordnance: oversees the development and production of naval guns, bombs, and torpedoes
CAP	combat air patrol of fighters over ships subject to threat
ceiling	height of the bottom of a cloud layer from the earth's surface
CINCPAC	commander in chief of the Pacific Fleet
CINCUS	commander in chief of the US Fleet, discontinued in early 1942 and replaced by COMINCH
CNO	chief of naval operations
COMINCH	commander in chief of the US Fleet
conn	the duty of directing the movement of a ship
course	the direction of travel in degrees, due north being 0 or 360, and due south being 180
cowling	metal cover surrounding an aircraft engine
CYAG	commander of the *Yorktown* air group
dead reckoning	navigation by keeping track of courses, speeds, and times to estimate position, with the course estimated by correcting heading for drift due to outside influences, such as the influence of wind on airplanes
draft	depth below the waterline of the lowest part of a ship
elevators (airplane)	panels on the trailing edge of a plane's horizontal stabilizer that can be angled

up or down by moving the control stick forward or back to change the pitch of the airplane

empty weight
: the weight of an airplane with no crew, cargo, munitions, or fuel

escort
: maneuverable armed ship that accompanies other ships to protect them from attack by submarines or other combat vessels, or similarly in airplanes, maneuverable armed airplanes, usually fighters, to accompany other airplanes to protect them from attack

fairing
: a smooth aerodynamic cover over a protrusion on an airplane, or a filler panel used to make a smooth curve between two surfaces having a sharp angle between them, such as the junction of the wing and the fuselage

FDO
: fighter director officer, who sat in a special radar equipped compartment on the carrier and directed the fighters defending the task force by radio

fetch
: nautical term for the distance a wind blows over the sea surface without interference, allowing the wind to raise waves

flag xxx
: person or property in the service of an admiral

flare
: part of the sequence of maneuvers to land an airplane, in which the angle of descent of the final approach is reduced until the airplane is flying level, with the wheels just above the runway

fleet up	a move up by an officer to fill a vacancy in a higher position in a naval unit
freeboard	the height of the main deck of a ship above the water
funnel	smokestack of a ship
general quarters	the highest state of readiness on board a combat ship, with all watertight doors closed and all personnel at their battle stations
grab-ass	military pilot slang for practice air to air combat
gross weight	total weight of an airplane, the sum of the empty weight and the useful load, including crew, cargo, munitions, and fuel
head	ship's toilet or restroom
heading	the direction in which a ship or airplane is pointed, in degrees from north, which may differ from the actual course due to influences, such as the wind, or tides and currents for ships
heel	temporary inclination of a ship toward the outside of a turn, caused by inertia
horizontal stabilizer	a small horizontal winglike structure on the tail of an airplane on which the elevators are mounted
hulk	a retired ship, stripped of useful equipment
in trail	a formation of airplanes in which they follow one behind the other
island	regarding aircraft carriers, the superstructure that rises above the flight deck on one side

lee	a sheltered place on the downwind side of a vessel or other obstacle
leeward	in the direction toward which the wind is blowing
leeway	the amount by which a sailing vessel is blown off the desired direction of travel by the wind, and hence generally the difference between a desired outcome and the actual outcome
list	a steady inclination of a ship to one side or the other caused by an imbalance or uneven support from below
LSO	landing signal officer
magnetic	when applied to directions, relative to magnetic north, the direction from the current position to the magnetic north pole, differing from true directions by the variation
magnetic north pole	a position in northern Canada that is the north pole of the earth's magnetic field, causing compasses to point to it
Main Navy	naval jargon for naval headquarters in Washington, D.C.
midships	adjective meaning near the middle of the ship
mountain telegraph	slang expression similar to "grapevine," "gossip," or "rumor mill"
NACA	National Advisory Committee for Aeronautics, the federal agency assisting with aeronautical research; a predecessor of NASA
NAS	naval air station

oiler	naval term for a tanker, a cargo ship designed to carry petroleum or petroleum products
overhead	the deck on top of a ship compartment, separating it from the compartment above; the equivalent of the "ceiling" in a structure on land
plane captain	person assigned to and responsible for the maintenance and material condition of a particular airplane
plebe	a member of the freshman class at the US Naval Academy, customarily harassed by the upper classmen
pitch	the rotation of an airplane around the transverse axis, causing the nose to point up or down relative to the horizon
power loading	gross weight of an airplane divided by its engine's horsepower; a measure of the responsiveness of the airplane to its engine
quarter	when used to indicate direction from a ship, roughly forty-five degrees from straight astern, with port or starboard to indicate which side
roll (airplane)	the rotation of an airplane around the longitudinal axis, in which the wings rotate downward on one side and upward on the other
roll (ship)	the unsteady inclination of a ship to one side or the other caused by wave action
rudder (airplane)	a panel on the trailing edge of the vertical stabilizer, which can be angled to the

	right or left with the rudder pedals, causing the airplane nose to turn toward the right or left
skipper	commanding officer of a ship or unit
spot	to park airplanes on the flight deck of an aircraft carrier in a specific arrangement
squawk	a discrepancy or defect in an airplane
strike	noun meaning a group of airplanes sent to attack ship or ground targets, or verb meaning to prepare for a promotion or new duty
strike below	to move an item from the main or flight deck to a lower deck
talker	man posted at a navy ship duty station to relay messages by telephone to and from other duty stations
tender (naval)	a ship equipped with personnel and supplies to maintain and repair small vessels or flying boats at locations away from naval port facilities
threshold	the approach end of a runway
true	when applied to directions, relative to true north, the direction to the north pole
useful load	the weight of the crew, passengers, cargo, munitions, and fuel in an airplane
variation	the difference, in degrees, between the direction to the north pole and the direction to the magnetic north pole
vertical stabilizer	vertical winglike structure on the tail of an airplane, on which the rudder is mounted
VHF	very high frequency radio

wardroom	the compartment in which officers gather to eat and relax aboard ship
wing loading	gross weight of an airplane divided by its wing area, usually given in pounds per square foot; an inverse measure of responsiveness of an airplane to its wings
yaw	the rotation of an airplane around the vertical axis, in which the nose of the airplane turns toward the right or left
yeoman	naval term for an enlisted man who performs secretarial and clerical duties

Appendix A: Miscellaneous Naval and Military Terms

All information is for the US military forces as of early 1942.

Fleet Aircraft Carriers and Their Designations
The US Navy had built eight fleet (large) carriers by the end of 1941, as follows:

CV-1 *Langley*:   First experimental carrier; converted from a collier (bulk cargo ship); commissioned 1922; 11,000 tons; converted to a seaplane tender in 1936.

CV-2 *Lexington*:   First of class; built on a battle cruiser hull that was surplus due to the Washington Naval Treaty of 1922; commissioned 1927; 33,000 tons.

CV-3 *Saratoga*:   Second of class; built on a battle cruiser hull that was surplus due to the Washington Naval Treaty of 1922; commissioned 1927; 33,000 tons.

CV-4 *Ranger*:   Smaller carrier; first carrier designed completely as such; commissioned 1934; 14,500 tons.

CV-5 *Yorktown*:   First of class; commissioned 1937; 19,900 tons.

CV-6 *Enterprise*:   Second of class; commissioned 1938; 19,900 tons.

CV-7 *Wasp*:   Smaller carrier to fit within treaty limitations; commissioned 1940; 14,700 tons.

CV-8 *Hornet*:   Nearly identical to Yorktown class; commissioned 1941; 20,000 tons.

Aircraft Carrier Deck Crew Color Coding

Carrier deck crewmen wore shirts and caps whose color indicated the crewman's function as follows:

Brown	plane captain
Yellow	deck control
Red	ordnance
Purple	oil and gasoline
Green	arresting gear and catapults
Blue	plane movers
White	medical corpsmen

Aircraft Carrier Squadron Nomenclature

Carrier squadrons had an alphanumeric designator. The first letter was always V, which stood for "heavier than air," as opposed to lighter-than-air aircraft, such as dirigibles and blimps. The next letter designated the purpose of the squadron as follows:

F	Fighting
S	Scouting
B	Dive-bombing
T	Torpedo Bombing

By late 1941, separate scouting and bombing squadrons continued to exist, but their aircraft, capability, and operations had become essentially identical.

Following the letter representing the purpose of the squadron, there was a dash, followed by a number that was originally the number of the carrier on which the squadron was normally embarked, but there was the occasional swapping of squadrons between carriers. If there were two squadrons of the same type on a single carrier, there was another digit, either a one or two, to designate those.

Examples:

VB-5	Bombing squadron from carrier CV-5, *Yorktown*.
VF-42	Second fighting squadron from carrier CV-4, *Ranger*.

Airport Runways (still applies today in 2016)

Runways are denoted by numbers that are the magnetic heading of the runway rounded to the nearest ten degrees with the zero dropped. Example: runway 29 (or "two nine") has a nominal magnetic heading of 290, though the actual heading is between 285 and 295.

Airport Traffic Patterns (still applies today in 2016)

Airport traffic patterns are rectangular, with the runway on one of the long sides of the rectangle. Turns are to the left unless otherwise noted. The pilot may enter the pattern at the crosswind leg, which is a short leg upwind of the runway, and perpendicular to it. He then turns left onto the downwind leg. The crosswind leg and most of the downwind leg are flown at the traffic pattern altitude, normally around 1,000 feet above the runway. The pilot may also directly enter the downwind leg, which is a long leg on the side of the rectangle opposite the runway. He flies the downwind leg until he some distance downwind of the approach end of the runway, and then he turns left onto the base leg, which is a short leg perpendicular to the runway. Finally he turns left again onto the final leg. At this point he should be lined up with the runway, flying toward the approach end. He then descends to a landing.

Army Aircraft Nomenclature

The army used an entirely different system from the navy. The first letter designated the type (purpose) of the aircraft, as follows:

A   Attack (light bomber)

B   Bomber

O   Observation (reconnaissance)

P   Pursuit (fighter)

T   Trainer, with a preceding letter P (primary), B (basic), or A (advanced)

In the case of experimental aircraft, the letter X was put in front of other characters.

The first letter was followed by a dash and then a number that indicated the sequence of all designs of that type considered by the army. This was followed by a letter indicating the version, and there was no indication of the designer or manufacturer.

Example:

P-40B   The fortieth pursuit type considered by the army, third version (two revisions, the first version had no letter after the number).

Military Aircraft Piston Engine Nomenclature

Army and Navy aircraft often had engine types in common, and they used the same nomenclature. Military aircraft piston engines had an alphanumeric designator. The first character was a letter designating the cylinder arrangement, as follows:

I   Inline; a single bank or line of cylinders with crankcase; air cooled.

O   Opposed; two banks of cylinders are arranged on a single crankcase directly across from each other; usually two or three cylinders in each bank; air cooled.

R   Radial; each row, or disk, had cylinders arranged radially, like spokes of a wheel around a crankcase: air cooled; most radials had only one row of three, five, seven, or nine cylinders, though a few had two rows of seven or nine, and one had four rows of seven.

V   Vee type; two banks of cylinders that were angled in a vee and joined on a single crankcase; usually six cylinders in each bank; air or liquid cooled.

This letter was followed by a dash and then a three- or four-digit number, designating the engine's total displacement in cubic inches. The displacement is the total volume swept by the pistons and was the accepted measure of engine size. The volume swept is the volume of the space that the top of the piston moves through as it goes up and down in the cylinder.

Military Aircraft Engine Cooling:

Air cooled	Ambient air was brought in and ducted to flow around the engine cylinders and particularly the cylinder heads; the cylinders and cylinder heads were extensively finned on the outside to increase the surface area for heat transfer. The heated air then exited through ducts. Air cooling was always supplemented by cooling the engine-lubricating oil in an oil radiator. This arrangement was reliable because it had few moving parts, and, except for the small oil-cooling system, it was free from leaks. However, this arrangement tended to have greater aerodynamic drag.
Liquid Cooled	Ambient air was brought in and ducted to flow through a radiator (heat exchanger) to cool a liquid coolant. The liquid coolant was circulated by a pump around the engine cylinders and cylinder heads and then back to the radiator. In military engines, liquid cooling was always supplemented by cooling the engine-lubricating oil in an oil radiator. This arrangement tended to have less drag than an air-cooled system because the cooling

radiator was relatively small and could be positioned and ducted to minimize drag, but this arrangement was less reliable and more vulnerable to combat damage. For this reason, the US Navy avoided it after radial air-cooled engines became available in the 1920s.

<u>Examples (these three engines competed directly with each other):</u>

V-1710	Vee type; 1,710 cubic-inch displacement; two banks of six cylinders; liquid cooled; made by the Allison division of General Motors.
R-1820	Radial; 1,820 cubic-inch displacement; one row of nine cylinders; air cooled; made by the Wright division of Curtiss-Wright.
R-1830	Radial; 1,830 cubic-inch displacement; two rows of seven cylinders each; air cooled; made by the Pratt & Whitney division of United Aircraft.

Military Ranks

<u>Navy</u>	<u>Marines and Army Equivalent</u>
<u>Officers</u>	
Admiral (Adm.)	General
Vice Admiral (VAdm.)	Lieutenant General
Rear Admiral (RAdm.)	Major General
Commodore (rarely used)	Brigadier General
Captain (Capt.)	Colonel

Commander (Cdr.)	Lieutenant Colonel
Lieutenant Commander (Lt. Cdr.)	Major
Lieutenant (Lt.)	Captain
Lieutenant Junior Grade (Lt. j.g.)	First Lieutenant
Ensign (Ens.)	Second Lieutenant

Enlisted Men

Chief Petty Officer	Master Sergeant
Petty Officer First Class	First Sergeant, Technical Sergeant
Petty Officer Second Class	Staff Sergeant
Petty Officer Third Class	Sergeant
Seaman First Class	Corporal
Seaman Second Class	Private First Class
Seaman Third Class	Private

Naval Aviation Petty Officer Abbreviations for Chief, First Class, Second Class, Third Class:

Aviation Ordnance Man: ACOM, AOM1c, AOM2c, AOM3c

Aviation Machinist's Mate: ACMM, AMM1c, AMM2c, AMM3c

Aviation Pilot: CAP, AP1c, AP2c

Aviation Radioman: ACRM, ARM1c, ARM2c, ARM3c

Naval Aircraft Nomenclature

The navy used an entirely different system from the army. The first one or two characters are letters that designate the purpose of the aircraft, as follows:

F	Fighter: Single engine; designed primarily for combat against other aircraft but can be used for light attack on surface targets.
B, SB	Dive bomber: Single engine; designed to attack surface targets with a single bomb that is dropped in a very steep dive; armed for defense against other aircraft. The S indicates that the aircraft is also designed for scouting (reconnaissance).
J	Utility aircraft: Usually a single-engine amphibian for communication between multiple ships or between ships and the shore.
N, SN	Trainer: Designed for pilot or aircrew training. The S indicates that the aircraft is also designed for scouting (reconnaissance).
PB	Patrol bomber: Multiengine flying boat designed for long-range patrol and horizontal bombing; armed for defense against other aircraft.
SO, OS	Scout observation: Single-engine float plane carried on a battleship or cruiser, mainly for scouting (reconnaissance).
TB	Torpedo bomber: Single engine; designed to attack surface ships with a torpedo that is dropped from horizontal flight at very low altitude; larger than a dive bomber because the torpedo weighs twice as much as the largest bomb; may also be used to drop bombs from horizontal flight; armed for defense against other aircraft.

In the case of experimental aircraft, the letter X was put in front of the other characters.

The next character is a single digit that designates the sequence of the designs for that purpose or type that were built by that manufacturer. For example, if the designation started off with "F4" it would mean that this was the fourth fighter design by that manufacturer. In the case of the first design (number 1), the digit is omitted.

The next character is a letter designating the manufacturer; before 1942, this was also the firm that designed the aircraft, as follows:

A	Brewster
B	Boeing
C	Curtis
D	Douglas
F	Grumman
J	North American
M	Martin
N	Naval Aircraft Factory
S	Stearman (division of Boeing)
T	Northrop
U	Vought-Sikorsky (division of United Aircraft)
Y	Consolidated

Next, there is a dash followed by a single digit, which designates the sequence of revisions of that design.

Examples:

XF4U-1   Experimental example of the fourth fighter design built by Vought-Sikorsky, first version (no revision).

N2S-3   Second trainer design built by Stearman, third version (second revision).

XBT-2   Experimental example of the first dive-bomber design built by Northrop, second version (first revision).

SBD-3   First scout bomber design built by Douglas, third version (second revision).

F4F-3   Fourth fighter design built by Grumman, third version (second revision).

On October 1, 1941, the secretary of the navy approved the official use of manufacturer's names for naval aircraft, such as "Dauntless" for the SBD and "Wildcat" for the F4F.

Naval Combatant Ship Types

CV-x   Fleet aircraft carrier: Large aircraft carrier designed to operate with the fleet or in a separate task force; maximum speed, thirty-plus knots; after the first carrier, they were named after early US naval ships.

BB-x   Battleship: Large surface-combat ship; heavily armed and armored; able to easily defeat other surface-combat ships except battleships; before 1942, maximum speed, twenty-one knots, except for two ships newly commissioned; named after US states.

CA-x   Heavy cruiser: Smaller than battleship; able to easily defeat other surface-combat ships except battleships and heavy cruisers;

	maximum speed, thirty-plus knots; named after US cities.
CL-x	Light cruiser: Smaller than heavy cruiser; able to easily defeat destroyers and small surface-combat ships; maximum speed, thirty-plus knots; named after US cities.
DD-x	Destroyer: Smaller than light cruiser; able to easily defeat small surface-combat ships; able to detect and attack submarines with depth charges; very maneuverable; maximum speed, thirty-plus knots; named after famous navy and marine persons.
SS-x	Submarine: Designed for torpedo attack against other ships while surfaced or submerged; for fleet boats of mid-1930s and later, maximum speed, twenty knots on the surface, ten knots submerged; many older types of lesser capability in service in 1941; fleet boats named after fish species, with first letter indicating class or type.

Appendix B: Bibliographic Essay

Introduction

Early in the project of writing this series of novels, I decided that I might never finish it if I indulged in original research, although I was sorely tempted. Therefore, the nonfiction parts of this book are based almost entirely on the original research and reporting of others, and to a very small extent, on my own experience. In what follows I have attempted to provide the reader with an idea of where I found important nonfiction information. The authors and numbers refer to the list of references given in appendix C.

I have also attempted to indicate the parts of the story that may read like history but are, in fact, my invention, hence fiction. I have tried to make the fictional parts realistic, based on my knowledge of the history and my own experience as a pilot and aeronautical engineer, including flying several World War II airplanes.

General References

A general chronology of naval events throughout the period of this book is provided in Cressman (1). The activities of *Yorktown* and her air group in late 1941 and 1942 are also described in Cressman (2), Lundstrom (3), and Lundstrom (4), and therefore much of the history for this book can be found in these works. The reader should consult these three works for anything not mentioned specifically in the notes for each date given below. A good overview of the entire war from a non-US viewpoint is given in Deighton (5). Costello (6) provides an excellent overview of the Pacific war. The strategy of the Pacific war, from both the American and Japanese viewpoints, is described in Lundstrom (7). Recent summaries of the Pacific war up through June 1942 are given by Symonds (8) and Toll (9). Tables of information on all US Navy ships and aircraft of the period are given in Fahey (10).

December 16, 1941

The event of the falling Wildcat is my invention. A woman in the Combat Intelligence Unit is my invention, although Mrs. Driscoll's leading role in US Navy code breaking is history. This invention allows Alan to have an additional insight into strategic matters that may not be entirely realistic. The lack of preparation for the German submarine onslaught on the East Coast of the United States is described in Hughes and Costello (11). Miller (12) covers the evolution of War Plan Orange.

December 17, 1941

Lundstrom (3) and Lundstrom (4) have a description of a typical carrier air group at this time. The development of the US fighter aircraft of World War II, including the Wildcat, is thoroughly covered in Dean (13). The development of the Wildcat is specifically described in Greene (14). Layton et al. (15) describes the activities and infighting in the naval intelligence community throughout this period. The Army Air Corps' belief that heavy bombers were unstoppable and could substitute for surface forces is well described in Olson (16). Williford (17) covers the reinforcement of the Philippines in detail. The loss of American air superiority over the northern Philippines and its consequences is described in Costello (18), in which the *New York Times* article is quoted and referenced, and Burton (19). A detailed description of events in the Philippines just before and after the start of the war is provided in Bartsch (20).

December 21, 1941

Information on the Panama Canal comes from Google Maps, Google Earth, and Wikipedia. That information states that the configuration of the canal remained essentially the same from 1941 until very recently, when a widening project was started. The evolution of the US Navy's attitude toward unrestricted submarine warfare is hardly mentioned in most histories but is described in detail in Holwitt (21).

December 22, 1941

I was able to read and copy articles from *Time* magazine on their website, from which the article (22) is taken.

December 27, 1941

The description of a typical World War II carrier squadron ready room is based on the display at the National Museum of Naval Aviation. I assumed that ready rooms did not change very much between US entry into the war and the period of the display, 1943–44. Operations on carrier decks of the time are described in a cursory fashion in many places. For a person familiar with airplane operations on land and having some knowledge of aircraft carriers, it is possible to deduce many of the characteristics of operations on an aircraft carrier. Some description is provided in Mears (23). A colorful summary is provided in Kernan (24). A detailed description of operations on the deck of a later Essex class carrier in 1945, with many photographs, is given in Atkins (25). An excellent general reference on navy aircraft is Bowers and Swanborough (26). The characteristics of the World War II dive and torpedo bombers, including the Dauntless, Helldiver, Devastator, and Avenger, are described in Mizrahi (27). The specific evolution of the BT-1 into the Dauntless is covered in Heinemann (28). The evolution of the Dauntless is also covered in Tillman (29), along with a description of a combat dive. The difficulties of dive bombing are described in Buell (30). Instructions for the operation of the SBD-3 and the layout of the controls are given in the Pilot's Flight Operating Instructions (31). The layout is given slightly more clearly and a diagram of the terminal phase of a bombing dive is shown in Peczkowski (32). Many details are also shown in Dann (33). Nevertheless, many details of the dive bombing practice exercise are my invention. A description of a recent flight in one of the few remaining flyable SBDs is given in Stokely (34).

December 30, 1941

Information on the San Diego area comes from Google Maps and my own experience living in the area from 1963 to '68. The layout and history of the San Diego Naval Air Station on North Island are given in Shettle (35) and Sudsbury (36). The history of Consolidated Aircraft is covered in Wagner (37). A description of tactics for launching carrier strikes is provided by Lundstrom (3) in connection with the Battle of Midway in June 1942, where he states that the *Yorktown* air group had used the running rendezvous twice before. Testing it at this early date is my idea. The history of the fast oilers developed by the navy in the late 1930s is told in detail in Wildenberg (38).

December 31, 1941

I have not read about pilots giving flight instruction to their gunners, so this is entirely my invention.

January 1, 1942

The air raid alert early on New Year's Day is mentioned in Lundstrom (3). Admiral Fletcher's embarkation in *Yorktown* and its implications are covered in detail in Lundsprom (4), along with the disposition of the airplanes to be carried as cargo.

January 3, 1942

The navy-wide promotion is mentioned in Lundstrom (3).

January 4, 1942

The loading and unloading of the six floatplanes is mentioned in Lundstrom (4).

January 5, 1942

The ill-fated relief expedition to Wake is covered in many places, but I have relied on Lundstrom (4). This work also covers the politics in Fletcher's and the *Yorktown*'s captain's staffs, and the consultations with the air group. The sinking of the submarine *Sqalus* and the aftermath are described in Maas (39) and LaVO (40). The history of torpedo design, the Newport Torpedo Station, and the defects in US torpedoes are well covered in Wildenberg and Polmar (41) and in Newpower (42).

January 17, 1942

The story of the navy's attempt to cover up the losses from the arrival of German submarines on the East Coast of the Unitad States is covered in detail in Offley (43).

January 18, 1942

Admiral Fletcher's efforts to inform himself quickly about aviation are described in Lundstrom (4). Cressman (2) describes *Yorktown*'s first refueling at sea.

January 19, 1942

The development of the YE-ZB homing system is described in Wildenburg (44).

January 22, 1942

The effort of *Yorktown*'s executive officer to redirect *Yorktown*'s role in the Pacific war is described in Lundstrom (4).

January 30, 1942

I got the details of the geography of Jaluit from Google Maps. The possible revelation of the presence of an American carrier by an unauthorized overflight of Howland Island is described in Lundstrom (4). In the actual historical event, two *Yorktown* SBDs did fly over Howland Island, against Fletcher's orders, but apparently the Japanese did not see them.

January 31, 1942

The executive officer of VB-5 (Bellinger) did disappear during the Jaluit raid, which is described in Cressman (2) and other sources. The resulting shuffle in the officer appointments is my invention.

February 5, 1942

Results of the attack on Pearl Harbor are summarized in many sources, quite succinctly in Cressman (1). There are quite a few works dedicated entirely to the attack, two of the best known being Lord (45) and Prange (46). The layout and history of MCAS Ewa was obtained from Shettle (47).

February 6, 1942

Google Maps provided the modern layout of Pearl Harbor and Honolulu. I found a 1942 map of Honolulu on the Internet. Useful background on life in Hawaii both before and after the attack was provided by the letters of an Army Air Corps pilot in Edmundson (48). A description of the effects of the attack on civilians, with numerous photographs, is given in Brown (49). Toll (9) describes the collection and burial of corpses after the attack. The big change in the economic organization of Hawaii resulting from the outbreak of war is described in MacDonald (50). The wrangling in naval intelligence is described in Layton et al. (15) and in Carlson (51), which also thoroughly covers the operation of, and atmosphere in, Rochefort's Combat Intelligence Unit. Both works also describe the role of Mrs. Driscoll in US Navy code breaking. Another perspective on the operation of the Combat Intelligence Unit is provided in Holmes (52), the same Holmes who has a role in the story. The presence of the four future intelligence officers aboard *Pennsylvania* in the mid-1930s is discussed in Layton et al. (15).

February 7, 1942

The operations of US Navy submarines are given in Blair (53).

March 6, 1942

Friedman (54) provides a complete description of the history of the design of US aircraft carriers.

March 7, 1942

The incident with the man on loan from the Combat Intelligence Unit is from Lundstrom (4).

March 10, 1942

The incident with the clogged fuel filter is entirely my invention.

March 14, 1942

The transfer of aircraft between *Yorktown* and *Lexington* is described in Lundstrom (3) and Lundstrom (4). The history of aircraft piston engines is given in Smith (55), and a more technical discussion is provided by Taylor (56). The TBD Pilot's Manual (57) gives many details about the airplane. The pioneering aspect of the TBD when it first appeared is nicely summarized in Trapnell and Tibbitts (58). The overrating of the accuracy of bombing with the Norden bombsight is described in Olson (16). The presence of a total of only fourteen Wildcats on the US aircraft carriers in the Pacific on December 7, 1941, is mentioned in Ewing (59). The development of the US World War II fighters is described in Dean (13).

April 2, 1942

King's orders to read the Kettering article are mentioned in Sears (60).

April 20, 1942

Google Maps was helpful regarding the geography of the Tonga Islands.

April 25, 1942

The shuffle of officers in the *Yorktown* air office is described in Lundstrom (4), and other changes, including the VF-42 mix-up, are described in Lundstrom (3) and Cressman (2). Skepticism within VS-5 regarding the fogging problem is my invention.

May 1, 1942

Buell (30) is an account by a US Navy dive bomber pilot of his experiences in World War II. He was the pilot who came out from Fiji and joined Scouting Five on May 1.

May 6, 1942

The incident in which Sherman did not get his way in arming the strike SBDs on the *Yorktown* is discussed in Lundstrom (4).

May 7–10, 1942

The Battle of the Coral Sea is described in detail in the three general references: Cressman (2), Lundstrom (3), and Lundstrom (4). I have deliberately allowed for a clearer understanding of the battle than was probably the case on board *Yorktown* immediately afterward, in order to make it clearer for the reader. In the attack on the Japanese carriers on May 8, the real pilot who made the monkey face and then made a heroic dive to score a solid hit and earn a posthumous Medal of Honor was Lieutenant John J. Powers. Pilots finding wounded and dead men stashed in their staterooms comes from Buell (30).

May 27, 1942

Most of the information about what was going on at Pearl Harbor and naval headquarters in Washington is from Lundstrom (4), Layton et al. (15), and Carlson (51).

Appendix C: References

1. Cressman, Robert J., *The Official Chronology of the U.S. Navy in World War II* (Annapolis, MD, Naval Institute Press, 1999).
2. Cressman, Robert J., *That Gallant Ship, U.S.S. Yorktown [CV-5]* (Missoula, MT, Pictorial Histories Publishing Co., 1985).
3. Lundstrom, John B., *The First Team: Pacific Naval Air Combat from Pearl Harbor to Midway* (Annapolis, MD: Naval Institute Press, 1984).
4. Lundstrom, John B., *Black Shoe Carrier Admiral: Frank Jack Fletcher at Coral Sea, Midway, and Guadalcanal* (Annapolis, MD: Naval Institute Press, 2006).
5. Deighton, Len, *Blood, Tears, and Folly: An Objective Look at World War II* (New York: HarperCollins, 1994).
6. Costello, John, *The Pacific War 1941–1945* (New York: Rawson, Wade, 1981).
7. Lundstrom, John B., *The First South Pacific Campaign: Pacific Fleet Strategy December 1941–June 1942* (Annapolis, MD: Naval Institute Press, 1976).
8. Symonds, Craig L., *The Battle of Midway* (New York: Oxford University Press, 2011).

9. Toll, Ian W., *Pacific Crucible: War at Sea in the Pacific, 1941–1942* (New York: W. W. Norton & Co., 2012).

10. Fahey, James C., *Ships and Aircraft of the United States Fleet* (1941; repr., Annapolis, MD: Naval Institute Press, 1994).

11. Hughes, Terry, and John Costello, *The Battle of the Atlantic* (New York: Dial Press/James Wade, 1977).

12. Miller, Edward S., *War Plan Orange: The US Strategy to Defeat Japan, 1897–1945* (Annapolis, MD: Naval Institute Press, 1991).

13. Dean, Francis H., *America's Hundred-Thousand: US Production Fighters of World War Two* (Atglen, PA: Schiffer Publishing, 1997).

14. Greene, Frank L., "History of the Grumman F4F 'Wildcat,'" *Journal of the American Aviation Historical Society*, Winter 1961, reprinted by Grumman Aircraft Engineering Corporation.

15. Layton, Edwin T., Roger Pineau, and John Costello, *And I Was There* (New York: Quill, 1985).

16. Olson, Lynne, *Citizens of London: The Americans Who Stood with Britain in Its Finest, Darkest Hour* (New York: Random House, 2010).

17. Williford, Glen M., *Racing the Sunrise: Reinforcing America's Pacific Outposts, 1941–1942* (Annapolis, MD: Naval Institute Press, 2010).

18. Costello, John, *Days of Infamy: MacArthur, Roosevelt, Churchill: The Shocking Truth Revealed: How Their Secret Deals and Strategic Blunders Caused Disasters at Pearl Harbor and the Philippines* (New York: Pocket Books, 1995).

19. Burton, John, *Fortnight of Infamy: The Collapse of Allied Airpower West of Pearl Harbor, December 1941* (Annapolis, MD: Naval Institute Press, 2006).

20. Bartsch, William H., *December 8, 1941: MacArthur's Pearl Harbor* (College Station, TX: Texas A&M University Press, 2003).

21. Holwitt, Joel Ira, *Execute against Japan: The US Decision to Conduct Unrestricted Submarine Warfare* (College Station, TX: Texas A&M University Press, 2009).

22. "World Battlefronts: Battle of the Pacific: Havoc at Honolulu," *Time*, December 22, 1941.

23. Mears, Frederick, *Carrier Combat* (Garden City, NY: Doubleday, Doran & Co., 1944).

24. Kernan, Alvin, *The Unknown Battle of Midway: The Destruction of the American Torpedo Squadrons* (New Haven, CT: Yale University Press, 2005).

25. Atkins, Edward, *Flight Deck: A Pictorial Essay on a Day in the Life of an Airdale*, 2 volumes (Pittsburg: RoseDog Books, 2006).

26. Bowers, Peter M., and Gordon Swanborough, *United States Navy Aircraft since 1911* (New York: Funk and Wagnalls, 1968).

27. Mizrahi, J. V., *US Navy Dive and Torpedo Bombers* (Sentry, 1967).

28. Heinemann, Edward H., and Rosario Rausa, *Ed Heinemann: Combat Aircraft Designer* (Annapolis, MD: Naval Institute Press, 1980).

29. Tillman, Barrett, *The Dauntless Dive Bomber of World War II* (Annapolis, MD: Naval Institute Press, 1976).

30. Buell, Harold, *Dauntless Helldivers* (New York: Dell, 1991).

31. *Pilot's Flight Operating Instructions for the RA-24 Airplane (SBD-3)*, Technical Order No. 01-40AE-1, Fairfield, OH, Air Service Command, 1943.

32. Peczkowski, Robert, *Douglas SBD Dauntless* (Sandomierz, Poland: Mushroom Model Publications, 2007).

33. Dann, Richard S., *Walk around SBD Dauntless* (Carrollton, TX: Squadron/Signal Publications, 2004).
34. Stokley, J. B., "SBD Checkout," article posted on the AvWeb website, June 22, 2003, http://www.avweb.com/news/skywrite/185203-1.html
35. Shettle, M. L., Jr., *United States Naval Air Stations of WWII*, vol. 2 (Western States. Bowersville, GA: Schaertel, 1997).
36. Sudsbury, Elretta, *Jackrabbits to Jets: The History of North Island, San Diego, California* (San Diego: North Island Historical Committee, 1967).
37. Wagner, William, *Reuben Fleet and the Story of Consolidated Aircraft* (Fallbrook, CA: Aero Publishers, Inc., 1976).
38. Wildenberg, Thomas, *Gray Steel and Black Oil: Fast Tankers and Replenishment at Sea in the US Navy 1912–1995* (Annapolis, MD: Naval Institute Press, 1996).
39. Maas, Peter, *The Terrible Hours: The Man Behind the Greatest Submarine Rescue in History* (New York: HarperCollins, 1999).
40. LaVO, Carl, *Back from the Deep: The Strange Story of the Sister Subs* Squalus *and* Sculpin (Annapolis, MD: Naval Institute Press, 1994).
41. Wildenberg, Thomas, and Norman Polmar, *Ship Killers: A History of the American Torpedo* (Annapolis, MD: Naval Institute Press, 2010).
42. Newpower, Anthony, *Iron Men and Tin Fish: The Race to Build a Better Torpedo during World War II* (Westport, CT: Praeger Security International, 2006).
43. Offley, Ed, *The Burning Shore: How Hitler's U-boats brought World War II to America* (New York: Basic Books, 2014).

44. Wildenberg, Thomas, *Destined for Glory: Dive Bombing, Midway, and the Evolution of Carrier Airpower* (Annapolis, MD: Naval Institute Press, 1998).
45. Lord, Walter, *A Day of Infamy* (New York: H. Holt, 1957).
46. Prange, Gordon W., *At Dawn We Slept: The Untold Story of Pearl Harbor* (New York: McGraw-Hill, 1981).
47. Shettle, M. L., Jr., *United States Marine Corps Air Stations of World War II* (Bowersville, GA: Schaertel, 2001).
48. Edmundson, James V., *Letters to Lee: From Pearl Harbor to the War's Final Mission* (New York: Fordham University Press, 2010).
49. Brown, DeSoto, *Hawaii Goes to War: Life in Hawaii from Pearl Harbor to Peace* (Honolulu: Editions Limited, 1989).
50. MacDonald, Alexander, *Revolt in Paradise: The Social Revolution in Hawaii after Pearl Harbor* (New York: Stephen Daye, Inc., 1944).
51. Carlson, Elliot, *Joe Rochefort's War: The Odyssey of the Codebreaker Who Outwitted Yamamoto at Midway* (Annapolis, MD: Naval Institute Press, 2011).
52. Holmes, W. J., *Double-Edged Secrets: US Naval Intelligence Operations in the Pacific During World War II* (Annapolis, MD: Naval Institute Press, 1979).
53. Blair, Clay, Jr., *Silent Victory: The US Submarine War against Japan*, 2 vols (New York: J. B. Lippincott, 1975).
54. Friedman, Norman, *US Aircraft Carriers: An Illustrated Design History* (Annapolis, MD: Naval Institute Press, 1983).
55. Smith, Herschel, *A History of Aircraft Piston Engines* (Manhattan, KS: Sunflower University Press, 1981).

56. Taylor, C. Fayette, *Aircraft Propulsion: A Review of the Evolution of Aircraft Piston Engines* (Washington, DC: Smithsonian Institution Press, 1971).
57. *Pilot's Handbook for the TBD-1 Airplane,* Technical Order No. TBD-1, Santa Monica, CA, Douglas Aircraft Company, 1937.
58. Trapnell, Frederick M., Jr., and Dana Trapnell Tibbitts, *Harnessing the Sky: Frederick "Trap" Trapnell: The US Navy's Aviation Pioneer, 1923–52* (Annapolis, MD: Naval Institute Press, 2015).
59. Ewing, Steve, *Reaper Leader: The Life of Jimmy Flatley* (Annapolis, MD: Naval Institute Press, 2002).
60. Sears, David, *Pacific Air: How Fearless Flyboys, Peerless Aircraft, and Fast Flattops Conquered the Skies in the War with Japan* (Cambridge, MA: Da Capo Press, 2011).

Made in the USA
Coppell, TX
06 August 2021